THE
HUNTING
ANIMAL

By Norman Bogner

In Spells No Longer Bound
Spanish Fever
Seventh Avenue
The Madonna Complex
Making Love
The Hunting Animal

Norman Bogner

THE HUNTING ANIMAL

William Morrow & Company, Inc. New York 1974

In the days when providential plagues
swept the cities clean, the individual,
in his capacity as survivor, inspired
with some reason a certain respect:
he was still a *being*. There are no more
beings, there is only this swarm of
dying creatures stricken with
longevity, all the more hateful in
that they are so good at organizing
their agony. To them we prefer
almost any animal, if only because it
is hunted down by them, despoilers
and profaners of a landscape once
ennobled by the presence of beasts.

—CIORAN

i

IN
STRANGLED
ORCHARDS

No mask like open truth to cover lies,
As to go naked is the best disguise.

—CONGREVE

1

Afternoons have a way of growing shorter for married men because evenings are the natural and not entirely painless childbirth of routine.

The existence of Kit and her house of horizontal refreshment inspires gloating memories and relieves vodka-enlightened conversations with wives. The mind runs recklessly along different paths, and the gray-edged meat loaf with its blood-yellow egg-eye, dished up in a slaughter of tomato paste, is transformed into a miracle of domestic invention. Even the midweek agony of a television repeat hums merrily along, mingling with that most picturesque fantasy imprinted by an afternoon at Kit's. The clean air of home, and those open fields bordering fledgling country clubs, do not quite stifle the boredom that is the very fruit of a realized ideal.

Thus Kit's and the smile on his face . . . and no further questions.

Stalled in the interminable snarl of cars that stretched from Exits 38 to 19 on the Long Island Expressway, Daniel Barnet sent himself a birthday greeting on this the thirty-seventh year of his adventure with fate. To his wife Sonya he mentally composed the valentine of a true sufferer. The billet-doux, sheathed in simulated strawberry velvet, would be placed on the toilet roll

he had located in the caverns of the linen closet downstairs, then
installed on the solid gold holder, where it belonged.

The valentine, devoid of rhyme scheme, would take the form
of an interrogation, four questions:

1. Why didn't you use the Pristeen last night? You could hardly
   say I was in any terrific hurry, so how come no douche when
   I went to the great expense of plumbing in a primrose (special order) bidet?
2. Why has that small junction I entered by accident eight years
   ago become the size of the New York State Thruway? Please,
   Sonya, don't give me that crap about childbearing, because
   I've screwed other mothers with two children. Compared to
   you they were like the I.R.T. during rush hour.
3. Why do you think I'm writing you this note? To inform you
   that there was no paper on the roll and you can wipe your
   own ass from now on? Or that I'm leaving you for a piece who
   knows more about blowing than you do? Not exactly.
4. Since you constantly remind me how important you are, how
   come I'm telling you to go fuck yourself?

PS. By the way, Sonya, unless you are immune to tetanus, I
   suggest you change your razor blade. It looks like you've
   swallowed the Wilkinson claims like the sucker you are. They
   do not last a lifetime and they do rust.

Valentine or not, it would not do for Hallmark. One day
though . . .

The traffic miraculously began to flow, and Daniel mentally
filed the note amid the debris that was their marriage.

A short stroll through the dismal actuality of their attempted
intimacy the previous night made him shudder. Sonya lay there
like a bloodless slab of meat. Kissed him afterward. Almost ab-
sentmindedly as a token of some dimly remembered affection.
It had been the kiss of an accountant dealing with a faltering
business over a long period of time. The black and red ink
wantonly intermingle until there is just a nasty fuliginous
smudge. He'd left her to finish herself as best she could.

He slipped his Rolls Royce Corniche (the only one on Long
Island) into a gap left by a Mustang. Owning this piece of Eng-
land and driving it along the rutted broken streets of New
York was an act of profound defiance.

But there was a bright side to his days, the constant services

of Kit and her handmaidens. New faces and old sensations that
Sonya had once provided during the furtive non-event that was
their courtship. What a mistake to have changed her status.

He'd wanted to leave her for a long time, but the impulse was
mysteriously divorced from action.

Sonya countered every disagreement they had with a searching
fundamentalist argument.

"How can you be bitter with somebody who changed her religion for you and is now in the B'nai Brith? It's like a black
psychiatrist. So stop complaining, Daniel."

Equating her reluctant enrollment in the local Sisterhood of
Jewish women with her performance in the sack was typical
Sonya logic.

"If not for me," he threatened, "you'd still be serving coffee
on Super Constellations to Miami."

"And married to a pilot," she said wistfully. "Daniel, I give
you everything you want."

By nature contentious, he could not survive without bickering.

"Like what? Like last night?"

"Well, isn't it a challenge to try to turn me on after all these
years?"

"Next time, don't save me the dance."

"Why doesn't he get into his new Rolls Royce and drive slowly
past the bus stop so that everybody's tongue can hang out. Fact
is, it's eight twenty-five and if you don't make a move you'll miss
all the mothers. I know my big boy still likes to cruise."

"You haven't got my number . . . not yet."

"I'll pretend I do." She patted his behind, edging him out of
the door.

"Are you patronizing me?" he demanded.

"I certainly hope so." She waved a limp hand as he opened
his car door.

"For Christ's sake, Sonya. Get those nails done."

"I knew there was something . . ."

Since attaining money, virtually overnight, Daniel continually
changed his will. Five of them over the summer and eighteen
codicils. On Monday, Sonya was usually out, and on Thursday,
with visions of tax savings, she was invariably reinstated. Tuesdays and Fridays he divorced her.

Theirs had been a prejet romance when National Southern

Airlines was phasing out its props and marrying off its stewardesses like Sonya. In common with early Monroe, she had been full of hidden promise and quixotic surprises. But no repressed grief, or lost loves, clouded her vision, dimmed her mind for just that instant when life would not be worth living. He kept an enormous supply of Seconal on her bedside table just in case melancholia might, one night, inspire the necessary degree of despair.

"Do me a favor and take an overdose," he pleaded.

"I'm going to outlive you by twenty years." She flaunted one of his own insurance tables at him. "Read it and weep. Life expectancy, Daniel."

Numbers you couldn't fight. No doubt about it, she was correct. If cigarettes or heart-lung didn't terminate him, she would find some other device.

In an effort to trace the mine shaft of his marriage, its warehouse of nadiral depressions, he did not have to be at all selective. A random sample served his purposes.

The logjam in Sonya's mouth had been dispersed by a smart buff-colored cap job and when she smiled now it was with enthusiasm, not merely lip pursing, because she was no longer afraid of how the world would react to crooked teeth. For her it was Sassoon wigs—three, all blond—and sometimes when Daniel felt generous he'd run her hair into Charles of the Ritz, so that the setting and styling would look a bit different from the local butcher's. Collecting it in a clear plastic box, and at a cost of fifty dollars, gave him an opportunity to gauge the logical craziness of his wife. In fact, with the box resting congenially on the passenger seat, he was happy to give it a lift, preferring it to Sonya.

Actually, in retrospect, it had been the National Southern Airlines uniform that had engineered the attraction. The body at twenty-seven—his first encounter with it eight years ago—had a tensile leanness about it, but he had discovered too late that it hardly compensated for a specific tendency to titlessness. And Daniel was, had always been, would continue to be, devoted to fine tits and the corkscrew form.

But the tits weren't cupcakes or even protuberances. Just hardened flesh-colored bits of plaster of Paris that had adhered to her chest. The nipples were done in a luminous glacé that formed hardened nubs even when she wasn't aroused. He was the man who had everything: breasts for a weight watcher.

No matter how he squeezed them together, there really wasn't enough *fleisch* to slip his dick into the gully and French-fuck them, planning to fire along the canal zone. In the attempt, they'd vanish, and Hotspur would erupt unexpectedly. A few times he'd glued her eyebrows together.

Leggy, yes, she was, but with one of those preshrunk asses that should have been tagged with "Sanforized" to warn people. His fingers probed bone when they tightened on her ass. How had she captured him? Certainly not with her Midwestern conversation, usually featuring tales of the invincible courage of airline personnel. Nor could her absence of wealth have persuaded him, for he had no commitment to the poor. No rescue operations for him. A leggy, small-town, lower-middle-class shiksa was what she was.

Sewing was definitely her strongest point. But who married for sewing? What kind of accomplishment was that? Should he tell his friends: "This is Sonya. Want to see her sew? She's also flown to Miami six hundred and eighty-four times. Seven hundred, darling? Who can keep up with your credits?" Should he show her photograph, the unrecognized celebrity, along with nineteen other girls grouped around, what else, an airplane, which she'd clipped and framed from the house rag? "That's her, among the finalists in the Miss Stewardess Contest. Pretty impressive. I thought so myself. I married it."

Getting back to the cap job. It had had a practical purpose behind it . . . er . . . not entirely cosmetic. A talentless suck. He thought if the bite could be altered, she'd improve remarkably, and wouldn't hand him back his cock with all those crazy-paved serrations on it.

Another factor, secretly, well, perhaps not so secretly, operating against Sonya was that she didn't like him to come in her mouth. A complaint . . . about the taste. The first time he'd heard of such a thing. To discourage him from the procedure, she developed the brilliant technique of lifting up her head at the first sign of spunk, and allowing it to spurt all over his pubic hair.

Catching his first load after months of test runs, she spat it back out into the rough.

When he protested, she said: "Where was I going to spit it?"

"Bathroom sink ever occur to you? It's frequently used for that purpose. Know what I mean, Sonya? Like when you brush your teeth with toothpaste, you wouldn't expect to drop it here, now would you?"

"Well, that's different."

Pointless to go on with this piece of schmuckbait. Capped, the teeth were no longer a problem, for now the marks were evenly distributed and not simply on the back of the head. This, for a thirty-seven-hundred-dollar dentist bill. Pushing deeper he found was a way of beating the teeth. But she wasn't thrilled about it.

"You're choking me."

"It's for a worthy cause."

"I still don't like the taste."

"Listen, you're not at the Four Seasons. . . . You don't complain to the maître d' about the *escargots* not being up to standard. You're sucking a prick, not dining out. This isn't something you drop into a stew to flavor it."

Sonya's one success in the French Grand Prix resulted in a certain remedial achievement. She caught the fly ball with a Kleenex, and the two of them spent forty-six minutes picking the bits off. Thussssss . . . WET STRENGTH TISSUES came into his life.

Out of his magician's hat he pulled a strange idea that fit into her world view:

"It's considered brain food, like fish."

"Really? I never heard that."

"Puts a different complexion on it. Another thing maybe you weren't aware of is that a special sucking poll was carried out by Indiana University or someplace equally prestigious, and they discovered a definite correlation between breast growth and swallowing jism. So if you'd like to cooperate I might be able to build you into a 34A by the year two thousand."

"I like my boobs."

"I was afraid of that. But look, aren't you curious about how your life might be changed if they grew a little, sort of got in your way?"

"It would destroy my tennis serve."

"What are you, a Billie Jean King or something? I've seen you hack balls around on a court. You're a lousy player because you're badly coordinated. Tits in this context is a red herring, Sonya."

Not a bad screw at all. She used to go at it with fervor, but at the same time with a nonspecific orgasm problem. Thirty-five minutes was her fastest time. The box had started out nice and tight, like a monkey's toehold. His daughter, Sylvia's, appearance in the world had converted it into Canal Street, with the same amenities. He'd need the discontinued Caddy model with the tail fins to enjoy the new dimensions and not his eighteen-centimeter *flèche d'amour*.

Sonya on the other hand—he hadn't noticed any serious objections—enjoyed being eaten. No protests to halt the proceedings. Salivaless after thirty minutes of her blue-plate special, he'd wander around the room, musing grimly:

"I must be out of my mind. What am I doing, scoffing this grounded *yold?*"

Loping naked down to the kitchen, Daniel would drain half a quart of milk from the container, the most effective method of spit restoration he'd discovered after searching experimentation. Celebrating his return from dehydration, he'd triumphantly brandish his equipment and slip into the pouch for a quiet pipeful of snazz, a view of her interior scenery. Like an airport road it basked in anonymity, a place of absent witnesses. Fearing the Pill, careless in the application of spermicidal foam, rarely able to locate at the crucial moment her diaphragm, she had devised the perfect contrivance for solo ecstasy.

Withdrawal.

Daniel and his army of one were forced to retreat with victory in sight. In the adjacent room, door open to guard against suffocation, Sylvia, his small daughter, trilled baby melodies to her daddy, who was firing loads on the green drapes and navy quilted headboard while Sonya, the target, shrank under the bedclothes out of range.

Cleaning up the mess was no picnic; and he would often find himself caught between washing his joint before the come had settled into starchy flakes that had to be picked off by a sharp fingernail, and the baby's three A.M. bottle. Thus, while the world slept, Daniel ran alone through the house.

"If only you'd gone to college instead of airline training

school. Maybe it would have made a small difference," he complained to the baby, who returned wind smiles for answer. "I just don't know what I'm going to do. This can't go on."

She also thought it terrifically funny to tickle him. It really made her howl and filled the void of her sense of humor, also nonspecific. A riot when she got him under the arms and his whip shrunk to a small hooded chicken wing.

When all was said and done, he really couldn't stand her. Didn't want her dead, but lost.

Her tastes before he introduced her to the delicacies of Jewish food ran to canned luncheon meats. Spam, ham, bologna, head cheese, Birds Eye fish cakes, Hoagies with limburger and onion, shit like that, which she'd batter to death with heavy lashings of French's mustard. Simply horrible. It took him a year to get Heinz Ketchup into the house, another year to put it on the table instead of the Snyder's muck she lapped up.

Three years had gone by before he knew what hit him, and she was still learning how to cook. Bagel freezing she performed like a genius. In fact anything that could be frozen she froze. One of his favorites, creamed spinach, she made once a month, and five weeks later he was still eating it.

"If you didn't know, you'd never guess it was frozen."

"Really? Then why does it taste like catgut, and why, Sonya, is it defrosting on my plate, and why, while we're at it, is the bottom hot and the top cold? Because it's frozen."

"I'll take it back," she said, making a grab for his plate.

"I thought the least I'd get from you when we were married was competent service. I mean to say, you took orders from people about what they wanted to eat, no?"

"Those trays were done before we got on the aircraft by the catering unit."

"I see. Do you suggest we sign up with them?"

The young landowner had seized his first property in 1966, in schlock Babylon, L.I. An instant community tortured into existence by one C. B. Luckmunn, who had fled when part of the development began to sink into the swamp upon which it had been built. Daniel had brought his parents out for an inspection tour when Sonya had returned west for a visit with her mother, just a week before the wedding.

The three had seen Sonya off, but his father still could not quite remember his future daughter-in-law.

"Which one was she?" he asked Daniel. "They was all dressed the same."

"The one that kept posing on the gangplank," his mother, the fastest answerer in the East, replied.

"Oh, that . . ."

His mother reviewed the color scheme in a state of noisy wincing. On the bed, a navy blue coverlet; green speckled curtains opposed the blue walls; charcoal gray wallpaper in the kitchen imprinted with odd-shaped wine gourds, mead vessels and muralized with an oxen roasting. All of it antagonizing her. It seemed to be the work of a schizophrenic.

"My, Daniel. You really made something of yourself," she said. "A tract house and a hilly billy shiksa that flies to Miami in airplanes for a job. Ever meet a Jewish girl flying like that all over the place?" His silence she took as an admission of a failed encounter. "You know why? They're in college. They got brains to feed. The brainless ones you can get running down aisles in the air carrying liquor bottles. Not a normal person. A dummy does that work. They name baby boys Riley and girls they call Bernadette. You think she'll learn how to cook? She'll start a fire, I'll bet you a million dollars, the first time she gets near a stove. They live on beer and pork, *chazerei.* Mister, I hope you bought yourself a giant freezer, because that's what you'll be eating. Ice."

"And that blue bedroom. What's it for? To remind her of the sky when she's sleeping?" His father's pithy comment.

"Don't aggravate, Hy. If Daniel wants to destroy himself after our sacrifices—and college wasn't a sacrifice, Mister Bigshot?—then let him."

"A New York shiksa at least is civilized," his father noted. "She's been among Jewish people, among their homes. She's had an opportunity to learn. I see only disaster before mine eyes."

Father joined son in a brisk walk to the car. Tenderness and advice was Daniel's for the asking, but he remained silent before the stolid, gray bentness of his father, entering his third decade as a handbag stitcher.

"My final word, Daniel, is you were stupid enough to get into this, now let's see if you're smart enough to get out."

"I don't want to," he protested.

"She's pregnant?"

"No, she's not pregnant."

"I only wondered because that might have been an honorable reason for going ahead." Not quite the final word, Daniel realized, as he opened the door to the Chevy, and his father, the sporty driver, slipped on his ventilated racer's gloves before segue-waying into a characteristically slick buck-pass that made tongues hang out of mouths: "If your mother had listened to me and named you Kenneth like I wanted, everything would have been different."

Five years later, Hy and Frieda were moved to bury their grievance when Daniel retired them to a condominium in sun-drenched Cocoa Beach.

When Sonya converted, became a Hebe for his sake, he was embarrassed by the whole thing: she understood nothing of the religion, the people, the culture. Making her Jewish was an insult, a horrible contradiction, completely unendurable. A slap in the face of historic struggle. Jews had died, been slaughtered, so that Sonya might become one? Absolutely absurd, a mockery of sacrifice.

When he questioned Rabbi Goldring about her progress, he'd been told by this exceedingly gentle man: "I'm sorry she didn't go to *chadah*. It's robbed me of the opportunity of hitting her. No insult intended, Daniel."

"I know how you feel, Rabbi."

"Where does she come from?"

"Somewhere in Indiana originally, then she moved to Denver."

"How'd they let her into the airplane business?"

In our time she was one of the finest reheaters of food purchased elsewhere; thus Daniel would only startle the distressed scholar with evidence of her solitary skill.

"Until I met Sonya, I genuinely believed I'd go to heaven," her divine guide complained. "Now I'm dismissing the possibility because I may be tried for killing her. Do you know she's still puzzled by the fact that *kasha* the food and *kasha* the question mean different things even though spelled and pronounced in a like fashion. So I told her, Sonya, dear, don't people in

English say *pair, pear* and *pare* with a knife? Never crossed her mind that such things exist in other tongues. Hebrew, she advised me, was a foreign language. Of course it's a foreign language, which is why she's studying it in the first place. Listen, there's a young man in Great Neck who has a reform temple. I've suggested she take instruction from him. He's got more strength than me and also happens to be a personal enemy. He's a rich kid who fell into a *schmaltz-greeb,* and your Sonya is just the one to make him realize that life isn't just a bowl of jello. Frankly, what set me off is that when I showed her the sanctuary, removed the Torah from its sacred place, this idiot starts making crosses over me. I got such hot flushes that I almost dropped the scroll. A fine thing for a rabbi . . . But when I looked in her eyes I felt she was mocking me."

Her greatest, deepest, most cherished ambition was to be mistaken for Janet Leigh. She had herself photographed constantly. She was the sort of nuisance who handed her Bell and Howell to strangers, so that they might capture her, fingertips poised on metal rails in parks, at the zoo, gibing at amusing animals who made her giggle while she obstructed the view of small children who came for a look at the lion. He'd walk away, leave her to the sweating men with eyeglasses who clanked against the view-finder as she personified some strange idea of infinity—La Gia-conda in a stewardess's uniform.

Also she gave the grass harp regular, seasonal trims, so that from time to time it seemed to him he was slipping himself into a tall man with a pointy Vandyke. Come springtime and it could have been the back of a Mohawk's skull. She took a particular pride in tending this most private of gardens, using a small, dangerous nippers designed for cuticle carving, forming strange topiary shapes on her lunar landscape.

"Maybe you should have been a chicken flicker," he moaned plaintively.

"A whaaaat?"

"Please don't let me distract you. Get the sideburns even for a change."

"I need a mirror," she said, then balanced a tissue-flecked handbag mirror between her thighs.

One summer she gave him a really nasty shock. Shaved it so clean that he thought he detected, when he examined the red lips snarling at him, some horrendous cavity from Dracula's past that had haunted his childhood. She certainly kept him guessing.

"Look, Sonya, I want to discuss your box with you."

"What is there to discuss?"

"I want you to leave it alone. Stop picking on it. Just keep it on Red Alert, ready to accommodate me."

In its nude, hacked state, he noticed it had five o'clock shadow and resembled a sweetbread waiting for its pastry coffin.

"Daniel, please stop making faces at me."

"I don't understand this baldness. Man is attempting to grow hair and you're shaving it."

"It's for the warm weather."

"I see. Well, frankly, Sonya, it disgusts me. I for one don't know what was wrong with matted hair."

"Got me all itchy."

Easing his chin up from the port of entry, he said: "This is perverse, Sonya . . . like copping somebody's scalp."

Always dry when he was ready to fuck, she invariably wet on her tongue the two fingers of her right hand to provide solubility for a basic penetration. Never washed her hands afterward.

"Listen, doll . . . when is everything you put on the table going to stop tasting of cunt? It's just infernal coming from the O.J."

In an attempt to remedy the unchanging tides of her Scapa Flow, she turned to various emulsified Woolworth balms, eventually settling on Pond's Cream for Dry Skin.

"It's like entering a hot marshmallow sundae."

He turned her on her side, worked out the proper angle of elevation.

"You are not going in that way," she said firmly, closing off the castle by sitting on her fanny.

"It's tighter, altogether a better fit."

"I don't like it."

"What, fifty million homosexuals are wrong?"

Swirling morbid cloud formations the color of chronic infections signaled his arrival in Manhattan. He peered down Forty-seventh Street, Kit's new location. Over the past years Daniel had followed Kit through a succession of apartments and to the background music of galloping inflation, which for many of her clients had been a dirge. Not for Daniel. He had made money. But . . . had it been better in 1969 at twenty-five dollars a throw, or now at forty dollars?

In a discussion of the situation with Kit one day, she had made an honest claim.

"From a percentage point of view, I've gone up less than sirloin. Pieces change and the price has to."

It made economic sense to Daniel. But the question still remained. Had the service been better, the ass more supple, the pussy less elastic, when she called herself Mildred Dalyrimple and was on Twenty-second Street, west of Fifth; Ruth Cohen of East Seventy-seventh; Lynn Harting, just off Lexington at Fifty-fifth; or now as T. R. Stevenson, First Avenue and Forty-seventh Street, where the amenities included a view of the United Nations?

The nine hundred-odd lays Kit had engineered for him had to add up to something more than serendipity carried to the length of folly, and the names of the girls, their remote places of origin, more than just a jumble of Scrabble letters. Had he signed an endless chain letter, joined a Pyramid Club without an eventual winner? Daniel Barnet, thirty-seven on Valentine's Day. Some kind of inside joke he never got.

2

Clerical black formed most of the furnishings of Daniel Barnet World Insurance Associates along with steel-rimmed glasses, the small, round unfashionable sort, and that curious compound of odors which springs from men who change their suits infrequently and shave inconclusively. Daniel was pleased to see the office as crammed as a free clinic. All of his clients were priests. While they justified the ways of God to man, Daniel and his salesmen justified their premiums, a nicely balanced quid pro quo.

Murmuring "Good morning, all," Daniel walked past rows

of desks manned by earnest young executives in dark suits, nononsense haircuts, the type of recruits favored at one time by the F.B.I. Daniel's employees, forty of them, not to mention bookkeepers and secretaries who accounted for another twenty souls. A grand total of sixty human beings whose lives he changed, who depended on him for their daily bread.

Daniel wore his height—six feet three from age seventeen, when all growth apparently stopped abruptly—in a defensive slouch, but he had a loose, active manner of moving that generated energy of a kind. He wore his hair neatly over the collar of his red shirt.

His face never tired of maneuvering, for he was subject to dozens of mood changes, virtually by the hour. He seemed to carry himself with the uncertain élan of a man who had a history of damaged pride, and he had that tendency of stroking his arms and face that was to be found among neglected children and disillusioned men. His nose had a small droop at the nib, but was lifted by an expansive bone which traced a tortuous route up to the brow. It appeared to have been gently broken at one time, but he had no knowledge of this, for he had never had a fist fight in his life.

Like God, Daniel was his own associate, although the image conveyed sounded corporate, and liability was of course limited. The associates were nominees on company stationery, lending depth to the organization line. Daniel was a closer, possibly the best the insurance business had ever possessed. The Church had rewarded his feckless genius by appointing him their insurer.

He entered his office. All glass, or at least on two sides. The visionary needed an unobstructed view.

"Just stay loose, baby," he said, greeting Rouault's suffering Christ (an original) which hung from the wall beside his desk. Frequently, when closing a policy, he'd get off his swivel chair, turn his back on the priest and address the painting.

"What do you think, Lord?" After a ten-second pause, Daniel would slip on his plain glass spectacles, zero in on the priest, addressing him like a golf ball he knew he could cream. An effective combo, Daniel and Christ in thorns. "Well, Father, how do you feel about the premium?" A hint of uncertainty and Daniel drew the painting back into the act like a Bob Hope stooge. "If He could send us a message, do you know what it would be?"

Looking up from behind the nettle of figures that Daniel had thrust upon him, the priest would find himself cut off before being allowed to take an educated guess at Christ's message, and Daniel would close: "He would say insure in the name of the Church. In My name. I am the beneficiary. Amen!"

An irresistible argument. David had discovered a little known fact about men: the more logical they were, the easier to sell, so his tactics were emotional and generalized. "Not only will the Lord greet you with open arms when you enter His fields, but St. Stephen's will be able to get rid of the dry rot and extend the Junior Parochial School."

The only photograph in his office stood stranded on his desk in a red morocco binding: the now dead Father Francis J. Aurelio, the man he held responsible for his business success and the reclamation, in the early days, of his marriage. Father Aurelio, benign with beard and moustache, his watery blue eyes impaled behind spectacles, had a good deal to answer for.

On a trip to the East, Sonya's spiritual mentor had arranged to visit his former choir charmer, a long-shot mission of mercy in view of Sonya's acceptance of another faith.

Pacing his transistor-sized living room in the nineteen-thousand-dollar Babylon kennel he had hocked himself to death for, Daniel peered out of the front window at eight hundred other houses, exactly the same as his own, built on lots the size of postage stamps. Car washing and gardening were the Sunday morning activities. He himself could not afford even basic implements, and he fended off the neighbors' gibes by saying: "First I need a microscope to find my garden. . . ." Fooling nobody.

Dressed in her baby blue sleeveless Dacron ensemble, Sonya, seven months pregnant, still had something of the airline stewardess and Howard Johnson Motor Lodge hostess about her. To Daniel she always looked naked without menus in her hand. She squeezed into her pumps, filling the air with a fine charge of Ammens medicated powder.

"Why would he want to see you?"

"Father was always terribly fond of me," Sonya replied. "And generous . . ."

"Which means that we have a generous priest who knew you

in Denver years ago . . . and I've got to pick him up at Kennedy on Sunday morning."

"What are you in a mood for?"

"Well, like we've got to feed him."

"Pick up some smoked fish then. Anyway, he prefers to drink."

"Oh, really."

Daniel vaulted from the windowsill and like a defender of children and the infirm embraced his solitary bottle of Haig Pinch.

"You are not hiding it again . . . when *I* have a guest."

"Sonya, I explained that this is for show, and in the event of a boy—God should so grace this mixed union—it will remain unopened till the *briss*. Anyway, at the rate I'm going I'll be out on my ass next week and I need the security of getting drunk. . . . Regard it as furniture."

She treated him as a small tortured boy constantly requiring assurances. Hooking an arm affectionately around his neck, she blew warm Colgate breath in his ear and forced his free hand on her stomach.

"Did you feel it?"

"Definitely the big toe."

"I thought it was the head," she said, taking the liquor from him while he placed both palms on her navel, where activity was constant and mischievous.

"This is a finagle."

"What about the job now?" she insisted, teasing the tax stamp off the bottle.

"Hoffman said I'm not producing and I'm on trial."

"I thought you were over that," she said with a hiccup.

"Last month's figures weren't so hot, so I'm dancing on eggs again."

"Did you stand up to him?"

"Actually he was standing and I was sitting and shitting in my pants. I think he likes height when he starts to scream."

"Daniel, you are not going back to another goddam freaking boiler room. I had enough of that the last time. So just sweat it out," she said, reverting to her high nasal Midwestern whine when the converging topics of daily life inevitably led to the ice rink of their finances. "One Spigleman is enough for anybody."

"He got caught, so that's why you're knocking him."

"Mistake, Daniel. He escaped and you got questioned. . . ."

"Okay, drop it."

"I think you better get a move on. Father will be coming in on Braniff forty-nine at ten EST."

Slouching into his Alexander's close-out special blazer, Daniel throttled his protests and decided to make a practical inquiry.

"What do Father and I talk about?"

"How about insurance? Maybe you can sell him."

"Now, Sonya, just once fucking well try to make some sense."

"I told you he was generous to me when I was a teen-ager . . . and his family are loaded. He's dedicated to spreading the Christian spirit."

"To a shiksa who converted? I now see why the Harvard Business School offered you a scholarship."

"Daniel, you haven't been able to sell anybody for ages. . . ."

"So I kiss his feet and make nice all day and he'll buy?"

She pondered the question, made conflicting braying noises, indicating to Daniel that a typical Sonya debate was in progress. Unverifiable evidence that so many hours in the air hadn't like radiation damaged the brain paths.

"Why don't you just be your usual loving self to me?"

"I thought you wanted to make a good impression."

"Maybe that's the way to go about it. Father Aurelio can't stand cruelty."

"I'm cruel to you?"

"No, not really. It's just the effect."

On his face she detected the mixture of contrite anger which like frozen food with preservatives was said to be unharmful. A warning she knew of his permanent threat of explosion. Unfused though, and merely volatile.

"A buck for gas," he demanded. "And don't tell me that you're broke again. Because, Sonya, I found thirty-four dollars in the chartreuse bikini panties—another investment that didn't pay off. My doll as sex queen with four matching bras."

"Don't act so desperate," she said with a smile. "It shows." She handed him five dollars. "Get Nova Scotia this time and not that cheap salty belly lox or else it'll only encourage Father to drink more. . . ."

At the airport he sat fuming behind the wheel. He spotted a black suit, the right collar too, gave the figure an amiable wave.

The priest came toward him, bent his head to look in the car window.

"Daniel Barnet?"

"Who else?"

Aurelio got into the car and tossed a small overnight bag in the back seat.

"It's a pleasure to meet you," he said. "I appreciate your coming for me."

"Just say a prayer for me and we'll call it quits." The priest laughed in a kind of heh-heh way that sounded thoroughly Catholic to Daniel.

Father Aurelio settled back to take in the countryside along the Van Wyck Expressway.

"How long you staying, Father?"

"This is a permanent move," Aurelio said. "I've been reassigned."

"Gotta make one stop," Daniel said, parking in front of Lox City. "No question of who's king here."

Over a piece of smoked whitefish, the two men began to warm to each other. Slicing bagels in the background, Sonya Barnet, the former Sonya Anderson of Muncie, Indiana, and Denver, felt nascent chills of satisfaction at this first confrontation between Father and her Jewish husband.

Delicately fingering a piece of sturgeon—Daniel had gone mad spending and driven on "Empty" for twenty miles—Father Aurelio made it clear that he understood and sympathized with Sonya's conversion.

"It was a practical decision, wasn't it, son?"

"Definitely. So that we could get a divorce if it came to that, and so Sonya wouldn't be uptight about getting an abortion. Actually, she's still fighting me on that."

"Daniel, she's in her seventh month."

"Her argument is purely on medical grounds."

"Don't believe a word he says, Father. You would be shocked to know the scene he made about me converting. Got me this old Rabbi Goldring who always had saliva running down his beard."

"That only happened when you became his pupil."

Sonya rubbed her distended stomach. Inside, spiraling slowly to the bridgehead of her womb, was what would turn out eventually to be Sylvia, the namesake of Daniel's maternal grandmother. Sonya and her pessary had struck out on the honeymoon. Daniel had got her drunk and refused to conform to the good olde rhythm method that had served so many so well before her.

He rose to refill Aurelio's empty glass. Daniel and his solitary bottle of Pinch had reached that point of abandonment where the host grimly mutters: "Fuck it, let him finish and choke."

"No water, right? I usually get it right the *ninth* time."

"He's so unbearably rude. I don't know if I can stand it another minute with him, Father."

"I can't understand all of this talk about abortions and divorce," Aurelio said with an ache in his voice. He'd undoubtedly been expecting a social visit and not tag-team domestic wrestling. "Daniel, you're Jewish and Jews aren't usually that quick to get divorces," he said amicably.

"Jews do what's good for them. Believe me, I won't fall out with my religion if I unload this yo-yo. It'll be a *mitzvah*, Father, a blessing, you know. My people reward one another for admitting a mistake. They don't punish. . . . No sulphur or visions of hell on my side of the street."

Sonya rose from the table, supporting herself on nails filled with cream cheese and chives. She shook, then extended her belly close to Father Aurelio's head.

"It moved, Father. Want to feel it?"

"Sonya, just in case you didn't notice, that outfit Father is wearing means to some people that he's a representative of the Catholic Church. And you don't normally ask such men to run their fingers over your stomach, unless you happen to be you."

"I hate him, Father. Christ forgive me, I do."

"I wish the two of you would stop this bickering. There is a child to be considered."

Tactically, Daniel took a complimentary line with Aurelio; pointless to offend someone who was polishing off his Scotch: "You're the first person I've met through Sonya who wasn't airline personnel. Maintenance people are her favorites."

Fretting, pouting, then stretching her eyes, Sonya's characteristic facial expression when angered, she surprised both men by breaking into a coughing, racking howl, a sound which ended abruptly when the tear ducts filled.

"The fountains of Rome. In your honor, Father. Sonya thinks of everything."

Father with a full glass accompanied Sonya upstairs for an hour's comfort, freeing Daniel for the Giants-Green Bay Packers early kickoff. He drowned their whispers by turning up the sound, and prayed that the performance begun in jest would not evolve into the bitterness that lay too close to the surface to be amusing. Staring gloomily at the golden pigskin with the teams' names inscribed, he had a terrified vision of himself on Monday morning at the Princeton Insurance office drawing the last of Hoffman's threats and given the reality of the street by Wednesday. He forgot his fear on the first series of downs, and only now and then, during beer commercials when celebrity guests were introduced, became aware of the fact that he was a frightened man who bullied on the instructions of a woman.

There was, although Daniel refused to admit it, a genuinely appealing side to Father Aurelio's character. He had sacrificed wealth and that grass roots precedence that comes with old expansive family connections to serve people like Sonya. Just beyond comprehension. While late scores and odd meaningless statistics flooded the screen, Daniel was relieved to find Aurelio calmly making concerned inquiries about his future. Sonya had gone for her daily exercise stroll down the block.

"How long have you been with Princeton Insurance?" Aurelio asked.

"I'm rounding out my first year," Daniel said lightly, but on the verge of opening his heart and confessing that the routine was throttling him.

"You earn a good living, don't you?"

"I'm one of the big producers. How do you think I managed to buy this house?" Daniel insisted in a militant voice which aborted echoes. His opening was as dead as Kelsey's nuts, he knew, peaking before he'd gained any momentum. Like the Giants, his fortunes had evaporated and he clued back into the one-sided game. At newstime, and with Sonya on her third great circle of community hellos, Daniel finally brought up the subject of insurance. He suddenly felt himself grow cold, knew that he had hit upon the single great idea of his life.

INSURING PRIESTS!

Giving birth to a preposterous hard-on which confirmed the

knowledge. He stood up good-humoredly and extravagantly splashed Father's glass. Not quite concealing his boner, he had asked again the simple question:

"You mean to tell me that you don't have any life cover?"

"I'm afraid I never got around to it."

Daniel stalked the priest, carrying out a fast visual medical. "How's your health, Father?"

"Good, I'd say," he replied, then sipped the whiskey.

"I hope I'm not being personal if I ask you a few questions, like your age."

"Forty-seven."

"What about your personal habits like drinking and smoking." Father Aurelio revealed three smuggled Havanas. "Good, the company can live with cigars, and I assume you're just being polite about your drinking," he continued, casting a suspicious eye at the quarter-filled bottle of Pinch. "Can I assume it's mainly in the wine line?"

"You can," Aurelio said.

"I've got a suggestion to make, Father. Firstly, when was the last time you had a medical examination?"

"Let's see. I think it was when I was in the service."

"That must have been years ago. You ought to have one now. It'll be free of charge, on the company, needless to say." When the priest demurred for an instant, Daniel pounced. "I mean, wouldn't you like to know where you stand healthwise?"

Aurelio smiled pleasantly, revealingly for Daniel. The teeth looked terrific. There were however two problems, which appeared like insane Kamikaze pilots diving on a battleship. The company Daniel worked for demanded urine specimens and Wassermanns for its medical. How could he ask a priest to piss in a bottle or suggest that he might have syphilis? Not even Daniel could work up that much nerve. Would Princeton Insurance waive the Wassermann for a priest? It was definitely worth a try.

Taking Father Aurelio through his medical paces proved a nerve-racking experience for Daniel until he got the all-clear sign from the doctor on Aurelio's cardiogram, which was the shit-or-bust part of the examination. In spite of gleaming choppers, Princeton could learn that Daniel was selling to another stiff who might not be around to pay his first premium. Apart from some minor albumin irregularities, Aurelio passed with flying colors.

If offices are not the natural breeding grounds of Marxists, pinks, Communist cells, and Maoists, then it is small wonder that they spawn people with demonic forehead V's, and crusty mouth-corner eruptions. These office impresarios have only rubber bands and paper clips and dockets and carbons and who's-stolen-my-two-hundred-Papermates as serious convictions for which they sacrifice personal freedom and which enable them to reconcile themselves with supreme ease to the disasters of anyone trying to get ahead. Their reason to believe: Saving the Company Money.

Usually located behind foundry-fresh gray-green steel desks with plastic cigar-brown signs as pedigree, they come to regard the Daniel Barnets of the world as their natural prey, taking a genuine, personal pride in their every conceivable failure.

No matter how hard Max Hoffman tried, Daniel refused to take any interest in the revival of spent, bled, stamp pads, and never accepted the need to account for every single penny of petty cash Max dispensed.

The dreary mind-bending routine of traveling to and from the office, parking the car at a midway point and hopping on a train to insure that he arrived punctually at eight-fifty drove Daniel to the fringe of madness. Tardiness Max noted, and responded to in a hectoring voice that was a model of tedious consistency.

"Daniel, when is this laxness going to stop? I want an answer. . . ." The clock showed 9:01. "And please do yourself a favor and don't give me that horseshit story about the Long Island running late or breaking down again. I take two buses and one subway to get to work and if I can use three kinds of public transportation, then you sure as hell can." Max brought out a street map and indicated his own domain in South Yonkers.

"You come in from Babylon and me from here, and I would say that, give or take an eighth of a mile either way, the distances are almost the same." Max rose from his desk and with an accusing finger continued: "And you've got better connections than I do. . . ."

Daniel had given up protesting and merely fretted his life away, revenging himself in the only convenient way possible.

On the principle that earning power doesn't know from sexual inclination, Daniel developed an office liaison with what happened to be Max's girlfriend, then his fiancée, ultimately blossoming forth as Mrs. Hoffman. Her name was Norma and through various stages their relationship was unencumbered by any fine sentiments from Daniel. All that remained constant were Norma's tearful scenes and Daniel's comfortable licentiousness. Norma was his gash at Princeton.

"One thing, Max, when I have my own big outfit, I'm going to hire you away from Princeton because I'd like you worrying about my nickels the way you do here."

"Listen, it's now nine fifteen, Daniel, and you're crapping up the morning. I explained you that last week. You got calls to make. A salesman at his desk is as bad as a reporter there."

Max peered at him through watery brown eyes that possessed the demonic ambivalence of cowering—the iris would retreat into the pupil—when in the presence of superiors, and blazing truculently if an underling required scolding.

"I told you, Daniel, to get a move on. You sold one lousy policy to a priest and you think you're hot stuff. Probably your first and last sale."

Daniel wiped off a speck of dust which had become ingrained in Father Aurelio's photograph, still bemoaned his premature death after only nine premiums. His first quarter-of-a-million policy.

Ignoring his stack of mail and the time-stamped telephone messages his secretary had placed on his desk, Daniel immediately got down to business.

He dialed Kit's private number. Her dazed sleepy voice, marinated in an ocean of Smirnoff's, still carried the lame crawl of yesterday's hangover.

"Kit, it's me, Daniel. I'm just checking in. . . ."

"At ten thirty? Only me here to bang, Daniel."

"Thanks, but your friendship is too valuable."

A pause. He assumed she didn't understand.

"Pauline's supposed to drag her ass in some time today."

"Do I get a crack at last?"

"You better have your premiums paid up, baby."

"Pauline Bianco, the kiss of death?" he said excitedly.

How could Kit be so matter-of-fact about Pauline Bianco? The effect of her name galvanized Daniel, brought a strange dizziness. A legend in her own time, it was rumored that two had died under her.

According to Kit, Pauline had established the house record: twenty-seven tricks in one day on the noon-to-midnight shift. Even in sleep, Pauline functioned.

"Some girls have an orgasm or fake it," Kit explained to him. "But Pauline is your out-and-out nymphomaniac. She starts coming and doesn't stop. Don't ask me how. The day she turned all those tricks I went in afterward to ask if she wanted to hit a few bars with me and Leo, or grab something to eat, and she was laying there with her eyes closed. But Pauline wasn't sleeping," Kit averred. "She had a dildoe inside her. Man, I could not believe my eyes. As I get close to her I see that there's the underside of a pair of red balls and I say to myself, 'Kit, you got to lay off the juice. It's destroying your mind. You're seeing red balls.' So help me, Daniel, it had 'Made in West Germany' on them."

Daniel knew only one man who had "encountered" Pauline. His former employer, the elusive Irv Spigleman. Yet again, The Fly was out of circulation; he'd failed to show at Kit's. Daniel hadn't seen him for months. Maybe he was at last dead?

The door opened slowly and a golden-maned head revolved at the top of the archway. Gary Rubin possessed this strangely evanescent quality of appearing, or of having said he appeared. People wondered about his identity. He was one of those elderly young blond men of prominent, unforgettable features and the personality of a broken safe. Balancing on his right foot, his left several inches off the ground, he conjured up weightlessness and the illusion of defying gravity. Daniel's oldest friend, two months his senior, now his employee, waiting for permission to enter.

"Happy, happy—"

"Thanks," Daniel said. They were booked for dinner with Gary and his wife Marlene, the only couple Daniel could tolerate, and then only occasionally.

"Come on in," Daniel said. Despising his authority over Gary, he grossly overpaid him, cut him in on the profits. Why not? The government would only get it.

"So how's the birthday boy?" Gary asked.

"I'm worried. I've been getting such heat from Norma that my piles might come back."

"I thought you were sitting kind of funny," Gary said with sympathy. His principal function apart from shadowing Daniel was listening to him.

"How do I swing Norma and Max into dinner tonight?"

"You're crazy to try. After New Year's Eve . . . This won't be a pillow fight." Gary poured himself a cup of coffee, splattering the saucer—a sure sign that Daniel's personal life was a burden God had inflicted on him. He toyed with the cups and saucers on the Louis Quatorze table which Daniel had bought as an investment.

"Marlene wanted to get you china for a birthday present. But I told her that Daniel's already got important china."

"I can't leave Norma out."

"Well, you can't leave Sonya out. Man, your wife . . . can you?"

Daniel stood up, worked himself into an angina rage, punched his desk, but not hard enough so that it would hurt.

"This time for sure I'm going to unload that cunt."

"Norma or Sonya?"

"Sonya!"

"Daniel, you've been saying that for years. What she do now?"

"Last night. My birthday screw and she was icky-sticky like a piece of bubble gum that's been chewed to death. How is it that a man of my abilities and intelligence . . . my money! puts up with vaginal odor?"

"Vaginal odor? Sonya? First time you've mentioned that to me," Gary said with the veiled hint that this might be another of Daniel's libels. "She's the cleanest chick in the world. Even Marlene, who hates Sonya, admits that."

Daniel sat flatly on his backside, eased his legs over the belly of his desk in a moment of tenuous reflection.

"I hate to bring this up," Gary said, justifying his appearance. "But I think I'm due for a new territory. Marlene's been breaking my balls."

This was an incentive scheme Daniel had created to reward his executives with a week away, ostensibly on company business, but actually a release from the bondage of marriage . . . and with one of Kit's traveling companions.

"Why not? You free around one?"

Gary thought for a moment. He was one terrific diary checker. Most of his day was spent filling it, duplicating it, but he was always available.

"I've got drinks on with Father Terry, but I can get out of it if I phone the church now. Why?"

"Pauline Bianco's in town and I thought we'd fuck our lunch today."

3

The marshland of black slush flying from passing cars thirty stories below Daniel's office provided another dismal greeting to Valentine's Day. Depressed him, so he popped a tranquilizer, then pressed a button, knocking out the flashing red lights on his executive phone board. One by one, the lights disappeared. The signal told his secretary Jeanette that he was taking no calls. Out. Not available. But . . . Daniel loved company, visitors. He cherished the moody role of: "Mr. Barnet's out, or in conference . . ." Actually, even the boy who delivered his sausage hero got to see him.

Ignoring Jeanette's tedious whine that Daniel was seeing no one, Milton Gershner barged into the office. Slimes, as he was known to intimates, had ingratiated himself with Daniel over a long period of time. He now performed an armada of unpleasant tasks connected with Daniel's real estate interests. Slimes checked tenants' credit; made horrible noises when rent was in arrears; threatened the helpless whenever possible. He had a sweaty vulpine face, the complexion of fried liver. Accustomed to stalking and patience, the dirt of strangers was his natural lodgings.

"Sorry about this," he said without arousing Daniel's interest, for Daniel was toying with a cluster of apartment-house models that he either owned or controlled for the Church. All the models were of similar construction: vertical cheese boxes built to house humans in the smallest space and at the highest tolerable rent.

Slimes groomed the remnants of his hair with the tips of his fingers. A deviated septum further aggravated the wound that was Slimes' face. When he talked it was in a series of disconnected snorts.

"Problems, Slimes?" Daniel asked. Every event and undertaking in Gershner's domain was treated as a crisis.

"The tenants are organizing a committee in the Five Hundred building to fight the rent increase. Last week I jammed the washing machines in the basement and cut off the central heating." He brandished an official document. "We got an order from the Housing Department to switch on, or go to court."

"What about a boiler breakdown?" Daniel inquired. "Can't you tell them that?"

"They sent in independent engineers who reported that there was nothing wrong with the boiler, and we can't throw a stink-bomb in our own building," he said as though denied the keynote of his strategy.

Slimes lit a Lucky Strike while Daniel pulled a folder from a gleaming mahogany cabinet built into the wall, leafed through several pages, then calmly returned to his desk, which, except for a Hoffritz clock giving the time all over the world, Father Aurelio's photograph, and some black crocodile Gucci desk ornaments, was conspicuously clear. Not a paper in sight. As a new school businessman, he had discarded in-and-out trays, masses of memo pads, all of the accouterments of the past. When he had something to say he said it on his Dictaphone.

"Technically we don't even own the building," he informed Gershner. "We're management. It's a leaseback deal."

"So let them take us to court?"

"No, I think we'll deal out instant doom. Have we got a free apartment?"

"Two. One on the third floor and a penthouse."

"The penthouse is fine. The apartment market stinks, so we don't want to sell them off, but we need a hike just to pay bank interest."

Daniel dialed a number, tapped his desk impatiently while waiting for a reply. "If he's drunk again, I'll shove him back on welfare," he said angrily to Gershner, who was skimming through Daniel's *Wall Street Journal.* "Elvin, is that you?" Daniel shouted at a voice. "Then get him." He turned his attention to Gershner. "Slimes, get off your ass, and phone the movers to bring in all the Salvation Army stuff to the penthouse of Five Hundred. And don't use the service elevator but the two main ones, and I don't care what gets scratched."

Hurrying out, Slimes asked: "Is it under control, Daniel?"

"I'm going to bust the block."

"Which one?" came a voice at the other end of the line.

"Five Hundred. Listen, Elvin, I want you and the whole gang to move in today. Elvin White sounds too respectable, so dream up one of those Muslim names."

"Hadj ir al Zibir."

"That's greatness," said Daniel. "I want you to get the full orchestra in tonight and also call a Panther meeting."

"How many people?"

"Anything over a hundred. Mogambo costumes, lots of feathers, and the cannibal cooking pots we used last time," he added, hanging up.

To combat legislation, and government restrictions in his apartment houses, Daniel and his attorney had developed one of New York's most successful block-busting operations.

Elvin and his family, which could be improvised to eighteen children and a hundred adults, would move into a luxury apartment house whose tenants were causing Daniel grief. African tribal drums, musical instruments attached to amplification systems capable of creating an unbearable cacophony would rip through the all-white building day and night. Elvin's friends and family, dressed in loincloths, carrying spears, bows, and arrows, would parade through the lobby. No law against how people dressed or who visited a tenant. The behavior of the black children doing their pickaninny number—eating watermelons in the elevator, throwing chicken bones out of the windows, ringing doorbells to beg for handouts—would finally drive the tenants to the point of insanity. Then at about six in the evening when most people were returning from work the kids would ring all the elevator buttons, forcing the tenants to wait hours before getting to the top floors. In two days, half the tenants would plead with the management to break their leases, forfeiting their security, and the other half would gladly pay the increase if Elvin could be shifted out. Eventually, when everyone had signed up, the drums would cease, the blacks disappearing in the middle of the night with Elvin their leader, until Daniel had another problem building.

When Slimes reappeared, Daniel was standing by the window, watching two parking attendants cleaning his Rolls.

"Pick up a lease, Slimes. Make it out in the name of Hadj ir al Something. Then clue in the super and the doorman about what's happening and say Elvin is a diplomat from . . . Uganda."

"Does such a thing exist?"

"The U.N. then. We've got a lot of green buried in those fucking bricks and I want them to produce, so get weaving."

"Daniel, one thing . . ."

Daniel turned, beginning to feel dazed by the tranquilizer and having difficulty focusing his attention.

"You didn't understand something?"

"No. I just wanted to wish you a happy, happy birthday."

"Thanks . . ."

"Daniel Barnet does not forget his old friends and I'm proud of my relationship with you."

Daniel no longer enjoyed the servility of his friends and the constant reminders of past associations. Even though this served to measure his progress, the monstrous assortment of wrong turnings along the way had the effect of intimidating him and calling attention to the sinister aspects of luck. Actually he was still only a stone's throw from the panicky young man who had been classified 4-F. Celebrating his rejection, he entered show business for a short spell as a dance instructor for Inez and Pablo Dance Studios at Faigenbaum's Cliff Hotel, amid Catskill activities, where he first became acquainted with Slimes, who was the summer bartender. Slimes had captured his imagination with his brilliant conniving, for he had devised the perfect and so far as Daniel knew the only reliable method of beating the bar. As the Faigenbaums did daily inventory checks of the liquor supplies and cash balance, there seemed no way to screw them, but the owners had not reckoned with genius.

"First of all, at a bar with everybody hustling pussy, no one in the world knows what kind of Scotch or rye or gin they're drinking," Slimes explained at the end of the season. "Vodka was invented for the purpose."

"But if Faigenbaum is counting pennies and measuring every bottle, then how?" Daniel asked like a child at a magician's entertainment.

"I bring my own change and my own liquor. I move two-three bottles a night when we're really jumping, and a bottle when it's quiet. I get twenty-eight shots out of a fifth which costs me two-fifty wholesale and at a buck a shot that's twenty-five fifty profit per bottle. Ten weeks of this and I go back to the city with a bundle."

"Then what do you do?"

"I'm in linen supply. Bartending in the city is too rough. Like hard work."

For the questionable favor of introducing Inez into Slimes' sack, Daniel was promised a job with Slimes' firm on their return to the city. In any event, Daniel had grown tired of being smothered by Inez's forty-two-inch water wings, her Juicy Fruit breath, and the noisy racket of Tito Puente and his mambonicks which she insisted be played during their nightly excursions. For dessert, Inez demanded nude merengue dancing by the boathouse, and kept time by tapping his balls.

Slimes arranged an interview for him in the back room of a social club on Mulberry Street. The place smelled of stogies, the only beverage on view was black coffee drunk from small glasses, and no one apparently spoke English. Daniel detected a single expression as he nervously passed through the club— a scowl graven on each face.

Slimes sat at a desk which seemed to have been rescued from an acid bath. Hundreds of initials were scratched into the scarred top, and the chair he sat on favored its left side. Daniel stood awkwardly in front of the desk. Behind Slimes was a grimy window and a partially opened door leading to a yard. Daniel followed him outside. An elderly Italian man sat sunning himself on a striped-canvas deck chair. At the rear Daniel saw a small weatherbeaten wooden hut which Slimes unlocked. He carried out a covered wire cage while the Italian man stared at Daniel.

"In New York there are thousands and thousands of restaurants, clubs, catering joints."

"Short and sweet, Slimes," the Italian man interjected.

"Right, Mr. Cappelli. The point is, Daniel, that they all use linen tablecloths and napkins. If they don't, we persuade them to start using. See, that's the business, linen supply."

"What if they've already got someone to supply them?" Lifting the cover off the cage, Daniel recoiled in horror. He'd seen them in films, once in the woods at camp caught a fleeting glimpse of one. "A skunk!" he shouted in alarm, tripping on the uneven paving stones.

"Don't worry," Slimes assured him, "he's on our side. You see, when we visit a prospective client, we bring our friend with us. The man don't want to sign up with us, we show him our pet." Out of a bin in the shed, Slimes picked up two menacing war-surplus gas masks, tossing one to Daniel. "We unveil, then we put these on, and we watch the guy sweat."

"They always signs on the dotted line and you leave with a check for the first quarter's installment," Cappelli explained.

"How do you know the skunk won't let off—?"

"We had the glands removed. It's psychological warfare. In the old days you made threats, you terrorized an owner. Nowadays we're gentlemen. When we put on our masks the guy we're hitting is going to believe that the skunk is going to shoot a load, or else why do we put on masks?"

"A hundred a week plus commission," said Cappelli. "That's if he can add and hustles real good."

"I'm a college graduate," Daniel protested.

"Then what the hell are you doing here?" Cappelli asked quietly. "You can't cut it in the straight world, that's why."

Daniel ignored the question, and the answer, merely nodding, faced with the futile but objective assessment of his worth. The land of opportunity had proved to be nothing more than a cul-de-sac for Daniel Barnet. He'd wind up with a career as an office manager, an achievement that would take years of plodding.

"I think this kid's mailroom material," said Cappelli. "Where'd I get the idea that Jews were smart? You're the only one, Slimes."

"I'll produce for you, Mr. Cappelli," Daniel said respectfully. The old man he realized was a fox, deceptively disguised so that people like Daniel would misjudge him.

"Okay," Cappelli said, his eyes lingering on Daniel's face. "We'll see what kind of balls you've got. You got yourself a new skunk man, Slimes."

Beginning with the yellow pages of the Manhattan telephone directory, Daniel discovered that most of the eating places listed would take months to cover. Overcome by the vastness of the enterprise, he applied himself logically to the task. Senseless to attack on an alphabetical basis, so using a city street map, he broke down the enormous list geographically. Slimes had apparently wasted time attempting to work luncheonettes that used paper napkins, and small bars without much of a food business. Daniel carried a shredded assortment of lettuce leaves and nubs of carrot to feed the skunk. Under Slimes' tutelage he was shown how to enrage the beast by tantalizing it with bits of cabbage, which he would demonstrate to an obdurate client. This was the premask sequence to the showdown which never came.

Driving along First Avenue, Daniel said, "Five boroughs, Slimes. We could spend our lives doing this."

"It's a beginning to better things." Slimes emphatically tapped the wheel of the new Buick. "You get looked after very well. This car for openers. Cash in my kick all the time. You meet people who are helpful and this leads to other things. Last year 'cos everybody was so pleased with me, I got a numbers drop on the West Side. You keep at it and give the people loyalty, they don't let you down."

Daniel proved to be efficient, conscientious, and remarkably inventive, the latter quality eventually endearing him to Mr. Cappelli. In his first month he opened a hundred new accounts, carried home almost three hundred dollars a week.

For a time, Daniel wondered why Jews rather than Italians had been selected for this type of operation. Cappelli reasonably explained that most catering halls were run by Jews and he believed that certain trades responded better to their own kind. "For jukeboxes and pinball machines I always stick with Italians because there I need strong-arm stuff when I don't get cooperation. For talking to other Jews, who better than you, Daniel?"

An unimpeachable argument. Cappelli controlled the entire business from his deck chair, and when the weather turned cold from a small table in the front of the Amici Social Club.

"I've got a suggestion, Mr. Cappelli," Daniel said one afternoon after knocking off for the day. He stood in front of the table, for he had never been invited to sit down and he looked directly at the two empty chairs at Cappelli's side.

"You want to sit, Daniel, don't you? Know why you can't? You're not a member and maybe a member walks in, calls 'Hi' to me and I can't offer him a chair at my table 'cos you're taking up the place. It's bad manners on my part. Now what've you got to tell me?"

"I think there's no point in continuing to hit individual places. Why can't I walk into a chain and organize them . . . ?"

"Go on, I'm listening."

"The people running the chains are sitting in offices, not wearing aprons. I go up to an office. I make an appointment with the owner and I give him a demonstration."

"What stops him calling a cop? The little guy you can muscle."

"The man in control of an organization has more to lose. You see a brand name that they advertise needs only one little piece of bad publicity and he's finished. Suppose you're Chicken Universe with two hundred outlets in the city, you advertise on TV. You spend thousands promoting your name. It gets in the papers that in a couple of the places skunks have been found and there's no explanation. Word of mouth, the public starts talking. Whenever Chicken Universe is mentioned, someone'll say that's the place they found the skunks in. If the boss does call the cops, that still doesn't prevent me from doing a job on him. I go to court. Extortion, menaces. I've got no record. My word against his. I'm employed by a linen supply company. What do I know about threats and skunks?"

"I love it, Daniel," Cappelli said. "Tell Slimes I said okay and you'll get all the help you need."

Riding high in his new role of syndicate financial genius, Daniel grew a shapely moustache to age himself, purchased his first cashmere overcoat, foraged through various hat shops until he came up with a dignified Dobbs medium brim which emphasized that he was not to be taken lightly, appeared regularly at sporting events with an assortment of past-it bar waitresses, all of whom he generically christened "Angie," and explained his wealth to his father with—"Don't worry, Pop. I'm connected. . . ."

Swarthy barmen in dimly lit cocktail lounges now greeted him with: "How's the boy, Daniel?" then surreptitiously leaned over, hoarsely whispering that there was a new chick starting work tonight who would crown the selection of beat, anything-goes girls he had accumulated like one-buck Scot ties. He told people his name was Danielli only when out of earshot of the Amici Social Club so that his claim might not be disputed. Recognition, the mellifluous sound of his name rolling off the tongues of strangers, heightened his newly born sense of pride and self-admiration. He scrupulously examined his face every morning, was ruthless with blackheads, took the occasional weekend off with Slimes to Atlantic City where among lonely, desperate, single women he built up a backlog of lays for the city; he assured them that if anybody was causing them trouble he would personally eliminate the pest, wreaking vengeance in bloody Palermo fashion. Bodies in deep freezes, hanging by thumbs, or by the collar on stevedore grappling irons, were the marks of the Danielli hit.

On a muggy August morning Chicken Universe eventually received the benefit of one of Daniel's business visits. He persuaded Slimes that he didn't need a backup man, could handle the action more effectively as a single. An appointment with the chairman he inveigled easily, indicating that he had new freeze techniques for chickens which would save them a fortune. Their offices were in a genteel brownstone on Park Avenue, and Daniel drummed a beat on the receptionist's desk, and stared at photographs of buttery capons jammed in their death cells.

The cage he carried, hooded in red velvet, he passed off as a new breed of succulent pullet. The chairman's secretary finally called for him and accompanied him to the executive suites. He shook hands with an impassive thirtyish man who introduced himself as Frank Blake.

"We're operating a franchise operation," Blake said. "The company has two hundred and fifty outlets which it solely owns and we've got another two hundred which are owned by individuals in partnership with the company. So if your gizmo is any good, Mr. Danielli, we might even sign an exclusive contract with you and also help you market it."

Daniel paced around the room, then stopped, took off the gray suede gloves and laid them beside the cage. He decided to begin low key. Menacing, if necessary, would come later.

"It's not exactly a new freezing technique I've got in mind."

"No?" asked Blake. "It was my understanding on the telephone—"

"—Your understanding doesn't matter a shit to me, Blake."

"What's this all about?" Blake said, perplexed, and removing his glasses.

"My organization operates a linen supply company and your people use thousands of aprons."

"We've already got a supplier. Good morning, Mr. Danielli."

"We can also supply all the boxes and paper napkins you use in your places."

Blake picked up a folder marked "Sales," put his glasses back on, and dismissed Daniel.

"You can find your way out by yourself."

Daniel slammed Blake's desk with the palm of his hand, scattering some I.B.M. punch cards.

"I don't think you understand my position or your own," Daniel said.

"What is this? Are you some kind of nut? I told you I wasn't interested. Now clear out."

Skunk time. Daniel lifted the velvet curtain, at last getting a rise out of Blake, who leaped to his feet and shouted:

"Get that goddam thing out of here."

"How would you like a couple of hundred of them running around your joints?"

"Are you trying to intimidate me? Because if you are, you've run into the wrong man."

"Okay. If that's how you feel." Daniel picked up the cage, and handed a gas mask to Blake.

"Here's a sample. I think you ought to get yourself a job lot of these for your employees."

Blake fingered the mask and in a fluster said: "Mr. Danielli, please sit down for a minute and let's discuss this . . ."

"Nothing to discuss." Daniel whipped out a contract. "You just sign this, and you'll never have to worry. My personal assurance."

"Your assurance?"

"Right! That's all you need and I give you a clean bill of health."

Daniel could see that Blake was thinking over the proposition, and he sat down on the sofa, examined the moons on his manicured nails, placed the cage on the floor while Blake turned the pages of the contract.

"I can't sign this alone," said Blake. "It also requires the signature of the treasurer and the secretary."

"Where are they?" Daniel demanded.

"In their offices."

"You better get them in now, Mr. Blake."

On the intercom, Blake instructed his secretary to get hold of the two officers, poured himself a cup of coffee and offered one to Daniel, who told him to go easy on the sugar. In a moment there were knocks on the door and Daniel, now in charge, admitted the two men, then fell back on the sofa and broke into a soft whistle.

"We've just been offered a take-it-or-leave-it deal," Blake began to his executives, who sat on chairs facing him, their backs to Daniel. "This man under the pretext of developing a new freeze has just told me that unless we contract to take his linen and his line of packaging that skunks will be let loose in our franchises." The two men turned slowly, glaring at Daniel, the man of respect, and waited while he revealed the skunk. There was an unexpected sound of laughter. Blake's loudest. Daniel jumped up in disbelief.

"You think I'm playing games?" Daniel stormed, then fell silent when one of the men turned around and pointed a gun at him.

"Hey, what the hell are you doing?" Daniel asked, sliding deeper into the sofa.

Never having been closer to a pistol than in 35 mm. on a wide screen, he thought he heard the snap of the safety released. Blake walked from his desk and sat alongside Daniel. He pushed his glasses back down from his forehead, examining Daniel as though in the presence of an extinct specimen.

"Whatever your name is, shithead, you better start filling us in on some details. Like who sent you here?"

"It was my idea," Daniel said, averting his eyes from the gun. Maybe if he didn't look, it would disappear.

"Do you know who we are?" asked the man pointing the gun.

"Chicken Universe?"

"We're Chicken Universe all right and we're from Detroit. That's where we started," said the third man. Possibly the company secretary, but Daniel did not inquire. "That's where the

family is, baby, that bankrolled this company. Now who the hell
do you work for?"

"Mr. Cappelli, Joe Cappelli," Daniel said, hoping the name
would drive the men insane with fear.

"Cappelli?" said the man holding the pistol. "Who's he?" he
asked Blake.

"An old Moustache Pete. Wonder that he's still alive. I guess
he must be about eighty now and his brains are soft. I mean to
say, sending around an idiot like this with a skunk in a cage.
Man, this is the twentieth century. That stuff went out even in
the old country."

The pistol was pressed against Daniel's right temple and he
was asked to provide Cappelli's telephone number. He thanked
God he'd remembered it as Blake dialed the number.

"Is Cappelli there?" Blake asked. "Then call him out of the
yard. Who is this? Frank Blaccaro from Detroit. I think I've
got one of his people sitting in my office." Blake winked
at Daniel in a friendly fashion. "Think of something nice, because you might not get the chance again. By the way, what is
your name?"

Daniel heard a voice give his own name, spelling it for Blake.

"Joe. Christ, who knew you were still alive? Have you got a
kid called Daniel Barnet working for you with a skunk?" Blake
put his hand over the receiver to inform the others that Cappelli had identified Daniel. "Honestly, Joe, why don't you check
people out before trying to muscle them? I'm running all Detroit money through my company and this Barnet threatens me
with a skunk. Now, come on, stop kidding . . . and if you want
some friendly helpful advice, forget about using animals. Make
a small investment in some stinkbombs. All you need is hydro-
gen sulfide and you're in business. Okay, but as long as you
behave yourself."

Bleary-eyed and in the midst of his first swoon, Daniel saw
the mass of faces closing in on him. His last moment on earth
and he was sitting next to a skunk gnawing wire on a cage in
anticipation of a last lettuce leaf from his diligent owner. Blake
picked up the cage, handed it to Daniel, and said:

"On your feet. Now listen to me, Barnet, get rid of your pet,
forget Cappelli, change your pants because you wet them,

fill out some forms at an employment agency, and get yourself a nice safe nine-to-five job in an office or a garage so you don't get yourself into trouble. It's a big, rough world and you weren't meant to buck it. Now, vanish."

4

Daniel's secretary was one of those noodle-soup-for-colds dears who, in spite of his pleas to leave him alone, had made a career out of trying to understand him. Obsessed with improving him, and insuring that he was universally loved (if he followed her instructions), she treated his office as her nature-wander path. She attempted to regulate his personal life in the same benevolently inspirational fashion as Golda in Israel.

She had taken Norma Hoffman, Daniel's mistress, under her wing and exerted a one-woman consumer's pressure lobby for precarious romance.

"When are you going to call Norma? She's been phoning since eight this morning," Jeanette said in a throaty whisper that was designed to avoid the outright scold, but rather to appeal to his conscience. Before he could reply, she added: "Norma only wants to wish you a happy birthday, so don't say you're out, I don't like lying to her."

"You lie to Sonya all the time," he said, pointing an accusing finger at the truth-giver.

"Sonya is your wife. A man's mistress sits in a bomb shelter," Jeanette said.

Not his firmly rounded, fruity Norma. Women, he realized, surrounding him like flies blitzing dogshit, were always forcing him to exert himself for *other* women. He clicked the buttons on his phone and shooed Jeanette out of the office, since elaborate commentary was another of her wretched virtues. He cut off the amplified squawk box, so that Norma's displeasure would not take the form of a public announcement, for there was no response a man might make to justify neglect.

On the fourth ring, Norma answered, impregnating "Hel-lo" with her chronic outrage and familiar grief.

"It's me. . . ."

"Oh . . . I wondered when you'd get around to me. The mailman came and went and no Valentine's card. I guess you're confusing me with Sonya. You're so soulless."

She orchestrated his guilt like a Tyrolean accordionist, mostly with wind. Their last marathon evening *au couchant,* she had described as a mercy hump just to put her out of her misery. He had naturally defended himself: "Are you serious? I left one of my lungs inside."

"Norma, it happens to be my birthday. And I sent you a greetings telegram."

"You did? I guess they're a little slow to deliver out here."

She and Max lived perhaps twenty minutes away from him. She had forced this move of convenience years before.

"Are we having dinner together at least?" she asked.

"I was wondering . . ."

"I have your birthday present , . . and Daniel I will not be stalled."

"Well, what am I going to do with Sonya?"

"Maybe we could eat in different restaurants and you get yourself a pair of roller skates. . . ."

"Ice skates," he suggested. "Look, why don't we do it this way: I'm booked with Gary and Marlene and Sonya of course and we're eating at Casa Brasil. Why don't you pull Max there and we sort of run into each other and I ask you to join us."

He thought he heard the sound of a growl, not the Bell equipment this time nor an F.B.I. bug.

"I'm not going anywhere near Sonya. You and I are going to have dinner with Gary and Marlene. This is an ultimatum. I'm not kidding this time, Daniel."

"I'll have to put a contract out on one of you."

"Try yourself."

"Norma, what is this attacking about? Please try it my way. I'll ask Max to join us and we'll make it a friendly business get-together."

"Fine, just don't bring Sonya."

She snapped down the receiver without allowing him a last word. And he lost the slender comfort of her anger, which usually made him feel better. Reproaches had circumscribed the wayward drift of their affair. Even after all of this time, he still found himself victimized by promises he refused to make to her.

Norma had been the easiest woman in the Princeton office to promote, but it occurred to him only after a time that her apparent compliance was really the visible proof of her love. She had come from Chicago to work at the insurance company as the doctor's nurse, and Daniel saw in her an inexpensive alternative to Sonya. She was twenty-three, he was thirty-one, and his only opposition to her affection had been Max Hoffman, then the office manager. He had developed a degree of antagonism with Max which matched his domestic one with Sonya. The combination of a freebie and screwing Max at the same time had proved irresistible.

Catching hold of Daniel's sleeve one afternoon on the way home, Max had sought to make peace: "Daniel, be fair. You're a married man and she's a nice girl who knows from nothing."

Decided to play the shits with Max.

"Max, I'm in a hurry to get home and frankly I don't know what you're talking about."

"Look, you got time for a drink?"

Gazing at Max's office gray-green complexion which now, during his unavailing and protracted courtship, he had sought to improve by regular sunlamp treatments, resulting in splotchy, dry, flaking skin, and further irritated by a noisy after-shave, Daniel decided to have a drink. Company policy prohibited office romances, and both men conducted their pursuit with the anonymous concealment of Colonel Abel.

Max selected a nearby bar that catered to free-loaders and offered two drinks for the price of one, and all the greasy meatballs and cold cocktail franks anyone would dare swallow. Daniel felt he could give Max about twenty minutes of his time. This would allow Norma to get to her apartment, make the bed, put out the ice and cheese dip, so that he could zoom in, rip her off, and still make the eight-thirty to Babylon.

"I know you've got a helluva long trek, so I appreciate this, Daniel," Max said, placing on the table a pair of vodka martinis the size of small vases.

"About me and Norma . . . Christ almighty, I don't know where you got that idea."

"Is that the truth?"

"Why should I lie to you?"

"That's true," Max said, nodding his head, sipping his drink and persuading himself instantly that he had brought a false charge. "Some married guy is giving her a hard time. I thought it was you."

"Norma say it was me?"

"No. I just sort of assumed . . . listen, I'm sorry. But you know, around the office I got the impression that she liked you."

"And you concluded that she'd be giving me head?" Daniel said with terrible outrage.

"Daniel, please, don't say such a thing about Norma."

"I swear a lot, Max."

"Yeah, I noticed, but you do around her and she don't seem to mind."

From the moment he had begun working at Princeton, Max had taken special, apparently prophylactic, measures to purge Daniel of his revolutionary office manners. The task was comparable to taming a Lower Saxony boar. He who hates longer and harder develops a natural arrogant superiority, and Daniel finally managed to reduce Max's balls to the size of cuff links. The sort of achievement which might fill any cannibal with pride. Daniel had made him give ground, slowly truckling, until Max, as was now the case, sought to ingratiate himself.

"I could give you a little clue . . . but Max, I hate squealing. . . ."

Max speared three meatballs on a toothpick, balanced them exquisitely and swallowed them as though they were rare micro-piked heads. Mystery made him ravenous.

"I know I been a little hard on you, Daniel. But it's been for your own good. I didn't want you fired."

"I guessed as much," Daniel said, draining his glass.

"You eating the olives and onions?" Max asked, for there was a generous assortment of this pickled hardware at the bottom.

"Go on, you have them."

"I'll get us another few setups," he said, looking at his watch.

The bar policy altered in precisely five minutes and the feathery cut-rate inducements became brutally overpriced. Max hustled into line, held up a quarter to the bartender to identify himself as a tipper, and of course waited his turn patiently. His subtle plan was to feed Daniel drinks to loosen him up, a typically sophisticated Max gambit which amused Daniel and virtually played into his hands. It had been Daniel's nightly custom—a training program of sorts—to knock back six or seven vodkas with Norma, so that he could actually wreck her for an hour or so and come when *he* was ready. After a concert of multiple orgasms, Norma would be limp, barely talk coherently.

"They give you a fair deal here," Max advised him, serving fresh drinks. "I'd really consider it the most terrific personal favor if you could give me a little info on who's giving Norma trouble. You notice the rings under her eyes?"

"Who hasn't?"

"There's been talk . . . ?"

"Whispers. Suggestions sort of. You know at your level, you don't hear too much," Daniel observed.

"What's the word, Daniel?" Max asked, his voice losing its industrial rasping whirr, which each morning had the spine-chilling, nerve-racking grate which a shoemaker trimming the uneven outer sole makes at his wheel. "There's a new wise guy in Casualty. One of them greasers which wears flowered ties," Max suggested.

"Top . . . echelon from what I've heard around."

"Top!"

"Exec. Look, Max, I don't think I can say any more. You know that expression about the wrath of gods."

"Give me a name."

"There's a theory . . . straight," Daniel emphasized the word to indicate the unimpeachable source of the intelligence, "from the typing pool. June let it out. Claims she was dropped for Norma by Andy." The office nymphomaniac and the executive vice-president had been carrying on a well-publicized T.G.I.F. affair from four to five-thirty during the year.

"Andy Robinson is my friend. He would never . . ."

"Max, didn't your father ever tell you that a single hair on a woman's pussy is stronger than a cable on the Golden Gate Bridge?"

"That mother. My friend . . . he wouldn't buddy-fuck me."

"Your friend?" Daniel said in a manner dispelling the illusion. "How? He invites you to his barbecues in Pound Ridge?"

"No, never."
"You call his wife 'Jennifer'?"
"I haven't met her."
"So what gave you the idea that he was your personal friend?"
"We work together for fourteen years."
"You just swat asses for him."

Daniel polished off his drink in two short gulps. Running right on schedule. Ten minutes on the subway to Sunnyside, and a three-minute walk to Norma's apartment, a few more drinks, and he'd be ready to dismember her.

"Daniel, thanks. I won't forget this."

Certainly not until the following morning, Daniel knew very well, when the engine would be cranked up, his raw red lips slicked with Chap Stick and yet another day would be stretched out in the nightmare vision of infinity that was Princeton Insurance, Inc.

"You can have these olives, too," Daniel said, slipping into his overcoat. At long last, Sonya had had the zipper repaired for the sheepskin lining and now it took a bit longer before he froze.

Norma usually behaved as if she were sitting *shivah* until he arrived. Noshing Max's balls had sharpened Daniel's appetite for Norma's post-office diversions. He'd have the full seven courses this evening, and ninety minutes was the time he allowed for the banquet.

He had a key and let himself in. One large room with a kitchen alcove behind a raffia screen; a bathroom that she kept as clean as an operating theater; a small round dining table by the window which gave onto a self-service gas station; a tweed-armored convertible sofa which enabled her to characterize the despondency of her living accommodation as a studio. Immediately below the room was a take-out Chinese restaurant ruled by steel-plated cockroaches.

She lolled nakedly on the sofa, sipping a vodka on the rocks, and he crept up on her and sucked on the small hollow of her shoulder. In the flesh he never had any doubt that he was in love with her. Her skin announced the unexpected union of scattered freckles and olive tone, pleasing Daniel, for it attracted light. But in her lonely brown eyes, the history of Sephardic movement found a permanent record. The expression playing on her lips, like a solitary child's, was one of unvarying sullenness. She was the sort of girl who always dieted on rotten men who made promises, screwed her, and left her for dead. Daniel had collected her after two broken engagements.

"You're a little late," she said. Even naked she wore her Embraceable Bulova, clock-watching for his benefit.

"I stopped off for a drink . . . with guess who . . . your secret admirer."

"Max?" Jacked herself up on an elbow. "How come?"

"He wanted to find out if I was putting you away."

"You didn't tell him?"

"No, I said it was Andy. You don't think I'd say it was me. Christ, Norma, I get enough heat from that tub of shit."

"He's not a tub of shit."

"A drink, please, and don't fucking well tell me what I can't say. This old fart gives you a little romance and trust my baby to start getting ideas."

He always whipped her, made her cower, then consoled her. She presented an image of carefully tended sensuality to men, but her previous experience had wrecked her confidence. Daniel had sailed into her the first week she began at Princeton, chalked her off on a Saturday morning and been going helplessly to the well ever since.

"I'm giving up the apartment."

"That's a relief. Where are you going to move?"

"I'm not sure yet. . . . I can't cut the rent."

"Norma, I'd help, but with Sonya and the baby and the mortgage, I'm being eaten alive."

"So I've heard. But, Daniel, life with you is getting a little one-dimensional. I'd like there to be more than getting laid between five thirty and seven forty-five . . . when you can make it. One movie and seven dinners in almost a year doesn't exactly convince me that you want to leave Sonya."

"I hate Sonya."

"Do you ever tell her that, or just me?"

She pinned up her waist-length black hair with enormous bobby pins and headed for the bathroom. He poured his own drink, sank a potato chip into his favorite cheese dip—chives with love—and trailed after her. Experiencing confusion, he waited outside for a moment, heard the thunderous explosion of water coursing through elderly pipes which cut into the rumbling cannonade of the el a block away.

She was in the bath. Her body slurping and swizzling through bubbles.

"It's like you're the one in a big hurry tonight," he said.

"Max's taking me to the theater and then out to dinner."

"How the hell can you stand him?"

"He's lonely and so am I."

"Where's he taking you for dinner?"

"Sometimes he makes dinner at his place. He's a pretty good cook."

"At his place?" The news startled Daniel, then jolted him into a frenetic adolescent bout of throwing himself about. Valuing convenience above all else, his energies were confined to weighing up the loss. "You better tell me what's going on."

"I sleep on the sofa. All better now? Please close the door. I'm getting a draft."

"What else?"

"He's asked me to marry him."

"He'll ask anyone who'll have him."

"I suggested that I move in with him."

"I suppose I should have expected something like that from you. You'd peddle yourself to anybody . . . just to get married."

"You've got cheese dip on your tie."

"I don't want you to marry him."

"Then just leave Sonya."

"Look, Norma," he was barking while she shaved a leg, "you and I produce some terrific fucking. Why make more of it?"

"When did I ever make more of it?" she asked, forcing him to swallow the lie he had imposed on her. "I never thought our relationship would amount to anything else." She paused. "Max, at the very least, is a decent guy. A friend who doesn't lie or bullshit me."

"We're not going to end it this easy."

"Then it'll be my decision and not yours. Now I want you to go before Max arrives."

For the first time since trivial childhood hurts, Daniel was aware of a sense of loss that usually inhabited some invisible undefined area outside himself. It orbited mysteriously, out of range. Norma had begun to make him grieve.

She came out of the bath. Bubbles clung to her back and he dried her with the still damp towel he had used the day before. He loved the curve of her round behind and the flat stomach. He would press his ear to her breast, imagining he heard the sound of eternity coming from deep inside her. But he enjoyed Norma only in her role as piece. Wife would have removed the attraction, he was convinced.

He bent down and kissed the top of her head while she sat on the edge of the tub powdering her toes. On her face she registered the resigned agony of a girl who had found passion, then had it misplaced for her.

"You'll get your name changed to Hoffman and you'll wind up collecting all the shit that goes with it."

"Daniel, do me one favor. I've had nothing but unpleasantness and flack since I met you. Is it possible to say *something* kind?"

"I'd sooner give up smoking than fucking you."

Their affair had been going on and . . . on. Each ending created a new beginning which tasted sweeter as time passed. Even on his birthday, he couldn't make up his mind about inviting her to dinner instead of Sonya. Irresolution had become the constant fact of his life. But Norma remained, as unexpected and as pleasing as a truffle.

5

Some meetings, some people, are impossible to duck or postpone. Lawyers. Possessed by a strange and wayward demon, Daniel was one of nature's most outstanding arrangers of meetings. He would invariably attend these get-togethers in a mystical union combining puzzlement and outrage. He would seldom remember the reason, not to mention the purpose, of the gathering and would fume and fuss at the loss of man hours, twisting papers into outlandish shapes until someone explained why in fact he

had to attend. Lately it had begun to embarrass him. Jeanette
sent him memos beforehand which he would never read. At the
end of the day she would religiously collect them off the floor,
pissing and moaning about janitorial duties. Daniel had in the
past year become the Charles Lindbergh of indoor glider flight.

"Daniel, Jack Sonnerman has been waiting outside for ten
minutes."

"Oh, yes," he said vaguely. "Do you know why?"

"He has an appointment with you. You called him yesterday,
didn't you?" Jeanette suggested like a detective leading a suspect
into a confession.

Sonnerman came through the open door and Daniel squinted
sheepishly at him.

"Happy birthday, my dear," said Sonnerman. He deared and
darlinged his clients to death. Daniel he kissed on both cheeks,
a practice among Jewish men which unlike the Mafiosa equiva-
lent is not farewell, but stay well because I need you. After a
course with Weight Watchers, he had gone from 230 pounds to
189, eliminating pastrami from his life in favor of organic foods,
and he carried in his pockets gnarled figs and bits of dried pear.
He opened his attaché case, handed Daniel a thickish foolscap
document, then distributed himself on most of Daniel's red-
leather Chesterfield, resting his chin on the high arm.

"So what have we got here?"

"Your new will," Sonnerman said, uncrossing his legs and surprised. "There were so many codicils on the other one that it
became meaningless. I drew up a new one as you asked and put
Sonya back in. Your kids get three-quarters and Sonya and
Norma divvy a quarter. Right?"

"I'm divorcing Sonya."

"Since when?" Sonnerman demanded, rising and edging over
to Daniel's desk. "Daniel, at the rate you're going you'll wind
up dying intestate."

"I really want to know if it's too late to get an annulment."

"An annulment? After two children and almost eight years of
marriage?"

"Can't Judge Mariolla fix it?"

"That good a fixer he isn't. I mean he can't invent grounds
that don't really exist. What is it with you, Daniel? Since when
has Sonya become such a menace?"

"I hate her."

"That's not grounds. . . . Look, you're building it up in your mind."

"I want to marry Norma."

"In my whole life I never met anyone who was so frequently in the market for trouble. A beautiful mistress minutes from where you live, a wife who is, generally speaking, an adorable person."

Daniel pondered the situation. He wondered what kind of figure Pauline Bianco had. Kit had been building her up for months, feeding him tantalizing bits of information about her performance. Now with Irv Spigleman banged out of circulation, there was no one to cross-check with.

"Jack, Sonya's got some stocks."

"Oh, Christ, I'm fainting. I advised you over and over . . . Did you ever come clean with me about how you felt? Or confide in me the way a client usually does?" Sonnerman asked, skillfully advocating the strength of his own position. "How much has she got?"

"A few million in unregistered stock from Spigleman."

"Nothing to worry about. The Fly's toilet paper'll never get a registration."

"Diamonds . . ."

"Diamonds? Real ones? Big?"

"A hundred big ones at least which I bought as a hedge."

"That's a gift and legally hers."

"The house . . ."

"A divorce at this moment, Daniel, is out of the question. That's my advice. Grin and bear it. Make nice on her."

Sonnerman raised his tinted bifocals to heaven while Daniel skimmed through this most recent addition to his collection of wills, braying moody sounds. His morning had taken on its usual negative momentum inspired by Sonya and the desire to screw her out of any claim she might have to his financial interests.

"How do you feel about a robbery?" Daniel inquired.

"What have you got in mind? And who is the burglar and for what reason?" Sonnerman asked captiously, zealously guarding the tarnished trunk of a reputation that required mudguards.

"What's wrong with me? I tell Sonya that I've heard there's

been a lot of robberies in the neighborhood and she should keep the ice in the vault at the bank. I then get knock-offs and replace them. The house I ask her to sign over to me because of tax or something like that."

"Really, Daniel, you're underestimating her. And I haven't heard a word about a robbery. I bring you a nice fresh will and you want to make me a partner to conspiracy. As it is, I'm facing disbarment proceedings over my brother-in-law's tax finagle. And my dear client," Jack added in a panic-stricken voice, "this morning I get news which I wasn't going to mention on your birthday. Audit!"

"I thought the audit examination went fine. We got the I.R.S.'s seal of good housekeeping."

"I thought so too. But this morning I had a visit from two Treasury lawyers. Kids, neither of them over twenty-five, but they got to start somewhere and they had a hard look at your financial structure and they told me they were going to reexamine it just so they could satisfy themselves that nothing was wrong."

"Will they take?" Daniel asked.

"Daniel, these two kids got their grounding with Nader in Washington. They were on the team that wiped out the Department of Commerce. You give them cooperation, not bribes." Sonnerman blinked in shock. "They've got ideals which haven't gone sour yet, but by age thirty they'll be sticking their hands in everybody's pockets like they all do."

"I don't see the problem. What have I done?"

"We don't pay income tax. It's that simple. I mean we're honest about it and we've got the law on our side, but it still looks bad when someone with your income shelters everything. You remember that piece of rock we flew to . . . Georgetown in Grand Cayman?"

"So?"

"The point is that I established a British company there to funnel all your money through. That company is charitable, or as it's technically known, a discretionary trust, and the reason we went to all this trouble is that this charitable trust has trading rights. In other words, Daniel, we then buy stock and property in any currency through the account in Zurich. We buy money, we buy gold bullion—whatever looks like it's going to do well. When the dollar was under pressure I bought you pounds at two dollars and thirty-eight cents and after the devaluation they were worth about ten cents more."

"Jack, I'm stuck with Sonya and Norma at dinner tonight. What do I do about that?"

"Daniel, for God's sake be serious. We're discussing money and not your sex life. Our charitable institution does not pay income tax and what I think these lawyers want to do is use us for a test case. The government foots the bill on their side and if there's a hundred-to-one chance that they can prove that you willfully evaded tax they'll go to court." Momentarily winded, Sonnerman lit an herbal cigarette.

"It sounds like a chickenshit case to me," Daniel said. "As long as you assure me that at the time we didn't break any laws."

"Technically, we didn't. But I still don't like the looks of it. Because if they think something is fishy they'll slap a jeopardy lien on all of your assets."

"There is a problem about assets," Daniel said.

"You've got nothing in the U.S. The apartment houses are legitimate tax shelters, and they're owned by a company."

"Sonya has some of my money, Jack. In a phony account . . ."

"And you dare talk to me about divorce? Are you insane? Divorce! Scandal! And you're selling insurance to the Church of New York. Another thing—have you eliminated Max Hoffman from the office yet?"

He'd been foolish to allow his personal situation to crisscross into his business. A bind. But it was too much trouble to unload Max inasmuch as he was oppressively diligent about every penny of company money that came in or went out.

"Eventually . . ."

"Eventually he may discover that you have been screwing his wife silly. And eventually he may rediscover the pride he stuck up his ass. And eventually he may bury you. He knows too much about your business, my dear. Daniel, get rid of him."

Daniel, now in a condition of some trepidation, accompanied Sonnerman to the outer office, to the elevator, reluctant to let go of him.

"You can't just walk out on me now. Fire Max, stick with Sonya, ignore Norma. That's advice?"

"The oracle of Delphi I'm not. You married the woman. You must have had a reason for doing it."

"Where are you running?"

"To court. To defend a more important client than you. Me!"

6

Walking in his customary Librium daze back through his office, Daniel was overwhelmed by the confusion of his current circumstances. Constantly exhuming shrapnel fragments of his life, he made a concerted effort to get to the bottom of himself. If only he could find a laboratory, better still a kitchen, so that he could weigh and examine the ingredients that made up the ever-changing recipe of his passions, he would consider himself fortunate. But today's ragout tasted of yesterday's gravy and there was always present a sweet-and-sour taste that alarmed him.

The progressive deterioration of his taste buds had begun with Miss Sonya Anderson when she ushered him to seat 16E on a tattered roach Super Constellation. The wayfarer was on his first trip to the winter wonderland of sunshine. Miami. Not that he preferred cold climates or winter sports. He had quite simply never made enough money to enable him to forage for nookie during Februarys.

"Here you are, sir," she said. "I'm your stewardess, Sonya Anderson, and I hope you have a pleasant flight."

She smiled at him through the stale motionless air that carried ancient ruins of vomit and a horizon composed of millions of airborne farts looming overhead like some deadly commencement of interplanetary warfare. Also it was 1:30 A.M. and the briskness of her performance amid the frenzied Cubans stampeding down the aisle, he thought indicated a high degree of composure. He'd sit on Miss Anderson's lap if they had to crash-land.

The source of Daniel's wealth, of recent vintage and alas to prove transitory, was a job selling stock at Spigleman and Associates. On Gary's well-earned Section 8 discharge from the army, Daniel had brought him to the firm, where he himself had worked up to the lofty height of Spigleman's aide.

"He's the most impressive guy I've ever met," Gary told Daniel.

At their first meeting Spigleman was dressed in his customary, hysterically electrifying pastel apricot flannel trousers which illuminated the burnished brown of his permanent winter tan. Virtually six feet, and with a navy-blue-black hair weave, Spigleman was falling in love with himself again. Gary had virtually stood at attention. Reclining under a sunlamp, and wearing black goggles, Spigleman conducted the interview. If importance is the embroidered lie of not being able to leave one's desk, then Spigleman was important.

Under the desk Gary observed that Spigleman's trousers were curtsying on his ankles, and a girl whose face he couldn't see was slowly consuming him. What further impressed, indeed astounded, Gary was that he'd never shaken a man's hand in these conditions. Unflustered, Spigleman said:

"Kit, don't crease the pants." Without a change of intonation, he continued: "Just have a seat. I'll be through in a few minutes."

Good as his word. When the sunlamp timer went "bing-bing," somewhat louder than a typewriter bell, Spigleman rose, hitched up his trousers and the girl crawled backward from under the desk; moved as though from a secure knowledge of the floorplan over to a door leading to a bathroom, plopped the sap into the sink, gargled, walked out, relipsticking as she traveled.

"Ever meet anybody busier than me?" Spigleman asked Gary, then went on, as he did not expect an answer. "I'm so fucking busy that I can't even get myself a lunch break. Now, I look after my people once I take them on. You can ask your friend Daniel, who's on his way to becoming a rich man. . . . By the way . . . Gary, is it?"

"Gary Rubin . . ."

"This is Kit and she or one of her friends'll look after you and your clients. We arrange to coordinate her and Daniel loading when we've got somebody we want to torpedo. Either we leave with every penny the client has to his name, or Kit leaves with his balls in her mouth."

"Tomorrow, Irv, unless you call me otherwise," Kit said, formally examining Gary and treating him to a mere mandarin nod. *"You* can contact me through Irv or Daniel. . . ."

All at once, Spigleman's telephone began buzzing, ringing, singing, as though the communication systems in his office were suffering from a nervous breakdown. Spigleman barked:

"Four and half-six. Seven and five-eighths—for a block of ten thousand. Check the pink sheets. Don't tell me I'm outta line, Steve. I'm making the market and I want you to give it till over the weekend before we start dumping. Let's run it up a little. Listen to me. So you've got a big position. I won't let you suffer. No, it's not going to be like the Medical Credit Cards. You'll get a registration of the paper. I swear on my life," he said, slamming down the phone.

Spigleman rose, went to his safe, and took out a six-foot-long box, opened it to reveal thousands of three-by-five index cards which listed the names, addresses, and telephone numbers of people who had filled out coupons in reply to FREE INSIDER INFORMATION offered by I. SPIGLEMAN & ASSOCIATES, ASSOCIATED WITH ALL LEADING EXCHANGES.

"Paper every one of these names with the prospectus."

"I'm not licensed or anything yet as a registered representative," Gary said helplessly.

Spigleman handed him a sheet of paper with a pen.

"Just sign it and you're registered. I predated it six months so you're in business. If you're a quarter as good as Daniel, you'll make a happy man out of me."

When a new issue was hot—and this depended on how much air Spigleman needed to inflate it—every broker became his own customer, bought stock for one of the phony names and sold off as soon as the high point was reached. Spigleman himself had about fifty of these accounts, and while most normal people were checking the *Wall Street Journal* to measure the temperature on the street, The Fly gave the impression of idling away his time in the lunatic diversion of reading obits in the Cleveland *Press*, San Francisco *Examiner*, the Cincinnati *Inquirer*, and hosts of other papers. At one time or another, he breathed life into a thousand different corpses.

The outer working-office was divided into thirty cubicles, each slashed by some sound-absorbing plastic opaque matter which prevented the various men pitching on the telephone from talking to each other or staring when they were spinning romantico *ficciones* to the innocent of the world.

Daniel funneled Gary into the cubby next to his, streaming with delight: "So you're in. . . ."

"What do I call myself?" he asked, still reeling. "A registered representative, or a customers' man?"

"Gary, I don't know how to tell you this. But you are now a *stockbroker.*"

Gary had slid into the business while in the army. He sold offshore mutuals to the regiment's red dog and crap-shooting hustlers. Gigantic capital appreciation and forced savings. That was the story.

"I want you to be aware of one danger," Daniel cautioned.

"What's dangerous about selling toilet paper on the phone?"

"You just have to be ready to cut out at a minute's notice. Because when The Fly" (Spigleman's *nom de guerre*) "just senses trouble—he doesn't have to smell it—he's gone. Vanishes. On Fridays which is payday, he gets guarded and tailed by everyone here. We work on a rota system."

It appeared The Fly had just several months earlier resurfaced after a two-year sabbatical, emerging tanned, pasteled, reeking of health, to set up his latest boiler room. A Cessna (for big danger) was stationed on a lonely Long Island airstrip all set to shift Spigleman to the outskirts of such scenic Mexican wonderlands as Tuxpan, or Poza Rica de Hidalgo, dropping him by parachute if necessary (for The Fly was a skillful parachutist) at about 3:08 A.M., when all Mexico was, for a change, asleep. The Fly would then hook onto the local banana-boat special and reconnoiter with his Hungarian wife Magda, who together with him held approximately twenty-two different nationalities.

Possessed of makeup kit, beards, all the paraphernalia required for flight, The Fly was apparently one of the few people in the world who could alter his height when it became necessary for him to cease to be.

"You ought to see him slouch," said Daniel. "Entirely different man."

"How'd he get back into the country? If everybody was looking for him?"

"He came up with a medley of hits for the SEC, and the F.B.I. Like about nine hundred people are in the shithouse and under indictment since he arrived back in town. My personal opinion is that Spigleman plans to stay for a while to make a big score."

Daniel handed him a batch of prospectuses.

"What's this stuff we're selling?" Gary asked.

"It's called *Fjord*. Our claim is that it's the celebrated Norwegian hair-restorer. The breakthrough. We hold the U.S. and Canadian licenses. We get it produced in Paterson and every kind of *drekh* is in it. Basically an egg-and-beer shampoo with lots of rosemary, basil, and tarragon so it smells nice. Instead of lanolin, the druggist puts in ground bones and marrow that he gets from the local slaughterhouse. Which is a great part of the pitch. Lanolin, everybody is fed up with. But imagine, marrow bones? It's so *mishigah* that it persuades people."

Daniel examined Gary's sucker list, which comprised names responding to the Spigleman heavy ad campaign and also others that he had purloined.

"He gave you a good one, because I insisted on no dead-ass leads. This is from Lombard, Chase, and Richter."

The Fly, in order to get the names of stock buyers, floated around various big-board houses. He'd get his hands on a few back-room clerks—the filers—offer them $1,500 in cash, plus a Minox, which they could keep after having used it for his purposes, then open another shop with the names of 100,000 actual buyers.

"Why'd you go to work for him instead of a legitimate house?"

"The Fly keeps phony books, pays half of the commissions in cash, lies about the tax contributions and social security, so if you need a stake in a hurry, this is the place."

Hysterical crisscrossing fugatos emanated from various booths as the men crooned melodies of instant riches, untold Texas wealth. Utopia. A counterpoint in madness. Gary, on Daniel's advice, stuck close to him and listened as Daniel made his first call of the day.

"I'm building a clientele for the future, Mr. Tomasi," he said with a snap like a Doberman. "I'm predicating all of my future business on this one single trade. So if I didn't think I could get you in and out in the short term with a hefty profit, I would not be recommending that you take five thousand shares of Fjord.

"It's Norwegian, and pronounced Ford like the car with a *j* in it. It's their waterways. They've got this special silt that divers drain from the fjords. A quart of it takes fifty divers working on a twenty-four-hour shift maybe a month to gather. And they can only work in the summer months before the great Norwegian night takes over. A thousand? Okay. I'd suggest you make it a joint tenancy. Angela and John Tomasi. Just a sec . . ."

Daniel rose from his desk, squiggled two questions marks next to the long-shot Daily Double he had worked on while riding the subway, in the office john, and over his container of coffee. He was at this period going through his pencil stripe and vest, sartorially splendid double-breasted fashion. Evenings he boned up on price-times-earnings ratios, and Magee's mysterious book on the alchemy of charting stocks, only dimly understanding either. But it did give the pitch a certain maniacal violent pizazz.

"What about that guy you've got on the phone?" Gary asked nervously.

"I'm building to a delayed-action close," Daniel explained. "First I want to see who Don Ackerman likes in the Double. And second, and more important, I'm going for a piss. Tomasi'll be counting his profits in his head till I get back."

While Gary waited in Daniel's cubby, the client alternated simpering hellos with off-key whistles.

A few minutes later, Daniel reappeared.

"Jesus, Gary, if I don't stop reading in the head, I'll never stop pissing on my shoes. Ackerman is going with jockeys," he noted contemptuously.

"Your client—" Gary pointed to the noisy phone.

"Testing the line." Daniel cradled the receiver. "Listen and learn. Here's a big bump. . . . Mr. T., the situation is serious now. David Rockefeler walked in, followed by Paul Samuelson . . . and if I'm not mistaken, Governor Scranton, who I only know by sight. They've gone into conference with Mr. Spigleman. Let me phone you back once I get word from the meeting."

Daniel hung up suddenly, then reexamined the sports page. "Maybe I ought to stick with basketball rather than ponies. . . . Come on, I'll show you the next step. . . ."

Strolling through the office, Daniel greeted various men, assured Gary that attendance and punctuality did not concern The Fly.

"Results equals commissions."

He stopped at what appeared to be the largest cubicle, where a man with 50 x 50 binoculars peered out of the window into a skyscraper across the road.

Without looking up, Gerald Slotnick sucked in his lips, emitting a spine-chilling saliva-through-teeth whistle.

"You missed them again," said Slotnick, a balding young man who oscillated effortlessly between twenty-three and forty-one, never juvenile, never old. He had been living with, from its infancy, the possibility of a lesbian romance in another boiler room across the street. "They were really going places, then somebody walked in for a nose powder. Must be married chicks with no place to meet. But, Daniel, they'll be noshing any day now."

"Gary Rubin," Daniel announced, "I'd like you to meet our security analyst, Gerald Slotnick. My friend Gary's just starting. If you can stand up without embarrassing yourself, we've got a load waiting to hear your voice. He's panting. . . ."

Slotnick examined the card listing Tomasi's previous big-board stock purchases. As this came from a stolen batch, purchased by The Fly, it was accurate.

"Supermarkets in Pennsy . . . what a portfolio . . . G.E., AT & T, Texas Instruments, Xerox . . ." A scorpion was hatching before Gary's eyes.

"We've got a Fjord load. But first we'll double-team him."

"Oh, I'm Borgia again," Slotnick suggested. "My favorite starring role."

He had been a clever accountant with a special gift for balancing consolidated statements on trapezes. But he had cooked too many books too well. Out of hemorrhaged earnings, Slotnick created black magic. He collected suspended sentences like a whore does promises. Maurice Stans was his hero.

"Lead me to him."

Passing Don Ackerman, formerly a lawyer, who was still sulk-

ing after having come out on the short end of disbarment proceedings, Daniel warned him that betting on jockeys was chasing
fool's gold. He dialed Tomasi's number again, switched on his
$12.98 tape recorder, sound verité from the floor of the exchange,
a melody of instant financial havoc for the client.

"Mr. Tomasi, this is Daniel Barnet calling again from Wall
Street. The noise? Oh, there's a panic about Fjord. Sorry, but
I can't talk any louder. The company's analyst, Gerald Slotnick,
just came out of the meeting. He and I went to school together
and our wives are cousins, so he's doing me a personal favor
by speaking to you. Wait! He's on a long-distance call to Norway
and there are going to be developments. One thing I ought to
tell you, he's very worried about your portfolio. You've been
stuck with a load of old-fashioned blue chips because you've
been brainwashed in the past by big-shot names and advertising."

Slotnick scratched his nuts, sipped some coffee from a container.

"What's going to happen?" Gary asked.

"A burial," said Daniel.

Slotnick seized the phone, fully psyched up for the encounter,
and began immediately out of left field, talking to the wall,
but conveying the impression that hundreds of people were
scurrying about, waiting for his command.

". . . you just tell the FTC that I'm tired of waiting for their
report, Miss Barnes. . . ." Gary looked for Miss Barnes. Invisible. "Get me the stock collation buildup charts on volume
and distribution of Fjord. Program the computer for DX minus
Beta. . . ." Then into the phone. "Hello. This is G. J. Slotnick.
Who is this?" A pause. "Tomasi. Yes, right. You're a personal
friend of Daniel Barnet's. To be absolutely candid with you,
Mr. Tomasi, I never speak to clients. It's unethical as far as
I am concerned. And Daniel is trading on our personal relationship. But—what? How did you know I was on the phone to
Norway? Okay, since you know . . . I'll have to be very brief.

"First of all, your portfolio, to put it as kindly as possible,
is one ungodly mess. Someone who must have hated you put
you into all of these things. . . . So you and your broker *have*
been on bad terms. Now, Fjord is a special situation . . . and
the company, to tell you the truth, has been seriously handi-
capped by the fact that they can't produce enough. The call I

received from Upheim has altered the situation. There has been a major silt find in the heart of the largest fjord outside of Bergen, which means that the synthetic component can now be completely eliminated and the various carbonated bituminous elements which presented such a serious problem are now solved molecularly. This means that they don't have to use the Steinmetz reduction process any longer. The company's scientific research department is positive. Now I'd like you to forget that this discussion ever took place. I'm putting you back to Mr. Barnet."

Daniel gave Slotnick the golden handclasp. "Look, Mr. Tomasi, can I call you John? John, when I asked if you wanted five thousand shares you told me a thousand. There is just no stock available. Wait a minute, there's been some movement. It's a buy from Lehman at five and a half. When you've got something good everybody wants to get into the act. You got yours at four and a half, so while we've been talking, you just made yourself a thousand dollars. Absolutely. Just get your check in to cover the trade by special delivery. I'll be in touch with you as soon as there are further developments."

As soon as Daniel hung up, he explained to Gary that on the next new issue, which The Fly was promising momentarily to the office, he'd pull Tomasi out of Fjord with a thousand profit, ravage his portfolio, and load him to death with the new disease.

"This one," said Daniel, "is going to get the works . . . cremation. The other thing, Gary, is we've been known from time to time to get clients up to the office with hunting knives, so if you get a comeback, call The Fly to the phone immediately."

"And he's so good he gets the guy off your back?"

"He's got techniques. Listen, the man knows what he's doing. He personally has killed more people than Ivan the Terrible."

"In the meantime, do you think I ought to start selling this marrow-bone soup for hair?"

"Too late. There'll be a wait till The Fly's lined up the new shit, so why don't we grab a plane for Miami or somewhere for a week?"

7

The plane wheezed to its leveling-off altitude, bouncing through turbulent air pockets, causing morose thoughts in Daniel's mind. Had the God of Vengeance decided on a crash for his generous ward? He nudged Gary, who had fallen into an instant doze, but received a series of grunts rather than the consolation he sought. Grabbing the stewardess's arm as she stalked down the aisle to silence a bongo player, he said:

"It's a helluva way to start a honeymoon."

"Is 16D your wife?" she said with a gorgeous, marzipan giggle. He'd broken the ice.

"We've got a full load," he said. "Can the plane handle it?"

"We'll be serving drinks soon, so we won't care, will we?"

"Going to my death drunk makes all the difference."

"I'll hold keys at the back of your neck if you prefer. Mr. D. Barnet," she added, ticking his name off her list. She winked at him. Liked what he saw. The open, guileless face, the soft lilting Midwestern accent, the straight stocking seams, the sweet little behind which could fit nicely into the palms of his hands. Drops of water from the air nozzles woke Gary and he lurched on Daniel's armrest.

"This may be the first time anybody's ever drowned in the sky," he said.

"Gracious, I've got to go get on the air and describe the use of the life jackets. No, hang on," she faltered. "I think it's my turn to demonstrate. See you, real soon . . ."

He'd seen, read, heard of people who commanded remarkable skills and coordination. But Sonya demonstrating the use of the Mae West was a unique experience, combining grace, functionality, and daring. She made it *interesting*. With the oxygen mask over her face he thought he'd never seen anything so magical, so helpless.

"If only I could fall into something like that," Daniel said, nudging Gary.

"Which one?"

"That stewardess. She's quality. Probably has a million guys lining up from here to California waiting for a date."

"Ask," Gary advised, his eyes flickering shut. "The ass isn't much."

"Well, it's not Marlene's, that's for sure. You couldn't put a tablecloth on it and have six for dinner."

"What's wrong with Marlene's ass?"

"She's your fiancée, so how would I know?"

"She cooks pretty good, she's learning to get a little perversion in the sack, and she's got one great job."

Marlene was an assistant buyer of children's underwear for nine hundred and seventy discount stores coast-to-coast, and she and Gary had been engaged for thirty-nine months. The trip to Miami he had lured Gary on, Marlene claimed, was instigated to break them up. Not exactly the truth, but Daniel, like most bachelors closing in on thirty, had a vested interest in keeping his close friends single.

Rather than Miss Sonya Anderson, Daniel reluctantly accepted the accrued evidence that he would marry either a black hooker, or some Marlene-like lump with a T-bone nose and not the stewardess's exquisitely snubbed organ tilting up to celestial bodies. His beast would have years of nose training with a clothespin, could pot meat like a luncheonette pro, swill a dozen egg creams at a sitting, and hustle Mah-Jongg on the campuses of Catskill hotels. Well, the likes of Sonya Anderson would never smile on him and he became resigned, consciously, to a life that would never be fulfilled. Merely empty, aery, dreams.

Mooning over such incidentals as Sonya's slender, aristocratic ankles, the brace of merry freckles which stippled each cheek, *not* so that she could be described as having a face full of freckles, but just enough to assure a secure place as a girl who was outdoorsy. The short blond hair was combed straight back, letting in a little light under the nape of her neck, which had the rutilant sheen of a Golden Delicious. Her face was set off by sunny warm gray eyes, giving her the friendly flicker of little girls in movies in which the horse is the star.

She came back into his life, flashing a germ-free Colgate smile that revealed cutely crooked teeth. Wheeling a drinks trolley with elegant miniatures. He ordered a double Johnny Walker

Red, for he admired the shape of the bottle. Employing one of The Fly's gambits, he offered to pay with a hundred-dollar bill. The Fly usually brought out a thousand for a steak sandwich and had developed innumerable credit accounts.

"I can't break that," Sonya said, casting a loving look at the bill, while female ice-cubes melted in the glass. "I'll pay and you'll owe it to me."

She took a single out of her pocket and stuffed it into the old-fashioned glass.

"You'd lay out for me?"

"I think you'll pay me back. . . . How long are you going to be in *Miama*?"

He sat stricken, never having heard the holiday mecca called anything but Meeyammy or Myammi. *Miama* held suggestions of foreign parts, golden sands, a place in a million to begin a . . . love affair. . . . O land of promise!

"I'm not sure. A few weeks in Miama, then maybe on to Puerto Rico. I'll see how things go. What about you?"

"I go back and forth."

"You stop over for a few days, don't you?" he asked.

"Usually about two . . . I am afraid it is beddy-bye time, Sixteen E," she informed him, walking to the rear.

The cabin lights dimmed, and he tried napping but couldn't quite ascend the slipstream of oblivion. Insomnia . . . a new curse in his life. Must have been airborne for more than two hours, and the eyeballs were becoming gelatinous, flaming red coals on which to cook the pupils sate-style. Went for a wander, for She had not returned to resume their intercourse.

He and a small boy paced the aisle, glaring at each other as though both waited for news and the first to receive it would assume a natural superiority over the other. He found her, came upon her, in that cabin office structure that adjoins the johns and the kitchen at the tail end. She was sitting on a jump seat adjacent to the entrance/exit. No light, but he cut out her silhouette.

"Can I help you?" she said officiously, obviously not recognizing him.

"Hi," he said, suspecting he had been guilty of some form of traveler's presumption.

"Oh, hi, there. Can't you sleep?"

"I'm not nervous or anything like that. I never could sleep on planes."

An officer sitting next to her brought out something that looked like a compass but had no pencil attached, and extended both its metal legs for some esoteric degrees-and-seconds calculation.

"What're you doing . . . ?"

"Oh, we're working on the flight plan. Weather control advised us that we might pick up some winds from Cape Hatteras," she said like Amelia Earhart talking to Lindy.

"And you'll fly over it?" he asked, sensing his foolishness among these professionals.

"We'll sure try," the officer said curtly.

At the magazine rack the kid buttonholed him.

"That guy sitting with the stewardess," he told Daniel, "is sticking his *hand* up her *dress*."

"What are you talking about?" Daniel said angrily. "They're doing weather charts so a little snotty kid like you doesn't get bumped around."

"Mister, you need glasses."

Daniel lifted his hand, then dropped it, plopping to his side as though following through a military salute. Probably a federal crime to whack a kid in midair, violation of interstate law.

He caught a short snooze, and woke up to the dazzle of startling navy blue clouds and scalpel-sharp filigrees of early sun.

Didn't have time for a rinse of the mouth or a gargle, before Sonya was there—at four in the morning!—with coffee and Danish, smelling of fresh mint, briskly moving, unflappably competent, and apparently the recipient of fourteen hours of sleep.

"Sorry I couldn't get back to you," she said.

"Where will you be staying?"

He whipped out his new brass-covered notebook with attached pencil that usually dropped a two-inch-long piece of thin Eversharp lead whenever he needed to make a note. It didn't disappoint him, and he jammed it back, like a rapist in the throes of panic copulation, and prepared to note details, holding it at an angle in midair while she evidently made up her mind about the future trajectory of their relationship.

"Most of the time in Motel Row," she said, shunting a tray

over another seat to a man eavesdropping on the tête-à-tête.

Why, he protested to himself, could he have no privacy with her?

"Where in Motel Row?"

"Pirates' Den or the Malasian . . ."

"Well, I'd like to call you. Maybe we could shoot out for dinner one night."

"Gee, I don't know about that."

Surely she could dine freely and in public with a man and not arouse the company's troubleshooters.

"Nothing unethical about that," he assured her.

"I'll see, okay . . . ?"

"It's Daniel Barnet, don't forget. I'll give you a call tonight."

In all of Daniel's air flights, he was characteristically first to bolt out of the plane, ignoring crew salutations, hustling down to the baggage area at full speed. But for the first time in his life, he shook a stewardess's hand, held it in his own, so that their flesh was one.

"I'll speak to you later, Sonya," he said softly. "And don't forget . . . I owe you a buck."

She yawned and he wanted to give her his shoulder.

"I sleep till about five, so not before, hon."

She called him "hon." . . . He reconfirmed the names of the motels, was troubled by the orthographical vagaries of Malasian, but decided against asking for the actual spelling. A man who could not track down a motel did not deserve an evening out with Sonya Anderson.

Exhausted at 6 A.M., Daniel and Gary were shunted to their room at the Hotel Versailles, which occupied the Midlothian area of Miami Beach, a stone's throw from Lincoln Road. Daniel's first trip to the Gold Coast and he assumed the role of an oriental potentate, ordered breakfast on the terrace and kept an eye on the Hertz Mustang they'd rented at the airport.

Gary came out of the shower, sat on a chair, and allowed the sun to dry him.

"How many girls have you ever met who were named Sonya?" Daniel asked.

"Listen, if you don't stop this shit, I'm going to get my room changed," Gary replied, holding his ears. "It's enough hocking,

Daniel. Just give that patsy a fuck and start walking a straight line. . . . I don't know what's wrong with you. She brought you a drink, shoved some coffee on your lap and you're crazy."

"Gary, we've suddenly lost . . . emotional contact."

"I'll say we have."

"Are you going to dump Marlene?"

"Steady employment, paid vacations, a box so immaculate you could eat out of it? Seniority, tenure, *nuch*, and I should give her a push? Until I started at Spigleman's who do you think has been supporting me? I'm into her for about three g's. At twenty-five dollars a throw I owe the girl a hundred and twenty lays and God knows if I've got it in me. Because with Marlene it's got to be a full performance and not like in and out with a thermometer. Energy is required."

"Well, marry her. Then it doesn't have to be so frequent. You can give her days of the month."

"I've been doing a lot of serious thinking. Her father'll spring us to a down payment on a house. We've been looking for a place. Saw a beautiful development around Babylon and they've got one helluva train connection, so that Marlene can get to her job with no hassle. Three hours a day on a train isn't too much to ask a woman who loves you, is it?"

"Where is she going to find another Gary Rubin at her stage of the game?"

"You said it. But in the meantime, I'll sing a song of freedom."

Reluctantly, Daniel returned to the subject foremost in his mind, creating swirling eddies. Mysterioso . . .

"As my friend, can I ask you your personal opinion of Sonya?"

Gary scratched himself, sipped some of the lukewarm coffee, and turned his mellow red eyes on Daniel, who seemed to be suffering from gastric pains to judge from his haunted expression.

"Honestly, what can I tell you? The girl said hello and good-bye to me. She handed me a pillow and a blanket, brought coffee and Danish and a ham sandwich that had icicles on it. She's a good fixer, that I know. A chair in one of the rows wouldn't recline, and she gave it a kick with her knee and it worked. She doesn't spill drinks. An olive she places in a martini. I mean, you want like depth analysis"—Daniel's face in the crotch of his elbow was reborn with every word Gary spoke—"and what else is there?"

"What about her body?"

"Her body?" Gary sat up on the bed. "Man, that chick was wearing an apron for most of the ride, so how could I study the body?"

"Well, in uniform she didn't impress you?"

"Daniel, just face the facts. You don't know a damned thing about her except that she's another flying boing-boing and the odds are she's logged in lots of flights and loads of dicks."

"I resent that!"

"End of discussion. I want to sleep and maybe you ought to do the same thing."

"Just don't talk to me."

Noonish the boys with their gray faces and carp-white bellies were taking a little sun at the poolside. The hotel invited its guests to sample a free yoga lesson, which was attended by a senior citizen, and in the pool a few ladies clustered on the steps discussing the lousy marriages that "children who had been given everything" had made. Daniel sprayed his face with old Coppertone in new packaging and computed the waste of his existence away from the incomparable Sonya Anderson.

She was staying at the Pirates' Den. He learned about that at one-fifteen. As he sat slick with oil and fidgeted from the pool to the ocean, the day seemed endless until he could make his call to her. He wondered if his time had come, felt an inexplicable yearning for fatherhood, a home, rather than his furnished apartment, a woman he could spend an evening with . . . talking . . . rather than forays with stray pieces whose faces he could not identify in the morning. He felt absolutely certain that Sonya was not the type to pressure a man into a coronary for the sake of an extra buck. Generous, obviously hard working, different . . . stock . . . pioneer.

On the phone at last, he observed chills which he attributed to Sonya and not his greed for the sun.

"Hello," said Daniel to a voice. "Can I speak to Miss Anderson? She isn't there? Didn't she leave a message for me? Daniel Barnet. Oh, that's better. The Poodle Room . . . ? I don't get this. . . . She said she didn't have a date. Who are you, please?

. . . Bunny. And you're her friend. Jeez, what's going on in your room? It sounds like a chick coming. No, I'm not being rude. Good-bye."

Three costume changes before Daniel settled on his navy slacks and pencil-striped seersucker sports jacket. Navy tie with the powder blue short-sleeved shirt. Sat on the balcony attending Gary in the final stages of scalp preparation. The hair was combed against the grain, so it would lie straight when shifted to normal.

"So we're off to suck city," Gary said, at last ready.

"That's a peculiar description of one of our country's finest and most beautiful hotels," Daniel said. "Not another hotel in the world like the Fontainebleau."

"The broads are six deep at the bar. It's a shopping center for snatch. And, Daniel, for a wise guy, act a little more sophisticated. If you run into that stewardess, don't drop a load in your pants. Test it first."

8

Daniel had seen crowds before, but never had he witnessed such a crush of bare arms, exposed cleavages, gold slave bracelets jangling on wrists. As on a merry-go-round, he was pushed every which way, losing Gary along the tortuous path. A tray of hors d'oeuvres narrowly missed his shoulder as a waiter hurtled through the infinite vector of tits surrounding Daniel. Hundreds of faces. Peculiar thing: whenever he passed a woman, it didn't seem to matter if she were drinking, talking, or eating, she would stop to examine him. The dreaded nervous stomach-rumbling shits pierced his abdomen as he was caught in that twitching no-man's-land of uncertainty that precariously informs all vaguely made dates. Tracked her. Every few steps and a little check over his shoulder to see if he had missed her.

Becoming crazy from the faces, he ordered a drink and collected it through a gauntlet of limbs as wildebeests grappled for a free dinner . . . promising promises through lips coated with orange smears and wagging truncated spareribs at nonsports who refused to pick up drink tabs.

A voice . . . He'd never dreamed, never thought to pathfind in that direction, clutched his chest in joyful surprise, his eyes went glassy.

SHE.

Her.

SONYA.

Singing on the bandstand. Hand-held mike, lyrically completing the final refrain of "Gypsy in My Soul." The casual phrasing thrilled him as no other sound had ever before. She was an entertainer . . . a woman who flew for a hobby, but her heart was in melody. No wonder she couldn't be bothered with him. The audience response seemed to him dismal, unappreciative. He clapped till his hands—never very strong—ached, then shoved through a crowd of high-stepping cha-cha dancers, and greeted Sonya as she was about to plunge the two feet from the bandstand.

"Hi, there"—he extended his hand to ease her passage to ground level—"you were sensational."

"Glad you liked it. I'm out of practice."

"I phoned and got your message."

She appeared puzzled.

"What message? I don't ree-call leaving a message."

"Well, I'd hoped we could have some drinks and dinner."

Glancing around the room, Sonya played roulette with the faces as Daniel engaged a comfy stool which he'd snared from three people.

"You're looking for one of your friends?"

"Serve him right, that sonovabitch," she muttered obscurely.

"Has someone offended you . . . ? Bartender, can we get a couple of setups," he shouted, a man for all seasons who could order a drink and clench a fist simultaneously to ward off anyone who threatened her.

"C.C. and ginger," Sonya said to Daniel who passed on the order.

Studied her dress, a wild silk kimono in astounding sea green which was printed with interesting patterns of crustaceans, and also what he took to be Eastern temple symbols and smart hexagonal figures that told some unfathomable story. He was tempted to plant a kiss on the sylvan, shapely, blond-haired, bronzy arm.

"I think your dress is gorgeous."

"I make all my own clothes," she said a bit more cheerfully.

"I guessed as much. The garbage they sell in stores could never come close to what you're wearing." Her talents and creativity intimidated him. Drinks were slid over to him. He waved his hundred-dollar bill and had his heart broken when the bartender changed it. "Can we drink to a first meeting with the hope that it will bring many others?"

"Sure, if you like . . ."

Her posture on the bar stool—ramrod-straight back—struck him as outstanding. No slouching, neckless hulk with boobs the size of medicine balls for him, but an elegant Miss Creamy Goodness who fashioned her own clothes. Not just following Simplicity patterns, but a woman who created originals, who brought a new dimension to style.

"Would I be inquisitive if I asked you about your singing?"

"What about it?"

"Well, are you on any regular show? Radio or TV, that I might have caught?"

"The piano player"—she pointed to a hunched-up little man in a maroon tuxedo jacket sweating over a keyboard—"and me worked together a few times in the old days."

"Old days? You're a child, for goodness' sake."

"I won an amateur singing contest with the Pepper Farson Orchestra in Denver."

"Pepper Farson . . . Hmmmmmmmm. I'm not sure—"

"Never heard of them?"

"I didn't say that."

"We used to hit the ski resorts at Aspen and around there."

"I see"—he wiped a blob of sweat from his eye—"you were on the road at resorts. I can't imagine why you gave it up, you're certainly as good as anybody around."

She digested this compliment, squeezed his hand very friendly.

"They got another girl who they claimed was better than me."

"If you had the right agents and managers sponsoring you, I'll bet anything you would have made it."

"Water under the bridge . . ."

Another talent, he thought bitterly, wrecked by the bitch goddess Success. Probably if she'd laid the right men, she would today have her own program. Well, music's loss might prove his salvation.

"Could you excuse me for a minute? Daniel? Yes, Daniel. I just spotted somebody I want to tell to drop dead."

"If you need any assistance whatsoever, just let me know."

Daniel followed her movements with intensity. She stopped in front of the airline officer who had worked the charts with her.

"What happened?" he inquired on her return. "Some sort of technical problem?"

"You might put it that way. They want to reschedule me and I told them nix."

"I appreciate that," he said cordially, offering her a new drink. "What about dinner?"

"Dinner. Anywhere your heart desires, Sonya, doll . . . I'll say so long to my friend."

He trotted across the dance floor to a small cove where Gary and two women were pawing one another. His eyes weaving to the interior tune of an alcoholic mazurka, Gary made an inquiry:

"What's my friend Daniel drinking?" He threw a mixer at the bartender, who responded to the call by turning his back. "Soooooo? What's it all about . . . this life?"

"Gary, I don't want to get into philosophical discussions. Just tell me what's the story with the room tonight? Like if I invite Miss Anderson back for a nightcap, will you be working there?"

"Great. You bring that stewardess back and we'll fuck the daylights out of her."

"*We'll?* Pardon me. My buddy you may be, but I fly solo with Miss Anderson."

"Who's that?" asked one of the women, shaking her arm to regain the collection of Mayan Miami jewelry sliding down it.

"You may have heard her sing 'Gypsy in My Soul' a few minutes ago. For your information, Gary, Sonya was a singer a few years back."

"We've got a 'Do Not Disturb' sign. I'll stick it on the door-knob."

"I personally would not like to arrive and at the last possible second discover such a sign. . . . So it's yours until midnight, then mine, say till two thirty."

"Fine, Daniel, whatever you say. We'll work it in shifts."

"Why don't you drop your Miss Anderson," said the blond-wiglet part of the combo, "and the four of us can party it up?"

"That was another life, honey," Daniel proclaimed. "I believe I've found the real goods now." Parting, he was overcome by a surge of displeasure. "I can't believe that you didn't catch her song. . . ."

In the exquisite rapture of the moment, Sonya called the Camera Hawk Girl, who shoved people out of the way and lined Daniel and her up at the bar. Two flash shots searing their eyeballs completed destiny's still of the happy meeting.

"I really love those rum drinks," Sonya said.

"I'm sure the bartenders here can cope with them."

"Nix. You've got to be in the surroundings. You know, those Peloponnesian places with palms and flowers and gals with printed sari skirts."

He gave a short *fonfer* over Peloponnesian, a little uncertain himself about the pronunciation.

"I know what you mean. If there's one that you're fond of, let's get a move on."

She had a fuzzy idea of where the restaurant would be located. Daniel took innumerable wrong turnings and came to the conclusion that she who flew with the stars as her backdrop might be forgiven for confusion on earth. A pump jockey tipped him off to a place on a causeway. Drove the car at fifty in high-density areas to reveal that speed was also his bag. At red lights he squeezed her hand.

And in the parking lot of The Polynesian Kai she treated him to a tongue-exchange kiss. She chewed Sen-Sen which didn't taste so fab on the receiving end. Never mind . . .

Inside. Perfection. Swivel-hipped girls in sarongs paved their way, enjoined them into a bar with a stupendous collection of rare voodoo furniture, Sonya explained to him. She who had been everywhere was taking the trouble to educate him.

"They represent various gods of the Samoans," she said, joining hands with him over the pepper mill, forging a bridge of palms and elbows.

"So much I don't know about. When you're in business . . . your reading is restricted to the financial sections. And when I go out it's to relax with a musical."

"What business are you in?"

"I'm a stockbroker," he proclaimed loudly, expecting heads to turn. "With I. Spigleman and Associates. I'm one of the senior associates."

"So you sell stocks?"

"Just the big blocks. I don't handle the chicken"—he caught himself in time—"small accounts. Like if someone's aunt wants a thousand I.B.M., a junior person handles that kind of trade."

"You must do very well," she said, pushing her face across to his and puckering her lips.

"I don't like to brag. But I'm thinking of retiring at the end of the year. In my bracket, I'm actually starting to lose money by working. Taxes," he added airily.

"You are such a young man. Can I ask . . ."

"I'm not exactly thirty," he said jauntily marching his fingers up her wrist. "And you . . . ? Dare I ask or would I be ungentlemanly?"

"I'm not exactly thirty either."

"Sonya, I find you . . . well . . . very witty and at the same time . . . sultry."

Shared their first double portion twin-strawed Scorpion. He wanted to pull the gardenia out and pin it on her dress, or tease it over her ear, but it was wet and the wiry green stem looked vicious. The second one and he was beginning to see double, kissed her fingers when intending to put a tidbit in his mouth. The drink was like delicately flavored kerosene. Leaving the voodoo bar, they walked over a bridge to their dining table. Daniel insisted on being placed by the soothing, tinkling falls set in front of a cave entrance, and an oriental glen upon which small cute kindergarten alligators frolicked. She handled her booze, he thought, with enormous skill, and furthermore she assisted him with the menu, patiently elucidating hidden meanings lurking in a Chinese oven. He wound up with chicken livers cooked in some type of translucent bag, and she with Bali-Bali lamb.

Didn't want to force his attentions on her, which meant returning to her room, where the presence of flying companions might inhibit her. Excused himself to telephone Gary.

"Daniel," Gary insisted, "dump that flying pig and drag your ass back here. These two aren't pros, they want to have a scene. We've just completed the first inning."

"Look, I don't want to argue, but please leave the room in a fit state. Gary," he added, "is there a fresh towel for us?"

"You're too fucking much."

Ooooooh, Gary was putting the friendship under serious tensions. Lumping Sonya with all the other pigs.

No ambiguity in the car, she let Daniel know at once she was in the mood. Nestled the lovely head on his shoulder. Fell asleep as a matter of simple fact and had to be wakened in the Versailles driveway. Shaky-legged, she marched with him for support through the deserted lobby.

The room was not simply a mess . . . in disarray, but might have been used for weeks by a kidnapper and his family of hostages. In the bathroom he tripped over towels, washcloths; encountered a spent tube of vaginal jelly in the sink; the toothbrush glass smashed to smithereens; part of the mirror had been employed as a palette for facial retouching. The toilet bowl contained a collection of tissues with red lip imprints. He flushed, flung towels behind the door, wiped the wet floor by skating on the bath mat, then rolled it up and flung it into a closet. Under the corps of wet towels hanging from the shower rail, he found a lonely straggler. Untouched.

Sonya waited on the terrace out of harm's way as he slapped the sheets down. The room improved when he switched off the overhead light, becoming a series of inviting corners and nooks.

He yanked her off the terrace. She was still wobbly, her thoughts in the sky. She fell deadweight on his bed, and it crossed his mind that he had never seen such a desirable woman.

Drunks he had banged before. Usually they lay like mummies for the first half hour, then after he'd dropped his load—never failed—they'd spring to life, become lively, encouraging, noisy, hungry.

"How's my girl feeling?" he inquired.

"Thirsty. Would you please—"

"—Get you a glass of water? Of course, Sonya."

"Those rum drinks can truly zonk you."

"So I've heard," he called from the bathroom, letting the water run. No lukewarm solutions for his treasure.

He held her head in the crook of his elbow so she wouldn't gag. She inspired tenderness . . . off an aircraft, and he kissed her face, unmindful of her rum breath or that a stocking had skittered down one leg. Some lucky guy would pick up a lost garter and win the Daily Double at the track. That's what Daniel thought. At Checkpoint Charlie (the top of her thigh) she trapped his hand, and he lamely withdrew. Her, if she said no, he'd leave alone. He didn't want to offend her, terminate their relationship for the sake of a first-date hat-trick bang. Wait. Patience. Still . . .

The livers in the bag had been unsatisfying, dried out, bitter, and he was snack-minded. He had left off at the thigh. Perhaps she didn't enjoy thigh tampering but would respond to a different arrangement? She was thirsty, he'd let her drink; he was hungry, maybe she'd let him eat.

Her panties came apart in his hand. He must have been generating the heat of a hydroelectric plant to create such a chemical reaction. He just could not understand it, and he tilted the lamp shade just enough to measure the damage but not so that Sonya would notice. A strangely moving encounter for Daniel—paper panties. He'd never known such a product existed. Made sense to him. Flying here, there, everywhere, who had time for laundry?

He couldn't make out if she were sleeping, resting, or suspended in some oriental state of relaxation. Soundless breathing. He counted himself among the fortunate of the earth lucking into a nonsnorer.

He disrobed, hung up his clothes, since she did not seem in a hurry to leave. As a final precaution, he attached the "Do Not Disturb" sign on the door to ward off Gary. Fine prospect, him grinding Sonya, and Gary noisily careening into the love chamber, probably demanding *his* turn with the goods.

He couldn't exactly pull down the panties; it was more an unwrapping procedure. His first privileged view of Lands' End made him talkative, rhapsodic.

"How is it that kings abdicate, empires fall, statesmen are dishonored . . . ?"

She sat up stunned, seeing only his face.

"Who were you talking to?"

"Myself . . . go back to sleep, doll. You need your rest."

Her head fell with a thud on the pillow as though he were a hypnotist commanding sleep. Back at operational headquarters, a major decision was taken which would affect the lives of others.

He decided to nosh a little, never having heard that this could harm the complexion of a sleeping beauty. Might possibly put a little rosiness in the cheeks. Working with the quiet of a saboteur, he crept stealthily below the top sheet. He held up a corner to light his path, then as he was just about to . . .

Noticed something.

A piece of string, hanging out of the sluice gates. Surely not . . . then what could this strange female textile be—as yet unnamed in the annals of his life—Celanese or something? Tempted as he was to pull it, he thought it worthy of discussion, rather than subject it to the same fate as her panties.

"Sonya . . . Sonya."

"Uh-huh . . ."

"I don't know quite how to put this, but there's a piece of—"

"—Are you the one that ripped my panties off?"

"Pardon? No, actually I didn't. When I touched them they sort of dissolved. There's a string . . ."

"Oh, shoot. Where are we?"

"Miami Beach. Hotel Versailles. And I'm Daniel Barnet."

"I should have been in L.A. for my monthly."

"Ahah . . . Look, you never mentioned it. I'd like to apologize. I thought, well, maybe it was left over from your panties," he said in a fluster. Felt all exposed. His dick was galloping over his balls like he had to make the fort or else them Injuns . . . Calmed himself. Became constructive. "I don't know if you'd consider other . . . modes of love."

"Like what!" She was fully roused now, and he was certain he detected a little hostility. "If you think I am going to— yeeeeeeeeeeeeeeech. On a first date?"

"Well, I'm sorry. But I am in one helluva state."

"Which is not my fault."

"I'm sorry to admit you're absolutely right."

She softened when he took the blame himself, made apologetic little-boy faces.

"All right, you lost your head. It happens."

"You're a very understanding woman. The most understanding I've come across in a lifetime of disasters. You're different, special, you really are."

"Come on over then," she said patiently to the naughty boy, "and I'll pull it off."

Good as her word too. He made an even distribution on a pillow that she set down under him. Who was he to object as she yaaaaaaaaaaaaaaaaanked? He had no right to criticize the technique of a woman who might aptly be described as a sexual philanthropist. He smiled gaily, wiping himself down with the last virginal towel.

The first thing she asked afterward was:

"Do you like lamb chops?"

"Of course I do, silly girl. In fact, Sonya, I think I'm in love with you."

"I'm sort of a little uncertain myself. . . ."

She nuzzled her face into the thicket of hair on his chest.

"Sonya, what is the most important thing to you . . . like what do you want most?"

"A house," she said with the speed of a bullet. "Sharing apartments and motel rooms with seven-eight gals isn't like a home."

"Doll, don't I know it."

Lost his heart to her.

Unforgettable.

9

Back in winter climes:

A period of paranoid Rachmaninoff rhapsody accompanied Sonya's introduction to The Fly and his den. At lunch at a White Rose bar she had said, sitting under a graying Carstairs plaque: "There is faaaat on this pastrami . . . and Daniel, in other words, you are totally full of shit and you are also one of that large group who like to fuck and . . . man, brag about fucking airline stewardesses. Am I reading you right?"

Scoffing his second helping of hot cherry peppers, a shortcut procedure for putting the fire back in his balls, he decided he didn't enjoy Sonya in this forthright mood. Under the light and in civvies, with a wishbone smear of deli mustard on her wrist, she looked positively green to him.

"We've got something big—gigantic—on at the office," he said.

To pacify his restless band, The Fly had promised to unveil

his latest virus. A new Spigleman black death in which Daniel enthusiastically placed great faith to revive the depleted fortune he had blown in Miami. He and Sonya in consort had rifled through eighteen hundred dollars. When he brought her up to the office to meet his colleagues, she had had a short session with Don Ackerman while Daniel was closeted with Spigleman planning the presentation.

"In other words—" she recommenced.

"Why, Sonya, do you start everything with 'in other words'?"

"Maybe I don't want to call you a liar to your face."

"Very considerate . . ."

"Don said he gave everybody there legal advice."

"Legal advice? Ridiculous. Don was disbarred last year."

"That's what I mean. Just about all your friends have some kind of case pending. I also heard from another of your associates that when you are not sure of payment from a client you are prepared to get this man mugged. That is quite a business, Daniel."

Did not want to contradict her, but she could hardly call a session with Kit a mugging. Perhaps a consultation. His high-flown corporate ethics had been partially exposed and he was determined to conceal what still lay under the rug. Shards of their Miami madness still remained and he found it impossible to keep his hands off her. Slipping a knee between her thighs under the table, he reminded her of the delights of his ardor. Like hashish the residue was potent, lingering, and addictive if consumed habitually.

"They put compost on soil to make things grow," she suggested.

"Doll, you've lost me."

"Fertilizer . . . shit, then you plow it and hope something in God's universe will come up from underneath."

"One thing, Sonya. You'll never have to worry about money."

"As long as *I* keep working. Daniel, I think I have been flying longer than I have been walking. I went from toddling into the sky."

"You're one of the lucky ones—you've got a profession."

She made one of those lip farting sounds, releasing a fine spray, but the shrinking chest spasm stabbing him, a code he broke easily, removed any lingering doubt that he now had a shot with a woman who was unique, country strong. No hint of gaiety crossed her face. Now or never, he thought.

Yes, there were so many wondrous qualities she possessed that he'd never before encountered. Too abashed to quote poetry aloud, he mentally compiled a list of her assets under the generic but lyrical canopy of: "How do I love thee . . ." Fuzzily, he counted four out of unspecified multitudes. Orchestrally the passage was *ripieno*.

Dearest, Darling, Sonya—
1. I love your manners.
2. I adore you because you're so amusing.
3. I love your fabulous walk and the sway of that adorable *toochis*.
4. I love you because you are so intelligent, competent, neat, and wise in the ways of the world.

PS. I want to marry you, doll.

Instead of this elegy, he offered her a batch of spongy napkins so that she could wipe the grease off her fingers, for she was ripping the fat from her sandwich and trimming him at the same time.

The New York segment of their affair had been conducted under the most romantic Transylvanian conditions. Under graying polluted werewolf moonlight and always against the pressure of time. No symphony, just a series of resounding codas conducted by voices constructed of microwaves in airport departure lounges. La Guardia, Kennedy, and Newark became his places of abode. He had come to love Newark, the jewel in the empire of metropolitan airports. At the Newarker Restaurant, he had his special table overlooking the runways, could make a reservation at a moment's notice. The headwaiter even recognized his voice on the phone!

"The house you took me to last week in Babylonia," Sonya said with passionate interest. "We can start there, can't we . . . ?"

"Babylon?" he suggested timorously.

"Least we've got your friends Gary and Marlene out there."

To close Gary, or rather "finalize" him, Marlene had sprung for the down payment and engaged a caterer.

Daniel had carried Sonya in his arms over the muddy tracts where roads were promised by the salesman, but the denizens wore trout waders.

"I have been living out of suitcases for too damn long, Daniel. I don't even have a toothbrush that isn't community property." She paused, opened her airline flight bag and brought out paint color charts, a card of fabric swatches, kitchen wallpaper samples. "I'll have to select," she added with a grimace, "in-flight. So all you have to do is put up the ten percent and swing a mortgage."

"Leave it to me," he said airily but with decision. "A home . . . our home. Sonya, it's going to be great."

"I will be back in three days," she said with a sense of fatigue that went to his heart "New York, Miami, L.A., Miami . . . New York."

Sonya had agreed to fill in for her bosom crony, Bunny Washburn, who had located a Pasadena shrink only too willing to arrange a fee-split with a grinder for the elimination of a casual fetus she had conceived how, where, when, and from whom, she could not say. The girls always stuck together when such occupational hazards struck one of their number.

"And, Daniel, when we've got one of our rare lunches in New York, please don't take me here again."

"The White Rose is all that's left of old New York. . . ."

"Well, how about some chrome place like the Four Seasons next time? The drunks there at least wear suits." She peered at her watch, alighted like a sprightly warbler. "I've got to catch my bus or I'll be late checking in. . . ."

He tugged at her arm and pulled her close for a Mach I kiss. "Where . . . when are you coming in?"

"Newark, fifty-eight at 2309. In theory . . . on my magic carpet."

Silent spring had come rather earlier than predicted for Spigleman and his flock. No cataclysmic mushroom cloud or vegetable poison had disturbed the delicate natural balance of the dealer in instant financial death . . . just a bull-necked man, wearing a brown sharkskin suit, rep tie, Shriner's tiepin, cuff links to the order of some thug labor organization and a resplendent duck's ass hair style. A customer had actually appeared in the flesh with voice so abrasive that it seemed to emanate from his bowels.

"*Marioles* . . . you've robbed me. I'm going to shoot everybody in this place." To dispel the possibility of ambiguity, the voice added: "You're all dead!"

In his cubby, Daniel was disturbed, but paid no heed, for he had just sent off his reservation check for nineteen hundred dollars to C. B. Luckmunn, the estate developer in Babylon, and also engineered a mortgage from a factor who had connections with a host of friendly fly-by-night savings and loan assassins.

Since most customers were regarded as merely prosperous ghosts, whom Spigleman called up from obscure regions, phones were slammed down under this threat of an office Guernica. They all followed the practice of Don Ackerman and hid—under desks, in the clothes closet, locked themselves in toilets. Only The Fly would dare open a window and walk the ledge to another office, but at this point Spigleman showed his mettle, and a man wearing pink trousers, a red shirt, and white cashmere sports coat in twelve degrees Fahrenheit, had to be prepared to defend himself.

"I am Irv Spigleman, the senior partner. Now would you be good enough to tell me what the difficulty is, Mr.—?"

"Rubuzzi, Joe Rubuzzi, and I say you and your outfit is a bunch of fuckin' shyster crooks. I come for my money."

Spigleman simply smiled, asked if Rubuzzi was not well, wished water, a Bromo, an Excedrin, was perhaps hungry and would be kind enough to join him for lunch.

"I just come straight from Pittsburgh and I'm not leavin' without my money. . . ."

"The Rubuzzi accounts at once," The Fly demanded in a curt but generalized way, for the office population had disappeared. "Come into my office, Mr. Rubuzzi, and let's see how I can assist you."

Taking a long glowering-fatal-look at Spigleman's doorman arm extension, Rubuzzi hesitated, then followed him in, still menacing.

"You ain't talking your way out of this."

Threatening a verbal shoot-out with Spigleman was all the ammo required. Doing an attendance check, Spigleman spied only the new landowner coming off the phone.

"Mr. Rubuzzi, I wonder if you'd like Mr. Barnet, the firm's security analyst, to join us."

Rubuzzi gave an "Awwwwwwwright," a sound which came from the throat of a dying cat.

Into the suite. The Fly immediately picked up his telephone, instructed his secretary to order lunch from Delmonico's, recommended the sweetbreads.

"Steak, medium rare, a wise choice, Mr. R. Delmonico's steaks are the best in the city."

Salad with green-goddess dressing, a triple order of french fries, and tutti-frutti ice cream sealed Rubuzzi's fate, for The Fly was just warming up.

"Nice office you got yourself there," said Rubuzzi.

"What line of business are you in?" Spigleman asked.

"I got me a couple of two laundries."

"Laundries . . ." Spigleman said ecstatically, as though Rubuzzi had touched on some long-standing but ultimately unrealizable ambition that The Fly nurtured in his breast, and which chance had denied him. "My father drove a laundry truck. And every Saturday morning I used to help him with his deliveries!"

"No kiddin'," said Rubuzzi. "What do you think of that there?" he inquired of Daniel.

"Mr. Spigleman came up the hard way," said the firm's analyst.

Within Daniel's hearing, Spigleman *père* had been a broker, banker, train conductor, miner, masseur, ditch digger, warehouseman.

"You learn a thing or two about life when you pick up and deliver a family's laundry," said The Fly.

"I'll say you do."

A waiter came with the lunch.

"Just check your steak, Mr. Rubuzzi."

"Yere, it's fine."

Rubuzzi's tale was that he had invested fifty thousand dollars, his life's savings, in a selection of Spigleman's toiletries and that his investment had now dwindled to eighteen thousand dollars. The Fly sympathized, made clucking noises, explained that the market prices depended on supply and demand, asked his analyst for some explanation.

"We were in a downside market," Daniel said. "Margin requirements were tightened. Lots of investors are waiting on the sidelines for positive sounds from Washington. Look at the redemptions of the mutual funds."

Rubuzzi turned to look, when Kit and another girl entered the office. The Fly then pushed a buzzer on his intercom to signal the operator to start ringing him every five seconds.

"No, I can't talk. I have Joseph Rubuzzi with me. One of the firm's most important clients. It'll just have to wait."

Rubuzzi took that in his stride, chest swelled, and his tutti-frutti ice cream turned to mush. His eyes lingered on four un-crossed kneecaps. Neither of the girls was wearing panties. They moved over to the table to join the men for coffee, and The Fly nudged Daniel. Time to shift.

"I'm going into conference with your broker, Mr. Ackerman, and the accounts department. And one thing I tell you, Joe, is when I want answers I get them," he noted in his soothing mellifluous Fly voice.

The standard procedure, a typical Fly tactic, was to leave the girls with the hysterical client. In about nine seconds they'd be fucking and sucking him into sillyville. While one of the girls was working on him, Kit usually shot off a few rolls of Polaroid snaps, so that the client would have a memento of his visit to bring home to his wife. Depending on his mood, Spigleman might reappear, catch the client *"in flagrante,"* as he called it, and ask the girls if they wished to call the police to take this rapist out of circulation. This ploy was used only when the client still wanted his money. If he quieted down, Spigleman would assure him that he personally would supervise the ravaged account and reconstruct it.

"Everyone into the conference hall," Spigleman shouted in the empty office. The men emerged from their shelters.

This was a large, well-appointed room with a real conference table and bridge chairs.

When everyone was seated, Spigleman paced with hands behind his back, coupled his thumbs in Prince Philip style and then whispered:

"It's called *United Leisure Activities.*"

Chattering among the men and many commendations were flung at The Fly's feet.

"Gorgeous . . . beautiful . . . a miracle . . ." all jumbled together as Spigleman in statesmanlike posture waited for order and the scattered applause to cease. The success or failure of a new issue depended entirely on the name. Didn't matter what if anything the company produced, or what they claimed in the prospectus, or how they were to improve mankind. The name! With a dull name, if they were making gold it couldn't be peddled. As a result, The Fly spent weeks and weeks in tortured self-doubt, struggling over nomenclature.

"We've got four hundred thousand shares at five bucks a share, which is a big position, and unless I was absolutely convinced that we'd be providing a real service to the community, you men know that I wouldn't go near it. The struggle I've had with Merrill Lynch, Allen and Co., Lazard Frères, not to mention the Rothschilds, who turned pretty sour when I scooped it away from them, to get United Leisure Activities for you men, you would not believe."

"The name's solid gold, Irv," said Daniel. "What does the company do?"

"It's a conglomerate in its infant stages. . . ."

"Like what does it conglomerate?" Ackerman inquired and got a look of disapproval from The Fly, like he was nosey and should mind his own business. Spigleman was accustomed to making announcements, constructing tautologies, avoiding specifics.

"What exactly is your question, Don?" The Fly returned, scowling.

"Well, what does United Leisure Activities do?"

"In other words, you're trying to pin me down? Would I get up in front of all of you to make a fool of myself? Don't I have everybody's trust and loyalty? Because this situation, if you're not interested, I can handle myself. Just make a private place-. ment with a fund and *fartik*. No aggravation. A phone call, you understand."

Spigleman went to the blackboard, drew triangles, squares, a three-dimensional cube, circles; then a parcel of zigzagging arrows, which confounded everyone; a square-root symbol! Reminded Daniel of plane geometry, but he could not for the life of him find a connection between the new issue and all of these clumsy drawings.

"The Fly is not known as the Father of Invention for nothing," Daniel informed Gary. "Just watch him go. Never knows what he's going to say. He just makes it up as he goes along."

"If you could all cut out the talking for a while, I'll explain.

. . . Here"—pointing to the cube—"is the infra-structure of U.L.A. and from here we segue-way into its component parts. First the circle. This represents the company's Scandinavian massage parlors fitted with sauna and wet steam and administered by company masseuses. The triangle represents the company's holding in nonallergic body paints. And the obtuse triangle contains U.L.A.'s investments in photographic equipment. Now just to give you an idea of how all of these elements are joined together. You're a business executive who's had a hard day. Want to unwind before heading back to ga-gaville. You go into one of U.L.A.'s clinics."

"Clinics!" shouted Slotnick. "This is clinics? Like which give medicine?"

"Relaxation," said The Fly. "Let me get back to my illustration. This executive wants to unwind, key down. He takes a sauna, maybe some steam. One of the girls gives him a massage. Then into the needle shower. He's feeling terrific. More active, you understand. He might then require some kind of artistic expression to project himself. So, instead of like an art instructor, he sort of becomes his own Picasso. He begins painting one of the girl's bodies. After he's through painting, possibly he wants a souvenir of the experience . . . his creation, so he can then take photographs of his work. You know, show the family and friends, even his kids, that he isn't *just* some kind of money-making machine. He's got sensitivity, talent."

Gary shook his head thoughtfully, suggesting a degree of skepticism to Spigleman.

"What's the trouble?"

"Well, Irv, what's the guy do if his *schmeckle* gets a little hard like?"

"I was waiting for that question. I anticipated it. There's a special *relief* massage, offered if the man wants to take the entire course, which is sauna, steam, massage, relief massage, body painting, and photography, which is cheaper than if he were to do each part of the program individually like à la carte. For fifteen dollars, he can get the whole treatment. If he signs up, say as he would for an evening college course, there is a special reduction. The course comes in ten, twenty-five, and fifty sessions. It's a complete package."

"So he pays fifteen bucks to get himself jerked off," Gary said.

"Gary, you disappoint me. When a man is laying on an osteo-pathic table and nothing but the finest linen touching his body, and the girl relieves him . . . how, in the name of God, can you call that a jerk-off? It becomes medical, you understand."

"If you say so, Irv."

"Now, U.L.A. already has a dozen clinics operating in the midtown area. As a result of public participation, the company plans to extend its operation to the suburbs and move out of state on a franchise basis. In a year there ought to be about five thousand clinics fully operative, and if anything, I'm under-estimating their target figure. The clinics will be geared to seven days a week, twenty-four-hour service. Because exhaustion don't know from time, or the day of the week. We're also going to hit all of the armed services bases, first at home, then abroad. It'll spread like wildfire and before you know it, the company will have a spearhead for an international setup. So now, I'm going to ask every man of you to come up with a target figure for his clients."

Silence, total, complete, so Spigleman decided to add a little hot fudge.

"Each client purchasing a thousand shares will be offered a free treatment at half the regular price, and a special founder member's reduction on courses. I myself am starting off with four thousand shares for one of Don's clients who came back from the isle of the living dead."

"How high are you going to run up these toilets?" asked Daniel.

"As high as I can. Maybe fifteen or twenty dollars a share be-fore we start pulling out."

The Fly gave a little bow, and spontaneous applause and cheering broke out. Another Spigleman winner, replete with poetry, romance—franchised whorehouses. Spigleman collected Daniel as the men stormed to their phones.

"Daniel, let's polish off the laundryman. . . ."

Back to The Fly's rooms. Rubuzzi was in the lav with one of Kit's operatives, getting the last of the spunk meticulously milked out of his peter, looking awkward with his trousers around his ankles and walking like Hercules in chains, waiting for the gods to issue his pardon. Smile on his face.

"I got him from every angle," Kit informed Spigleman. "Any

trouble, and his wife will hang him from the nearest tree if there are any in Pittsburgh."

Rubuzzi sheepishly hitched up his trousers, tightened the thick worn black leather belt and got all his organization geegaws reassembled. Spigleman opened his arms to envelop him, in a cluster of fraternal love, which further perplexed the shame-faced Rubuzzi.

"Holy hell, Mr. Spigleman, I'm sorry. I didn't mean to . . . it kinda just happened."

"Listen, my sister is a big girl and she can do anything she likes," said The Fly, inspiring a convulsion in Rubuzzi.

"Your sister!"

"Oh, forget it. Look, I checked on your account and I moved you out of the stocks you had. You've got eighteen thousand dollars and I bought you four thousand at five dollars a share of my newest underwriting: United Leisure Activities."

"That's twenty thousand dollars."

"It's okay. I'm guaranteeing your margin requirement. It'll wind up costing you next to nothing. Just a third in interest. You've got my word that I'll pull you out at the top."

The Fly picked up his telephone, instructed the secretary to get his car and chauffeur to the office on the double, since one of his most important clients had to catch a plane back to Pittsburgh immediately. He also sprang Rubuzzi to the $22.50 air fare. Anything to get rid of this nudge. Rubuzzi embraced The Fly before departing.

"I've never met anybody like you and your sister, Mr. Spigleman."

"Let's cut out this formality. Just call me Irv. And whenever you want any information, just pick up the phone and call me collect. I'm here to serve you, Joe."

Beautiful. Daniel had fallen into a money-printing machine with U.L.A. Couldn't believe that destiny had at last found his unlisted telephone number and was sending all those dollars to him. Building a future with Spigleman, part of the great American investment community, flashed his business cards to everyone he ran into. With pride. A genuine sense of achievement.

He and Gary had developed an act that was becoming a great double-play combination. The two had moved thirty thousand

shares of U.L.A. and were owed thirty thousand dollars in commissions by The Fly, who mysteriously developed trancelike
forgetfulness when it came to paying out and became afflicted
with writer's cramp—the fingers would freeze up, shake, jerk,
palsied, paralytic—on check-signing Fridays. Spigleman also took
to playing truant on that day of the week, and when spoken to
would suddenly become vague, amnesiac. One Friday he turned
up late in the day with the right hand in a cast and supported
by a black, funereal sling, pleading an ice skating mishap. The
office sharpshooters were openly gossiping about him, attempting to anticipate the direction of his flight. Maps of Mexico,
Central, and South America were pinned to the bulletin board.
The offices of Aeronaves and Varig were contacted every few
hours to check out Spigleman's possible flight routes.

Daniel was handed a secret memo from Ackerman. The Fly
had been followed that morning to Berlitz, where Ackerman,
after intensively questioning the school's personnel, learned that
he was taking a crash course in Portuguese.

"That spells Brazil," said Daniel.

The results from a straw vote were in, confirming a poll
Daniel and Slotnick had carried out, and it was agreed to push
The Fly from his own office window unless he paid all com-
mission checks.

But Spigleman disconcerted the entire gathering. An emana-
tion, without his cast.

"I've just come from the bank," he said grandiloquently. "I've
made arrangements with Chase for a ten-million-dollar credit
line. You can all pick up your checks right now"—he flexed the
putatively injured wrist—"because I'm writing."

Seeing thousands of dollars dancing around the maypole of
his illusions, Daniel embraced Spigleman. With these funds, he
would be able to pay off the house overnight. He and Gary lined
up at the cashier's privy, behind which Spigleman was merrily
humming to himself and *signing* checks. Daniel received one for
fifteen thousand dollars, the largest sum he'd ever seen attached
to his name. The atmosphere was like a wedding. Slotnick and
Ackerman removed their assassin's rabbit-lined leather gloves
and broke into a wall-to-wall tango.

"Let's get the girls and have a big lunch," Gary said.

"That doll is winging in from Atlanta," Daniel explained.

"They had to set down there this morning with a turboprop failure," the authority on aeronautics informed a baffled Gary. "If I cab down to the airline terminal building, I'll just catch her," he added sprinting through the office. "I'll be back with her. Wait!"

Through a motley army of gold teeth, blaring La Playa Sextet mambos, and ponging of Dos Veces fumes, the Hispanic cargo was disgorged from a Carey Line bus, and he saw the beat, wan face of his beloved. He lifted her off the jump step, throttled her in his arms.

"I have had nothing but *mahzel*—luck—baby, from the moment we met."

"I am shagged into stuporization," she said. "And sick to my tum. One of them was eating candy with stuff moving in it . . ."

"Ant brittle, doll. It's their Hershey's. Don't let it upset you."

He bustled her into his waiting taxi, smothered her face with a mixed assortment of wet and dry kisses and noisy ear-licks.

"I ought to get my bag deloused."

"Everything new, Sonya."   .

He flashed the check before her inflamed bloodshot eyes.

"Can it be cashed?"

"Sonya, don't you trust anybody?" he complained. "It bears the signature of Irv Spigleman."

"That's sort of what I mean. Daniel, I am starved. Can we get a burger or a hero somewhere?"

"We can do better than that. A little nose powder, eye-liner perhaps, and we are going to the Four Seasons for luncheon with Gary and Marlene."

"Walllll, I can't be forever. I'm filling in for Phoebe Jansen tonight. She's got to have her nose cauterized."

"You are filling in for nobody. You are finished flying. You think I can spend my life pacing the floor worrying about turboprop failure and tail collapses? Not to mention my recurring nightmare of metal fatigue?"

She slumped on his shoulder, sound asleep. Short abortive noises were transmitted from her bunged-up nose. A threnody of exhaustion which brought out his perfectly camouflaged instincts for protecting the infirm wreck his glorious fiancée had become. He wanted to wake her to help him solve the dilemma his check had created. A diamond ring after lunch, or should he pay off the house and join the select of American life—a man without a mortgage? He informed the cabby to keep the motor running, possibly the most inspired decision of his business life.

"Don't kidnap the sleeping beauty," he informed the boils on the driver's neck.

Entering 40 Broad Street, *his* building, he came upon a peculiar sight. A limping Negro handyman in animated conversation with Gary. Since his introduction to the brokerage business, Gary had become totally unscrupulous in his hunt for new clients. Approaching Daniel, the handyman slammed a broom at his shoes.

"What's with you and this creep, Gary? And where's Marlene?"

Ashen-faced, Gary turned to him, wordlessly gesticulated as sweat links dribbled from his sideburns.

"*Los Federales* are upstairs," the handyman said in a synthetic hispañola accent. "With *pistolas* drawn."

"Irv . . . Irv! Is that you?"

Under the brown makeup and turbulent shock of chicken-wire hair, The Fly's features were discernible to the initiated.

"Rubuzzi blew the whistle. He confessed to his wife," said Spigleman with rancid distaste for the most unspeakable act a grown man might commit. "Lucky I got tipped off in time."

"Thank God I was waiting in the lobby for you," Gary said.

"What are we supposed to do, Irv?" Daniel said, reeling dizzily. "I've got my fiancée asleep in a taxi."

"Vanish," The Fly advised in a voice that was definitely sepulchral. "Or else it's The Tombs."

"Our checks?"

"Yeah, Irv, what about those fucking checks?"

"Good as gold. But if you deposit them or try to cash them, you may get busted."

The three huddled by the gleaming brass mailbox near the newsstand as Slotnick, screaming, and Ackerman, demanding his civil rights along with the entire lair, were led through in handcuffs.

Out of the rear exit into the streaming daylight, Spigleman floated. A black mote in gray cleaners' overalls.

He tried to tell Sonya the truth when he regained his breath.

"Daniel, you are not one of nature's great thieves. It's sad, screwing little guys, so why don't you look for a job?" She handed him an abandoned *Times* from the floor of the cab whose meter had crescendoed to twenty dollars. "And please, buy me a goddam hero before I starve to death."

10

Daniel's involvement with his friends had become a lifelong ac-tivity, as aseasonal as his quest for the perfect piece. With his thoughts constantly on this afternoon's activity at Kit's, he real-ized that it was too late for coffee, too early for lunch, and too wildly impertinent to begin fucking at eleven-fifteen in the morning, birthday or not. He had reached, virtually without being aware of it, that early success pinnacle in business which corresponded to the tragic ejaculatio praecox in primates. His insurance operation virtually ran itself and he, chairman, presi-dent, holder of all stock, had as his daily grind nothing whatever to do except to seek from the far corners of the earth, trouble.

Security had been his undoing, and when the Church of New York had removed all financial doubts from his life, he had gradually begun to fall apart. They had given him a contract to insure all of their clergymen, having recognized that they had in him the perfect unprincipled dealer to husband the fortunes that they not only refused to admit existed, but also disclaimed.

Monsignor Braughton had called Daniel "The Perfect Sin-ner." The beauty part of the arrangement was a get-out clause, enabling the Church to abandon Daniel either for moral reasons, or if his chicanery embroiled them in legal difficulties. They could neatly plead innocence and dissociate themselves from him.

Although it might be supposed that perfidy was to Daniel what bricks are to a builder, no finger of accusation was pointed against him. Those whom he touched prospered, and spoke his name in saintly prayer. Canonization might be premature, but turning over money is still the best way to build friendship.

Crossing swords one day with Braughton, chairman of the Church's Financial Committee, Daniel had angrily established his own preeminence.

"Look, I pulled you out of Harlem and most of the slum firetraps that were causing all that bad publicity. You're on the respectable East Side now. Nobody starts riots or fires there. Closed-circuit TV, not a single murder yet, and only our door-men have guns."

"I accept that, and all you've done, but some of the investments you're making touch sensitive ground, so please bear that in mind. We keep a dog, but occasionally we like to do our own barking," he had said, gently rebuking him.

Daniel did not take the implied criticism lightly, decided on a good roast, without basting.

"What happened, Monsignor, when you and your whole committee lined up against me on co-ops?"

Braughton was justifiably reticent. They'd attempted an in-unity-there-is-strength line with Daniel.

"Our advisers on property . . . previous advisers," he corrected himself, "well, they made out a strong case . . ."

"Just a damned middle-class mood. Death to us as investors and impossible to sell. Soon as inflation hit us we would've been buried. I fought for the classic three-roomer, or the Junior Four. Rent! You get rich by collecting rent, not paying it. Follow your advice," he said derisively. "How would you like to be sitting on seventy-five co-ops at four hundred thousand dollars apiece at this moment of time?"

Braughton unconsciously rustled his beads.

"Daniel, just a little discreet care, nothing more."

"You may not like my aggressive approach or my manners, but let's stick to our original agreement. You worry about sin, and I'll build capital."

"We both have our failures. . . ."

"Depending on where you're sitting, it's a toss-up about whose are more expensive. Let's just remember the sign above the bar: 'In God we trust, all others pay cash. . . .'"

A delegation spilled over from Gary's office to Daniel's—informal as usual. Daniel's custom in his one-man war against company bureaucracy, for he was wise enough to know that profitable investments are not made by appointment. Yet another meeting Daniel had overlooked, the Wednesday financial discussion.

The nucleus of Daniel's corporate team possessed shrewdness, a knowledge of the law, skilled double-dealing, and they knew exactly whom to bribe and how much it would cost. This small but effective group nursed the Church's pension funds which had grown as a direct consequence of the insurance aspect. Dead priests insured for millions with the Church as beneficiary had created enormous funds. Out of thin air.

Daniel surrounded himself with those he could trust and only in Gary, Don Ackerman, and Gerry Slotnick could he find undying loyalty. The boys had grown up and were now respectable. He retained Max Hoffman for personal reasons, but Max pulled his own weight. As financial comptroller, he was in charge of mercantile credit checks, actuary advice. Max also had all the wiretapping and bugging connections the office required. Their tortuous employee-employer seesaw added piquancy to the staleness of a relationship yet to be resolved.

Birthday greetings trilled through the air, and Max even sang a few bars of "Happy Birthday." Nothing, however, could dispel Daniel's ugly mood. Buried in him like some doomsday warheads were the conflicts of his personal life.

"Can someone tell me, like right now, why I had to be bothered with Slimes this morning?"

"I didn't want to take the responsibility for busting the block," Ackerman said, meticulously pulling up the knees of his four-hundred-dollar Cardin suit. "So I memo'd Gary about it."

"It was a straightforward rent hike. Max showed me the bank charges last month and to meet them we needed an increase."

"The law—" Ackerman began, but Daniel interrupted.

"Fuck the law. Since when are we concerned about legislation and shit like that. So don't give me the law. Baby, this is New York City and anything goes. Now, Don, let's block-bust anything we have to. But quietly . . ."

"I'm tired of jiggling the books," said Max, "especially when I have to pull us out of good things before our info gives us a peak."

The three men were nominally responsible to Gary, but he merely served as an interpolator. Whenever a quick yes or no was required Gary was bypassed. For his part, Gary was grateful.

At seventy-five thousand dollars a year, sitting on his can and go-fering for Daniel suited him fine. Indeed, his function at a business level was as the charming bagman who carried cash to whoever required the green sweetener.

"I have some good news," said Slotnick. A two-thousand-dollar hair transplant had changed his life and returned him to a boyishness that had never before existed. He and Max devised recipes for cooking books.

"Hit me," said Daniel, wondering how in the name of—well, nothing was sacred—his peace of mind, he could arrange to place Norma and Sonya at the same table that evening.

"I'll cut right through the shit."

"That's a change from your usual style," said Ackerman with a grin.

"Daniel, you remember that unregistered paper Don found for us two years ago?"

"Which one? He's located so much *drekh* for us . . ."

"The canning factories, Daniel," Don said, bounding up. "And it was a fucking good investment," he added irately. Don always said he made fucking good investments.

"Somewhere in the state of Washington. Yeah, I recall that you pulled my prick for us to take the paper."

"We got a registration this morning," said Slotnick.

"So it wasn't toilet paper, was it?"

"Don, I'm congratulating you," said Slotnick. "Don't get moody. I want to hug you."

Max handed Daniel his clipboard with facts and figures. He was never without it, finding both comfort and serenity in numbers.

"Daniel, our position was a million shares at a quarter a share. Gerry unloaded them to a go-go fund at six dollars a share. A private placement."

"Where's the green sheet?" Daniel asked.

The green sheet was an office code, devised by Daniel, of which no copies were to be made. Daniel personally destroyed them. The sheets indicated who had been bribed, the amount, the reason, and the eventual plan of action.

"Why'd the fund pay so much?" Daniel asked.

"I know you didn't read the technical report I prepared at the time, but Gary did," Ackerman explained.

"Some kind of canning process . . . who knows. For tuna or salmon?" Gary said, invariably close enough to the facts so that he did not appear a fool.

Admiring his reflection in Daniel's window, Don said expansively like a seer:

"Well, before everyone got hysterical about ecology and the preservatives used in food, I found Washington Canning and Packing. They were using a natural bean oil and not monosodium glutamate. That caught my eye. Last week they got exclusive contracts from two coast-to-coast chains for own-brands. It runs into millions."

"Then why the hell did you sell?" Daniel asked.

"We've got a five hundred and seventy-five percent profit, Daniel. And there are a whole batch of new situations that require liquidity. We've got rights to buy stock at ten dollars a share which we can exercise if we see any movement. And we've been fighting for a registration. So the smart thing was to run with a profit."

Studying the green sheet, Daniel grew exasperated.

"I'm sorry, I never would have approved. According to this, Gary delivered fifty thousand dollars to the vice-president who advised us to step in. The family that started the company had lots of property and plants. They were stupid investments at the time, because they couldn't put up plants in downtown areas, but now they're perfect for hotels. We bought the registration for a hundred big ones, so our investment all told was two hundred and fifty for the paper and one hundred and fifty in envelopes. This was an asset strip operation. . . ."

"I know what you're implying," said Slotnick defensively.

Daniel was buzzed through on his line and heard Jeanette whisper:

"I've got Norma and Sonya on two and five. . . . How long should they hold . . . ?"

"Till they stop breathing," he said, cutting her off.

"Daniel, listen, the funds aren't idiots. They're not going to buy paper without an investigation. I couldn't sell a shell."

"Gerry, the important point was the registration. Next the strip, then we look for idiots. I'd find them and hype them in for a few bucks a share. Just think of the kind of poetry a fund could write about natural preservatives to justify buying it. People read these fund reports and they think, my fund is right out front. Now except for the property where we needed liquidity, what was everyone in such a hurry for?"

Finally he had climbed over the morning's drears and felt himself coming alive. The astringency of dealing and the mystery of his afternoon appointment with Miss Pauline Bianco at Kit's were the solitary factors that excited him. But none of the new ventures tempted Daniel. A one-third interest in the Golden Grove, a Las Vegas hotel and casino, he dismissed.

"If Hughes got out of Vegas and the Mafia are frightened to go near the place, how can we take the chance? There are government agents sleeping on the streets. The skimming is over and we'll have Treasury people climbing up our ass. There's also a moral consideration. We're playing around with the Church's money, and even though we've got a stake in it, how can I justify putting them in the gambling business? No!"

Hoffman suggested opening a chain of employment agencies and also providing finance to a group of wiretappers who needed expensive electronic equipment.

"The employment agencies are over. Most of the fly-by-night shops are being investigated by the state. The legal terms of the contract that they make a stiff sign are being disputed. Read the papers, Max. One court case after another. And who needs employment agencies when there's so much unemployment? There are no jobs. As for putting two hundred and fifty grand into bugging equipment, what happens to the shit if there's a federal seizure or one of these *goniffs* gets caught? We've flushed our money down a toilet. The stuff is impounded, and if we want to be so stupid as to mount a claim we find ourselves at the wrong end of a federal indictment."

To Ackerman, Daniel listened sympathetically for almost half an hour as an elaborate scheme was outlined. Charts were brought out, photographs of building sites displayed.

"Don, with all due respect. What the world does not need now is another new offshore fund. IOS and Gramco finished that for the likes of us. Do you think I want to spend the rest of my life in litigation with half the countries in the world? Do I want a palace in Switzerland for my offices, or Hugh Hefner for my friend? No, thank you very much. I want a little peace of mind, and I'd like you to continue concerning yourself with little companies that no one knows about and getting in on the ground floor. You're not a property speculator. You like the sound of the

Bahamas. You want a vacation there? Take off a month. Smarter people than us have gone bust there."

The room was silenced and the men turned from one to the other in a state of suppressed irritation. Daniel had never been so negative, so adamant in knocking down their ideas.

"The fact is, Daniel," said Slotnick, "that we have all of this money now in cash."

"I'll think of something," he said. "Maybe I'll go the other way. Because when I present the pension fund accounts to Monsignor Braughton, I'd like for once to have some balance. Like conservative business tactics, so he doesn't have to ask why I'm shoveling money into a company just starting up. One thing I can't ever explain is a large cash balance. For that he doesn't need us. He can stick it all in a savings bank."

The men rose, gossiped quietly, then moved toward the door.

"Max, hang on for a second, will you?"

Carrying his collection of clipboards like a schoolmaster after a lecture, Max waited in the corner of the room. Daniel no longer baited him, but still made him distressingly uncomfortable.

"I screw up too . . . ?" he asked, while Daniel buzzed through to inform Jeanette that he was going to lunch with Gary and was ready for his car.

"No, don't be silly." He paused, distinctly awkward. "I've got a little birthday dinner tonight. Gary and Marlene, me and Sonya . . ."

"Have a good time. Listen, I got you something. Just hasn't come yet. The trouble with ordering . . ."

What if anything did Max really know about their tangled relationships? And how could Daniel just tell him he was through?

"I wondered if you and Norma were free . . ." he stumbled. "If you'd like to join us."

"Thanks, I'll check it out with her first. Let you know later, okay?"

"Fine."

On his way out, Daniel stopped. The office, led by Gary, were singing "Happy Birthday," forcing him to smile. For once the constant witness of other men's anxiety seemed vulnerable.

ii

WINGS

Ever let the fancy roam,
Pleasure never is at home.

—KEATS

1

Over the years Wings had developed a deadly technique for tossing off Sonya which involved seizing between his big toe and
its mate a section of her vulva and manipulating it until the
chemical magic of coming had been reached. He could perform
this prehensile act even while reading. Not indicating a lack of
affection, but a familiar and friendly exploitation entering its
ninth year. In its on-off-on-off sporadic style, it had preceded and
run parallel to Daniel's entry into her life.

Daniel had siphoned off nearly eight years, and what remained
of their marriage were the splayed threads of an angry friendship
both were reluctant to end, or for that matter admit even existed.
Sonya did, however, sense that their annual going-out-of-business
fire sale might this time be an honest claim. Not simply the sign
their friends had laughingly hung, then ignored, over the entrance to their violently palatial home in Kings Point. She had
instigated the move when he left Princeton Insurance, but he
made sure she had nothing to do with the architecture or the
furnishings.

Sonya had at long last reached the clearing in the woods
Daniel had inadvertently guided her to, only to be deserted. No
other word for it. Daniel came home, when he did, to visit his
daughters and to use the facilities: the heated pool, enclosed in

winter, open in summer; the sauna; the golf driving range; the all-weather tennis court; the poolroom. A sportsman for all seasons, he attended games played by the Jets, Giants, Yanks, Mets, Knicks, and Rangers, not to mention boxing matches. In between of course the lie of constant business crises at the office. But the intimate of athletes and friend of champions, dripping cronies and swarmed upon by a legion of ass-kissers, hardly ever fucked. At least not her.

Now with Thanksgiving buried, she could relax and resume her real life. Only Christmas stood between her and the birth of 1973, her thirty-sixth year. She looked forward to her birthday with uncharacteristic elation, for she had Wings' promise that they would finally "cut out all this hidin'."

Peering over her copy of *Different*, she watched the movement of Wings' toes. Had a memory of an old war movie from TV. Was this the pincer hold favored by Montgomery in his pursuit of Rommel's panzers? More like a beached crab fighting for its life against the skilled tortures of a small kid. When caught in this position one day by her friend Bunny, she had denied that this was proof of Wings' indifference.

"You're being taken for granted," Bunny Washburn said.

"You're kidding. We're always in action. He's going to leave his wife."

"Wings said that? I seem to recall a similar remark some time back when you told him you'd marry Daniel."

Truth unfortunately seldom invited excitement, invariably silence. Her affair with Wings started on the Miami run before Mr. D. Barnet of 16E had conceived of a winter holiday. Wings in his capacity as navigator of the crate, having located Charleston, S.C., would saunter down the aisle at 2:20 A.M. EST meeting Sonya just as she had dimmed the cabin lights and taken her last order from a querulous passenger. Both would enter the toilet, lighting the *Occupado* notice.

Though neither might dare lay claim to having initiated the airborne screw, they might honestly boast of having logged in dozens of hours and could certainly operate with limited oxygen and sudden losses in cabin pressure. Dining on Sonya at twenty-three thousand feet with her spine impaled on the safety grip—almost costing her a disk—Wings could ply her without coming up for air. He also helped her overcome her poison complex, inch by inch, a fact which could not very easily be explained to Daniel.

The ignominy of first love prolonged into an affair had dismal consequences for Sonya. Along the way there had been others, and when Sonya thought about them, they came under the vague heading of MISCELLANEOUS.

Wings was still blond, now forty-three with the same teen-age doll face which showcased fine wrinkles. His light green eyes were small and he never seemed to use them on anyone but himself.

Familiar with every single mental and anatomical quirk of his partner, Wings extended his bare legs over the come-crusted pillow and introduced himself to Sonya's palm. He continued a Wankel interior massage. Their private parts were usually given love names for each meeting. Originally from the South, he took advantage of that fact in Queens, among women, naively convinced that regionalism abetted seduction. As good a theory as any. In a molasses accent which lingered like a Colonel Sanders heartburn, he said:

"Say hey to the S.S. Pedro."

She wrapped her fingers around his dozy boner. More ghostly than menacing.

"Hey, San Pedro," she said with a shrill giggle. In everything she needed to be led, but once led, never retreated. With the characteristic enthusiasm of a newcomer, she had become more revolutionary than any of the others. Sonya had introduced games into their lives.

The constant diet of Daniel's once-over-lightly sorties had brought out her desperate, suspended mood for adventure. She had become . . . experimental, edging toward some unknown depth. She'd heard stories about Daniel, the master of discretion, and his pickups. He had been banging anyone . . . into rough trade. She hadn't troubled to get the rumors confirmed. Wasn't it enough that he always came home on empty?

"Now, Wings, you say 'Good afternoon, Miss Emma.' "

The salutation was delivered silently with his big toe. Her guy, *again.* Her initial feeling for him—love?—had been twisted into a brittle form of jaded rapture which she couldn't quite control. He'd been married when they met and still hid behind the protective custody of the institution, his three teen-age kids, and the flimsy net curtains of a lapsed Catholic. This had the doubleheader effect of making her laugh and want to puke, yet another wedding of incompatibles she presided over.

"Don't," she said, flicking his hand off her breast. Both Wings and Daniel had *some* common ground. They were nipple twiddlers.

"Get's 'em hard."

"But it hurts. And my idea of a lazy afternoon does not include pain."

The front door opened and they heard Bunny's voice: "Anybody here?"

"Just us," Sonya replied from the bedroom.

"Sorry to disturb you."

Bunny was the organizing genius behind the apartment, which was located on Queens Boulevard, next to the Lee Foo chink joint, fording several delis, a minute from Pep Maguire's teeny-bopper discotheque, useful for generation-gap joy riding, and ominously situated across the street from the Department of Correction's tidy monstrosity. Bunny had brought Sonya into the fold after another stewardess had dropped out. Rotten marriages, held together by the short hairs and who-played-blind, unified the group. Old friendships formed the basis of its cohesion, and secrecy was the formidable weapon of survival.

"Bud's not in yet," Sonya called out.

The rent was shared by three men and three women, and an amicable communal lifestyle had developed. There had been an "apartment" before, in Astoria, but incursions by blacks had terrified them. And Bud had logically pinpointed the problem:

"How do I explain to my wife that I've been knifed in Queens when I should have been hijacked to Algeria with the rest of the passengers?"

The group comprised:

SONYA ANDERSON	(Stewardess, National Southern. Ret.)
BUNNY WASHBURN	(Flight Dir., Alaskan & Terr. Airways.)
PHOEBE JANSEN	(Stewardess, National Southern. Ret.)
LAMAR "WINGS" CONNOR	(Navigator, Nonscheds.)
BUD VAN ALLEN	(Flight Engineer, Intercontinental.)
CAL BEASLEY	(Navigator, Nonscheds.)

Not a pilot or a single among the men. Never mind . . .

Sonya still wondered, but no longer cared, if she had been recruited back into the group merely to help with the rent in their new apartment. She was sharing again. Back into airlines . . . in a sense. It certainly filled in the afternoons and evenings. Relieving her of such morbid activities as B'nai Brith meetings; cruising Great Neck and its environs in her snappy blue Corvette Stingray; and the relentless team of aging Princesses who'd walk into her home uninvited, unannounced, to check out if she'd purchased anything they couldn't afford. The women in the area had the same complaint (neglect), belonged to the same golf club (Windy Knoll), and owned the same nose (Dr. J. Herbenstein, the artist who had brought obsolescence to his métier).

The chief offender and intruder was a fortyish woman from the mansion next door, who pleaded with Sonya to join a local Gal's Luncheon Club and could never contain her curiosity whenever giant Mack trucks swiveled around the crescent driveway.

"Is that chandelier from Fortunoff's or Sloane's?" she'd ask while Sonya still had a toothpaste smear on her lip and was tapping her egg.

"It's from Daniel."

"You got yourself one helluva guy. My Sy would rather get leprosy than go near a furniture store."

"How'd you get in here?" Sonya asked politely.

"How? I just walked in. First I rang the bell, then I entered."

"I'm going to have a bath."

"Go on. I don't mind. I'll have a little wander. Your room sizes . . . I thought *we* had roominess. We're living in a cottage next to you. How come no one ever sees that wizard you're married to?"

"He's out fucking most nights."

The remark caused the Weintraub woman to break out in a frenzied spittle laugh.

"Some sense of humor you got, Sonya. Dry . . . And so what do you do to keep in trim?"

"Me?" An ad in *Newsday* had caught her eye. The New School was flogging wisdom to the lonely and the overhill underachievers. "I take courses at the New School . . ."

"Now I know you're smart. One thing before I depart. Please

ask your Daniel where and how much that chandelier went for. Looks to me like it could only come from a Parke-Bernet auction."

The flippant answer to Weintraub had accidentally set Sonya in motion. She registered at the New School for Urban Psych., and a survey course in History of Western Civilization. Attended class three times, and when she was out, as was now the case, her notes to Daniel bore the sacred imprimatur of adult education. She still maintained a passing respect for appearances and loaded the bedside repro bombé with $73.86 worth of textbooks. The impressive display of potential scholarship amused Daniel.

"Next thing I'll know is you'll be leaving me for Bobby Fischer."

"I'd rather just string you out, Daniel."

"Time is your friend and my enemy?" he asked.

"Slow and painful."

"Oh, Indian style . . . Hey, where the fuck's my Vitamin E?"

"You swallowed the entire bottle as usual. Doesn't seem to do you much good." He'd heard about the remarkable restorative powers of this most recent sexual philosopher's stone. A panacea in search of a plague.

"It's for my skin. They say it stops the corners of your lips from cracking."

"Maybe if you changed your company or didn't lick them."

"Oh, you're studying medicine also. What a bargain I got."

"Could be you are heading for an early menopause."

"I'll make sure about your lobotomy tonight. Definitely temporal lobe," he theorized, while powdering his balls. "Doll, one thing you can count on. When you're rocking with stomach cramps and the hot flashes are crippling you, I will be knocking off the fresh stock of nineteen-year-olds. Now hang in there with your psych."

The only genuine friendliness that either evinced was when departing. Love glows burned in their eyes at leave-taking. Perhaps they had been wedded to some optimistic view of human nature rather than to each other.

Wings had started to doze, and having come with alarming regularity, in multiples, Sonya wondered if rousing him for a precocktail finale was at all advisable. His red-raw meat was on its way to tartare.

Flipping through *Different,* a hard-core publication from the bowels of San Francisco, she examined the photos. No limp V-2 dum-dums in this magazine. Pure action. She studied the faces of the girls caught in various extremes of ecstasy, and they possessed a reality on film that transcended the actuality of her and Wings lying there naked and whipped. On the faces of the men, she thought she detected appreciation for their partners. On the merchandise page, she observed mechanical appliances, pussy blenders, dildoes, wooden torture devices, shank irons, leather corsets, all the aphrodisiacs known to man and God. The Sappho Society and the under-eighteen Platonists were reopening their memberships, but "birth certificates required" for the latter. It didn't seem likely that all of the underground weirdos of the world had taken asylum in America overnight, or that permissiveness was in and restraint out. Something deeper, and she sensed she herself was a part of it. The lonely of all ages, sexes, practices, had ripped through the earth's crust and were about to join hands in some massive convulsion. No leadership qualities inspired Sonya, just a simple desire to be noticed. To be identified.

When she wanted attention, she always addressed him as: "Lamar! Get this."

"Fell off, I guess," with self-pity in his voice.

The correspondence section of *Different* yielded radium.

Sonya began reading in her clearly modulated stewardess-on-the-air-Mae-West-instructional voice:

" 'Sir, In an illustrated book on sexual techniques, recently I read about rubbing the penis between a woman's breasts . . .' "

"Where's he been?" Wings asked.

"Do not interrupt."

" 'I had not heard of this before, but it seemed a challenging notion, and since my wife has been generously endowed, we decided to try it. By squeezing her breasts closely together so that a small entry remains, it is possible to work up a considerable degree of friction. But the activity is much more stimulating if you can slide the penis through the breasts and into the woman's mouth. I must confess at this stage, for it is a give-and-take event, that I yielded to my wife's darker urges. Since receiving her Weight Watcher's diploma for outstanding effort, she has been nagged by a wayward sweet tooth. With great reluctance, but since we are married folk, I allowed her to introduce my erect dickey bird into a pot of honey whereupon she licked it dry. With a little practice this can be managed quite easily and makes a most interesting variation.' "

A short hiccuping gasp signaled Sonya's touchdown orgasm. As ever, a nonscheduled arrival, which surprised Wings.

"Miss Emma, I do believe . . ."

"Getting there is half the fun," she said.

"Sonie, you are gettin' absolutely spatial. An' I dunno if I dig it."

2

Gunning her Stingray through the belligerent anarchy of late-afternoon traffic, Sonya pulled into the Den's parking lot. She'd stay there until the rush hour was over, since there was hardly any compulsion to punch clocks for a husband anxious to see her and to relate the activities of his day. When in doubt, she either went for a drink with Bunny or Phoebe, both if they could make it, or if she was on her own, and wanted to avoid the bar scene, she'd have her hair done. Not because it needed doing, but to put off the interminable evening that stretched out like some illimitable, unconquerable Gobi Desert.

Before resuming with Wings, she had frequently allowed herself to be picked up, gone for a fast rip-off with a stranger. Afterward, her conscience did not trouble her, nor was she given to self-chastisement. The demands of the human body could not be overlooked, and *what* was wrong with being an easy lay?

Mr. Angelo the hairdresser had done her hair for years and at odd hours. He catered to the airline stewardesses and lived by their fiendishly irregular hours. He was aggressively heterosexual but came on daisy camp, so that husbands and boyfriends did not feel threatened. She got in before the crush of secretaries and singles with early dates who Angelo now needed for economic survival. He could have you washed, set, and dry in an hour. It was a factory.

He was well over forty, and had that ageless continental insouciance that could only be achieved by a man who had never been abroad and been born into hair. It went well with his long shaggy locks, open print shirt, sunlamp chest tan presided over by a medallion of some obscure faintly religious order. She and Angelo had that perfectly rare relationship of never having exchanged confidences.

"By all that's sacred and profane, Sonya!" said Angelo. "I haven't seen you or your wigs for ages now. Where are you all keeping? What can I do for you?"

"The works."

"Looks like you had it done this morning, but Mr. Angelo never argues with a client."

He pecked her on the cheek. Still on Acqua Di Selva and himself in the third person.

"Saw Bunny and Phoebe last week." He paused and in a cordial voiced called to a young girl reading *La Prensa*. *"Isabella, por favor, toma, la señora."*

"Since when with the Spanish?"

"Since everyone quit working in this city. I speak Spanish *and* I'm nice to my girls. My manicurist, I have to make an appointment with to get her in here. She works five different shops and I'm going to get her on meatless Tuesdays. In any case, your nails look fine."

Sonya smiled at herself in the mirror and had the delightful sensation of falling in love with her image. Sanity was to be found in self-love. If not for Daniel, she might have made it as a model. "No question about that," she said aloud. But she'd preferred the security of an airline job. Could not blame him for her failure as a model or film star. In her prime, according to a consensus of *Cosmo, McCall's* and *L.H.J.,* the sacred trinity which kept her in close touch with herself, advising her on how she ought to be reacting to diet, fashion, and orgasm. Multiple affairs were the rage, and the use of the battery-operated vibrator was no longer a cause for despair. Just come, smile, and get on with your life. Civilization was making huge strides. Advancing from the rhino horn to the new dawn of electronics . . . the cosmic climax.

As an old customer, she had a range of privileges, and turning on with a joint that Angelo laid on her in a little curtain-drawn cubicle illustrated his trust and her tenure.

Toking off the joint and watching the irises of her gray eyes darken, her shampooed hair created the impression of a Medusa head, certainly classical, still Monroeish.

"*Es buena?*" Isabella asked.

No soap in her eyes, so she couldn't complain. She had long since lost the fricassee Esperanto she had employed in dealing with Latin passengers. Sonya pointed to her hair, but Isabella indicated the spiff.

"*Esta.*" She beamed, displaying the family jewels, her gold teeth. "*Yo he traido marijuana.*"

"*Si, si,*" Sonya replied. What service—the connection was doing her hair. In the friction part of the wash, Sonya wanted a little more el springo in the fingers, but Mr. Angelo's Lemon-ized Bouquet Garni rinse was applied before an interpreter could be called.

SMASHED.

Nothing under the sun, or in God's universe, had yet begun to compete with the dual pleasure of the high hair wash. Wandering between the fulfilled gloat of rocks off and the possibility of an as yet undefined starring role in someone's life, her thoughts treaded water then sank without trace when the specter of Daniel arose from the depths. Where was her wonder boy now? A study of his previous behavior, even just as he was leaving Princeton, had been recorded by so many witnesses that not even the Supreme Court could dispute the facts or object to the evidence as hearsay and imagined.

But she had set the chain in motion, advising him to commit the unforgivable offense.

"Lose the master lead sheet," she had insisted.

"I'd rather get gangrene or jump from the *Dakota*," he said. "Max is the boil on my ass and the company won't increase my commissions."

Nursing him along down the path of the estate to the car-park where his secondhand but still prime Olds Toronado spoke of a healthy climb, she clutched young Sylvia in her arms and made the decision for him. In her tum, but barely visible, Noreen, their second accident, was on the way.

"Either you squeeze the boil or lance it. How near are you to closing the Bishop?"

It was to be his giant step forward, giving him an unprecedented three-million-dollar year of policy writing. A million-dollar endowment policy to a youngish bishop with unlimited mileage on his speedometer. Daniel had spent six months in pursuit of the priest, who eventually succumbed to his blandishments and agreed to go to higher authorities for the premiums. This would be a direct link to virgin territory, Jesuits and Dominicans.

"I should hear today."

"Just don't back down. And let me know what happens."

"Don't I always, doll?" Yes, in those days he did.

At the office he registered that remedial blankness which precedes shock when he found the large manila envelope on his desk, tremulously opened it. It had been signed, and *witnessed* by the Bishop's secretary.

Daniel's first act, after a maniacal shriek had informed the four hundred and twelve people that he had arrived in the office, was to tear his lead sheet into small bits, then light the master in a dangerously small ashtray at Max's desk. Max charged toward him.

"You're late again, Daniel, and why haven't you turned in your lead sheet? And I want to see a comment before each and every name."

"I lost it."

"You lost your lead sheet? Where is the master?"

"That I just burned," he added and skipped to his area. Max followed him through row upon row of desks where clerks were at their grim tasks, punching adding machines; typewriter keys bounced in the pool, where women with earphones machine-gunned at one hundred ten words a minute, the awful impersonal drone that comprises business communications.

Daniel reached his desk and opened a container of coffee and peeled the waxed paper off a prune Danish, which gleamed as though from shellac.

"You get off your ass when I talk to you," Max demanded. "And wipe that smirk off your face. You think just because your wife is pregnant, I won't get rid of you? My Norma's also pregnant and I don't behave like you!"

Daniel injected two drops of sweetener into his coffee. The concoction tasted like hot Joy and he pulled a face.

"Why do I get coffee from the luncheonette every day?" Daniel asked. "The piss from the machine is just as bad."

"I don't want to hear any more complaints about anything. And I drink the machine stuff every day and it doesn't bother me."

A woman clerk broke in for an instant front-line decision from Max.

"I'm sorry to interrupt, Mr. Hoffman, but are you signing Mr. Reece's correspondence while he's out sick?"

"Why don't you pp. it, Miss Mann?"

"It's to an important account."

"Let's see then . . . ?" Max pondered for several moments. "Add as a PS that in view of Joe's illness, 'Max Hoffman, Manager' is dealing with it. And send me a carbon."

"June is out sick," said the woman.

"Again! What is it with her? That's twice in the last six months I've had to redistribute her work," said Max calamitously.

"I think she's having an abortion," said Daniel, aiming the empty coffee container and shooting it into the wastepaper basket. "Dead eye . . ."

"What do you mean abortion?"

"That's the rumor circulating, Mr. Hoffman," Miss Mann observed disapprovingly.

"I think it's one of fourteen guys in Accounts," said Daniel. "Billy is the office favorite."

"Well, the company doesn't recognize abortions as a legitimate illness."

"Dock her, Max."

"Don't worry, I intend to. If she can find time to fool around, then she can use her own time and not mine to pay the consequences." He waved the typist away and was about to turn his attention back to Daniel, who had just picked up the phone for an in-coming call. He listened to Daniel say:

"Right, I can cut out after lunch. That should get me there at about three if there's no traffic, which'll give us a couple of hours of serious fucking. Bye."

"Even a million-dollar man doesn't get away with that," said Max.

"According to the office clock, it's nine fifty-five, so why don't you grab somebody's *News* and go for your shit, instead of pressing your ass cheeks together and leaving off at my desk."

"That's it. You're out."

"Really, Max, after all this time, why don't you get wise to yourself. You can see Andy and recommend my dismissal, but everyone knows that unless he okays it, you can beat your dummy. So if I were you I'd reorganize the crap in the typing pool and threaten a temporary."

Max seized a piece of paper and began to list Daniel's sins aloud.

"One: filthy and foul language in front of female personnel; two: lateness each and every day; three: loss of lead sheet; unaccounted expenses is four; five: using office time and the company phones for immoral reasons."

"Just a minute, now, Max. Since when is screwing somebody else's wife immoral?"

"This time you're not going to worm out of it. I got you right in the palm of my hand."

Daniel wondered if he had in fact provoked Max to his thinskinned limit. Had he missed something? The Church Financial Committee under Monsignor Braughton was seriously considering Daniel's proposal. The signs were encouraging. At Sonya's behest, he agreed not to eat meat the next Friday.

"Max, you're in a bind and I don't know how to advise you. Should you have your shit first, then see Andy, or take the chance of blowing your special V-2's in his office and hitting him about me. It's a true test of a man's fiber. What comes first? Company loyalty, or your bowels?"

"How Andy hired a dead-beat boiler room guy in the first place is still a miracle to me."

"I produce business. And that is the name of the game."

"Start clearing your desk, Daniel, and don't waste time," Max announced peremptorily.

"Oh, me, oh, my. The office manager who knows every company rule threatens a little salesman like me. I get a month's notice for every year I've been in this toilet, which adds up to four. Furthermore, our vice-president, Mr. Andrew Robinson, has to interview me, then send me an official letter before the deed is done. Isn't that standard practice?"

"It is," Max admitted sheepishly.

"So what are you waiting for? It's ten ten and you, Max, are crapping up *my* morning."

Max darted off, down the long corridor which started with ugly green striped tiles and abruptly built up to navy blue thick-pile carpeting in the executive section, along with simulated wooden doors; decently dressed secretaries; spick-and-span exec johns, the floors of which no mail clerk had ever pissed upon; the latest intercom gadgets; voice boxes for conference calls; nifty steel percolators which produced drinkable coffee; a bar area in teak; all of the mass-produced articles that constitute executive success, and from which Max had been excluded during fourteen years of loyal service. Daniel trailed after Max and waited in the reception area of Robinson's office as Max had the secretary buzz through. His fat cheeks were puffed out, red, choleric.

"We'll see who's boss now," Max advised him.

"I haven't run for the hills, have I?"

The remark clearly troubled Hoffman, but it was too late to do anything. Robinson was able to spare him two minutes. Robinson in charge of personnel and day-to-day company operations was one of those friendly executives whose door was always open. And open it remained when Hoffman recited his complaints.

"Andy, last week I reported to you on the subject of Barnet's behavior like when he told me when my prick reaches my ass I should fuck myself."

Robinson, a tall gray man, began strolling, nodding, appearing to lose hair as Hoffman whined on.

"Yes, Max, I recall. What now?"

"He's killing office morale. And his expenses," brought a lyrical quivering tremolo to the Hoffman monotone. "He put through a hundred dollars in restaurant bills. When I asked who, what, why, where, and no receipts, he goes to his desk, and pulls out one of those pads that waiters carry and he writes out four bills for twenty-five dollars each. Is this any way to run an office?"

"I'll speak to him about it."

"What about when he has girls come up to the office and sit by his desk. Listen, I'm the last man in the world to be prejudiced. We've got plenty of blacks and Puerto Rican citizens working for us, but believe you me, I know spade hookers when I see them. They march in and out like they're on shifts."

"I'll speak to him about it."

"I think he ought to be fired. In fact I fired him this morning and it's gonna look bad if you don't back me up. It'll undermine my authority."

"You fired him?"

"Well, first, of course, I would have consultations with you."

"But you just said you fired him, Max. You can't fire and you know that."

"Well, I'll reinstate him and you can fire him according to policy."

"It's a problem. This year Daniel has already hit a batch of priests for two million dollars' worth of business. Endowment, Max. And they were under forty with track backgrounds from Georgetown. They can go on for fifty years . . . you know what that means to us in premiums and word-of-mouth recommendations?"

"So pay him his commissions and move him out."

"My dear Max"—Robinson tired of walking and slumped on his office couch—"the priests love him. We've got information that Monsignor Braughton is contemplating handing him an exclusive contract for the diocese's complete insurance."

"But why him?" Hoffman protested.

"Why? He sold them, that's why. There's a chemistry in selling which our trainees never understand."

"I don't know what is happening to our high company ideals and American business ethics in general when a Daniel Barnet can hold a gun to our heads."

"Max, he isn't holding a gun to our heads. He's got our balls firmly in his hand and if he decides to squeeze, it's going to hurt."

"So you're not going to fire him?" Hoffman asked incredulously.

"No, Max, you're going to give him his expenses . . . and . . . apologize."

"Never."

"Well, Max, if I have to apologize for you, on your behalf, you understand, your future at Princeton is likely to be . . . somewhat insecure."

"Would you believe it?" Hoffman said, shaken, nodding, helplessly caught in some vise that he could not free himself from. Max passed into the outer office, saw Daniel smiling through him, turned to regard Robinson with his arms open waiting to receive Daniel.

"Max," Daniel whispered as he brushed by, "there's a conspiracy against you. Didn't I tell you he was fucking Norma? And now he's fucking you. . . ."

At Princeton, as in all large impersonal offices, paranoia was an even more intoxicating element than oxygen.

"Never. I don't never believe you, smart guy."

To celebrate that day, Daniel traded in his Olds for a brand-new Lincoln Continental, in opalescent gunmetal gray. And with a reluctance he never bothered to conceal from her, he treated Sonya to an expensive on-the-town evening and dinner at Pietro's, a smart new joint.

For ages she had been advocating group policies for the Church to Daniel, similar to the type she had had at National Southern. Daniel, the genius, had presented the idea to Monsignor Braughton, who could add and subtract as well as anyone. The proposal received a favorable response, and Daniel was biding his time, but was still too insecure to make the break with Princeton.

On the drive back from Manhattan along a deserted Long Island Expressway, Daniel gently eased his new Lincoln up past fifty mph. The salesman had told him to treat the car gently for the first thousand, but Daniel, with a small boy's mischievousness, found himself disobeying.

"Daniel?"

"Yes, Sonya?"

"We are going to get a lot more of the Church's business."

"I am," he corrected her.

"Then we'll be rich, won't we?"

The snappy bucket seats made snuggling a little difficult, but Sonya overcame the problem by placing her hand on his fly and testing for life by tapping her fingers on him.

"What's that for?" he asked, adjusting the climate control to sixty-five degrees to see if the gadget really worked, and wasn't another of those sales hypes.

"I'm expressing appreciation, hon."

"It's appreciated," he replied, fobbing her off for the thousandth time. The problem, one among a sinister line of them,
was that in all of the years he'd been with her, she'd never been
capable of the impulsive crazy act that would make their sex
anything more exotic than mowing the lawn. Just once, he
thought, couldn't she run out of the house naked, jump into
the car and put her ankles through the passenger straps, or sit
in a restaurant with a napkin cloaking his dummy and pull him
off while the world quietly got on with eating their steaks.

"Hey, we were holding hands," Sonya said as she walked with
him into the kitchen.

"Here's five dollars. Say goodnight to the babysitter. I'm going
to bed."

"I thought we could have a talk. We haven't for days."

"I've been running around, Sonya. Writing policies like a
madman."

"At the rate you're going," she observed with approval, "we
ought to be ready for a house in Kings Point by next year.
Should I start looking?"

"Why not? What else have you got to do with yourself?"

"A good deal, Daniel. What with Sylvia, the Sisterhood luncheons, running a home, I'm also on the go day and night."

"You know that plunger I bought and never used?"

"Yes, it's in the broom closet."

"Did you ever think how pleasant it would be if you shoved
the handle in your cunt and jacked off for me? We could sub-
stitute that for the late movie one night. What do you say, kid?"

"I'm not going to talk to you when you get real filthy."

"Is that filthy? It sounds to me like a human activity which
I'd prefer to the TV."

"I am not a whore."

"Don't I know it."

"Maybe you ought to get yourself one of those siphed-up
black sluts on Forty-second Street."

"Why does she have to have syphilis, be black, or operate out
of Forty-second Street? Couldn't she be a nice happy-go-lucky
Litvak from the Bronx or Smith?"

"I don't think that type conversation would go down awfully
well with priests."

"You'd be surprised. They're human and curious. If a man

is a man, he has to spend a certain amount of time considering his relationship to pussy."

"You're disgusting."

"I get big commissions just the same."

"This sort of talk about sex turns me off, if you want to know the truth," she said, carrying a tray with milk and pie up to their bedroom.

"Sonya, have you ever wondered if there's a direct link between your consumption of Sara Lee Brownies, skimmed milk, and the absence of 69 in our relationship?"

"Good night. I'm going to sleep in Sylvia's room."

"I think I'm going to sleep in my car."

"Daniel, will you eff off."

"Darling, just once, once, angel, say Fuck Off."

"Anything to please you, Daniel. Fuck off, then." She giggled with amusement.

In the corner of her pink bedroom, just below the dancing animal wallpaper, Sylvia, the world's tidiest sleeper, drifted through her nightly twelve. And Sonya, with all pretense of excitement abandoned, lay crumpled in an exhausted heap. But Daniel would not let her off so easily. Success had brought with it the special tortures of newly won self-confidence.

He approached the bed where she feigned sleep and tapped her cheek with the throbbing head of his dick.

"Wha!" She groaned, shocked into rigidity.

"Look," he began, "I came in to apologize. What I said about the toilet plunger was pretty outrageous and in poor taste."

"You're forgiven."

"I'm not going to stand on foolish pride. Do you think we could work out some kind of compromise and use a Coke bottle instead? The brewers got hip and changed their style to cans and wide-mouthed jobs, and I wouldn't want you to endanger yourself foolishly."

He ruffled her nightdress as she gasped at the entrance of his joint in her mouth, then rejected it like bad coffee.

"Is that your idea of marital accommodation, Sonya?"

"Will you get the hell out of here. We've got a child sleeping who can hardly breathe because of adenoids."

"I'm afraid the connection between Sylvia's adenoids and the state of my cock is a little too subtle even for me to understand."

"Get out, Daniel."

"Will you come into the bedroom so that we can settle this?"

"I'm not budging. I'm sleeping. Why don't you try it by yourself?"

"Because at my age there are certain convictions I have. Beating my dummy doesn't fit in my world view. Now drag your ass out of that kid's sack."

Pulling flimsy maize nylon over the looseness of her relaxed dormant parts, Sonya came out into the hallway with him.

"What's brought on this crisis?"

"The condition of our sex life. How about that?"

"What has got you in such an uproar?" she asked.

"Specifically, my balls. They are in an uproar because they can't exist on a diet of low-cal pies, skimmed milk, or that flying wheat germ which greets them every morning after a bad night's sleep. To be absolutely specific, Sonya, they survive on a diet of pussy. Take that single life-giving food away from them and they begin grumbling."

Considering his point through the decaying smear of some variety of brown eye-shadow, she nodded, apparently finding some merit in his argument.

"All right. What do you want me to do?"

"Be enthusiastic for openers. This isn't some act of mercy. You're not pulling a kid out of a lake. I want you to get out of that fucking *schmata* first of all and put on your old airline raincoat with nothing on underneath. Then we're going to get into our new Lincoln Continental and drive to the center of town, and park in front of Neisser's Haberdashery. We'll get out of the car and while I appear to be browsing for a necktie in the window, you'll take my prick in your mouth and blow me."

"Daniel, it's two forty-five in the morning."

"Try to be relevant. Why is time against us? If anything it favors the enterprise. The only one likely to pass then is a patrol car and since I've insured most of those crooks under a group policy, what do you think they'll do? Arrest us. We go to court. Pay a fine. Explain to the judge that we're sorry, but close with the fact that even though we've been married for some years

and have a child from this union, we still maintain a desperate
overwhelming animal passion for one another. That ought to
be good for a suspended sentence and a chuckle. No more than a
ten-buck fine, which I can well afford. How does that scenario
grab you, Sonya?"

He peered down from what appeared to be a great height at
the shrinking withdrawal of his cock, shamefacedly retreating
like a tortoise head into its doughlike air-raid shelter.

"We've solved the problem. It's gone. Let's get some sleep,
hon. I'll have it sucked locally in the morning before I get to
the office."

The memories, and a headache induced by her high, and
Mr. Angelo's hair drier, and the scalp stabs of clumsily placed
rollers, brought Sonya down with a jolt. She tipped Isabella a
deuce and was about to flee, when Angelo caught her by the
cash desk.

"Don't be a stranger, now," he said. "And how's that millionaire you're married to?"

The propinquity to wealth always made him tremble. Tonight he'd be telling total strangers that Sonya Barnet was in
today.

"When Daniel had nothing he was a prick, and now that he's
made a fortune, he's a bigger prick."

The first legitimate confidence he and Sonya had exchanged
caused him to grimace and add with faltering dismay:

"Doesn't anything nice happen to my clients?"

3

Shortly before Christmas, an abundance of rumors concerning
Wings begun by Phoebe and confirmed by Bunny brought
Sonya to a delicious state of schizophrenia, so that the rift between what she heard and believed was a compelling exercise.
Physically it agreed with her, and she thought with some justice
that she'd never been lovelier. Hair cosseted in a velvet Alice
band, she was returning to mad innocence.

"I don't believe it," she said to Bunny on the phone. Daniel was within range and double-talk was necessary.

"Can you get out? Now . . . ?"

"Of course I can. Daniel and I are keeping our record intact. We haven't had dinner together for a week."

Her husband for all seasons was sitting at the far end of the sixty-foot living room in a disoriented stupor. He had pitched both ends of a doubleheader at Kit's that afternoon, canceled Norma for the fourth night in succession, and had decided to get home early, have a sauna, and play Daddy, a role he enjoyed occasionally. At his feet, his two daughters, Sylvia, almost seven, and Noreen (Sonya's Momsey's name during the misadventure of her life), were giving their full attention to a repeat of "Sesame Street."

"Daniel, I have to go out," she said.

"I'm in for the night."

"It's to see Bunny. She is in one sorry condition."

"Again? I thought she had the pipes disconnected."

"Daddy, how can a woman get pipes disconnected?" Sylvia inquired.

"Your mother's friend can."

"Not that at all. Just a personal crisis," Sonya explained.

"How can you tolerate that goof-ball? She's like an abscessed tooth—should have been removed years ago."

"What toof?" Noreen asked Daniel. She had an enchanting lisp, but Daniel had been told that speech therapy was inadvisable for a four-year-old.

"You, you're still up?" he said, affecting shock. His portrayal of the loving father invariably took the form of buffoonery. He swooned in disbelief. "Noreen, by the time you're twelve, you'll need the bags lifted and not even my major medical will go for that. . . . Your mother's back to when I found her. Flying in circles."

"Don't listen to him," Sonya said, dragging her black diamond mink on the carpet and creating a small wake of fluff. "I want you two in bed by seven."

A short abortive squawl symphony traveled directly to the fifteen-foot ceilings.

"Daniel, will you—"

"My belt."

"You don't wear one," said Sylvia. "That's why his pants fall down," she apprised her sister with a fiendish giggle.

"Sonya, if you run out of gas this time, try the A.A.A."

"Good night, all you lovely people."

She'd gone back to calling Wings, Lamar. Lately he'd been secretive, unenergetic, and broken dates with her. Hanging her up at the worst possible times as far as Sonya was concerned. After she'd showered at the apartment and lay expectantly on the bed, there had been abrupt telephone calls. Bud Van Allen, the long-standing soulmate of Bunny, had caught her in this position and the two of them had got pretty close. . . . But betrayal was alien to Sonya. She felt a weary gratitude to Wings for relighting the dead ash of her sex. This brought with it certain gruesome notions of fidelity that she'd buried along with her Catholic girlhood.

At the La Guardia Sky Lounge, she saw Bunny at the bar charging through her preflight allotment of double Cutty Sarks. Her hair platinum blond through the ages, both she and her body lived on a diet of skin foods, and estrogen balms. Upon retiring, Bunny had to strip her face like a car chassis before the possibility of skin—an underneath—emerged. When not airborne, she had taken to wearing a weighted belt around her tum, now heading for the point of no return: thirty inches. She was Sonya's oldest, dearest friend . . . her mentor. All that separated the gals from holistic oneness was Bunny's seniority and her two marriages. Moving off the bar stool, Bunny signaled Sonya to a booth.

"What's the urgency? No one cracked—"

"—No, dear me. I'll be up in Juneau for the week. Got myself a real unhappily married guy." She flashed one of those bracelets with a trillion diamond chips that used to be presented to actresses nobody remembered on the dance floors of nightclubs in movies of the forties, causing song, a kiss, and conga lines.

"That's tremendous."

"It's really outstanding, isn't it?"

"You better believe it," said Sonya enthusiastically. She shielded her engagement ring which by contrast suffered from acromegaly and which Daniel had christened The Star of Kings Point and purchased as an investment hedge.

"But what about Bud . . . how's he taking it?"

"Bud and I have always been Friends with a capital F. And we get together when we're both sort of in-between. I think I know every little one of his shakes better'n my Canadian Exercises. We do more talking than actual . . . therapy."

"Bunny Washburn, you did not pull me out to discuss this. Now, sis, let's get down to it," said Sonya, toying with a lemon twist.

A few attractive evening traveling executives with expensive attaché cases cruised over to the bar, and Bunny narrowed her eyes to check them out. They were not, alas, she knew instinctively, flying to Alaska.

"Bud finds you Enchanting. Capital E, and well, he was feelin' me out."

"Sorry, I don't get this."

"Have we shared . . . ?" Bunny demanded.

"Dammit, of course we have."

"Money, apartments, toothbrushes, our troubles . . . our friends now and then?"

"I think you've had too much."

"If I can't fly smashed, then I do not board the aircraft . . . you know old Bunny. But I am not, repeat, am not, remotely close to necessary highness. On the q.t., Bud passed on some info about Lamar and this is not bushwa. . . ."

Sonya's knees quivered involuntarily under the table.

"Get us another pair of the same, hon," Bunny told a waitress.

"So . . ." in her gleaning of undesirable intelligence, Sonya invariably became succinct.

"I will not have you two-timed again."

"Again and again and again," Sonya replied with an absence of lightheartedness.

"Trouble is, Sonya, is you always have taken a little fooling around too seriously. Not like me." Bunny paused, then smiled, proudly revealing the silent wonders of gum-recession treatment. She burst into a soft ditty: " 'Put on your old gray panties/ The ones that were your aunties/And we'll go for a tussle in the hay, hey.' That is me but not you, Sonya."

"What did Bud say?"

"Not for your ears, but he can't stop me sounding off. Lamar has signed on with London Charter Club. Gambling junkets."

"Dammit, I went to all that trouble trying to get him with Delta."

"What with those dolly birds on the King's Row, you will be seeing less and less of him." Leaning over as though to avoid a treacherous bug that John Mitchell may have had planted and then forgotten about, Bunny continued: "He also has himself another woman. . . . But Sonya, this did not come from Bud. Understand?"

In the crevices of her heart, Sonya felt the arrival of winter.

"Lamar," Sonya said, "is so damn dumb and insensitive." She refused to break down. Daniel's special guerrilla training course enabled her to develop the blank look into a work of art.

"I knew you would take it in the right spirit. But . . . all is not lost. Bud has a Yen, capital Y, for my dearest friend. Know what he told me, Sonya?"—she was no longer listening—"he respects you."

Bunny was too, well, sisterly and delicate, to come out in the open with the suggestion of a switcheroo, so she picked at it in the manner of a small child warned off scratching her chicken pocks for fear of permanent scarring.

"You find Bud attractive?"

"Attractive?" Sonya asked. A year ago, possibly longer, before Sonya had joined up in the apartment, she and Daniel had run into Bud one evening at the Homestead Steak Restaurant. Bud had given her a wink and made a clucking sound, attracting Daniel's attention.

Daniel had said: "Hey, doll, you won't believe this . . . But I think you made a hit with that Martian at the bar. You better look after me, Sonya. I'm the only living witness you've got who could swear in court that something wearing pants made a pass at you."

"Bud would like to see you."

"Well, I don't know," she said, for talking herself into another conversion of the spirit struck her as impossible.

"Bud has enormous—vitality. I can't wait to see my man in Juneau," Bunny said, uncrossing her legs and thrusting them into the aisle as though to allow the giver of the bracelet an imaginary passage into fields ready for crop rotation.

"Well, I've got to get going, or Daniel will hit the roof," Sonya said hollowly, bundling into mink herself and the package of small miseries that constituted her romance with Wings.

"Me too." Bunny guzzled her drink. "You would not believe this, but the drugstore ran out of Binaca the other day and I am back to Sen-Sens."

She phoned Wings' home, informed Mrs. Connor that she was with London Charter Club and instantly required his where-abouts to advise him of a change in schedule.

The Easy Acres Roller Skating Rink in Woodside was located in an area of warehouses and forgotten shells off Woodhaven Boulevard, and Sonya circled the place half a dozen times, so that she could control the fluttering of her hands and the imaginary husk that had settled in the back of her throat.

She paid eighty-nine cents for her ticket at the hot dog, candy counter in the lobby of the rink. A man in a gray-white apron on which black fingerprints were recorded dispensed tickets and the offal of such places. He thought she looked familiar.

"You with the Roller Derby?"

"No, I'm not," she said, brushing by him when he lifted up a check pad and pencil and the suggestion of an autograph hovered ambiguously before her face. The man released the turnstile, admitting her.

"You certainly could be Marie Dynamite's double."

"I can't even skate," she protested, passing through into a wide circular arena where some hundreds of people who had failed at bowling whirled and reeled round to the tinny thump of a mazurka.

The piss-filled toilets flushing noisily at the side of the en-trance smacked her right in the face, and her nostrils curled. The odor of sweaty feet and greasy burgers over which disin-fectant lagged, and the maddening grind of skates, entombed a history of social disorientation. Here were the beer-drinking bar-flies, seventeen-year-old girls with intolerable acne conditions, the fat secretaries, and loose middle-aged women whose looseness no one cared about. And there was also Wings with a can of Rhein-gold by his side, on bended knee tightening the skates of a bubbly-legged redheaded woman who wore glasses with rhine-stone frames. What was more he wore the skate key around his neck. She watched him for a while, skating backward, forward, waltzing to *Tales of the Vienna Woods* and jiving to "She Loves Me."

The woman and he skated with arms crossed and held each other's hands. His partner. Sonya found a place for herself in the empty mockery of stands, littered with crushed peanut shells, and moldy blue hot dog rolls from which even the vermin retreated. Wings and his woman rejoined their beer cans, and Sonya painfully observed affection between them. From a distance, it seemed as though they'd known each other for years.

"Christ," she said to no one in particular, "he's not *even* with his wife."

No reason to linger, she thought, when several male skaters attempted to catch her eye by lifting a leg and holding their skates in the air. An invitation. She click-clocked on the concrete floor and walked toward Wings. When she was a few feet away from him, he saw her, and in a splutter, he hurriedly explained Sonya's presence to his partner, then excused himself.

"How come you heah?" he asked. "Somefin' wrong?"

"I didn't know you skated," she said. "And I didn't know you took the job with that charter. I went to a lot of trouble trying to get you on with Delta . . ."

"The pay was stinko," he said, flicking a cowl of blond hair that matted to his forehead. He was sweating and ill at ease, and when he got close to her his breath expelled sour beer.

"What is this? Your weekly skating evening?"

"Tha's right, Sonie." He pointed to two teen-age girls and a boy in that nowhere gawky stage between twelve and fifteen. They were grouped around a pinball machine that they continued slamming after the tilt sign came on. "I got me some passes and took the child'en wiv me."

Sonya herself had been a child of passes, slipped to her mother from the palms of strangers, and she thought she hated passes more than anything in the world.

"So you're going to London with the junket crowd."

"Money's real good."

"It's seasonal and you know it. You're just going to screw around."

"Not true," he protested feebly.

"And who is that dose you're skating with, Lamar?"

"Happens to be an ole frien'. I resen' you callin' her tha'."

"She take her kids, too?"

"She ain't married."

Glaring at this Houdini who had opened her up day and night in all sorts of conditions over a gulf of forgotten years, she had no mercy for herself. She smiled at him, and slapped his shoulder with her leather gloves.

"And you with *your* kids. They're the excuse you gave me years ago."

"They ain't no excuse."

"I am going to roast you, Lamar. And peel the skin off your back inch by inch, you bastard."

Betrayal again, the only constant in her life, tore out some primordial Midwestern streak of meanness inherited from her dead Momsey, a woman who had worked as a cashier, handled bills, and was always broke.

"Lamar, I want the five hundred dollars you borrowed from me, right now. You get those fucking skates off—"

"—Stud fee, darlin'. An' if you thinkin' of tellin' my ole lady 'bout us, I will make a point of visitin' you husbin. Jes' anover bill you run up, baby, an' you got you'sef a yid to foot it foh yuh."

"He's got more balls than you. . . ."

"But they ain't for yuh. . . . Sonie, I nevah met a woman tha' wantid her ass whipped more'n yuh," he said despairingly.

Wings, the daredevil on skates, performed an eagle turn. He pulled his partner off the bench, and she cast a detached glance at Sonya, then glided off with him to the poignant yip of a faraway Perry Como tune.

4

Nursing herself back to a semblance of normality—not that Daniel noticed—Sonya plundered the stores on the Miracle Mile. Buying, buying, buying. Serenely unmethodical. Persistently confusing her were the peppy voices on TV and the radio, warning the population that Christmas would be upon them before they knew it and shopping days until the blessed event were disappearing. To Sonya, they just multiplied.

A vacuous smile indelibly engraved on her mouth, Sonya concealed her hurt in a finely spun cocoon, so that the malignancy of her anguish might appear to be some other, some foreign emotion, which Daniel characterized to the girls as "Your mother's sense of humor. She doesn't need a joke. She has herself." To Sonya: "Since you stopped sewing your own *schmatas*, you've really changed. Get back to needle and thread, doll. It's therapy, recommended by some of our leading yo-yo's." He would chortle and the girls would laugh uncomprehendingly along with him. "She is the price I have paid for total unhappiness. She's irreplaceable. You want the best car, you get a Rolls. For misery, Mommy." Jolted to the outer limits, Daniel's wasp sting virtually absorbed itself.

Turning into the split-level mausoleum that Daniel had constructed as a tribute to himself, Sonya wondered why the hell she'd come home at all. She'd had a few calls from Bud, met him once for cocktails at the Den and debated with questionable logic a point of some philosophic interest to women: love was out, but was sex still in?

The answer for Sonya was a remorseless yes. She had always required men on a regular basis, but the stray moonlighting husbands she'd collected since Lamar's departure had the combined disadvantages of "another appointment," and suffered from the four-minute-mile syndrome that a new piece they'd never practiced with imposed. Disappointed by their own speed, strange men blamed her for their own unskilled labor. Thoroughly shock-absorbed, Sonya eked out a paltry sexual livelihood at transient airport motels and began seriously turning over Bud Van Allen in her mind. Two cast-offs might yet make a team.

She wasn't surprised to see workmen, four of them, outside the house. What did astonish her was that they were placing an enormous tree, a Christmas tree, on the small island of potted plants that forded the entrance to the house. Barking out orders at the curb of the island, her mate.

"It's out of alignment. C'mere," Daniel told a workman. "Now either my neck is crooked, my friend, and I happen to know it's not, or else you people've got to get rid of those soft lenses and go back to glasses."

Nor was she surprised by the commando figure of Adele Weintraub patrolling the perimeter of the estate, another failed infiltration. Adele casually waved a pinky finger and leaped across a ditch to indicate that clandestine activity was over for the afternoon.

Sonya was home. On the landing, her soft little girls, small mice, peered out of the staircase window to keep tabs on Daddy and the workmen.

"Oh, look what just arrived," Daniel said, noticing Sonya.

"What is this, Daniel?"

"I thought that maybe you'd get it right on the first guess. It's a Christmas tree, Sonya."

"Must be twenty, twenty-five feet high!"

"What an eye for detail."

"Daniel, I don't understand why you changed your mind about a tree and all," Sonya said breathlessly, pleased.

"Straighter," he shouted. He buttoned up his suede Aquascutum fur jacket, waved a friendly greeting to the girls above, then cast an eye on his wife. "I thought, why not, we've got the driveway for a tree of this kind. It's twenty-three feet high, so you weren't far out."

"More like thirty," Weintraub shouted.

"Who is that woman, Sonya, and how did she hear?"

"You were shouting."

"Doll, I come home early and I find this thing with more eye black than Carl Yastrzemski and a two-year-old Sassoon hairdo, like lurking. I think she was going through our drawers. One of your friends?"

Weintraub crept in closer for a more detailed inspection of the skyscraper tree.

"Hey, I thought you were Jewish," she hollered.

"Can't you tell *goyim* when you see them?" Daniel returned.

She held her stomach from the pain of laughter, and Daniel with an audience of one in tow welcomed her.

"Now, no photos," he said. She still must have been a good fifty feet away, and Daniel seemed perplexed. "Hey, how could you hear what I said from way back there?"

"Some people are farsighted. I hear . . . at great distances."

"Your husband must love that."

Sonya fitted in a word edgewise.

"But, Daniel, all the things you've said about celebrating *Chanukah* and not Christmas . . ."

"This"—he pointed to the monster growth, branches splaying in the wind—"is a Norwegian fir, Sonya. Not one of those shrubs you get from Vermont. Believe me, even when it comes to Christmas, it takes a Jew to show the world how to do things."

"You said it," shouted Weintraub.

Sonya was too enraptured by the sight of the tree even to contemplate a protest, and blew a kiss to the girls.

"I'm thrilled," she said.

"It's a small improvement over our first Christmas," he said. "Farewell, Babylon . . . forever. In any case," he added, appropriating the gesture for cold fact, "we're going to have loads of priests over. We'll be swimming in crosses. Good for business and it's a tax write-off the way I've manipulated it. So you'll be surrounded by all your old pals and you can work the Hail Marys out of your system."

"Are we going to have a party?" she asked.

"What a clever girl."

"I'll have to prepare."

"What, prepare? I got G and B."

The Island's pre-eminent caterers. Daniel had served time with them as a bar mitzvah booker and coined their slogan. "When you speak of prestige, you speak of Gernstein and Budnick."

"How'd you get G and B?" asked Weintraub. "Me they told they were booked solid until 1975."

He beckoned her forward within striking distance, made a fist and struck the air.

"*You* are not Daniel Barnet and you are on his property."

"I thrive on abuse. That's my bag, you doll."

"Oh, help, Sonya . . ." he called plaintively.

His one cry for assistance, she answered by bolting inside with a maddening giggle. Outside she heard him bellow to the workmen.

"Get the star straight, *schlemiel*."

"Straighter," Weintraub appended. "So, Daniel, who is coming to your party? Some of your neighbors, I hope."

Sonya's coat was taken by one of the maids. There were five in staff, and they kept coming and going so frequently that she never got any of the names straight, calling them all Smitty. She embraced the girls and walked with them into her bedroom.

"What's with Daddy?" asked Sylvia, trailed by Noreen. "I don't understand what he's up to," she said, her voice like delicate chimes.

"Just give me a minute in my room."

On her dressing table, along with legions of perfume bottles, skin food jars, creams for other creams—the condiments of the rich—she found a note.

"BUY A DRESS AND SEE THAT IT FITS THIS TIME."

Attached were seven crisp hundred-dollar bills that smelled as if they'd been fried in fresh butter. Daniel hated dirty or old money. One of his many quirks.

"That's seven hundred dollars," Sylvia said excitedly, fingering the bills. "We're going to have a party."

"How wuzth New York, Mommy?"

"Crowded and dirty. Slush everywhere," she explained to Noreen. Her mission that afternoon had been to purchase their Christmas presents. That she'd done so weeks earlier, storing them in the five-car garage, mattered not at all, for she had developed a degree of adeptness at lying to people's faces that had about it the placid embrace of truth.

"Get some hot coffee for the men," she heard Daniel ordering a Smitty. "Schnaps after the job is over."

"What kind of dress are you going to buy?" asked Sylvia.

"Black, I guess. That way I won't get into trouble."

"What did Daddy mean—'Farewell, Babylon, forever'?"

"Living in the present . . . Now Mommy's going to have a quick bath and then be down to keep you company for dinner."

"Can we watch?" asked Sylvia, conveying that awful sense of emotional starvation endemic to the children of the rich.

"Not now."

Sonya dismissed them, fearing that some trace of her afternoon bout, possibly the devil's stigmata, might be seared across her skin. "Pan Am. Motor Inn." In any case she'd left her bra and panties there, could not bear to touch them afterward. No explaining that to little girls who had frequently been admonished for forgetting to wear underclothes. She filled the deep, circular, black marble tub, switched on the Jacuzzi attachment and listened to the sleek purr of moving water. Outside, Daniel's voice rose above Weintraub's in martial combat.

When she got into the tub, for the first time she could recall, Sonya felt content. There had been such happy times in Babylon and she clung to the memories of them for comfort like a child rubbing the satin corner of a blanket. She pined for the old friends they'd lost. Intimidated and made uncomfortable by Daniel's wealth and status requirements, one by one they'd dropped away.

The rescue from the Babylonian Captivity most frequently employed was the Saturday Night Party, and Sonya eagerly attended them. From the confines of the Venice-like estate—it too suffered from slippage, back into the canal from where it sprang— she and Daniel had seen most of the gay watering spots.

During their four years' tenure, what stood out were Phyllis Melnikoff's "Evening in Paris"; Libby Kantrowitz's masked "Roman Holiday"; Jo-Jo Eisenwieg's "Madrid Matador" for which the boys had paraded around in ski trousers and thermal underwear as representative torero habiliments. Some of the men, unable to find or invent the torero cap, wore crumpled black silk yarmulkes held down with stretch-ease elastic. Walls of the houses were decorated with travel posters clipped from the local travel agency.

Sonya had also tried her hand at one of these costumed soirées, the theme of which sprang naturally from her past. Airline Travel.

Fifty of the revelers came attired as stewardesses, pilots, stewards. Daniel wore earphones for the occasion and suggested he was a flight controller, and glared at TWA, Pan Am, Eastern, National advertising slogans all evening long. Sonya remained consistent to her theme, serving frozen dinners in the manufacturer's ready-to-heat tin-foil trays. She had, however, placed typed stickers on each that read "Fly Barnet Airways" over the Birds Eye and Stouffer labels.

Brenda Lieberman's "Notte de Sorrento" promised an array of nobleman's gear; blue jeans, a colored shirt, and creased hat for instant gondolier or peasant guise. The women would lug out of camphorized plastic bags last year's New Year's Eve livery, pin on a rose or some piece of costume jewelry, so that all the other women would compliment them: ". . . Oh, is that new . . . ? Well, I never . . ." frequently rang through the air.

In spite of Daniel's moaning that he felt ridiculous walking six doors from his house in some form of strange, ill-fitting frippery just to see people he merely hello'd during the week, or politely waved to on food-shopping Saturday mornings, tonight's party would be rather different from the usual grab bag. Brenda could cook, was a vocational homemaker who had tried to train Sonya in such mysteries as breaded veal cutlets and lamb stew. The attempt failed miserably. Mo Lieberman was the estate's Mr. Fix-it. Anyone with the problem of drilling a hole or filling one with raw plug invariably asked Mo's sage advice, his assistance if it wasn't imposing.

Walking with Gary and Marlene, Sonya kept quiet as Daniel criticized her dress. Filled with the bountiful richness of Noreen, due virtually any hour, she had gone to extraordinary lengths to dress attractively, letting out an evening gown to accommodate her belly.

"I asked her just to wear her maternity slacks," Daniel said. "Most of the time Italian women are pregnant, so she'd be right on target. . . ."

"You know how it is," Marlene suggested, "when a gal's pregnant. She wants to look her best because she's self-conscious."

"And you think a purple evening gown with silver spangles achieves this?"

Gary said: "We'll be in shortly, girls."

"Where are you two off to?" Sonya asked.

"Gary and I are going to smoke a joint if it's okay with you."

"Then I suppose you'll eat like pigs, demand Sara Lee Brownies, and shove off home for the ten thirty movie."

"That sounds pretty good to me," Daniel said.

"Oh, I don't know . . . I wish I could relate," said Marlene. "The fact of the matter is I can't for the life of me see what you get out of smoking that stuff. Can't you drink like normal men?"

Sonya and Marlene had the same complaint. The boys could not hold their grass.

"Blow," Gary said.

"I will not be spoken to in that manner," Marlene complained. "Now don't be too long."

Marlene in her embroidered peasant-girl blouse and high black Italian boots drifted off, and Gary and Daniel found one of the empty benches on the concrete verge where the kids played touch football and softball. A smell of newly cut grass lingered like some memory of lost innocence in the barrack-constructed estate. Saturdays everybody, save Daniel, mowed the lawns of their twelve-by-eight rectangles which were referred to as gardens. Sundays, cars were washed, and men sniffed around each other, bucking for raves on the new secondhand Bonnevilles they had recently put down payments on, then shot into their houses for the highlight of the week—the Sunday game. Everyone met up in the evening at the take-out Italian kitchen or the chink joint.

The girls waited for them outside the Lieberman house, which Mo had distinguished, individualized, from all others. The Liebermans had painted their front door yellow. Sonya's relationship with Marlene was governed by the unromantic conclusion that Gary exploited Daniel's affection, borrowed money, forgot about paying back, testified on his behalf whenever Sonya caught her husband in an outright lie. She did not like users. Dopey and giggling, the men staggered forth.

"This is what I mean, Daniel," Sonya said, but Daniel thrust open the door and fell on Brenda, who was wearing a black lace gown, carrying a cheerleader's baton around which Mo had stapled red velvet, suggesting a scepter, and intimating that her forebears sprang from the crazy heights of the Italian Renaissance.

"Countess Lieberman," Daniel said, *"buena sera."*

"My two gangsters have arrived."

"I think the Princessa Barnet needs to go to the bathroom." He examined Brenda under a green Venetian lantern. "What is this, a high neck, Brenda? My only reason for coming was to check out the boobs."

"Oh, Daniel, you're terrible."

"Listen, Gary needs a little cheering up. Can you possibly fit him in for a frenching session during the course of the evening?"

"Looks to me like you've been smoking weed again. You're going to wind up a basket case. . . ."

At these parties, Daniel had a certain improbable charm that Sonya found irresistible. His naiveté was most apparent when he attempted to seduce the gals. He would pee with the bathroom door partially open, see who took the bait, then when chided by one of the women, he would feign Harpo's loony confusion which always amused Sonya.

In the salon, the carpet had been rolled back for dancing, and a selection of Mario Lanza's imitations of Caruso blasted forth from the gargantuan speakers. Mr. Fix-it had constructed an enormous wall unit from a mass of disparate parts.

Phyllis Melnikoff seized Sonya's arm, dragging her into a corner of the packed room. Everyone was shouting to be heard over Lanza, and Phyllis had this habit of holding on . . . physically, to the wrist of her listener. She implanted a sloppy, wet, neighborly kiss on Sonya's cheek and she took it like a sport. Phyllis' stock in trade was venomous criticism.

"I'd lay off the wine, Sonya," she said anxiously, as though this were a Borgia dinner party. "They've got Chianti bottles on show, but it's some Algerian slop that Mo got on a wholesale special. I think it costs a dime a bottle."

Sonya tasted the wine. Not exactly a rose from Burgundy, but not all that bad.

"See what I mean?"

"It's not great, but drinkable."

"They've cut corners all along the line. Loads of pasta which lays on your stomach all night. Now you be careful. . . ."

"Well, Phyllis, it isn't 'Evening in Paris'—"

"You're telling me. Al and I worked like dogs for two days. We served the best Prince Noir on the market and the coq au vin I made, wasn't it a treasure?"

Before she could reply, Daniel, trailed by Al Melnikoff, broke in on them.

"I hope you warned Sonya that the food is shit," said Al. "And, Daniel, keep away especially from them sausages because if you have to drive Sonya in the middle of the night, you don't want to be schlinging your guts out."

The grudge bearers on the estate were numerous and vocal. In fact, it seemed to Sonya that everybody in the room had something against everyone else. The men and women all watched each other like mongooses to determine who was doing well. The present of a fur coat usually served to insure that a woman would be truly hated. The women eyed each other enviously in the hope that the status quo would be maintained, and no one would break out of the economic confines, praying they would all sink together in the morass of bills and dunning letters.

Illness was another popular subject in Babylon and when any

man indicated he was feeling poorly, the immediate cry was heart attack. Who would get one first? Whose biopsy or smear would show the positive evidence of cell destruction? The sympathy theorem was frequently invoked. If one couple could pity another, then they had an edge. Which marriage would falter first? They all had a vested interest in one another's failure.

The motto and life principle were one and the same: keep up a front. Living in each other's pockets, they could assay, value, estimate, appraise, to the last cent, how much any of the men earned. When a man lost his job there was positive rejoicing, and people would say that the man had been a big shot and deserved to be cut down to size. No cruelty matched that of women with futile dreams, and Sonya played down Daniel's success.

Among the men, most of whom had married from the secretary classes, Sonya was considered a dish whose glamorous flying past lent a degree of exotica. It shook Daniel, the gradual apprehension that he had triumphed—won—the glamor-puss in the conjugal sweepstakes. The accidental elbows and surreptitious feel-ups that male neighbors inflicted on She who'd been accustomed to these attentions at thirty thousand feet, flying over cloud formations with ten trays in her hand, were responded to with cool professionalism. Soared above these physical attacks. Another facet that Daniel found disturbing, incomprehensible, was that the boys preferred to talk to Sonya, seeking her advice on bedroom matters, resorts, the rearing of children.

"How is that sugar doll feeling?" said Al Melnikoff, presenting Sonya with a kiss. She inspired slobbering among the also-rans.

Phyllis tugged a speared piece of Italian salami away from Sonya. "All you need is an upset stomach from this *drekh*. Did you ever see such crappy decorations?"

"Garbage," Al confirmed his wife's opinion. "Will somebody talk to Mo about changing that lousy record. I mean to say, shouldn't guests have some kind of choice?"

"It's disgusting the way they copied us with the travel posters," said Phyllis in the hope of producing an entente to support her views. "And I don't like criticizing, either."

The drinking was heavy and indiscriminate, moving from the sociable stage to the loud, imperceptibly. Guffaws that sounded hysterically hollow cut through the room. Men lined up at the bar for more wine, which Mo pushed ruthlessly, giving a sales pitch with each glass he poured. Several people brought bottles along, a practice which hosts encouraged.

Mo and Brenda were milking the evening, so that by midnight —still no food, except olives, dried bits of salami, peanuts, and celery filled with cream cheese—the course of events turned into drunken staggering, with men reeling and women groping, slurring words, dancing close together without moving.

After dinner, the hard-core local hell-fire organization gathered in corners to introduce more mature festivities.

Could Hal Eisenwieg be prevailed upon yet again to get his projector and set up the blue films Daniel had walked out on six times running. How many times could he watch the same dismal women with forties hair styles getting screwed, screwing each other, then joined by the archangel from Mombasa, a hirsute person with a surprising cherub expression, and a schlaung the size of a kayak. The director as was his wont invariably displayed it in closeup. From this position it looked (could have been) somebody's fine ebony banister, fit for a townhouse. Never failed to create an aura of consternation among the local Pedros, and groans of awe from the assembled group of Missuses, culminating in, yes, a movie star's moment of ultimate triumph, applause. Invariably these noisy dimly lit films inspired one of the ladies to do a grotesque striptease which the audience of hard-up men encouraged by more applause and raucous cheers.

Setting off a further chain of events. The small percentage of swappers would attend to their business while those less courageous necked and petted with the wives of neighbors. Discovering each other, only to cut each other dead, shamefaced on Monday mornings. When this moment was reached, Daniel and Sonya checked out, fending off accusations of spoil-sport, chicken, gutless wonders. They would alternate with Marlene and Gary, and gather in one of the kitchens for coffee, Sara Lees, and postmortems, swearing that they would never attend another of these parties.

"I need to get to bed," Sonya said apologetically to Mr. Fix-it, who was busily searching in Jo-Jo Eisenwieg's panties for the promised land.

"Daniel, you are not going," Brenda protested, moving his hand to her breast.

"I have to. Sonya's tired . . . and I'm loaded."

"I told Mo to ease up on the booze, but he never listens to me. I wanted to serve at eleven, and he made me wait till after twelve," Brenda chattered on, blocking the exit. Some form of Aegean male dancing broke out in which empty Pepsi bottles were surrounded, then kicked.

He took Sonya's arms and guided her into the fresh air and at these moments they usually happened upon a few of the revelers puking their guts out on the service road. In the morning, astride their cars, all the men would deny they were the ones who could not hold it, and the clarion whine of gossip would last until Tuesday, when the desperate economic weekly grind wiped the smile and good humor from all the wives' faces. Difficult to positively identify Saturday night's siren pushing a load from the laundromat.

"If we don't go," Daniel began, "we feel we missed something."

"I don't like all that smooching around. And those movies . . . well, I could do better."

"Oh, sure. My Miss Stewardess finalist. The world's great head specialist. Just forgot to tell me about it, right, doll?"

"If there is one thing I have learned from you, hon," she said sharply, "is that you don't shit where you eat." They were building . . .

"Gary pleaded with me to try to get him into Princeton."

"Don't," she counseled. "Four years ago he could have left boiler rooms . . . the way you left Spigleman. But he was too damn lazy."

"Gary is my friend," Daniel said.

"Don't you think it is time he started worrying about his own problems instead of bringing them to you? And you are not going to get him with Princeton because, Daniel, you have had enough of Hoffman. You are going to work for yourself."

"It's a big step. They might offer me a deal that I couldn't turn down."

Switching on the living room light, she felt the contractions hit her, eased her legs on the sofa.

"What deal is better than being your own man?"

"You all right?"

Smiling and rubbing her stomach with the cold tips of her fingers, she said:

"We'll wait a bit longer, then go to the hospital." He cradled her head on his lap and she squeezed his hand. "You were right about the slacks, I would've been more comfortable."

Coming out of the bath, she overheard Sylvia patiently explaining the facts of life to Noreen.

"Mommy has not let us in the bathroom because of the tree. It's upset her. Next time we won't have a tree and we'll be able to watch her."

"I like the tree," said Noreen.

"Which do you like better?"

"Mommy," replied Noreen unequivocally. "But why she upthet?"

"Because we're Jewish, you dope."

Sonya put on a long black velvet hostess gown which had cost a king's ransom at the Designers' Salon at Bonwit's, and clattered down the marble steps with her daughters noisily chattering behind her.

The workmen had completed their job on the tree, and the driveway now resembled a smaller version of Rockefeller Plaza. Daniel had brought the men into the living room.

Sonya didn't quite understand how he always succeeded in implanting an easy, friendly relationship among people who did some kind of work for him, since he invariably broke their balls. Part of the explanation no doubt stemmed from his characteristic remark—"I'm such a heavy tipper that your arm'll fall off when I come across. . . ." No question about it, he usually inveigled his way into the remote hearts of strangers. Here they were, drinking his best Scotch. Twenty-five years old.

"The blacks have knocked the shit out of the city. Sure they've had a rough deal, but so have we yids, guineas, micks and let's not forget your basic WASP. We dragged ourselves up, and we gave something to New York. We didn't just pull the meat off the carcass and leave the bones for vultures." He was holding forth and no one disagreed. Fair comment, she wondered, or the warm room and the old Scotch and the promise of largesse. The men rose, except for Daniel, when she walked in.

Going into his regular sales pitch to the men—the enormous benefit of group insurance—Sonya switched off. A visit to Daniel's, no matter by whom, usually meant signing a document of some kind. Like certain New Jersey *amici* who entertained at home, the visitor either agreed to a proposal or didn't leave. Dismissing the men with fresh twenties for their work, Daniel extracted pledges from each of them. They'd phone his office for medical appointments.

"It just goes to show," Daniel told her, "that if you're unscrupulous enough, and motivated by pure greed and selfishness, you can't fail to help people. I've done those guys a real favor." He handed Sonya a list of names. "I know this is going to require stretching your mind but the people who are employed in this household have names, none of them Smitty, so try to learn them by the end of the week because walkouts at Christmas are going to distress me."

"They keep coming and going," she explained helplessly.

"Sonya, a wall of resentment is being built up against you by your *own* kind. Me they like but you they can't stand."

"You're always slipping them money," she protested in a shrill voice. "That's why, dammit."

"Do you in your wisdom know of any more thoughtful gesture? And, Sonya, isn't that what I do to keep you sweet?"

"Your trouble is you oversimplify people to suit yourself."

He put on his jacket and ventilated racing driver's gloves. Recently he'd fallen head over heels in love with Jackie Stewart.

"Married to you, I have to oversimplify. Also, I'd like you to get out of your zombie trance. Understand? I'm out for the evening."

He did not bother to tell her where he went, or to pay her the courtesy of an excuse. Sonya no longer asked. In fact she had stopped listening.

5

Tangled in the mesh of anti-saboteur wire that Daniel had placed around his life was his chronically painful involvement with Norma.

Their affair had become as tiresome and demanding as his marriage. Just as it appeared that both she and Princeton were behind him in the dead file he consigned unpleasant experiences and forgotten lays to, Norma had risen from the morgue to haunt him. No Phoenix this, just an interminable moooooooooooan.

He circled her house in Glen Head. Max's car had been tucked into its garage, but her Camaro lingered at the curb. He could see through the window that they were still at table. Max did his fucking with a knife and fork, never having found a more desirable piece of ass than Norma's pot roast, or was it her lamb stew?

For a change, Norma was late for a date he did not wish to keep. She was still squandering the precious irreplaceable capital of his life. His time. Daniel shoved Diana Ross into the tape deck, adjusted the speaker balance and modulated the volume. Requiring a second or fourth wind, he lit a joint and parked at the end of the crescent. Nothing however could dispel the wretched sensation of imprisonment or the recherché bummer his various attempts to escape from the Hoffmans induced. The Willie Sutton of office protocol and flagrant infidelities was still a lifer.

From the moment Sonya had forced him into legitimate employment at Princeton, she had cautioned him to bide his time until he could spring himself. While suffering a series of false delivery notices with Noreen, Sonya had brought him to the boil in that serene manner which comes so naturally to women excluded from knocking out a living.

There had been a strange chill in the Princeton office which Daniel noticed and Sonya explained away as the big boys' fear of the little guy. Daniel wondered if the arrogant threats he had been making around the office would be taken seriously. The Church had agreed provisionally to his representing their insurance interests for a six-month period. An option get-out on their side of the course dampened Daniel's enthusiasm. Strictly performance.

Daniel assumed that the news had filtered through the Princeton hierarchy. Still, no positive action had been taken either to sway him back into the corporate fold or to prevent his leaving. But . . . Hoffman and his stooges kept well away from him.

Returning from a leisurely lunch, Daniel pushed open the glass door, but halted midway between his desk and the punch-card section. Grouped around the anonymous steel slab he had occupied for years were five men who seemed to be on a guided tour of the honeycomb, led by Andrew Robinson. From their photographs in the company's annual report, he recognized:

CHARLES BENTLEY HUGHES—Chairman of the Board
G. S. MORAN—President
WILKINS RUSHING, JR.—Executive Vice-President in Charge of Operations
LELAND RICHARDSON—Vice-President, Marketing
CLINTON BRITNER—Vice-President, Industrial Relations

A mirage of executives whose names were seldom spoken, for they resided on some breathtaking and remote mountain crest. In many ways they seemed not to have any connection with Princeton at all. Just names that he occasionally came across with no visible identity. Robinson did their hackwork and was the only employee who apparently had seen any of them with his own eyes. They seemed, as he approached, to be friendly, affable men, who were delighted to see him. He heard Robinson say:

"That's him. . . ."

Their talking ceased, as though a courtroom were called to order, and Daniel hesitated before his section, looked over to Hoffman, who had papers piled high on his desk and was determined not to notice him. The men made no attempt to leave and he awkwardly resumed his pace toward them.

"Gentlemen, this is Daniel Barnet," he heard Robinson say hazily. "Daniel, the board would like to have a meeting with you."

"Why don't we push off upstairs," said Hughes, offering his hand to Daniel. "We're very proud of you, Mr. Barnet. I don't think any member of this management team can recall when an employee has made as outstanding and unique a contribution as you have."

Daniel was amazed to discover that these men actually came to the office, that they worked at various jobs just as the company report stated, for there seemed some odd intangible quality which cut them off from the ceaseless reality of economic necessity. Under Hughes' thumb, some twelve thousand living, breathing, worried, fearful people labored, struggling not to rise above their station, but merely to maintain it . . . to go unnoticed by the omnipotent ruler of the universe. Robinson, Daniel observed, was both deferential and extremely nervous, since Daniel and the other salesmen came under his jurisdiction. Daniel was his responsibility, and so long as he remained a drone, did his share of business, his individual non-organizational talent could be condoned. Daniel was aware, as he filed out with them, that he had now become a threat to the smooth functioning of a corporate machine, and was too dangerous to ignore for a moment longer. What had begun as a desperate attempt to peddle just another insurance policy had now taken on the implications of big business.

Daniel expected to be taken into the board room. He had heard that one existed, set off alone, mysterious, a place in which millions of dollars were shifted around from one pocket to another like the small-change compartment of a street vendor. He coasted into a room, furnished as though it belonged to an apartment. A clubby room with comfortable chairs, sofas, a small bar in the corner on an antique dresser. It struck him as disquietingly casual.

"Have a seat," said Britner, a tall blond Aryan man in his midforties. Daniel had heard of him through Robinson and Hoffman. The mention of his name made them shudder. He was the company killer, and when anyone from middle management was called in to see Britner, he could order his cemetery plot, for his life with Princeton would be over. His achievement had been to keep the unions out of Princeton.

"Would you like a drink?" Moran, the company president, asked, ready to play bartender to Daniel.

"No, thanks. It's sort of too late and too early."

He assumed that the room was bugged and that whatever statements he made would be recorded and shipped over to Monsignor Braughton to demonstrate his lack of ability. Hughes ambled over to the sofa, sat on the edge. He was a small man who resembled a beautiful piece of wood, lovingly polished for thirty years. All of them in fact had that well-cared-for surface gleam which kept out the dirt and grit of the polluted city, traveling each day in some hermetically sealed container. An act of course, Daniel realized, for they were about to soil their hands with him.

"Andy's awfully high on you," said Rushing in one of those well-bred voices in which inherited wealth replaces corpuscles. "Judging from what we've heard, he and we have every right to be pleased with your performance." The endorsement could not hurt him with Braughton. "But do you really believe you're equipped to handle an account of the Church's size on your own?"

He'd been waiting for the sting.

"I don't think you're in a position to ask me to defend myself," Daniel replied amicably. He smiled to show that there were no hard feelings.

"Point for Mr. Barnet," said Hughes. He might have been scoring a rubber of bridge.

"Why do you think Braughton handed you their account on a plate?" Moran asked.

"I came up with the idea of insuring priests on an endowment basis. He knows that priests die, so why shouldn't the Church collect insurance?"

"Well, why didn't he approach the directors of your company?" Rushing asked. "After all, you're just a salesman."

"I guess I'm a pretty good one."

"Point two for Mr. Barnet," said Hughes grandly. "You're doing extremely well."

Britner picked up a thick file, made certain that Daniel saw his name on the dossier. A history of his sins and small triumphs.

"Now that you've got me here," he told Britner, "I think you're better off asking what you want to find out rather than flashing my employment record in my face."

"All right then," Britner said flushing, somewhat caught off balance, for the dictator's role was one that he assumed unconsciously. "How did you do it?"

"I told Braughton and his committee the truth and he knows the facts of life when he hears them. As an employee of Princeton, I'm obliged to accept your rates of interest."

"They're fair rates, Daniel," Robinson interposed. "We're not out of line and you know that."

"They're competitive rates," Daniel said. "As an outsider

representing the Church's interests, I can go to any one of a thousand companies and demand a better rate. If we're talking about insuring five thousand priests, with the Church paying annual premiums of two thousand dollars a year per stiff, and I can get a hundred dollars knocked off the top, why shouldn't I? I'm not going to pocket the money, they are. Is Lloyd's, or Mutual, or Fidelity, going to say no we don't want your business? Would you turn me down if I could eventually move two hundred million dollars' worth of business to Princeton?"

"Obviously not," said Rushing, a chilled disconsolate expression suffusing his face.

"As my employer, you can take the position that you're not going to make an exception of me. You've got hundreds of men selling insurance and they'd be entitled to the same reduction as me."

"We're not getting anywhere," said Hughes. "We want you to stay on here and we're prepared to make life very sweet for you, Daniel. We recognize your ability."

"Funny how for four years you didn't. I've been running scared for all that time."

"That's not true, Daniel," Robinson said as the eyes closed in on him, a noose hovering over his head. For blame somebody they would. "Except for your first three months with us when your commission didn't come close to matching your draw, you've done very well. I took you in off the streets because I believed you could sell."

"How do I weigh up the terrible indignities of being a wage slave? Andy, if I'm a minute late, Max tears into me. I'm thirty-three years old, I have a wife and in a few days my second child, so I was trapped here."

"Do you feel any loyalty to this company?" Britner asked.

"Of course not. Don't be naive. If I didn't hit my target figures would you feel any loyalty to me? You'd just memo Andy: 'Subject: D. Barnet. Get rid of him'."

"You make it all sound so mercenary," Britner, the assassin, complained.

"I think I speak for every man in this room and those directors absent," Hughes, now somewhat unsettled, began, "when I assure you you'd find a happy place on the board of Princeton and a salary and profit-sharing plan commensurate with your talents."

"I'm resigning," Daniel said, "effective immediately. Hoffman can chop up my accounts for the other salesmen."

"Won't you give us a chance?" said Moran with a shudder. "Listen to our proposal?"

"I don't owe you even that basic courtesy," Daniel snapped back. "Not the way this company treats people . . . but go on."

"You're currently earning on average twenty-five thousand dollars a year. We'll up you to seventy-five thousand, ten thousand for expenses, include you in the stock options open to board members, and get you a prestige car that goes with the office of vice-president." Moran seemed relieved to get the proposition off his chest.

"What is a prestige car?" Daniel asked.

"A Lincoln or a Caddy, say."

"I want a Rolls Royce."

"My God, that's about thirty-five thousand dollars now. . . ." Rushing groaned.

"Well, working on my own, I'll be able to buy one, won't I?"

He had sowed the trouble deeply. His absence would be revealed at the end of the year on the consolidated corporate balance sheet.

"You do appreciate that we could get unpleasant and legally hold you until your notice is worked out," said Britner.

"Well, of course you could and there isn't a thing I could do about it. Except never place any business with you again, Mr. Britner. Isn't it standard practice to do business with people you like if it's at all possible?"

"Wouldn't joining the board of a major American company please you, Daniel?" Hughes asked softly. "Wouldn't it demonstrate to every person who knows you that you're an outstanding success? We'd make an announcement in the Times and the Wall Street Journal to that effect. You'd take up your position not at seventy-five, but a hundred thousand a year."

He saw himself for a moment as a captain of industry who'd escaped from the rat hole through a fluke, and the image pleased him. A member of the team . . . the introduction to a new lifestyle. The position would naturally neutralize his commissions, which would go into the corporate basket of gross profits, a device employed by big-board brokerage houses when a man's commissions outstripped the partner's profits.

"Actually, I don't like being employed, and I'd still be an employee, director or not. I don't like working for a company, being held responsible by people over me. And the truth is, Mr. Hughes, that I would have to account to you."

"It's the nature of the beast. Is there any way we can hold you?"

"You'd have my goodwill, if that's worth anything, by releasing me right now."

Daniel rose, sensed the air of resignation drifting like some poison gas through the room and received his last handshake from Hughes.

"If it doesn't work . . . you'll always be welcome to come back."

"I'll make it work," he replied.

He returned to his desk, with the nervous relief of having bluffed and succeeded. The speed at which office gossip traveled exceeded even Princeton's new I.B.M. computer. The news and unconfirmed rumors of what had happened preceded him. There were many reasons for leaving Princeton, but they were mostly Max. When Daniel saw the doleful brown eyes, the white-on-white shirt Max wore religiously with the cuffs rolled up, and the Tie City ninety-nine-cent solid that men like Max Windsor-knotted in offices for purposes of identification, he felt he had come to the end of hostilities.

"Is it true?" Max asked apprehensively.

"What true, Max . . . ?"

"The board terminated you. 'Cause if that's the way it went, I'm sorry. I had nothing to do with it, Daniel. I know you're in pretty fair financial shape, but I also know that Sonya's due. Me, I got love in my heart. Norma came through with a boy."

"*Mahzel tov.*" He examined his desk, and discovered that there was nothing he wished to take. "I terminated the board, Max."

Shifting his weight from one foot to the other as though to restore his balance, Max puffed out his cheeks.

"Unbelievable . . . but I seen it with my own eyes." He extended his hand, and Daniel took it reluctantly. "I wish you well. I guess with you gone we can't call the place a lunatic asylum anymore. Misrepresentation." He laughed. "Listen, I'm sending out invites to the *briss* and I hope you can make it. But what with Sonya ready to pop and you getting yourself organized, you don't show, I'll understand."

On his way out, through a few waves, but mostly hunch-backed clerks' indifference, Daniel was handed a telegram by June during one of her rare appearances in the office.

"I signed for it, Daniel," she said thrusting forty-inch can-nons in his face. "All the guys I've fooled around with here, and the winner I missed."

"I'm the kind of guy who likes a hard time."

The telegram made him quirkily nervous. Had Braughton reconsidered, and was he going to terminate Daniel? The pros-pect of a law suit with the Church of New York over a broken contract made his hands tremble. He'd contemplate his own death with greater composure.

He opened it in the elevator and stared at the signature be-fore reading the message. It was signed Norma.

URGENT YOU COME TO SOUTH YONKERS HOSPITAL
IMMEDIATELY (STOP) NO PHONE CALLS

NORMA

The message troubled him. After ringing his home and con-firming to Sonya that he had resigned and learning that she had not quite got there but the signs were encouraging, he made the long trek up to the hospital to see Norma.

He blitzed along the Saw Mill Parkway with justifiable anx-iety. If she were going to die, had heard some dreadful irreversible news from the doctors, it seemed plausible that she would want to impart the news to the "great love of her life" before Max heard.

Norma had that fruity splendor of a woman fulfilled and he repressed unhealthy thoughts that bubbled to the surface. She had even managed to get her hair done, and seemed healthy, well endowed, and actually regenerating before his eyes. His own pancake had yellow bags under her eyes, squeezed the milk from her breasts and proposed to nurse. Norma had no such intention. She dropped pills, took shots, would leave the infant boy to the bottle. Almost against his will he heard himself utter what had once been in his heart.

"I should never have let you marry Max. I should've dumped Sonya and . . . well, what's the use of talking?"

"You know, Daniel, some things are never too late."

Through an adventitious course of events, perhaps in retrospect merely calamity and an even-money bet, Daniel had fallen victim to the occupational hazard of philandering. He had apparently inseminated both his kosher mistress and *trafe* wife during a darkling November week of unmemorable weather, thereby producing a pair of Virgos.

He hadn't seen Norma after she had entered the dangerous sixth month, phoned her once a week and suggested she ought to rest and avoid exertions. Blasting a pregnant woman required a stronger stomach than his, and so he set her aside and began his regular attendance at Kit's while the two ladies in his life laid preparations for *kinderzimmer*. Kit, under her virginal pseudonym, Mildred Dalyrimple, had opened shop on Twenty-second Street, and had contacted, in true boiler-room style, all the leads she herself had developed before her work had become strictly managerial.

He occasionally thought about his relationship with Norma and wondered now that she was about to expunge Max's child whether it wouldn't be best to let what had been simply fading, die a natural death.

Norma moved off the bed and sat down in an armchair opposite him. The blinding sun made Daniel squint and he shifted his chair.

"The baby's blood type is O." She paused, waited for Daniel to swallow. "I'm O as well."

"I'm O too, practically everyone in the world is," he bleated.

"Max isn't . . . he's AB. That's all there is to it."

"Who else have you been fucking behind my back?" he said in the tone of a prosecutor.

"Daniel . . ." she gave him a brilliant smile, squeezed his hands in hers, and her eyes left him with no room to retreat. "Just you, darling."

"No, I don't believe this."

"Is it so awful for you to be the baby's father?"

"In these circumstances, you're damn right it is."

Norma undoubtedly planned it. The act of premeditation struck him as unjust and yet human, understandable. She had married Max to spite him. Events that he had purposively initiated had closed ineluctably, and he despondently accepted the decree of fate—he had become his own victim. Norma's logic overtook him. Married to a man she tolerated, rather than remain in that nether world of part-time mistress Daniel had assigned her to, she had outwitted him.

His child.

A *son*.

The schematic maneuvers of business, he knew, contained an element of make-believe when placed alongside the determination of a woman. Despite the predicament Norma had created for him, he detected a new emotion which both puzzled and infuriated him. He respected her. She had outsmarted him in the grand game of deception he had played with her over the years.

"Does Max know it's me . . . ?"

"I didn't tell him. I'm his wife and it's his son as far as he's concerned," Norma said evenly, intimating that the state of affairs could not be taken as unnatural.

"Don't you think you could have told me you were planning this?"

"Honestly, Daniel, you're behaving like the injured party."

"Suddenly I'm beginning to feel very confused."

She had never before had him at a disadvantage and the prospect frightened her.

"You're pretty flip about it," he replied, becoming alarmed by the daunting reality of Max taking possession of what was rightfully his.

"I wanted your baby and I've got him, so stop sitting *shivah* for us. We'll make out just fine. Whatever Sonya can do, I've done better and I haven't had to put up with you as a husband."

"That hurts."

"Only the truth," she said, closing his neck in her arms and kissing him affectionately on the mouth. "I guess we'll be together in some shape or form for a while yet."

Some of the natural starch that held Daniel together oozed out of him. Just as he imagined he had taken control of the wayward forces insidiously ruling his life, he lost his grasp. Two children, neither of them planned, confounded him. They had been thrust upon him. Impossible now to retreat or advance. The consolation of his financial prospects dimmed before this outrage. He couldn't blame Sonya . . . *and* Norma.

"What're you going to call the kid?"

"I'm going to leave it up to Max."

At his moment of triumph, a paternity claim had been lodged against him. He could not refute it either. The boy did not even need a name tag. A hybrid of his own parents. Could have been their son in fact. Wore his mother's petulant expression, and carried his father's familiar L.B.J. earlobes, but would bear Max's name.

"Daniel, I didn't plan this."

"Does it really matter?" he replied in a quarrelsome voice.

"But now that you're out of Princeton, there are some problems." He allowed her to pause. In this instance, he refused to come to her aid. "How are you going to be able to see your son?" Her voice came at him like an unexpected hail. "With us in Yonkers and you on the Island. I won't bring our son to a motel for a visit with his father. Now come on, be reasonable."

"Well, what're we supposed to do? Live together in a commune?"

"Nearby would be more convenient."

"What're you suggesting?" The oppressive humidity crept through the air-conditioning and his underwear clung to him like a counterman's wet rag. "I'm not staying in Babylon."

Her eyes had that clever, Sephardic trader's habit of keeping off what she wanted to purchase.

"The grapevine from the office has it that with the big commissions you've been earning, you're looking for a house in Kings Point."

"What's wrong with that? I've worked for it. No one laid it on a plate for me and said—'Here, Daniel, it's yours.' "

"Max makes peanuts."

"The shells he deserves."

"Well, I don't see how I can bring up your son on seventeen thousand five hundred. Doesn't he deserve the best his father can provide for him? Do you think you'll just slip me a few bucks without anyone noticing?"

"Calm down, Norma."

She was crying, clinging to him, losing her breath.

"Oh, Daniel, don't be so hard-nosed with me. What have I done but present myself whenever you asked me to?"

"What do you want me to do?" he asked quietly, holding her on his lap.

"You're starting your own business. Wouldn't it make sense for Max to be working for you?"

"Never. You're crazy—"

"—Allow you logically to see us. Give you access."

"I can't stand him, and he'll never quit."

"He's wanted to leave for ages."

"I won't, Norma—"

"Your standard of living for your son!" she pleaded.

"Max working for me?"

Daniel shuddered at the realization that Max Hoffman of all people would not only name *his* son, but also parade around with the boy on his shoulders, take him eventually to sporting events, slobber, coddle, *play* with him. He himself knew what magi devotions the firstborn received from parents. But . . . wooing Max to come in with him in a new business?

"You'll be the employer this time," Norma said by way of reassurance.

"What's the alternative?"

She got off his lap, dropped a pill that she'd apparently forgotten to take, narrowed her eyes in the glaring sunshine. She wanted to pull down the shade, started to, then stopped.

"Alternative? Well, I'm not going to run to Sonya and tell her. Not me. I don't blackmail, Daniel, that isn't me. Yes," she added, shaking her head, "the alternative is entirely yours. You know what the situation is, and you know I'm not lying. I will just leave it to you."

The mortification of going to Max, praising his abilities and offering him a better salary coursed through Daniel's brain and was precisely what he did do at the *briss* of Benjamin Paul Hoffman. Norma had managed to sneak-thief in his middle name, to the boy, establishing some farfetched extralegal connection. Over more Scotch than he'd ever consumed at ten in the morning, and an abominable variety of stale cookies and rock-hard sponge cake, he said:

"Max, the writing was on the wall the day Andy wouldn't let you fire me. In a big company they slowly take away a man's authority . . . Humiliate him . . ."

"You're right. Norma and I have had discussions about it so many times. It wasn't just you, but everywhichway I turned, I saw them cutting me down. June I wanted to get rid of . . . She's still there, smirking at me."

"It's twenty-thousand and a one-year contract."

"Make it three. We're three people," said Norma.

"Three then."

"With a salary review at the end of the first year?" Max said in the softest voice Daniel had ever heard.

When he confronted Sonya with the deed, she had leaped out of bed and rushed toward him.

"Daniel, I don't understand you. You're actually going to hire Hoffman? He made you eat crap for years!"

"He's a good man in an office," he replied lamely. "I need somebody experienced beside me. Max knows how to run an office."

"This is just plain insanity."

"Look, Sonya, don't tell me how to run my business."

"I should have left you at Spigleman's and run for my life, you fool."

He saw Norma get into the Camaro, then start it up. He beamed his brights at her and she returned the signal. They were still flashing lights on darkened streets.

Daniel did not so much support people as subsidize his mistakes. He and Norma kept a room at a sprawling motel outside of Westbury. The Clipper was always making additions and room extensions, in order to keep up with the increase of general infidelity ripping homes apart but putting the smiles back on the faces of parents. Fucking was good for business—its permanent convention—and the Clipper was used by neighboring community headhunters for quickies. No seedy, lurid dump this, but fully air-conditioned and with bidets. On fine days a man might pitch and putt while waiting for his piece. The resort motel for all seasons with the emphasis on indoor sports. An evening search by the police for a mad killer would yield 237 John Smiths and Tom Browns.

During the week it hosted obscure Boondock luncheons which couldn't afford Manhattan prices, so one was likely to run into paint salesmen, area Chrysler-Plymouth staff whom the dealers were blowing to one of those dinner-dance events, or an occasional firemen luncheon that served prime ribs au jus, with a twig of bent parsley to lend class, and baked Idahos the size of a bull's testicle.

One of Daniel's old boiler-room friends, Eddie Farber, general-managed the place, claiming a piece of the action but fronting for investors who stockpiled funny "green" and wanted to escape from their wives. A tall stylishly dressed man with a beard the color of coffee, Eddie always seemed to have his arm extended ready to shake, called his name as soon as he entered the lounge:

"Daniel Barnet! An honor on any evening, but tonight a special honor," he shouted across the room. "Herbie, mix us some bull shots if the bullion is fresh, or else—?"

"Bloodies," said Daniel, shaking Eddie's hand for the thirty-five thousandth time or thereabouts, for Eddie was a remorseless greeter, as well as the North Shore's most astute and accurate ass handicapper.

"You know who finally got topped in twelve thirty-nine last week?" Eddie asked rhetorically. "Weintraub, the luggage king's wife—your neighbor if I'm not mistaken. She come in with some boing-boing traffic cop from Syosset. Disguised, too, in a navy blue wiglet, carrying a nine-hundred-dollar croc makeup case. What's the world coming to, Daniel?"

"Weintraub?" he asked.

"Outta court settlement for speeding. The depravity of these married cunts! Where is loyalty, honor, and trust?" Eddie hocked.

"Bring them back and you'd be out of business. You sure it was her?"

"Tongue longer than the Throg's Neck Bridge and a mouth the size of the Lincoln Tunnel?"

"Her," Daniel said. "She's been interviewing me."

"Where is Norma?"

"Powdering her nose or something like that."

"You in action tonight? I'll check out the housekeeper to make sure you got towels and linen."

"Conversation, if I can get away with it."

"Herbie," Eddie called to the bartender, "what's the story with limes? Talk to me of limes."

From the far end of the red leather tufted bar, Herbie shouted: "They're corroded."

"Corroded limes, Daniel. My apologies. You and Norma gonna have a bite . . . ?"

"I'll see if she's hungry."

"How's the kids, and Sonya?"

"They're all fine."

Eddie agilely jumped off his stool, got his hand ready, and trotted to the entrance. They were beginning to fill up with the exhausted troops of marrieds who had somehow wangled a pass from their mates, leaning on company Diner's Club cards for a chisel to pay for a bang. Daniel looked at the familiar faces in the bar mirror, received nods, acknowledged them. The Muzak volume was turned to high, the air filled with the hazy fug of filtered cigarettes, the garbled alcohol giggle of women who'd come to get laid between vodka martinis and Kahlúa coffee. The air-circulating machine carried the loitering miasma of feminine hygiene products, for these women were sprayed for action, brainwashed into believing by big media spending that a little whiff of cuntiness was a crime against nature.

Two with-it white voodoos with Afro hairdos gave Daniel a lift of the dark glasses to check him out, followed by a compliant eye. A no-money-involved scene, just drinks, dinner, then the preference test. Either of them, or both, in a friendly free-for-all, then their phone numbers written with a smudgy eyebrow pencil on one of his business cards.

Daniel had worked with Eddie for a time at the Spigleman academy. A brilliant opener, but he could not close his own fly.

"The directors want to expand the business. And they're looking for some up-front green and they'll lay off five percent of the action. I said I'd mention it to you."

"More rooms?"

"No, a resident abortionist. For kids. And if it clicks, a small AB factory. We've got the grounds for it."

"For that you need a single population. Most of these married beasts have their own butchers."

"Not all of them. Stragglers ask me for favors."

Norma came up behind Daniel, beminked, wrapped her arms

around his stomach and pressed her head against the back of his neck. For appearances they traveled in separate cars.

"You're not trying to borrow money from Daniel again?"

"Who should I ask then, failures?"

"My man," Norma said, pushing against the inside of Daniel's thigh, "waiting like a good boy with all these luscious ladies ready to snap him up."

"Just don't forget it." He moved off his stool and kissed her. "Norma, you're the only woman who looks good on my money."

"Who's that woman looking at you?" Norma said. "You know her?"

"Never saw her before," Daniel exclaimed, for once innocent of the accusation.

"She seems to recognize you," Norma continued hammering. "I'm a well-known Long Island civic figure."

Norma had warned him that she would put up with anything so long as he remained faithful. She had the mistress's traditional sense of humor: none. Even when he went to the men's room for a pee and a discreet pick of his teeth with dental floss, she asked why he'd been so long. If he said hello to any woman under sixty, she made threats, assured him that he'd never again see Benji, that "this time" she'd go to Sonya. Almost in the name of male survival and definitely for remission, he had to go to Kit's. Fortunately Norma was buried out on the Island and away from his *courvah* club.

He was beginning . . . to feel even more ambivalent about Norma, practically adoring her when the two could appear in public among the initiated.

He favored seats at the bar, the munificence of liquor bottles stacked on shelves reflected by dim lights and mirrors, the fragrance of lemons, the skillful speedy mixing of bartenders who didn't rattle when orders were flying. There was also another darker reason to which he clung: bars made the exchange of deep confidences more difficult. Tables in corners he avoided, and Norma knew this.

"I'm a lady and I don't like sitting or standing at bars."

"But you are not with a gentleman, Norma."

They had been through this from the beginning.

"I'd like to sit down. Now, Daniel."

Eddie led them to the window table through a recent reforestation of the uncrossed legs belonging to available women, the groping, grabbing hands of men slipping feels under table-cloths. The room's royal box had a perfect view of the activity.

"Give a think about that proposition, Daniel. It's a gold mine," he said holding out Norma's chair.

"Eddie, dear, Daniel has many ambitions, but becoming a pimp here is not one of them."

"Seriously, Norma, this is a legit situation."

"Then, obviously, Daniel wouldn't be interested in it."

He noticed her staring at him—obviously a prelude to intensive questioning—and he ran his hand through his gray-flecked hair, another of his roles: the moody maestro, preoccupied by his very own financial wonderland. When this failed to inspire the necessary respect, he studied the menu, affecting confusion. But the adventurer usually stuck to prime ribs with the bone—hold the au jus—and kept at bay the blueprint of daily existence she constantly demanded.

"Have you spoken to Sonnerman?" she asked.

"I'm going to have Lyonnaise potatoes and mushrooms with fried onions," he said.

"It doesn't agree with you."

"Lots of things don't," he admitted, hoping that her question would be absorbed by his dinner choices.

"Daniel, what did Jack say?"

"Sonnerman?" When hadn't he spoken to Sonnerman? "I speak to Jack every day."

"About us?"

"His advice is to wait."

"It always is."

"Norma, I have a brilliant lawyer. Am I supposed to tell him to fuck off and stick his advice up his ass?" Daniel was aware that he had become a long, nagging complaint in her bodily process, shooting adrenalin into her blood, then ultimately slashing open her veins, so that she was losing her ability to arouse him. Younger than him by eight years, the malaise of thirty and an indefinite future crept up on her. It was not a case of their affair developing mechanically or losing its novelty. A more basic function worked against her. Daniel was using her up—her time, her body. Inadvertently, of course.

"Do you want to go upstairs after dinner?" she asked.

"If you do," he said, lifting her hand and kissing her finger-tips, unsettling her.

"You didn't mean that as an act of mercy?"

"Don't take it in the wrong way," he said. "I'm working myself up for the big push."

"When is that due? With the spring thaw?"

"Things have to be worked out. There's big money involved, property, Norma."

"I'd starve with you."

"I wouldn't starve with myself. And let's not get melodramatic about it. Jack's advice is to hang on till after the New Year."

"What do you get? A tax rebate?"

"That's enough heat."

"I've got a lot to look forward to."

"I love you. Isn't that enough?"

A waiter placed their unordered hors d'oeuvres on the table.

"The last of the crab claws and Eddie said they were for you, Mr. Barnet."

"Thanks. Look, Norma, I'm having a New Year's business party—nineteen seventy-three is going to be my biggest year. . . . You'll be there. Jack too. Why don't you discuss it with him? Plan something."

He burst open a claw, dipped it in mustard sauce. Delegating the assignment to his lawyer was a form of razzle-dazzle end-around play with no ball carrier involved. While everyone was looking for the pigskin, Q.B. Barnet plunged a yard for the T.D. on a sneak.

"What sort of plan?" she sounded interested, making progress. "We get Sonya certified and committed?"

"Norma, I have Max working for me at your instigation. A lot's happened over the years."

She flung down a crab claw and splattered his jacket, but he did not protest or look up. Another scene. The bar would have been safer. Her tears spared him an exertion in bed, for they had long since passed simpatico embraces in bedrooms which made up for blood spilled at the table.

"Look, Norma, shoot down to the Conquistador and we'll have a few days together. I promise." She continued crying. Tonight's was of the shaking silent variety.

"I never met a woman who had more ways to cry."

"It took you to bring them out," she blubbered and for an instant she reminded him of Benji.

"By the spring . . ." he said.

"Promises, Daniel."

6

Sonya . . . *sinking*? Almost. But not exactly and not yet. New man with a sportsman, Gentile odor of unoffending Dr. Scholl's footpowder and Yardley's lavender water. Slender in an invisible sort of way, he was defined by his airline uniform. Almost like being out with a serviceman just returned from subduing dinks and she was doing her little bit for the war effort. She liked his blanched almond complexion and the faded blond beard, completely unlike Daniel with his black marauding sideburns. A woman could see Bud Van Allen's ears.

A gentleness in Bud, too. She fancied he was just the type of man who'd be happy to change fuses and attend to faulty wiring upon request. Neighborly, serious, she could camp out with him on a fishing trip. He'd be kind, never have the suggestion of garlic on his breath, keep a pipe rack, could read a light meter, and assemble children's toys at Christmas. He was, she realized, her true American in a nation of hybrids. For once she'd found herself on the side of the majority. How had she missed these virtues in Bud? Bunny had certainly proved she was her best friend.

Sonya insisted on driving Bud home after cocktails at the Den.

"It's on my way."

"You sure, Sonya? I wouldn't want to—"

"Now, Bud Van Allen, let's not hear another word about it."

On the slushy highway, Sonya sat perched close to the windshield and with the radio tuned to WPAT's "Gaslight Serenade," humming along to Frank Chacksfield's film-music hits, while Bud got confidential, revealing personal facts: a seventeen-year-old daughter who was bright enough to already be preparing for a career as a dental hygienist, a fifteen-year-old boy well on his way to the glories of Eagle Scout, and a wife called Marge who was in a pretty terrible state, just having had her tubes tied and not fully covered on Blue Cross. A catastrophic oversight, she observed.

"Do you and Marge have a little from time to time?"

"Not in years," Bud said with relief. "We did our bit with the kiddies and have just been going on and on. She's a fine person of course. Civic-minded but the only thing we share in bed is *Newsday*."

"I am married to a sex degenerate."

"That'd be Daniel."

"Daniel, yes," she replied plaintively. "He constantly tries my good nature and I am at the stage where I just don't know any longer. It's been all-out war for years and we just keep at it."

"What would happen if you left him?"

"He'd have the locks changed in five minutes flat and an army of lawyers threatening me. Oh, marriage stinks. No fun in it."

"Routine," Bud observed philosophically, "wrecks a human being's individuality. Kids now have it psyched out pretty good. Live together . . . then, when you get tired, change them partners like you would a bum tire."

"I'm not sure I'd go along with that. Something nice and sneaky and romantic, too, about married people's affairs. The meetings, the quiet dinners, the stolen weekends."

"Sonya, you're a romantic."

"I guess I am."

Bunny had returned that day from the great north with her unhappily married man. He was called Rog, had a splendid beer gut, ears muffed with thickish hair to protect him from Alaskan inclemencies. Bunny couldn't make up her mind about becoming his mistress more or less permanently, or simply robbing him.

Sonya had spent the afternoon in the apartment watching Rog demolish a quart and a half of Harwood Canadian whiskey, after which he had decided to see if his capacity for passion had been impaired by a warmer climate and jerking off at his first visit to a blue movie . . . on Forty-second Street, Times Square, previously the center of the world.

Without duenna, Sonya and Bud had passed a pleasant gossipy few hours. Bud had cautiously plied Sonya with chin tucks and revealed an interest in cinema equal to hers. In fact, had it not been for the crying demands of "moola," he had desired a career as a film maker rather than a flight engineer for Intercontinental. Not entirely disinterested and up to his ears in debt, Bud had it on no less an authority than Wings that Sonya was free and easy with a buck. If he coddled her, she'd be prepared to come across.

She stopped the car at one of those potbellied meandering garden developments over which transatlantic flights culminated their stacking patterns. Home.

"Which film should we catch?"

"Well, Bud, dear, I have seen just about everything around. Only one I would check out again is *Clockwork Orange*. Did not understand it, but the rape scene was worth it. Wowwie." Her giggle was most infectious. "Suggestion: we might see the rape scene, which is at the beginning, then walk out. I'd treat of course."

"Could do better than that. Catch us a couple or two hard ones round Eighth Avenue."

"Is it safe?"

"Good point, Sonya. Now if you want to hang on, I'll just poke my head in to see Marge's all right and we can take off."

"I'll be at the luncheonette and meet you up there."

She phoned Bunny, who sounded dismayed. Bunny's $284 visit to Bloomingdale's had disagreed with Rog. So he planned steaks at Tad's, a tour of exciting First Avenue bars Bunny had tempted him with up in Juneau, then a rack in with her at the Taft Hotel where his wife would certainly be calling at 5 A.M.

Sonya decided not to advise home that she'd be out for dinner. It was her Psych night at school.

Over a thirst-quenching egg cream at the counter and a peer through the *Post*'s movie clock, Bud had tapped her shoulder.

"Not a movie in town," she said with a pained expression.

"I'm free and clear for two hours. Then I've got to be home to see someone who's hounding me. . . ."

"Bunny and Rog are going out. . . ."

"When?" he inquired, applying heavy pressure to her thumb.

"Slow you are not, Bud Van A. But I have forced you into a date that maybe you did not want."

He picked up quickly. She needed a coax.

"Never heard such nonsense. This, Sonya, with you, will be my privilege."

"Your privilege?" Slowly the frowning corners of her mouth perked up, the *Post* found its natural home on the floor and the toe of her shoe tat-tatted. Men like Bud knew the signs and the small games of desperate women. A man waited a lifetime for a bedworthy horny check-grabber, and Bud was not going to wait one second longer.

She gave him the keys to her car. At a light, he slipped his hand between her thighs and she smiled, too discreet to admit that practically the thought and not the deed had got her to a saturation point.

"I feel a little like I'm cheating," said Sonya when Bud helped her off with her coat in the apartment. "If Phoebe or Cal come by, what'll we say?"

He gazed at her mauve cashmere twin set. Must have cost more than his suit. The matching lizard handbag and shoes, not to mention the mink and the Patek Philippe wristwatch he'd seen advertised, were worth thousands. A fortune on her back. Something wrong with that Daniel to let this loose on the streets.

"Love?" he suggested. Worth a shot.

"Love . . . oh, Bud. Bud, can it be?"

"Why not? It happens if you get lucky."

"Christ, you are right."

"Every day. A brother-in-law falls for his sister-in-law. Friends, cousins. Hits them."

Her shoes were off and she reeled into the hollow of his shoulder. Firmer than either Wings or Daniel.

"For real?"

He embraced her. Without her heels they were the same height. Dazed by ecstasy, Sonya saw herself standing on a large clam shell in the middle of the sea joined by a winged Bud, wearing a helmet and whirling through the air beside her. A god en route to a seduction.

"Bu-ud . . ." When the romantic glow highlighted her eyes, Sonya was apt to add syllables, extending her emotion. "I have an idea. A real kinda cutey-cute one."

His asshole buddy Wings told him she liked to yap; read aloud; get herself crazy. He'd listen to anything. Working off the tap principle, Wings instructed him that a few extra gazumps might be necessary before hitting her for a loan to pay off Household Credit, who had stopped sending Bud letters filled with menacing legal phrases. The previous week a collector had caught him at home, grabbed him by the throat, and quite clearly called him a motherfucker who'd get his wagon fixed but good if he didn't pay what he owed, he had told Wings in a panic.

"I'm listening, honey."

"Uummmmm. Should I? Or shouldn't I?" she said positioning the heel of her right foot so that it bisected her left arch. A modelly, ballerinaish stance, which emphasized the straightness of her back and the absence of curves. Chin a little tucked out, sensual, provocative, a woman born to create controversy in the lives of men. "It is sort of . . . well, I wouldn't want you to get the wrong idea about me," she said, a moral rear guard action justifying the untoward. "It's . . . I mean, you are very handy with a camera. There is no question in my mind, Bud Van Allen, that you are a talented man."

Bud accepted the compliment in a state of shock, lost the thread actually.

"Thanks, but could you tell me how I'm talented?"

"Your photography, silly. Filming . . ."

"I handle myself pretty well with a Polaroid. The only time I missed taking a picture was when I bought some defective film."

"That's exactly what I mean about you, Bud. You are modest to a fault."

"I see." He narrowed his eyes, focusing on Sonya's ankles, slender enough to carry off wearing a slave bracelet with dignity. In his price range; twin hearts was what he had in mind.

"Could you handle a movie camera?"

"I don't see why not. Little while since I used one. Kids were photographed pretty regular when they were growing up."

"But you know how to use a camera, you don't forget, do you?"

She leaned into him, frontally, in a seductive lower-body smooch which expressed willingness.

"I guess I could take movie film."

He pecked the little button nose, then his mouth wandered to above the eyebrows.

"I love eye kisses," she said.

A simple enough request, Bud kissed her eyes, then inquired: "Ears?"

"So-so. There's a spot on my neck, under my hair." She made the necessary adjustment of hair and Bud tasted her.

A kind of ummmmmmmm in her mental orthography was shaping up, during which the twin possibilities of a more perma-nent record of her activities with Bud and burning Lamar's ass became betrothed in her mind.

"I have always wanted a little movie of myself." He demurred, and she pressed her case. "All done in the spirit of film making. Are you following me?"

"We film ourselves? Or I film you?"

"Us . . . in action, Bu-ud. We'll put the camera on remote control," she said, giggling.

It brought him out in a nice, fine, cold sweat. Could he wear a disguise, a dark wig? A Lone Ranger mask? No wonder Lamar-got rid of her. Behind the doe smile, she was wild. The idea began suddenly to appeal to him. Sonya on film would be like an annuity.

"Or we could ask Cal to run the camera."

"I guess I could tell him what to do," he said, nodding.

"Do you know what type of equipment we'd need?"

"Offhand, no, but I guess I could find out."

He busied himself with a small area of nape and ran his fingers across the cashmere. Her nipples hardened, sent spiky messages to his fingertips. He liked her breasts. No waste, no excess. Most of them taken up with nipple and pink flower. Very little white flesh on view. Yes, his kind of breasts, unlike Bunny's which mostly hung over his firm chin, bellies quivering like mer-cury, all in all, a poor fit. Sonya's he could swallow whole, in their entirety, like a TV dinner designed for convenient consumption.

Midway between sashay and a fox trot back walk, Bud high-stepped Sonya into the main bedroom.

All hands, he grappled with her garter belt, placed his smolder-ing Raleigh Tipped in the ashtray, and went at her neck with pecking wet kisses of short duration in an effort to cover as much territory as possible before he was due home. He shifted his head below stairs. A very thorough man.

"Bu-ud, you're getting me all hot. And my skirt is going to be one mass of creases."

She sat up on the bed, gave him her Bambi-eyed slack-mouth look, and placed a hand over her shoulder.

"The sound of a zipper always turns me on," he said.

"Even when you open your pants?"

"No, my own zipper doesn't affect me."

"Mine . . ." She shoved a willowy shoulder, bleached with powder, under his chin and he made short work of the top. She slipped it off and he began munching her. "What time do you have to leave?"

"No later than seven-thirty."

"Gives us about an hour. How many times do you think you can . . . ?"

"That we'll have to discover. I'm not what you'd call real fast and not exactly delayed action. If you're worried about here today gone tomorrow, don't because"—he checked his watch—"a half hour ought to see us safely there and back. A repeat performance, well, I just don't know if we can squeeze it in."

"I like your scheduling," she said, unhooking her red bra, constructed so that a nipple might peek through. She had recently purchased two hundred dollars' worth of "desire" lingerie in an assortment of colors, all featuring some aspect of kindly voyeurism. The matching undies had a diaphanous patch in contrasting red.

"What do you think?" she asked.

"It looks a little like a stripper's gear."

"Theatrical," she said correcting him. "There is a difference. I mean to say, this bra is what you'd expect an actress to wear in a movie. My understanding is that go-go gals and strippers wear just pasties." She sat squatting on the bed, holding court, just a little contemptuous of his attitude toward lingerie.

Thin-legged, wiry in jockey shorts and with his V-necked T-shirt, Bud seemed the type of man who spent a great deal of time jogging, a natural leader of air cadets. His St. Christopher's medal dangled from a chain and he switched it back to front in order to avoid thrashing Sonya with it. He flattened down a shank of hair which like a loose floor board had popped up from the Vitalis base.

Sonya reclined, waited regally. He began with her ankles, kissing both sides, advanced to the knees with calculated deliberation, unlike Lamar who just plowed ahead on a wing and a prayer. Bud was, she thought with confidence, going through an instrument check. He paused at her navel, disposed of a small lint deposit, then proceeded to lap her belly in gradually decreasing circles, obviously a stacking pattern. It would be a dilly of a fuck if he ever got to it. Something of a technician, he'd probably studied manuals, working according to the book. He darted through a series of ear kisses, then gathered a breast in his mouth. She'd seen his wang any number of times, but never before had had an opportunity to fly solo with it. She decided it was shapely, albeit somewhat hooded.

They were airborne before she knew it, and she wondered if the sound she heard was the undercarriage locking into place. She kissed him on the mouth fondly, for he was opening up with real power. Those Rolls Royce engines never failed. Coming away from his mouth, she noticed that he had stopped breathing audibly. Was he following some obscure regulation imposed by the noise-abatement society? She slipped her hand through the jam of legs and clasped his balls firmly in her palm, applied gentle pressures until he began once more to breathe. She'd have to ask him about holding his breath . . . but later. There was an air of professionalism in Bud's performance, completely different from any she'd previously experienced, which contrasted sharply with Daniel's acrobatics and Wings' tiring uncertainties.

As promised, a true pro, Bud came in on schedule at seven sharp. He unloosened himself from her like a belt buckle, handed her a flotilla of Scotties to stem the tide, and hopped to the bathroom for a towel and running water.

"Your E.T.A. was right on the button," she said affectionately. "How'd it go?"

"A round trip, Bud," she said, tissuing herself, and too lazy to get to the bathroom just yet. She lay back in his arms, noticing prominent and steely veins in the muscular forearms. A man who carried loads, a man she could trust. "Bud, why'd you hold your breath?"

"It kind of builds up wind."

"I thought it might. Had me worried for a minute."

A pleasant relaxed giggle.

"Now wouldn't it be nice if we had a record of this . . . this event in our lives?"

He got the message loud and clear.

"It could be pretty expensive. You know, you have to leave deposits. Film isn't cheap, neither. They can soak me . . ."

"How much do you think it would cost?"

He reckoned to himself, then made up a number.

"Three-four hundred possibly."

"I thought five hundred plus," she said unblinkingly, then picked up her handbag, pulled out a sunflower yellow checkbook.

"Four hundred, then," he said nervously.

"Who do I make it out to?"

"Just 'cash'."

"One thing, Bu-ud."

"Anything, Sonya." He'd happily yield to any lunatic request. He'd waited all his life for a mark. "Name it."

"Next time, let's not wear our watches."

7

Checking Sonya out New Year's Eve—a ride with a real shortage of thrills, Daniel thought, as he made a last-minute inspection of the house—he cast a critical eye on her dress and accessories, discovered something missing and frowned.

"Listen, we've got a ten-carat blue-white piece of my life locked in the safe which is in the shape of an emerald and it begins with D."

"My ring."

"I'm so glad you remembered."

The purpose of the party, apart from an annual salute to the new year, had a rather practical turn. Daniel was not merely going to show off, but to unveil "the house that God built" to the Church's finance group, who had after all made the place a reality by placing their business with him. Exterior Corinthian columns in sandstone were set off by an architectural free-for-all inside where Ionic and Doric minuscule examples revealed Daniel's apparently catholic tastes and the confusion which attended the building of his temple. The rooms were all high-ceiling jobs, the floors Italian marble, the library frowned under oak paneling which Daniel had insisted be stained a dark mahogany brown after he discovered that he'd selected the wrong wood. Sets of Trollope, Ruskin, and Richardson gathered dust in the bookshelves. The furnishings were eclectic and, in the main, reproduction Louis Quatorze, with here an Italian bombé and there a Yankee secretary.

"Doll, have a sherry."

"I'd prefer C.C. and ginger."

He sat her down on the autumn-leaf-patterned tuxedo settee, one of a pair he'd bought at Widdicomb, eight feet long and indicative of gracious living.

"Sonya, before dinner, sherry, champagne, but let's cut out the C.C. stuff."

"Why?"

"Breath, baby. We've got priests coming and for them whiskey's okay, but for you, well, let's discuss elevation for a minute. We're sitting in a house in Kings Point that cost—conservative guess—four hundred grand, and frankly, I'd rather *plotz* than have you drink that crap. So elevate, Sonya, and we'll all be one happy gang."

"Champagne then," she said indifferently.

Daniel snapped his fingers and two of the G and B waiters in tails came forward. The grande dame of modern catering, Fay Budnick herself, was taking personal charge.

"Madame and I will have champagne. You know," he said turning to Sonya, "that you look very nice tonight. Black suits you."

"I enjoy wearing black," she said.

He picked up his glass and left her sitting in the enormous room. She looked like a miniature, and for a moment he was overcome by the hopeless resignation that *this* was the mother of his two daughters, and that whether he got rid of her or not, she had occupied more than seven years of his life. A big dent.

The most remarkable aspect of their marital entanglement resided in their ability to heal all rifts without resorting to apology, striking him as a form of invisible mending which de-

fied calculated guesses and certainly all known laws of rational-
ity. Where did it spring from? he wondered. This ability to go
on . . . and on . . . and on . . . in a situation of interminable
conjugal lockjaw. Something almost dialectical about the process, a will to live what had become essentially lifeless. A casket
bound by the pastel-colored ribbons of two small girls, with
baby teeth, their mother's blond hair, who spoke barely in-
telligible words to him and made a fetish of dependence.

The girls were away for the night, staying with neighbors.
But even in their absence he was overwhelmed by their presence.
The odors of his prewomen haunted him. Sylvia, named for his
grandmother, rather cinnamon; and Noreen, named for Sonya's
mother, a tart herbal smell, which, he realized, came from the
variety of bath salts Sonya used for them.

Saddened by himself in a way that he found impossible to
convey, he lived captive to his household of three women. The
distance increased daily, and he came to the conclusion that big
money, screwing hookers, and a loveless marriage were his un-
redeemable lot.

Examining his reflection in the hall mirror, Daniel adjusted his
black butterfly bow tie, smoothed down his pink dinner shirt,
which along with his stomach had begun creeping outside of his
trousers. Lint-free and with the warm smell of a recent press,
his dinner suit by Cardin (who else?) and patent black loafers
(also signed) gave him an aura of European mystery—the owner
of racehorses cheering his stallions at Longchamps; member of
a titled English family, equally at home in the City of London
and Wall Street; escort to international beauties at a villa in
Portofino.

"Sonya, I'm feeling kind of European. You know, a little
desafinado."

"You want to go to Europe?" she asked, flicking a thread off
his collar.

"How about the two of us in Denmark this summer for a few
days? The Danes have come up with a new miracle. A rubber-
ized pussy that you can't tell from the real thing. It doesn't
talk. I thought I might order one for you. Any particular hair
style or color? Maybe a crew cut for those Indian summers,
doll."

Pebbles hitting a shatterproof windshield, causing her merely to blink. Daniel had done a remarkable emotional moving job for her, he had removed tears from her life, so that she was able to reside on a plateau without weather changes or wind, benumbed.

"Anything special for me to do tonight?" she asked.

"We'll be sitting at opposite ends of the table, so if you don't look at me, I promise not to throw a bottle of wine at you again."

They could afford everything now, even the unpleasantness. Time and again she'd wanted to dump him, but the comfortable collusion of their anger miraculously united them.

"Daniel, have you ever thought of divorce?"

He turned around, spluttering with laughter, and embraced her.

"What is my doll reading? *Cosmo*? Divorce! Do you mean to tell me you'd rob me of the one pleasure you give me . . . ?"

Before he completed his sentence, they found themselves enveloped by a swarm of guests. Daniel had invited a hundred people for nine and it appeared as though half of them had arrived at the same moment. The hallway was a clutter of fur coats, men's hats, and a nostril-curling mélange of perfumes. Sonya comfortably lost herself in the crowd, neither mistress nor guest. Mrs. Daniel Barnet, or the lonely woman's guide to anonymity. She recognized the basso profundo of Monsignor Braughton, who had paved Daniel's way through an obstacle course strewn with crosses and dollars.

"Monsignor, you'll never guess what I got you?" Daniel was saying as she started up the stairs, determined to get Bud on the phone to wish him Happy New Year. "Now if you don't tell the F.B.I., I won't either. Havanas, rolled in the pre-Castro style." Daniel seemed everywhere at the same time, shaking hands, kissing women, telling jokes, a one-man football team, offensive and defensive units. "The pity is that Father Aurelio isn't here to join us. He's up there calling signals for St. Peter, I'll bet you anything. . . ."

Their bedroom was also gigantic—Daniel's insistence on space had given the house a certain glandular exaggeration, and the rooms suffered from architectural expansiveness—with a lily-of-the-valley motif, eternally spring, a field of clover even to the dappled green carpet which would remind Jersey cows of home.

She picked up the telephone, an awkward antique object in screaming brass which might once have been placed in the hallway of a Saratoga boardinghouse, a decorator special on which Daniel had been clipped for three hundred fifty dollars and which he had justified by telling her that it would appreciate in value. Always ice-cold too. She dialed Bud's number, praying that his wife would not answer.

"Bu-ud, it's me," she said breathing in sharp reports. "If your wife's there, say it's Wings."

"Hi, Wings," said Bud. "How are you?"

"Bu-ud, I'm feeling so lonely and empty . . ."

"Can't talk," he whispered.

"What're you going to do tonight?"

"We're having some friends in. It's Wings," he shouted.

"Do you wish I was there with you?"

"You know I do."

"Happy New Year, Bud, darling. Maybe next year will be our time," she said solemnly, hope as dead as his cash balance.

"Yes, well, Wings. If you can get by—I told you it was Lamar—" she heard him interject. "I'll see you real soon."

"Love you, Bu-ud. We'll meet at the apartment the day after New Year's . . ."

"That's fine with me. Happy New Year—"

Sonya dropped the phone, chipping a lump of wood on the bedside table. Only Daniel would notice, fine with her.

Closing in on her were a pair of startled dark eyes, set off by a winter Puerto Rican tan, black hair in an upswept waterfall with dancing ringlets. Norma gave a short gasp. She had not expected to find Sonya there and she hoped that Sonnerman would get waylaid before coming upstairs. She was really angry, for Daniel had arranged the meeting.

"The only room that isn't used is the workshop."

Obviously he'd forgotten to mention this to Sonya.

"You can leave your coat downstairs," Sonya said evenly without looking at her. "No one steals anything here."

"Sorry, I didn't realize this was your bedroom." Norma did a short survey and found herself rooted by the door.

Only the annual office clambake and softball event brought them together, but Norma had never before been inside Daniel's home.

"It's like a palace," she said with enthusiasm.

"Little men like big places," Sonya replied, trying to draw her out.

She had heard about Norma ages ago, filed her, another of Daniel's past performances. In need of a reconditioning.

"What have you got to complain about?" Norma asked.

The unmentionable bubbled slowly to the surface. Sonya patted a section of the king-sized bed.

"The great man sleeps here."

Confounded by the direction of Sonya's remarks, and the sly foxy expression on the mouth, Norma drew into herself, fearful of disturbing the balance of whatever plan Daniel might have in mind to divest himself of Sonya.

"You know, Sonya," she began tactfully, "a lot of people are grateful to Daniel, and even though he acts a little crazy at times, they do think he's great."

"At what?" Sonya asked, calmly sitting at her dressing table. "I'd like to be the first to know that."

"I guess your husband can't ever be a hero."

"Well, Daniel isn't so much of a husband as a lover. But you know, he must be awfully like Max in that respect. The boys all like to vary their diet . . . variety," she added ominously. Catching an involuntary muscle twitch on Norma's face, she pressed on. "How's Max treat you? I suppose he still is the model of regularity. Gets home, gets up, goes to bed on the button."

"Sonya, what're you getting at?"

Sonya dented the armor and Norma leaned against a louvred wardrobe.

"Nothing, really . . ." Norma received one of Sonya's special dumb-dumb looks. "I just wondered if it was just the same for you?"

"What's the same?"

"Married five years or so . . . you know what, we should have a lunch together some time." She gave Norma a naughty-girl giggle. "Cunt to cunt."

"I'm not a cunt."

"Well, to . . . er, Max, you are."

"Like hell."

"You are misunderstanding me."

"Doesn't everybody?"

"Daniel understands me . . . only too well,"

"Really, I don't get this at all."

"What are you afraid of, Norma? Pretty woman like you with lots of men no doubt pestering you. Just Daniel's type. He likes them safely married, so he can bang away without fear, then run for the hills if it gets too serious. Wouldn't surprise me one bit if Daniel wanted to give you one. *I* would surely understand."

"Yesterday afternoon," Norma said sarcastically, then laughed, threw her hands in the air embarrassedly to indicate that she had just made a joke.

"He's got his charity lays like they all do. I do not mean you of course."

"What's this got to do with me?" Norma asked. She had a tendency to sweat under the eyes when in distress and Sonya was wrecking her makeup.

"Sit down here, Norma, and fix yourself up. Don't pay any attention to me, I just sound off now and then."

Norma allowed herself to be guided to Sonya's seat at the dressing table, and stared with dismay at her when she flung herself on the bed and lifted up her dress, revealing that she was without panties.

"I never can tell while I'm waiting for the great man to return from his whoring if he will want to grab me and ram it in. Bet Max is more considerate of you."

"Sonya, cut it out."

"Imagine yourself sitting here night after night in this fucking ugly place . . , well, a woman has to have lots of staying power. I do. Actually, no matter what he does, I won't leave that kike motherfucker. I do not care. I have my own life. My secrets too, Norma."

Edging toward some undefined border that combined outright lunacy with ambiguity, Sonya touched her at some unfathomable depth. The cackling laughter, stopping and starting, was like a weird hieroglyph disguising a void she too felt.

"Hey, you all right? What are you crying about?" Sonya asked, but Norma couldn't answer. "My Daniel hates criers, runs for his life. They terrify him."

They both turned to stare at an unannounced, unbriefed Jack Sonnerman, awkwardly standing at the bedroom's entrance and trapped in the no-man's-land of advance-retreat.

"Jack, why good evening. You know Max's wife, Norma."

"Good evening, ladies. I seem to interrupt a—"

"Nothing, Jack. Norma and me were just having a gal gab and the man's lawyer was sent up for . . . what?"

"My coat?"

"What is it with my bedroom and people's coats? We are using the study for a checkroom. You put coats on a bed, Jack, how will . . . ? What's that legal phrase about justice?"

"So many," he answered, retreating.

"Justice must be seen . . . to be done? That right?"

Norma walked past her, then uncertainly down the stairs, a skittery muscle in her calf, held onto the marble balustrade. Daniel looked up at Norma, gave her a friendly wink and continued talking to a group of clergymen. Out of the corner of her eye, she spotted Max carrying out a guerrilla raid at the hors d'oeuvres table, his plate unbalanced by caviar, smoked salmon, herrings, a champagne glass uneasily tilted forward, weaving through backless dresses and dangling chignons. Her bald swain in action, while Daniel lived with, supported, slept with—he must have in spite of his denials—Sonya. Slipping behind her and firing a parting salvo, before dissolving into a crowd, Sonya said in a measured, but determinedly casual voice:

"I'm so happy to have you in my home at long-long last."

A welt was born on Norma's cheek, and she pressed the back of her hand against it to flatten it. What she needed was a coin, preferably a cold one. Sonya crept into one's bones, turned them gelatinous, caused skin eruptions. Daniel had created a monster.

Tugging at Daniel's sleeve, but failing to interrupt him as he racked up points with a clergyman, Norma waited for a convenient moment.

"Everyone criticizes this country. Our people, our institutions, our food, Father. But consider mustard. Why aren't articles written or documentaries made on the varieties of our mustard? Gulden's Spicy Brown, Gulden's Creamy Mild, Heinz's Brown, French's, not to mention deli mustard. Why is there no one to praise our mustards?" Daniel concluded, baffling the others.

Turning his head a few inches, he whispered to Norma: "This banana's a fiscal comptroller. . . ."

"I want to talk to you."

"Find a corner."

Norma remained by his side, casting furtive glances over her beaded shoulder strap as Sonya's demented giggle pierced eardrums.

"I've never considered mustard in quite that context."

"Another thing I'm certain you never considered, Father Prichett, isn't it?"

"Right," said the man. He had one of those florid, freckled complexions, a shock of red hair which stood straight in a burr cut and sideburns that might have been machine-gunned. His face possessed glare, hurt Daniel's eyes.

"Correct me if I'm wrong, but every human being, no matter what his faith, sooner or later dies." Daniel waited three seconds for the priest to demur, then pressed on. "Now even though I'm not a member of your faith—mine came a bit before yours and in the old days my people joined anything that was going because they didn't want to be left out, and, who knows, there may have been group discounts in those days too when it came to hiring camels or buying food in bulk, so history determined that I should be a member of the tribe, a homeless people who have known historical adversity. They may have been said to have invented adversity. The point being, that Jew and Catholic die. Priests die. The way I work is that we take tax-free money, insure priests, and make the Church beneficiary . . ."

Monsignor Braughton, smoking one of Daniel's Havanas, puffed amiably and with his short body looked like one of those small metal smoke pots farmers employ to chase insects away. He joined arms with Daniel. The ice-gray eyes, however, told another story; they were not kindly.

"Daniel came up with this remarkable idea when he was working for Princeton," he said.

"And you made it a reality," Daniel exclaimed, becoming nostalgic and weasely.

"Well, we couldn't find anyone more unscrupulous than you. To defend our position, you understand, Father Pritchett. My committee and I agreed that we'd found the perfect sinner in

Daniel Barnet. Someone anxious to expiate his guilt and fall from grace for the Church's profit. You are my most successful convert," Braughton said with a laugh.

"I never thought about it that way," Daniel said with wonder-. ment. Then as Braughton edged toward some pretty women, Daniel resumed where he'd left off with Father Pritchett.

"If I were a betting man, Father Pritchett, I'd put money on your ability to judge a man by his face." Daniel brought out his pat hand from the stacked deck. "Look into my face, my eyes—the window of my soul—and see if you can find deceit, evasion?" Daniel insisted, thrusting his face about four inches from the priest's.

"Frankly, at this stage I don't know what to say," Pritchett replied. "It means committing millions of the Church's money."

"Feel free to discuss this with Monsignor Braughton. He'll tell you the kind of job I'm doing for the Church of New York. Just mix and mingle and enjoy yourself."

He took Norma by the elbow, handling it in such a fragile manner that even a gossip would have to say he was crossing an old lady.

"Looks good tonight. Calèche on all the parts. But, Norma, darling, please don't interrupt when I'm closing a priest."

"How does Sonya know about us?"

"Sonya knows?"

"She does."

"Could be I was talking in my sleep. Maybe I was praising you. Were your ears hot when you were in Puerto Rico?"

"I waited four days there for you."

"My fault I'm important? People coming to see me, calling me day and night. What do you think I'm running, a chicken-shit operation? Did you get your tits brown at least, so that I can justify my investment in you?"

"Daniel, she's really upset me."

"That's impossible. Sonya can't even upset herself. She's not smart enough."

The Rubins interposed themselves between Daniel and Norma, or rather Marlene did her aggressive, place-jumping number. Daniel got himself kissed on both cheeks and the mouth.

"It's incredible, Daniel, the taste."

"I take full credit, Marlene. Look up, Norma. That's a sixteenth-century Italian crystal chandelier, not a Fortunoff's special."

"What's with the Christmas tree though?" Marlene asked.

"That's the way I make my living, in case you hadn't heard. Doesn't Gary talk to you? Oh, I forgot, Marlene—you do all of the talking."

Gary enclosed him in a bear hug.

"Always my defender."

"In the unending war between husband and wife," he said, patting Marlene's cheek.

Rapid electrical impulses twisted through Norma's mind. Had the moment come for her to legitimize her relationship with Daniel? Sonya had always been represented as yielding, a foam rubber pillow, but she now appeared more formidable to Norma, with a hard core of resistance.

Max crept up on her and gave her ear a loving pinch.

Daniel studied the couple: his employee and his mistress, a cup and saucer with no obvious crack, forged in the crucible of his life, the union of disparities which he had wielded together.

"Max, I thought you were a lover of food."

Max brandished his plate—a wedding feast—on which the food had been laid out with the meticulous care of an office manager.

"What's missing?"

"Sugar-cured brisket," said Daniel to get rid of him. "I want you to report on it."

Sounds of music embattled the room. The mobile discotheque unit Daniel had hired were now fully operative, and he gripped Norma's hand and moved out on the parquet dance area that adjoined the living room and was referred to in the architect's plan as the orangerie. Domed with glass, it caught the sun. Potted plants on the window ledges, a swirl of palm frond, served as Daniel's ecology display and grass-smoking eyrie.

Daniel smiled at his guests, hurtling disks out of place, and nodded to the young black couple who ran the discotheque. Norma lurched into motion, grinding, swiveling, here a hop, there a grind. Ages since they'd danced, since they'd been a couple in public.

"I'm glad Sonya knows about us."

"What does she know? A lucky guess possibly. How's Benji?"

"You don't bother seeing him, so why ask?"

"Norma, stop hurting me."

The boy called Daniel "uncle."

"Just give me what's rightfully mine."

"Don't worry. Jack and I are working on it."

Into their lap danced Adele Weintraub and what must have been the luggage king.

"How did—?" he began, but was outdrawn.

"—Naughty, naughty, kids," Adele fired, then fled.

At the entrance, Sonya crooked her finger at him and then flashed her watch.

"Duty calls," he told Norma. "We're switching on the TV in the living room."

Supper was scheduled for midnight and as the second hand flashed over the mobs on Times Square, Daniel felt his hand being held, looked up and saw that Sonya had threaded her way next to him.

"Yes, okay, we'll try . . ." in automatic response to Sonya's request that they forget about the past and begin again. Standing next to him at the head of the receiving line as guests embraced them, he was astonished to hear Sonya remark to Norma when she kissed him: "You still here? I thought you left."

Only one tactic to employ against a revolt. Smother it, instant repression. He squeezed Sonya's chin so hard that she began to squeal.

"Doll, I guess maybe I forgot to mention it. But when people come into our home, and they're called guests, the hosts, you and me, have an obligation—"

"That hurts!"

"—to see that they are treated with courtesy . . . that they enjoy themselves, leave with a pleasant taste . . ."

"Cut it out, Daniel."

He released his grip.

"If Mrs. Max Hoffman disturbs you, then don't talk to her. You nod to her and forget she's alive. But when you open that shiksa rat-trap while I've got business people I'm entertaining, then I'll take you and throw you through that jolly bay window. Now drag your ass to the table and put your napkin on your lap and stuff the face with caviar, even though you don't like it. Pretend, Sonya, that you're into the better things of life. Have we got it all clear in our head?"

He shoved her ahead of him through the dining room door, sat her down, and with a playful smile spread her napkin on her lap, then walked to his own seat at the head of the table, pausing for an instant next to Norma: "We're letting her stay up with the adults on the condition that she behaves herself. . . . I apologize."

"Christ, why do I love you?" she asked rhetorically, spooning some Sevruga on a piece of toast and munching it near his ear.

"I make you come with consistency. I've spent a fortune dressing you like a film star. I am the father of your son. I pay your husband's salary. . . ."

"I wonder if they're still good enough reasons."

Toward the end of dinner, amid compliments from everyone, even the ascetic Father Pritchett, on the Beef Wellington, Daniel rose to make a short speech. In the doorway his employees and their wives clustered, applauding before he began, for the Christmas bonus had come to 20 percent of each man's annual salary.

"Since none of us can stand after-dinner speeches, I'm going to make mine short and sweet. I'd like to thank you all for coming tonight and wish you a happy, healthy New Year. Prosperous we know it's going to be for all parties concerned, so on behalf of my wife Sonya and myself, Happy 1973."

Nothing spectacular. He didn't like making speeches, felt exposed, self-conscious, liable to ridicule. Crowds had always worried him. He caught his breath when the tables emptied and guests shifted back to the dance floor. When he got up to pass through the dining room, he was cornered by a group of priests led by Monsignor Braughton.

". . . with the market climbing, I don't see why we can't get a little more adventurous with the pension fund," said Braughton.

"Monsignor, when I took over, you had a portfolio loaded with high fliers, and to call it by name, garbage. We've had steady growth in the last few years, so how can I justify selling off solid investments with high yields to buy speculative stuff? We became liquid when there was blood on the street, so we bought prime companies that were at their lows . . ."

"That sounds like solid thinking to me. I like the conservative approach," said Pritchett.

Out of the corner of his eye, he observed Sonya detaching

herself from the Rubins. He'd been right to rub her nose in it.
She headed toward him, obviously with her tail between her
legs, and he excused himself for a moment and stepped back:
"My wife . . ."
"Daniel, this is a New Year's resolution."
"I'm listening, don't be too long."
"For humiliating me in my own home, you are going to be
so very-very-very . . . sorry."
"That it? I'm sorry already. Now squirt a little Binaca on
the breath because it smells. And Sonya, drunk or sober, just get
lost."

8

Sonya out of sheer obstinacy had actually regained her gaiety,
but Phoebe Jansen, Miss Nebraska Junior College of 1957 and
Sonya's second dearest friend, stared at her with fascination. The
apartment was stifling hot, smelled of incense, and was bright
as Shea Stadium. Phoebe also shared the place with Cal Beasley
when they could dispose of their respective mates.

"Frankly, Sonya, I think you're flipping out." A small dark-
haired man threaded a wire under her chair, requiring her to
lift her feet. "Oh, excuse me."

"Sorry to inconvenience you, but I've got to use this socket.
The other one's got a fault."

"That's Mickey," Sonya introduced the man wallowing in
black cable, an arm inserted into a leather halter strap upon
which hung a small powerhouse of batteries. On a lariat of sorts,
a light meter and view finder dangled.

"He looks like he's gonna blow up something," Phoebe suggested.

Sonya applied a shield of Johnson and Johnson Baby Oil to
various parts of her body from one of those leakproof plastic
bottles, currently the rage of travelers, which was why Phoebe
lost her train of thought. Glazed like a honey-roasted ham,
Sonya examined her shoulders, tried a quick three-quarter-

angle pose with shoulder tucked under chin to test the provoca-
tion value of a partially revealed nipple bud. Used balls of
cotton were carefully aimed like foul shots at the basket across
the living room. Turning to the underside of a thigh, the land-
locked Andorra between leg and ass, she careened an arm awkwardly to insure that the oil slick was evenly distributed. Sight-
ing another unseasoned perimeter—the back of the arm—Sonya
contorted herself to reach funny bone.

"What exactly are you doing?" Phoebe asked in the spirit of
scientific inquiry, nervously coiling her legs around a green
cushion. "It looks like some basting process."

"It's an ancient practice of the Grecians," Sonya explained.
"When they were going to do their sculpturing, the models used
to take these olive oil baths to tone skin."

Phoebe's lips puckered and she nervously squeezed a relief-
sized blackhead onto her purse mirror, then applied a spotch
of Clearasil to conceal the eruption. Sonya had made her truly
jittery.

"How did you hear about this . . . this oiling?" She couldn't
imagine Sonya in a library "researching" among papyrus scrolls
or indeed reading a book.

"If you kept up with the articles and correspondence sections
of *Different* you'd know a thing or two about what is going on
in the world, Phoebe Jansen. Prominent sexicologists write these
articles about methods and variation of methods every month on
the month."

Slick and oven-ready, Sonya accosted Phoebe for a final inspection of her parts, causing her friend to grow even more flustered.
Even the bush gleamed, also having been newly greased.

"You don't mean that California mag that prints all that
smut?" Phoebe asked.

"A lot you know," Sonya replied, standing on tiptoe and extending her arms in a swanlike movement. "I am afraid you will
always have the mind of an airline stewardess. Expand!" Sonya
exhorted her. "Free yourself, Phoebe. Don't be so darned con-
ventional."

"You mean . . . take part in this whole thing? Practice cunty
linctus with another woman?" The suggestion drew a deep sun-
set flush to Phoebe's cheeks.

"I am talking about *sharing*. There is nothing devionic about

it all. You should of studied these ancient Grecians and their
poetics to get a little sidelight on the art of life, then you'd know
that a woman can befriend a woman and still like men. You
never did lie with a woman, did you?"

"No, naturally. But I once filled in on the European run.
Summer of . . . ? Sixty-seven. And I was in Greece for a lay-
over. Athens." She moved suddenly back into her chair, folding
her ankles underneath, a fail-safe carryover before she began
putting out. "They have not changed one iota, then, these
Grecians because their food is greasier than hell. And no wonder.
Putting oil on their bodies, what can you expect them to do
with meat? Correction, Miss Know-All—lamb. I was eating lamb
day and night. Sight of it made me sick to my stomach for a
year."

"Athens is not necessarily Greece," Sonya said didactically.
"Just like New York is not the whole of the States. You went to
tourist traps."

Raising her eyebrows to reflect her distress and to counter-
attack, Phoebe let fly.

"Really! Well, let me tell you that I was with a Grecian man
all of my time. And, let's see, his name was Adis or Iadis or
something like that, and not only did we get to all of the native
places where they were sopping up lamb, but this Adis did not
impress me as a rep. of an ancient cultural thingummyjig. He
kept on rubbing my ass all night long, which was not all that
bad, but then he tried to give me a screw in that place. And
what with me running to the john every five minutes shitting
out bits of lamb, which is why I think they feed women in that
manner for starters, to open them up. I mean this weirdo didn't
even come close to the proper port of entry, where there was a
possibility of him succeeding like a normal man. Just show 'em
that ass and they become raving maniacs, start jumping on
glasses, tying their ankles with hankies . . . I just don't know
about you anymore, Sonya."

"I am devoted to art, and Bud and I have agreed to do an art
film."

"You are smashed out of your skull. I dread to think what
Wings'll do if he finds out."

"Not *if*, but *when*. And I will pick that particular moment."

Phoebe blinked, belted down the last of her highball, poured herself a refill but appeared too frightened to get over to the bar for a Canada Dry Ginger Ale chaser because it meant going past Sonya, who still stood over her. She had sprung a minor chassis leak and oil slowly streamed down the backs of her thighs to the dip behind her knees.

"What do you think, sir?" Phoebe asked the man, still wheeling cable.

"About what?" he returned without stopping.

"This whole discussion."

"You mean whether to make a dirty movie or not?"

"Exactly." A glare at Sonya reinforced the correctness of her position. She gave the man a chalky smile, her ally.

"I think people ought to do what they want to do. One thing— I don't like dogs."

"Dogs?" Sonya leaned over interestedly.

"Yeah, dogs. I took one filim for some people out Jersey way." He paused to pin down the locale. "Last year. Asbury Park way. And they had this here schnauzer. Nice woman, too. With a lovely smile. Well, like I'm hired. Like you hired me when you phoned up my phone listin' in *Different.* So, you know, I get paid my money, I don't care what people do. But this damned schnauzer, they got lousy tempers. They like bark and all when you want to just give them a pet. Man, he was roarin' away while I'm doin' my setup, till this nice lady with what I'd call an Ipana smile jam him between her legs. Like in a headlock. Wow, he quiet down." He lifted up the sole of his Thom McAn loafer. "That tongue was maybe as long as the sole of this shoe. Never seen nothin' like it."

"That's downright disgusting," said Phoebe. "See what this could lead to?" she warned Sonya.

"What were the men doing, or weren't there any?" Sonya asked.

"The Jaspers? Well, they was like standin' there, watchin'. I think they was drinkin' Old Crow or some other bourbon. Gettin' bombed durin' the entire filim." He shrugged his shoulders in some perplexity.

"Did you run the film after for them?"

"Yeah, sure. That's part of my square deal. Half now, half on production of the print."

"Well, what was it like?" Phoebe asked solemnly.

"The dog come out the star, no question about it. He hogged the whole filim. Man, they loved it. They was pettin' that dog like he was God."

Into the fray, in a terrycloth robe, stepped Bud, a bit pasty-faced and shaking water from his head. He greeted Mickey, ascertained the condition of his health, apparently "in the pink," and sat down on the sofa, waiting for the bell. Having followed Sonya's plan down to the last detail—the hiring of a Keystone 8 mm. camera with a 10-28 mm. zoom lens; 4 photofloods of 500 watts by Mole-Richardson; tripod by the redoubtable Linhof—Bud ran into a small snag that threatened to jeopardize the entire production.

Film.

Yes, it was simple enough to buy. A cinch to load. He even got the hang of reversing it.

But . . . who was going to develop it? Kodak? Ansco? Agfa? He approached various dealers of cameras and learned that all movie film had to go to the manufacturer's laboratories for processing. No way of beating it.

He had pocketed three hundred dollars of the check. Out of danger and with no chance of making this film, he had been behaving with startling bravado, until he realized that Sonya would not accept defeat gracefully.

"Where is your ingenuity, Bud Van Allen?" she had asked scornfully.

For days, well into the middle of January, Sonya had puzzled over the development obstacle while she and Daniel maintained a cold peace. With the arrival of the January *Different,* held up because of the Christmas post, she turned to a little-perused section. *Different*'s MERCHANDISE MART. And thereupon struck pay dirt with Mickey.

"Mickey, dear, how long do you think you'll be?"

"Not too long."

"I am only asking because it is now eight-fifteen and my class in Urban Social Psych. at the New School lets out at about ten, so with my drive home, I shouldn't be later than, shall I say, the bewitching hour?"

"No problem. I just wisht that you'd a let me bring my own gear. This junk is ancient history. Anybody know where the fuse box is?"

"In the hall," Bud said.

Entering the hallway, Mickey removed his flashlight and shone it until he was rapped on the neck by someone entering the apartment.

"Who may I ask are you?" Bunny said, fanning her lashes at Mickey. She was followed by Cal, who suspiciously pressed his head over her shoulder.

"If it's a junkie come to rob us, don't look at his face and give him your money," said Cal, a man who prudently avoided heroics.

"I'm shootin' the filim," Mickey explained.

Sonya oiled almost by pointillistic technique extended her bare arms to the two, every inch a modern hostess.

"Come as players or to watch?"

"We'll see," said Bunny. "Bud doesn't look too happy with himself."

"If you're hungry there are some deli sandwiches in the kitchen," Sonya said.

"No thank you, we've eaten," said Cal.

"I wouldn't mind a deli sandwich," Mickey said, inserting his flashlight back into the leather holster attached to the back of his trousers. "I been here since six."

"Help yourself, but we are running a little late," Sonya reminded him.

"I can eat while I'm shooting. If there's any chicken salami, I'll go for that." He licked his lips. "I can eat chicken salami three times a day."

"How about rolled beef?" said Bud, offering him a teepee of waxed paper from which a pickle had begun to escape.

By way of reply Mickey seized the sandwich and found no difficulty scoffing and talking, directing the principals to the floodlit bedroom. He cautioned them to be careful of the wires, which lay on the floor like dozing snakes, springing to life only when trod upon. Sonya in a hopscotch jump arrived first to the bed, laggardly pursued by Bud, who apprehensively peered over his shoulder each pace to clock the reaction of the spectators. Stopping in his tracks when he heard Cal's twang.

"This is one for the fee-reek-in' books, Phoebe!" Phoebe adjured him to silence, but he could not restrain himself. "You mean to tell me they gonna start in humping on a movie.

Ker-rist, nobody don't tell me a goddam thing. I'd sure as hell liked to been in."

"You're drunk again," Phoebe said captiously.

Mickey ceased munching for a moment.

"You might yet," he said. "I done hundreds of these and I tell you, I seen guys freeze, you know, panic once them cameras start rollin'. So my advice to you is to keep your dick stiff." He resumed chewing.

"Mickey, dear, how's my position?"

"Listen, pal," Mickey continued to Cal, "you never can tell when a guy can get cramps in his nuts, so stay loose."

"Mickey! Will you stop that chattering and answer me. Is my position all right?"

Mickey studied her for a moment, one hand supporting his chin, the other supporting the elbow, ruminatively. He lowered the tripod several inches, looked through the view finder. Sonya heard tense whispering going on in the background. All very distracting, so she cupped her hands around her mouth and said for all to shush.

"Let's see, I can use this setup but . . ." A further check of the instruments. "This lens is not much of a zoom, so it might mean like creepin' in behind this gentleman's balls. Better still, Sonya, if you just prop your ass up on a pillow and let me check the angle from there." Sonya with head stiffly tilted up to the camera, practicing her smile on the Keystone iris, arched her back and slid a pillow under her. "That's better, Sonya. Give me a little less chin. Tuck it in." He'd started to sweat, and corralled Cal with his arm. "Listen, could you step back, you're creatin' shadows on the set, and I'd be grateful if someone could seaboard in a can of beer or a Coke."

In the background the three confounded spectators looked on with keen technical appreciation as Mickey stepped back and forth, light meter in hand, making small adjustments to floodlights.

"Mickey," Phoebe called his name respectfully.

"Yo."

"Here's your beer."

He slurped foam from the can, turned his head from side to side to frame the shot, then got behind the camera as Sonya remained immobile, hardly breathing, in a pose. Bud sat on a stool puffing a butt down to the inch level and cracking his knuckles. On what appeared to be a mere whim, he rose and hopped on his left leg. Mickey moved away from the camera, and said: "Pardon?"

"Pins and needles in my arch," Bud explained to Sonya who peevishly sucked in her cheeks.

"Okay by me. I just wondered . . . been around some pretty strange Jaspers in my day and I thought maybe you was hottin' yourself up."

A director-star conference took place at the head of the bed during which Mickey demonstrated certain . . . trade techniques from his wealth of experience. Thus, Sonya found Mickey's mouth tugging on her breast while Bud nodded, and Mickey rising for a breath asked—"Have you got that?" Mickey placed the remains of pickle nub in the ashtray on the bedside table, then let his chin stroll down the promenade of Sonya's stomach, halting at the high-grassed savanna, home of big-game animals, ultimately mounting it awkwardly with a jaw that might have been constructed with Land Rover springs. If not for the quick step of Sonya's hand at the mouth, Mickey might have passed through with impunity.

"This is the toll bridge, Señor," said Sonya.

"Right. Now there's no costumes you want to get in and out of?"

Bud's eyes appealed to Sonya. She had vetoed his Lone Ranger mask.

"None," she replied.

"Boy, that saves time. You got no idea how long it takes for people to get in and out of clothes. What about instruments and such?"

"What kind of 'and such'?"

"You're astin' me? I dunno. There's people like to work with bananas, Philly cream cheese, pliers, knockwursts, dildoes, hammer handles. Some chicks like bicycle clips put on their tits. One person, a terrific gal I know, her bag is havin' the guy's meat on a plate which she spoon feeds inter the La Bonza, all the time makin' ummm that's delicious, yum-yums to the camera. See, it's your filim. I'm here to advise as well as shoot. Another guy of my acquaintance goes in for blindfolds, then binds the young lady's arms behind with leather straps." He scratched his head. "I mean there's as many ways of doin' this as there's types of food. Another instance is the bandage fanatic: a suit and cloaker out of Mineola. He and the chick bandage each other up and make music by unravelin' the gauze. Like mummies. Man, that's too much. Three filims, I done for him. So give it a think. It's your ball game."

Turning a definite Fresca lime during this, Bud pressed his ear against Sonya's mouth to record her whispered instruction as Mickey paced on the threshold asking how the weather was outside or if anyone had caught the late result from Hialeah.

"What about an earring, Mickey?"

"An earring?"

"All right if I wear a single one on my ear?"

"You could wear a hundred and ten and it's okay by me."

Sonya took out a longish gypsy loop from the dresser drawer, draped it coquettishly on her right lobe, gave her newly set wig an affectionate pat through the lacquer and said she was ready to go.

"No prelims, just right away with the action?"

No reply. He stood behind the camera, created a nought with thumb and index finger, signaling the start and finally calling:

"Action."

Rather tentatively and with genuine diffidence, Bud un-raveled the tie across his bathrobe. A pack of Raleigh Tipped dropped out of his pocket and he bent out of shot to retrieve the coupon. The camera whirr distracted him and he walked toward it, peering quizzically into the lens.

"Man, back off," Mickey shouted. "I'm shootin' neck and nothin' else."

"It's that damned noise," Bud complained.

"You know of a silent movie camera?"

"How'm I doing?" Sonya asked through the tangle of men, checking her legs to ascertain the symmetry.

"You, you're beautiful. It's Jasper which is lousin' up."

"I wish you wouldn't call me Jasper."

"Bu-ud, now you are flying off the handle."

"Temperament," said Mickey with a sneer. He repositioned

himself behind the camera. "Sonya, there's a perfect shot of the Suez, so give yourself a little tickle there and maybe we can get Warren Beatty over there to liven up. Give a few groans so's he can audio himself into the mood."

"Got it," Sonya replied.

"Action!"

Complete with audible sighs, moans, devilish passion, Sonya began a fond caress. Baby hiccups brought Bud, still on foot, closer to the head of the bed. Sonya's head revolved from shoulder to shoulder à la Gilda, the heroine she most admired from her early movie years. Bud backed out of his Hush Puppy loafers and drifted toward the eye of the vortex, still wearing his expression of perplexity.

"Beam in, Jasper," Mickey barked.

Caught apparently by surprise, Sonya's eyes fluttered open, revealed her shy Miss Stewardess smile, which had remained Daniel's perennially favorite photo, and gripped Bud's tool in the palm of her hand.

"Couple of herky jerks, Sonya, but don't shift off the piller 'cos we sacrifice angle."

Toying with the obviously abashed Bud, she failed to get any response. He hung limply like a thread over her pinky ring.

"I forgot to take off my marriage band," Sonya said, sitting up.

"I promise not to tell. Just keep goin', Sonya, you're doin' great. Jasper needs an assist." He spun around to the silent spectators. "I think he needs some sideline cheering, so that he can run it up."

The others vaguely cheeped "Come on."

Action stopped as Mickey deftly reversed the film. In a flash he was ready to go again. Bud gravely examined his equipment, but it failed to react even to the special pleading of Sonya's mouth.

"Have a shot at the Canal Zone. Could be that'll light the fire."

Bud mounted her and visuals gave way to hickey sucks. Flailing energetically, he still looked like a small scout lost in the forest.

"That's it. Kissin' is your story."

"He's romantic," Bunny informed him. "Thrives on love."

"A romantic. A lover. May be true, but the fact is he can't fuck for shit."

"That's enough!" Bud stormed from the tousled sack. "Just about enough of your jiving."

Mickey dropped his hands apologetically to his sides. A sense of frustration tugged down the corners of his mouth like dragging trouser cuffs. Snorting through a blocked nasal passage, Mickey broke the silence.

"I'm only tryin' to be helpful. But that's a cocktail frank, friend, and on filim it'll look worse and not like any R.C. Cola bottle."

"I disagree one million percent," said Bunny pushing forward, headlights asserted against Mickey's chest. In her supremely puissant training manner that combined enthusiasm with trust Mama, she bent on her knees and tenderly started to gulp Bud.

"Hey, that's not bad," Mickey exclaimed as Bud increased. "All the time we had a stock with growth potential . . . a real sleeper this Jasper. Pity you're not on camera."

Bunny led Bud by the emerging extension to the bed, and Sonya shifted over, flustered.

"Here's how," said Bunny as the camera whirr recommenced. Weaving and bobbing in the flighty style of the elusive Kid Gavilan, Bunny nurtured her long-standing partner.

"Startin' to look real respectable, Bud," Mickey said encouragingly. "Real good." Indicating Bunny, he continued: "Young lady, lift your fall back as you work, 'cos you're obscurin' the entire head of the gent's dick and we'll wind up with a lot of fall movement and no visuals. Sonya, keep on! Bud, slide over and see if you can jam her this time."

"So we are winging it," Sonya complained.

"He jams me!" Bunny shouted indignantly.

"Do we got a stiff wang in the house? It's lookin' real good. Okay lift up your dress. Jasper, head for the Dardanelles."

Walking surreptitiously past the side of the camera, Cal Beasley unzipped as he avoided cables. When he reached Sonya she yanked him into shot.

"Great. It's all straight stuff, but very good. The new gobbler's got to drop his pants or I'm shootin' belt loops."

"Hey, now just you all wait a minute," Phoebe protested, her voice a trail of sharp stones. "Cal, you cut it out with Sonya, you hear." She darted before the camera, pulled Cal's hair and slapped his face.

"Keep it up. We got a fracas."

"I've got a good idea to do the film man," Phoebe shouted.

"No dice," said Mickey. "End around, sister. Box to the camera and instead of waitin' your turn, stake a claim when one of the girls lets up. We'll finale with spunk firin' to the camera. Aim straight if you can."

Nearing eleven and with the film budget a matter of history, the contestants sat leisurely in the easy chairs in the living room smoking, sipping beer to relieve parched throats, catching the late news, the morning weather report. An air of conviviality and reconciliation was evident as Mickey packed to leave. Sonya, also behind schedule, patted her shiny nose with a powder puff, then went around the room saying good-bye. She took Mickey aside, gave him an until-we-meet-again cuddle which was to be at the beginning of February when the print would be ready.

"It turned out great," she said. "One thing I wonder, though, Mickey dear. Have you ever made one of these movies with people who are in love?"

"Love? That passenger didn't arrive here."

"Oh. Right."

iii

AFTERNOON
AT KIT'S

It seems more than complaisant
to provide gratuitously what may
afterwards be sold for profit.
—HART'S RULES

1

The snow trucks were already out spraying salt. Daniel drove cautiously over the pitted roads filling with snow that stuck like adhesive. Commercials jangling thoughts of eternal love wheedled the population to buy heart-shaped boxes of chocolates, quilts, and to watch for skidding cars. It struck Daniel as an unaccountable paradox that he should have been born on this day, which served only as an armed rehearsal for the rest of the year.

Alongside him, Gary continued clucking warnings as repetitious as the newcaster's interruptions about the freeze-up.

"Max and Norma for dinner with us is just looking for trouble. First thing you do is blast Norma's head off and cancel."

Out of the office he was an expert on life, and Daniel's struggling *consigliere.*

"Gary, stop noodging me."

"If you think God watches over cheaters, you're mistaken. What do you gain by having Norma join us?"

"It's more trouble getting out of it than not."

"I think you want to see what happens when the shit hits the fan. It may be your birthday, but it's also the anniversary of a massacre."

Daniel pulled smoothly into the curb at the Carriage Top. The doorman took his keys and greeted him with an abridged version of the weather report.

"Afternoon, Mr. Barnet. Motherfucking cold, isn't it?"

Daniel slipped him five bucks to make him forget. He waited for Gary, who made no move to come with him.

"I have to skip lunch. I'll see you at Kit's."

"I insist you have lunch with me."

"In the office you can insist all you like, but Marlene asked me to pick up your present. By the time she gets to town the store'll be closed."

He felt a sudden surge of antagonism toward Gary for asserting himself.

"Marlene wants to get me a present, she can pick it up. She's not making an errand boy of you."

"It's okay, it's for you, and I'm used to it," Gary said, brushing the snow from his muffler and hair. His opposition was made of such small change. "Now call Norma, and save your hard-on for Pauline and not your friends."

At the bar, a voice as musical and as sweet as an Italian tenor's *da capo* welcomed the last remaining innocents of the world into his lair. The Fly was alive and well, beaming confidently and of course:

INSTIGATING BUSINESS.

The first words he spoke to Daniel were: "I have just asked Henry Kissinger to join the board of Spigleman Industries. Mrs. Waterman, this is not he. This is a man of even more local importance. He has more money. This then is DANIEL BARNET."

Only The Fly could introduce him and pronounce his name in capital letters. Weaseled into a neck brace for a two-million-dollar whiplash case that was pending and which he'd thrust upon Daniel two years ago, The Fly cautiously turned his head.

"What's with the case?"

"They offered three hundred fifty bucks, take it or leave it."

"I told you to go with Melvin Belli if we wanted a big settlement."

"Irv, he won't take phony cases."

"Did you mention my name to him?"

With his tan perennially intact, Spigleman was wearing a plum-colored Ted Lapidus jumpsuit, and from his wrist a medley of gold bracelets dangled. He had obviously heard that hip-looking financial whiz kids were in vogue. He was whipping up new insane froths and creating his special havoc for a middle-aged lady supporting the largest collection of lunchtime diamonds Daniel had ever seen.

"Mrs. Waterman, just study the prospectus for a sec."

He cornered Daniel at the waiters' serving hatch.

"Irv, Henry Kissinger? Have a heart."

"Here's the letter I wrote him."

A piece of paper was thrust at Daniel.

"Can't call me a liar, can you?"

"He'll never reply to this."

"I should hope not."

"What happened with you and Pauline Bianco? The boys said you were dead . . . again."

He pushed Daniel to the side and hooted for the barman.

"Chas, keep feeding us with Dom. Daniel, I need you to back me up. Just a few minutes."

"What about Pauline?"

"She in town?" The Fly asked coyly. "My advice is to wear a sock on your dick. I did for weeks after she screwed me. Contusion of the urethra. Now get your mind off pussy for a minute. Momma at the bar has this yo-yo fag son who I sent up to Kit's the other day, and he busted out on me. Insulted all the guys. Unfortunately, I haven't got the energy to turn this trick."

"Know why I like seeing you, Irv? You make me feel normal."

"I want the kid's name on my company paper. *Waterman*, Daniel. The layette fortune."

Smiling honey, Spigleman with Daniel virtually handcuffed to one of his bracelets slithered back to Mrs. Waterman. He pulled something from her hands.

"We mustn't be greedy with my worry beads," he said.

"What about Miss Bianco, Irv?"

"We'll deal with that later. Have a look at the new Gulf and Western, Daniel."

It was called Spigleman Industries, and registered in Andorra.

"Where is Andorra?" Daniel asked.

"It's a crotch between Spain and Italy. You have to hold up a magnifying glass to find it, or have ten-ten vision."

"You really believe my Bernie will be happy working with you?" asked Mrs. Waterman. She had a wattled chin and appeared to have spent her entire life losing weight. She had succeeded, and, in place of fat, her loose skin hunted for vague fleshy definitions.

"I will straighten him out."

As Daniel scanned the death certificate Mrs. Waterman was also anxiously inspecting, Spigleman peered around the crowded bar for other familiar faces to assist him in this interment.

"Did Eddie Farber mention the abortion factories for juveniles we're building? Tip of the iceberg in that field. Daniel, from there it's a short step to cut-price hysterectomies and all-in curettage packages. So we don't have to rely on kids who get knocked up."

"Irv, you're the only one I know who banged Pauline."

The Fly wasn't listening. He was taking calls at the bar, and shrieking at people to buy or go short. Under Spigleman's umbrella, Daniel read of such new wonders as:

ECOLOGY
Two hundred thousand all-denominational burial plots.
PROPERTY DEVELOPMENT
Asbestos siding and shingles. Exclusive rights in Gulf States.
HEALTH SERVICES
Gynecology clinics.
BANKING AND CREDIT
Dental credit cards.
SPORTS PROMOTIONS
Exclusive closed-circuit TV rights to cockfights.

Daniel handed him back the paper, and said: "Irv, as always it's beautifully printed . . . but cockfights?"

"Daniel, your trouble is that you're rooted to the present. The gambling and breeding scope of this enterprise staggers the mind. I've got a plan for syndicating cocks like they do racehorses. I've invented a new sport. Just think of the violence and real blood on the screen. It can't fail to enlist huge spectator support and believe me, my friend, this is the moment to step in and take a big position for the Church's pension fund."

"Was Miss Bianco worth the two-hundred-dollar clip?"

The Fly got up very close to him, and Daniel backed off. He had inseminated his cheeks with a strangely smelling cucumber after-shave.

"I'd rather talk of prison than the Kiss of Death," Spigleman said with the suggestion that he was exorcising a demon. He'd done four months upstate in an asylum for stockbrokers after returning to the States from Paraguay. The Internal Revenue, at the instigation of the Treasury Department, had dropped their case against him, for The Fly had fingered three major heroin shipments for them. "In prison, Daniel, the worst thing is when you arrive and they strip you down, make you spread the cheeks of your ass and a guy looks in for a weapon search. Humiliation but no physical pain."

"Kit didn't mention pain to me," Daniel said.

"You know those guys that play jai alai and the speed and power they get on the ball when they whack the frontón. That's what happened to my balls."

Daniel recalled small, slippery fast Cubans climbing the sides of walls and hurling the ball from the basket racquet with such bewildering force that spectators followed the sound.

"Come on, Irv, it wasn't like that."

"Agony. You haven't seen me since Kit's Christmas party. Everybody thought I was in trouble. Health reasons."

"My information was that you owed Kit some money."

"That's a lie. Now get into Mrs. Waterman with me."

How could he explain, without hurting Spigleman's feelings, that he was now a millionaire, and pitching old ladies or stealing the inheritance of minors was behind him. He'd passed Spigleman by on his trip up the mountainside.

"Isn't she a lovely valentine?" Spigleman cooed of Mrs. Waterman. "She's stepping in as a director with young Bernard."

"If we ever find that boy . . ." Mrs. Waterman said, turning mother-suffering brown caramel eyes on Daniel.

"He's trying to find his feet," Spigleman explained. "I treat him like a younger brother."

Daniel wondered, was beginning to have doubts, about Spigle-

man. Perhaps this accounted for the unisex gear and the beads
and scents.

"Irv has been so helpful about the personal things that we
have become good and dear friends," she said as though this was
an early-bird item for a gossip column.

"Daniel was once my employee and now he's financial adviser
to the Church, and . . . Spigleman Industries."

"Our lives started to fall apart with the untimely death of
Bernie's shrink." She laid a gnarled veined hand on her heart,
and Spigleman lifted it off and clasped it on the bar. "When he
died, forty thousand dollars' worth of conversation went with
him."

"Once Bernard is on the board of S. I. he'll be too busy counting money and making deals to worry about shrinks. He needs to
be kept busy," Spigleman advised her. "Don't you agree, Daniel?"

"No question that he's building a future with S. I.," Daniel
noted deferentially. The Fly liked to be accorded enormous respect in front of patsys.

"Once we find him again. I have Burns Detectives searching
for him, Mr. Barnet."

"Where is he?" Daniel asked, shifting off the bar stool and
about to make a dash for freedom before Spigleman got him in
any deeper.

"I don't know. He was only back from Tangiers the other day.
Brought with him a friend. I have had aggravation from Bernie,
but this is entirely new. I should know from Morocco that they
have Arabs. I thought there, wallets, fine leathers, a handbag for
Mother. But when I'm left notes in French which I got to get
translated that an Arab pisher wants hair straightener, the end
of my patience has approached. In my co-op not even a Gentile
would consort with Arabs."

Spigleman rattled his worry beads and Daniel got up to leave.

"Irv, I'll speak to you at the office. It's a pleasure to have met
you, Mrs. Waterman, but I'll have to meet Kissinger at the airport."

"Before you go, Mr. Barnet, have a look at this. I found it in
the Arab's handbag." She held up a pair of tweezers. "What
would he use it for?"

"Roaches or . . . eyebrows. Conceivably both."

Daniel headed for the checkroom, but The Fly was still on his back and in fact blocking the entrance.

"Some friend you turned out to be."

"Irv, I'm legitimate, and the last time we had lunch I had to stand bail for you."

"I didn't pay you back?"

"That's not the point. I ask you for some form on a piece that Kit has been bending my ear on and you make me help you close an old lady."

"Okay. But I wouldn't go near Pauline, because the truth is that she fucked me into oblivion. I wasn't able to go near Magda for weeks. My tool was black and blue."

"How'd you explain it to Magda?"

"God did not give man a tongue for speech alone."

"You mean to tell me that you've been eating your wife for all this time?" Daniel poured the last drop of champagne, motioned for another, in a state of incredulity.

"Magda only wants to come, no questions asked."

"Wasn't she even curious that you're suddenly—"

"I told her I was on a cunt-eating trip."

"Have you been eating her regularly, over the years?" Daniel asked, for the exercise seemed to him not entirely devoid of merit.

"I think the last time was on our first date. I wanted to impress her and there wasn't much more I could do in bucket seats parked outside the New Yorker on Eighth Avenue after a Sunday Tito Puente danset. I didn't want to get too heavy. You know how it is. You meet a girl and if you whip out El Pedro immediately she might run for it, or call a cop. But nobody, and I mean nobody, says no to getting eaten; and I don't care if it's the ugliest guy in the world doing it. He's quiet, he's down there out of sight, *fressing* away, and the girl could think maybe it's a Steve McQueen or a Sinatra. I should have tried that on Pauline. Because she didn't just throw me a bang, either, she did an internal plumbing job on me that I didn't know if I had a gallbladder left."

The Fly had such delightful De Quincey notions about ass.

"Irv, you better get back. Your victim is still moving and showing signs of wanting to leave."

"You'll be at Kit's?"
"Where else?"

2

Surfacing from the jackknife dive into his past, Daniel, like a human dactyl, appeared to have the stress in the wrong place. His life had never been relieved by the desire to develop a grooved golf swing, by tennis of any description; no elderly, cracking, worn, stained handball gloves were to be found residing in abandoned trunks in the basement of his home, nor any warped squash racquet, cobwebbed from disuse, to remind him of the simple athletic joys of past sweats. His was a history devoid of games, and the trophies, while human, were the immaterial dockets of passing glandular secretions. No letter for athletic prowess would ever adorn his blazer, announcing his achievements to a world clued in to the symbols of sport. The code of the married cheater was necessarily enveloped in secrecy, for the world always condemned that which had to be bought; and the familiar needle—"he's got to pay to get it"—oversimplified, mocked the quest for diversity. And so the stale passage of time was elevated by heightened moments at Kit's.

Her place was just around the corner and he turned up First Avenue, walking with a measured gait. To avoid the barking wind, snapping at his legs like an angry dog, he kept close to the buildings and store windows, catching his face from different angles, so that the shifting composite of his features had the sharply ominous effect of a cubist study, revealing to him what was, what is now, but concealing the possibilities of what *would* be. Like most possessed men, Daniel was on the trail of himself, a preoccupation that he had never outgrown. From his mind, both Norma and Sonya disappeared, spumes of gray evanescent smoke.

Daniel became himself. The Night Rider, keeping an appointment with his other, separate self.

A pilgrimage of sorts attended by a habitual chaser. He re-

garded Kit's as a sanctuary. In search of variety at first, he began
to suspect that he was looking for something more. Some mystery
that combined an inconceivable emotion with the act of animals.
When Daniel reached the lobby, the Puerto Rican handyman
filling in at the door nodded sullenly in his direction. Daniel
waited endlessly for the wackily programmed elevators to come
down and heard his name called from behind. He recognized the
voice, and the food smell which clung like athlete's foot to John
Reno's person. A tall, wasted man, thinning on top, blossoming
at the sideburns, Reno's last name was a source of speculation
among Kit's regulars, who years before had christened him after
the capital of his principal human activity. Divorce. Married
seven times and liberated the same number, he balanced the fragile equation of his existence with biweekly visits to Kit's.

No one knew where or how he came up with the money, but
season in, season out, Monday and Wednesday, he appeared at
Kit's. A rumor among the wealthier clientele had it that Kit
charged him only twenty-five dollars a shot because he was well
behaved, occasionally took over the cooking chores, and never
occupied a girl for more than twenty minutes. He worked the
big commercial delicatessens as a meat slicer; moving from
Blarney Stone to White Rose, recently reaching his peak appointment as a career counterman at Deli City. He shook Daniel's
hand. The matter under his nails recorded the deaths of a million salamis, and the immersion into pickle barrels for the perfect cucumber had spotted his hands with bracken discolorations.

"So Daniel . . . ?"

"So John . . . ?"

"The spick at the frank counter never showed," said Reno.
"You'd think he'd give a call. Not those bastards. Probably smoking his eyeballs. He'll come in tomorrow all reefered up, burn
himself on the griddle and holler to the union for workmen's
compensation."

The elevator came and Daniel let Reno in first. He carried his
usual shopping bag, invariably a white Deli City job, perhaps to
allay suspicion, and conceal his practices, for the bags had never
housed a pastrami or purloined side of Nova, but Reno's equipment, without which Kit said he could not perform.

"I hear Kit's got a fresh supply of nookie in and she's changing
girls every few days 'cos the outtatowners got piss in their pockets

to spend and business girls can't make a dime unless they drag
ass into the Big Apple."

"You get engaged or married since Monday?" Daniel asked
with a sly smile, for all the regulars checked out Reno's status
whenever they saw him.

Reno's standard reply never varied,

"I orways leave the door open."

"Ready to go to the bat rack for a Louisville Slugger."

"Gun shy I ain't, Daniel. Seven times I been to the well.
Nothin' to be ascared of. But I smartened up. I get my licks
here."

Daniel knew that the claim was to be taken literally, since
Reno's *mishagas* lay in the area of slipper licking, several pairs
of which were carried in the shopping bag. He was the perfect
gentleman so long as no one showed him a slipper. Then the
tongue came out, a long bister-pink organ like a small flounder
belly with which he could miraculously touch the point of his
chin in a feat of lingual acrobatics. This skill had apparently not
been viewed favorably by the seven previous Mrs. Renos, who
cited him with monotonous regularity for mental cruelty. In a
confessional moment, when Detective Lieutenant Christopher
raised the salient point of his performing this novelty act without
it costing a deuce a minute, Reno said:

"I don't get no charge unless there's an ankle in the slipper."
Called upon to elaborate, Reno clammed up: "Let's change the
subject, guys. None of youse'ud be here if you didn't have problems with your old ladies."

As the elevator arrived, Reno said: "I hear Kit's considerin'
barring Spigleman after the stunt he pulled. Sendin' a faggot up
here which like sneers at us and calls me a 'square schmuck.' If
Chris dint bounce him I would of. No cocksucker can get away
with that. Fact is, Daniel, I think The Fly's getting like 'fem-
inate."

A violent antipathy existed between Reno and Spigleman,
which Daniel believed stemmed from Reno's disapproval of
Spigleman's financial plundering. The Fly always carried hundreds, Reno fins, and Kit in revered capitalist tradition catered
to the big spenders.

Daniel pressed the doorbell, heard Kit's slippers trounce the
uncarpeted hallway, then placed his face several inches from the

peephole for purposes of identification. Three bolts snapped, the chain was unlatched, and Kit, definitely on bourbon for the day and not vodka, reached up to give him his daily peck. Her breath smelled like one of the processes of sour mash on the way to becoming Jack Daniel's and rejected by the company's tasters as unfit. But somehow, wondrously, Kit had managed to conquer the heavy, lazy, lingering odor of pussy, employing some potion which he'd smelled only once before, in the elevator of the Ritz-Carlton in Boston. Both managements refused to divulge the name of the aroma, which suggested oleander, lemon, a hint perhaps of marjoram, a mystery as exquisite and haunting as the Sargasso.

"Did you see Spigleman downstairs?" Kit asked.

"I saw him at the Carriage."

"Kit, is it worth upsettin' the hard core of clients by puttin' up with that nut?"

"I love all my nuts, Reno."

Daniel draped an arm over her shoulder, tickled the back of her neck as he followed her. She had a sunny snub-nosed face, decorated with freckles on her forehead, three-inch-long dirty-blond hair over which a variety of wigs paraded on some rota basis. Today's was semi-auburn or thereabouts with a touch of carrot thrown in for highlighting.

Daniel passed through the living room, which subsisted on disconnected furniture accumulated during Kit's various moves and all indicating different motifs. The merchandise dozed on their feet, and the clientele were at their usual quarter and a half poker game. Greetings were called from the group, and Kit fixed Daniel a scotch.

Gary sat at the table squeezing his cards in the hope that he might lance out an ace.

"What took you so long?" he asked.

"I ran into Spigleman. When did you get here?"

"About one thirty. I ripped off a quickie. You know me," he said chuckling. "I came, I saw, I banged. By the way, there have been some calls from Switzerland. You want me to get back to the office now?"

"No, Jeanette'll catch me here if it's important."

Kit slapped the drink into his hand and ground a dropped ash into the carpet.

"Which one is Pauline?" Daniel asked.

"Doll, she's on her way."

"Kit, this is not one of your familiar stalls." He knew her well. The hangup specialist. The giver of Arpège to men with stiff schlaungs. "I thought she'd be here, ready to go."

"Daniel, I swear she called me. She was catching a plane from Baltimore. She's probably cabbing in from the airport right this second. I don't have to tell you about traffic."

"See what she makes us go through," Reno said. "She'll do anything for a buck."

"John, fix yourself a drink and kibbutz poker for a few minutes, please," Kit entreated him.

3

Something called Carmelita, a stacked Puerto Rican, smooched up to Daniel on the sofa. She came with Kit's highest recommendation: "Daniel, just while you're waiting, shoot into three" —the principal bedroom with bath ensuite—"with this kid. She drills assholes like she's looking for oil."

Sitting back, he observed the oil diviner, pink and healthy, then inched away. Carmelita wore one of those perfumes with brand names like Cada Hora which caught one coming and going, and made his nose tickle. And her voice—midway between the whine of a Chihuahua and malicious damage to a cello— went right through his bones. She edged closer to him, stifling him into a corner.

Kit would not tolerate arrant nudity, thus the girls displayed themselves in a variety of veily, diaphanous materials, or tight circulation-stopping trousers. Most were booted up to the femur as though shooting rapids or trout fishing were natural functions of their vocation. A redhead arrayed in a simulated-snakeskin vest, allowing fluid chest movement and expansion, had a decidedly familiar look to her. Another, with her blouse two sizes too small, had unbuttoned herself to permit air circulation to closeted regions.

Kit ran . . . well, a discreet, mannerly shop. She frowned upon necking, suggestive cuddling, kneesy, "positively no dancing," monitored loud radios and blaring phonos which might cause neighbor complaints. It was evident that a sense of graciousness had once adorned her life, then like a guest over-staying his welcome had been politely shown the door. Certainly Daniel had never seen actual *activity* practiced in the public rooms. Goosing was forbidden, scorned by all as a tasteless de-vice of schoolboys. But strictly speaking neither rule nor man-agement blandishment ever restricted freedom.

Slow comers, whom Kit referred to as "commuters," were never abjured to rush, since satisfaction and not speed harkened back to Kit's genteel past. Herself unfashionably alcoholic, she allowed the smoking of grass on the premises, and of course con-doned pills, which all the girls popped like jelly beans, but drew the line on hard stuff, fearful of her reputation and federal nosybodies who'd bust her if the mere suggestion of H came to their attention. Not exactly caviar and definitely not proletariat, Kit's had a certain classless, gamy atmosphere comparable to a ballpark, where the rich and those not so fortunate rubbed el-bows in a spirit of equality. The place, so Daniel thought, profited by the absence of pimps, a species of being Kit spoke of contumeliously.

Daniel finally rose from the sofa because Carmelita had en-twined her toes on his ankle and was surreptitiously hiking his trousers. Striding past Reno, Kit, playing a zone defense, inter-cepted him.

"Doll, why don't you go for a quickie?"

"Never was a fast-time guy, I'll sit it out until the star arrives."

She glowered at her twenty-one-jewel Bulova, the only present that she could honestly attribute to her old man, the classy former apprentice jockey, Leo Cardoza.

"Man, that chick Pauline . . . waaallll . . . I don't know why I put up with her. Girls calling me for a booking day and night and I've got to wait on her," Kit, entering her early after-noon slur, complained, then went back to the bar for consolation.

"I want greatness," Daniel said. "And for that you can't be in a hurry."

"Oh, all right." She sat down on a high bar stool, fingered the plastic tufting on the bar, and flicked a finger on one of the

nailheads. "Everybody's sittin' here, playin' poker and warmin'
their keisters."

Since her bitching was as unremitting as an arctic winter, no
one in the game paid heed to her except Detective Lieutenant
Frank Christopher (suspended) who had folded his cards and
joined Kit at the bar. After his starring role on TV at the Knapp
Commission Hearings, Christopher was detached from the bunko
squad and given a floating assignment in his precinct which
quite literally meant sitting on his ass. He hadn't blown the
whistle on his superiors, but he had made some fruitful contributions, nailing various patrolmen and cooping specialists to
the commission's cross. Now in limbo, Christopher spent his
days at Kit's on a freebie basis, banging whatever he wanted in
a reciprocal trade agreement with Kit. He kept the vice squad
off her back, and provided her with protection.

"How's the boy, Daniel?"

"Getting older, I'm thirty-seven today."

"Hear that guys?" Christopher bellowed, his beer belly jiggling as he turned. "Daniel's birthday. We got to party. Kit,
beer me."

Staring at him through the daze of bloodshot eyes, which she'd
been feeding with Murine as tenderly as a mother nursing an
infant, Kit became offended.

"Chris, you've knocked off I don't know how many six-packs
today. Man, this is not a saloon."

Christopher retreated to Daniel's side. On his battered
stubbled face there was a look of distress.

"When you're down," he appealed to Daniel, "everybody
wants to get in a kick." He scratched a sweating patch of
scummy Brillo pad that remained from his head of hair. "Daniel,
what I dream about, and every cop I know does too . . . is
making the big H bust. There it is, five million dollars' worth
of junk that Mr. Big is cutting up. You slam in through the
door. Hands up! Okay, you shit, against the wall. Then they
start in pleading. Deal. Let's make a deal. Ten percent of five
mil is half a mil, so I settle for that. I'm a rich guy. I get myself
an account in Switzerland with its own numbers. Man, my
numbers, 'cos they don't tell anybody about the numbers except
the party concerned. How can you say no to that bread? Impossible. I got fifty thou to lay by for my boy's college. I'm a

big shot in the market. He becomes a lawyer. I get myself a top-flight piece of ass. Shack up with it for maybe a year. Bang-bang-bang. I'm tireless. I never stop. My dick's like granite." He pressed it against the bar, working himself into a hysterical sopping-wet rage. "And this one is givin' me a hard time about a fuckin' six-pack."

"Chris, if you're through talking to Daniel about your mighty dick, maybe you'll sit down and play," said Guy Rabinowitz, a pale straw of a man who had five eyeglass shops, and was reputed to have made big green through shylocking. "I'm hoping, Kit, dear, that the name Spigleman that you brought up from the back of your throat like phlegm is not appearing. Because if so, he gets an ice pick in the balls for sending up that *faigle*. No one, not even God, refers to Guy Rabinowitz as a piece of snot. Especially when it carries a handbag and has the breath of a poison pen letter. You hear me?"

"I hear you, Guy. But there are things from years ago between Irv and me. And if he needs me, I can't turn my back."

"I started with him, Guy," Daniel said, "and I couldn't kick him either."

"Ooooh, a conspiracy. I might pack in this place and find myself a massage parlor with normal customers," said Guy. He wiped his glasses with a pink lint-free cloth which gave his name and the addresses of his shops, then directed his attack on Daniel. "I'm really surprised at you, Daniel. Going to bat for that motherfucker. I thought you were a friend of *mine*."

"Guy, what do you want me to do? Irv bounces up and he deserves encouragement."

"Never had a job, that lousy creep," said Reno bitterly. "I been working since I was twelve. He's a con man and he's screwed everybody up here."

"Not you," Daniel said. "Me from the old days he still owes eight-nine million. But you he hasn't hurt."

"My head is fucking exploding," Kit shouted above the din. "I'm runnin' a place of business, and not some gambling den."

The latter remark Anthony Palazallo took as a personal affront to his profession. Frequently on the telephone to garner his action, the bookmaker was a client of long standing and a major spender.

"You want I should take my custom elsewhere, Kit?" he said

threateningly. "Plenty of joints in town that'd be glad to have me there."

"Tony, what are you gettin' in the act for? I didn't mean you."

"Well, Kit, spell it out in future," he replied, buttoning up his shirt as though his departure might be imminent. "Now who's in the game?" he asked, washing the cards. "Chris, you playin'?"

Christopher scratched his belly through an open buttonhole in his shirt.

"How's my credit?"

Rabinowitz held his nose and said: "From hunger."

Lodging a further appeal with Daniel, Christopher wrapped a gorilla-like arm around his shoulder, and rolling his head in a circle to free some kink, he slapped a flat palm on the bar, which made Kit jump.

"Hey, you scared me!"

"How do you like this, Daniel? These guys are s'posed to be friends and they're freezin' me out of a quarter and a half game."

Daniel slipped him a fresh twenty. It was worth it to get the arm off his shoulder and the breath out of his face. Christopher, with a broad smile adorning his tobacco-stained teeth, sat down heavily at his place in triumph. Most of his time was spent wheedling five here, ten there, thus twenty from Daniel without a hard-luck story seemed to him a victory of heroic stature.

"That's good money thrown after bad," said Palazallo, who mercilessly needled Christopher into tyro poker errors. "This lard-ass can't play with four aces."

Daniel's attention wandered to the other room. Five girls. Kit's cornucopia of pussy all performing various ministrations to their person. Carmelita was painting her toenails an opalescent pearl; another's mind was hooked into the thrill-a-minute of Matt Helm; another occasionally slotted in a word in *Dell's Fourth Crossword Puzzle*; a fourth daintily picked the burned buns off a mound of greasy, cold burgers which had that stomach-chilling appearance of simulated meat used for displays in slum grocery shops; the fifth, the redhead who had struck a familiar chord in Daniel's gash records, was tuned into the afternoon NBC serial, nibbling at her fingertips as the aging bag who played the hero's wife admitted infatuation with the neighborhood G.P.

The girls inspired a certain admiration from Daniel for having had the guts to *choose* their particular form of emptiness. Not entirely contemptible, inasmuch as Romance, like Civil War Georgia, had seceded from their lives. The day of hard luck stories which plucked at heartstrings was over for good. Kit's handmaidens screwed vocationally and without complaint. A hard, brutally ugly world, it at least possessed the virtue of honesty. By thirty, if they hadn't quit before, they'd be worn out and probably slinging hash in a diner, involved in petty crime, or connected to a married fifty-year-old who didn't want to rock the boat out in suburbia, but frankly, candidly, and perhaps blamelessly, could no longer make it with the fifty-year-old lady sadly going through her changes and unable to dye, conceal, or pretend that the silver threads among the gold landscaping the tunnel of love was anything more than encroaching, icy, old age. So the men, even the reluctant ones, cheated.

Kit had begun to stagger, reaching the midway point in her daily booze-up. A few stumbles and drinks later, she'd be well on her way to drinking herself sober, a singular cyclical process which attested to her recuperative powers and probably an immortal liver which she was bent on destroying with a ceaseless bombardment of alcohol. She was trying to forget . . . precisely nothing. Drank from habit, the unutterable boredom of a life of confinement. Almost her only contact with the outside world was over the telephone when she'd ask clients what the weather was like. She received her clothes by mail after spotting an ad in the daily papers. Delivery boys brought food.

When the spring weather came, she'd open the terrace doors, slap some baby oil mixed with iodine on her face and swallowing ten-ounce glasses of gin and tonic eventually . . . of course, pass out. In a sense, she disapproved of climate of all kinds. A couple of evenings a week, after midnight closing, she'd get out with Leo. Never for air or shop windows. Just directly down to the underground garage, slide into the passenger seat of her white Eldorado Caddy, and remind Leo to prop a pillow under his behind so that he could see the road. And off they'd zoom into the night to one of the dike bars downtown where she held court in a world of jiving, drunken bimbos, the hunters and prowlers of female society.

Sometimes the field trips had a practical value and she'd scoop up some lost kid, rescuing her from the smothering arms of a leather-jacketed bull; ask her to come by one afternoon for a drink. Then the inevitable process of "turning out" the girl would be accomplished in the course of a few days' training. The specialist wheedled, cajoled, tricked, promised big bread to these young bust-outs, since she had the unshakable conviction that lesbians made the best hookers. The intimation that a svelte young piece really dug chicks whispered into the ear of an up-tight client yielded astonishing results, and the guy would stand there and hem and haw because eighty dollars for a possible half hour—if he lasted that long—stretched him out on a clothesline.

"I'm not pushin', doll," she'd say collusively, "but, man, this kid is the most incredible switch-hitter I've come across in years."

The client always gulped his drink, real quick, then would excuse himself to go to the head: to count his cash.

"Like I'm a little short, Kit. Seventy is all I can come up with."

Noting the pleading croak in his voice, Kit would respond: "Okay, this once, but don't be forever. I'm doin' this as a special for you." The regulars were never subjected to this technique.

The phone rang and Kit irritably left the bar stool.

"I'm payin' that fuckin' service two hundred a month and when I tell them I got a full house and to message me, why won't they listen?" she asked herself.

She picked up on the tenth ring, moaned to the service operator, then wrote down a number.

"No more calls," she insisted. "Except Miss Bianco. I don't care who it is." She dialed, asked for a room number, then went into her routine.

"Charlie, doll, when'd you get in? Uh-huh, I know. I hear the picture business is dying a death. I saw your name on TV the other night. Man, it's been a cold one. Sure I'd like to get to the Coast. Who knows, maybe next month. I've got winners. Hang on, I'll see what's cooking." She muffled the phone, examined the room. "Big tits, he wants. Who'd like to hit the Plaza for a *short time*? Carmelita. Okay. But listen, this guy is Mr. Bullshit himself, so get the money first because then he'll come on with flying out to the Coast, all the movie crap. He's got four kids and he's only a shit-ass associate producer on a series, so yes him till he's blue in the face, but collect first!"

Releasing her hand from the mouthpiece, she continued, staring at the ceiling.

"Charlie, my love, are you still aboard? Great. Now, I'm sending you over the private stock. This girl's not really in the business. You saw the Miss World contest?" She knew he hadn't. "She represented one of the South American countries. Came in fourth . . . Which one?"

She waved a hand at Daniel. "Clue me a spick country, Daniel." Daniel wrote a name down on a cocktail napkin.

"It's Costa—right. Costa Rica. Coffeeville. What do you mean, is she built? You asked me for a brick shithouse and that's what I'm sending. It's one dollar," she concluded.

Daniel heard the man griping at the other end. The rates of hookers on the phone were always given in cents. A dollar indicated a price of a hundred dollars.

"What do you mean it's too much? You're here on expenses or else you wouldn't be at the Plaza, Big Spender. You want to come by, then it's fifty cents. This girl's got half a dozen dates lined up. Put your hand in your pocket and see what you can find. Listen, yea or nay, I'm packed out. You can see her seven thirty here if you want. You got calls? Whose fault is that? Doll, shit or get off the pot. You're tying up my phone. I gotta run. You think a dollar is high for Miss Costa . . . a girl who's only been in business for a month. It's like a virgin, tighter than a frog's ass. Twenty minutes. Yeah, I'm looking forward to seeing you too. Bye."

Rubbing her ear with the palm of her hand, Kit addressed the hussy *mickvah*.

"My ear's numb from talkin' to that jack-off . . . bustin' my scullions. Hustle it, Carmelita, and make sure it's a hundred in cash. This comedian could have traveler's checks, but tell him to cash them himself. They might be stolen and I don't want to take a fall for somebody else's wallpaper. I made that scene once. Dryin' out with kooks on the funny farm as an accessory. If he wants to go twice which I doubt very much because he's a single shot and not a Daisy repeater, lock him into a half-price before you get started. Two shots at one five o. You know, strictly between the two of you and what Kit doesn't know . . ."

She rejoined Daniel at the bar. He was quietly smoking a joint which Gary had tossed to him.

"It's like I'm running a luncheonette with a send-out business," she said topping up her glass with four fingers of bourbon. "How's that wife of yours, Daniel?"

"Still a bum lay."

"Blame yourself," she said sniggering. "I don't eat all this women's lib garbage, but a man has to pave that garden or else it gets overgrown with weeds, and somebody comes along who doesn't mind pulling them out."

"Oh, you're into philosophy."

"Me, never. I bless marriage every day. Who is my business? Married men. The single guys are out bashing the married women."

"I could never get that lucky," Daniel said.

For the life of him he couldn't remember the redhead or what if anything she'd ever done for him. Trouble was after so many years of Kit's everybody started to look familiar.

"Kit, who's the redhead?"

"Pamela. I don't know if you've seen her before."

"Was she here last year?"

"Could be. You were going through one of your screwball scenes about this time last winter. Man, Leo and I prayed: when is Daniel going to be normal again and come back to the club?"

He nodded. Quite accidentally and out of the enervating tedium of coming each day to Kit's, he had sought a little something out of the ordinary. A little dangerous diversion. For a month he'd been half of a Swinging Couple.

"Now I remember . . . Pamela and me in Pompton Lake."

No intention of persuading either Norma or Sonya to get into such a scene. In fact if they were prepared to accommodate him, it wouldn't have had such a tangy flavor. Through a publication devoted to keeping couples together, Daniel had fallen into several wife-swap clubs. He himself would bring along one of Kit's pieces for a dollar, introduce the girl as his wife, and sample the actual goods while Mr. John was taking his pleasures with a pro.

"I almost got shot because of her. She gave him her phone

number and offered him a cut-price rate and said she was actually a business girl."

The husband had nearly fainted and pulled out an unloaded pistol while Daniel had run for cover behind his car.

Kit gave him a schoolmarmish slap on the wrist.

"You, Daniel, are always in the market for trouble."

"Why? He thought he was screwing my wife until she squealed."

"But you were whaling his for real."

"No difference."

"One day, you will find out . . ."

Daniel glanced furtively at Pamela, still locked into the TV, which had altered to Graham Kerr, galloping through the morass of fudge cake. The alchemy of late afternoon recipes. Wasn't the Philosopher's Stone within the grasp of all housewives?

4

Breezing through his second afternoon joint, a meretricious concoction of black resinous hash laced with opium, sealed with camel shit and attributed to Nepal, further compounded with an admixture of Congolese grass, resulting in a BOMBER, Daniel compiled a mental list of his transactions with Kit. The manufacturer of the device, none other than Pamela herself, who on their date had scorned working and smoking combos, had now evidently altered her stance. In the intervening year several hundred dicks had doubtlessly been shoved in her face, making niceties of behavior—her procedures—a form of entirely dispensable hypocrisy. Seizing his elbow, she said:

"Don't hog it, man." Then leaning over the bar top, her breasts splaying the stippled salt and pepper Formica surface, she gave him a quizzical glance which succeeded in marrying invitation to interest. She spread-eagled her elbows, so that one partially rested on his wrist. "Don't I know you from somewhere?"

"Once upon a time we did a number together." He could just

see her reeling wide-eyed through an inventory of lays which was never up-to-date, pondering while toking the joint to cold ash. She pointed it in his direction to collect a fresh light, and shook her head dimly to activate the stagnant pond of her collected memories. The habitual lethargy to which this process had fallen victim strangled the exertion, and only the fuzzy, mucky silt, like fish waste, rose to further encloud the recognition. "I bet you don't even remember the name you were using then."

"What happened?"

"A man tried to shoot me."

This admission drew a negative response, a moan of dismay, and a reckless scratching of her forehead which dislodged one of her hastily glued phony nails.

"Don't worry, they're always falling off," she said to allay what she imagined to be his concern. "Shoot you? Because of me?" she asked, but did not remember.

A smile uplifted the down-turned cocksucking mouth, the top lip of which, supple in his recollection, had been worn down by chronic head. Like a kid's first arithmetic soap-eraser, attrition had dwarfed it, and her God-given stocks, never again to be replenished, literally wasted away before his eyes. The commerce invariably had this effect on the veterans, wiping their minds clean as a kindergarten blackboard on the first day of school. Amnesia was, Daniel knew, one of the occupational hazards of the game, for volume destroyed the tracks of experience. The client was no more fortunate. Who wanted to remember?

"Why don't we make up for lost time , , , errrrrrr?"

"Daniel."

That still didn't help, but put them back on a first-name basis. A facile intimacy to which he charitably contributed. The figure still retained a certain buxom sinuousness, assisted by a ridiculously small waist which created a sense of hyperbole in the fixtures. Classically proportioned, no, an eyeful in a badly lit crowded bar, jammed into a skin-tight sheath and camouflaged by cigarette cumulus would be the extreme limit of her definition. She was past it at Kit's, for daylight abused her, inciting contempt, forcing the buyer to make comparisons from which she could hardly benefit. Middle-aged at about twenty-seven, her natural splendors squandered, she might make it bar-hustling for a few more years; then if she continued, she would land out on the street whistling for rough trade. Another instrument for muggers to practice upon.

"Why don't we go for a while?" she asked, handing him back the joint. Her mouth curled in a hopeless smooch, her tongue unleashed as though from a spring flared around the upper lip in her hit parade number of arousal. Trouble was, it had stopped working, and she knew it.

"I've got a date with Pauline."

She clutched his sleeve.

"So what's wrong with while you're waiting?"

"I'm not ready right now."

In the business, anger compensated for little, and high-strung fillies were shipped out real quick to the massage parlors. Blowing up at a John upset the equilibrium, gave guys the shits when they heard a raised voice. Could be them next. The shots were called with mellifluous whispers, and hard-noses could wait till doomsday for another booking. Since there were many stables going, all the girls relied on the good word . . . references! A shit list from Kit, and it was pretty cold outside. Pam stifled the rejection, giggled inanely, wallowed in it plaintively, determined to maintain her reputation as an easygoing, no-trouble chick. Daniel, minus his name, had been pointed out to her on entering: Kit's pet. He dropped green like piss, was a good guy to know in a jam, once helping Kit to get a bust quashed. She owed him . . . and the instructions were, not to fuck with him.

"I think Guy's ready," Kit told Pam, as the optometrist, frail-looking, but forceful, cast an aerial view around the room to gauge the topography that suited him.

"I'm ahead seventeen, Daniel. Not bad for two hours, huh?" he said slipping next to Pam's unguarded flank, and resting his pointed chin on her shoulder. He'd probably go with Pam, Daniel thought, knowing the eye man loved those smooth old B-29's. The young stuff wore him down too fast. Daniel considered recommending her to Guy, backing up any claim she might dare offer.

"This is a beauty, Kit," said Guy of Pam, fingering a tuft of hair as though an authority on rinses, dyes, tints. "Red's my favorite color."

"Mine, too," Pam agreed, cuddling his chin in her fist, then yanking it gently.

"Are we going to do wicked things?"

"They call her Wicked Pam," Kit said, helping to bait him. "She's a specialist, Guy."

"Oooooh, a specialist. A specialist in which field?" he asked, faintly beginning to pant, his specs jostling down the septum.

Through closed teeth, Pam's tongue slowly and lithely emerged as though waking from a winter sleep and greeting the green world of spring.

"Ahhhhhh. Linguistics," said Guy. "One of my favorite subjects." Hooking an arm into hers, nothing genuinely suggestive, he eased up his glasses and peered down to chart the depth of the gorge which held an intrinsic fascination for him. "That is architecture, no, Daniel?"

"You like it, Guy . . . ?"

"I was there," Gary piped up. "It's AT & T."

"What's not to like?"

Pamela turned from one to the other. The fact that her fate for the next thirty minutes was hanging in the balance moved her not at all, reduced curiosity to a yawn. Either/or. Both? Nothing apparently could interest her less.

"Give it a draidle and discover which side it stops on," Daniel advised.

Aware perhaps of some obscure blood lineage, a spiritual consanguinity, Pamela fueled the fire, by suggestively taking the arms of both men at once.

"I've fucked for money and for pleasure. One and the same thing. Had orgasms both ways, so what the hell's the difference?" she demanded in rhetorical fashion. "And that's no question. Made it with two brothers together and you know what they were doing? Fighting out the old squabbles about who was the favorite son. It's all battles, about old ground that nobody really gives a crap about . . ." she faded into speechlessness, having had her disconnected say. An old hand at creating appetite where there was none, she detected a more pronounced and elongated attentiveness from the optometrist.

"So both ways you've come?" Guy said with an air of speculation.

She had struck the golden, *lost,* chord. The suggestion, nay, the possibility of bringing a business girl to the throbbing rapids of unsimulated orgasm, replete with ecstatic groans, screams, if possible . . . wildness, often aroused a potential client, enabling him to visualize cliffs of madness.

"Do you swear . . . like curse when you're getting your rocks off?" Guy asked, tamping a cigarette on his wrist, warming up to the subject and indicating the modus operandi of his sexual apparatus.

"I'm like an echo chamber," Pam suggested, not slow when it came to picking up signals.

"Could you give me an example?" Guy asked, almost tilting on her shoulder for support. A practitioner of parlor pseudo-analysis, he appeared to be compiling mental notes, blocking out a student outline which he might develop into a disquisition.

"Only in performance," Pam, a real pro, replied.

"Not even a hint?" He was persistent, a wheedler who temporized on the trivia of female confidences. "A for instance, please."

"When you give it to me, you'll hear all about it."

Guy did a fast stock-taking in the other room, Richter scaling the vocal quality of the other girls. Without ceremony, he abandoned Pam for a snoop. Carmelita ensconced in a billowing fur that cried weasel to the observant re-entered.

"He woo not go a secon' time, Keet."

Guy did not enjoy the exchange with a blond collegiate type who made a testy accusation about Carmelita. Obviously her bag was candor.

"Oh, she's back. A few million farts found a home in this sofa after she left."

"I reesen' tha . . . Keet. *Ella es una hija de puta . . . una chica sucia,*" she cried as swallowed tildas flayed the air. "She jealous on me."

"Now cut it out, you two," Kit said stepping between the two rabbit punchers. "This shit's bad for business, so unless the both of you want to disappear, shut up!"

Guy retreated to the bar, where the ladylike and demure Pamela lowered her eyes.

"You don't talk like that, do you?" he demanded.

"Love words only."

He decided to have a short conference with Daniel at the

expansive bay window which overlooked First Avenue. Sipping a whiskey, he indicated a certain hesitancy in choosing.

"So, expert, what's your opinion? You give her a rap before? Gary's opinion is not so strong."

"Your life's not exactly hanging in the balance. You don't like her, then Kit'll send someone else in . . ."

Making sense to Guy. He nodded sagaciously. He relit the dead joint, provisionally took a few drags, restrung the Ace Bandage on his right wrist, permanently sprained, which made going to the cash pocket an arduous form of navigation and was invariably accompanied by chilling Baskerville yelps—"I can't bend it, it's like paralyzed"—and creased his features into a series of ashen grimaces. Kit's advice—"Turn southpaw, Guy" —brought him to the point of incoherent babble, for the innuendo was clear to everyone and Guy didn't like to consider the possibility that the world was hip to him and the wrist.

"Across the street, nations are deciding the fate of the world," said Daniel, pointing at the U.N., "and you're in conflict about a hump?"

"Hollering, Daniel . . . a *schrier* that makes the walls come tumbling down is what I want. Turns me on."

"I don't think Kit'll go for auditions."

"That's the trouble. How will I know? Not until it's too late and I'm locked in the playground. Once I had a screamer" —he kissed his fingertips like Charles Boyer testing a vintage for a sycophantic sommelier while Hedy through the gauzed lens cracked a smile—"she was like an Yma Sumac. She could crack a watch crystal."

"Fascinating." Guy's *schpiel* had gone on unabated for all the years Daniel had known him: the quest for the perfect pair of lungs. "Ever wonder why this is your particular craziness?"

The limp wrist flexed, looked like it possessed the latent power of Rod Laver's, as Guy pondered repressed matters—the Rabinowitz Primal Scream, here and there a Guyish trauma culled from his mental archives—which accounted for his compulsions. As he puffed away, the U.N. gradually fogged before his straining eyes.

"My mother," he said at last, as thoughts collided in his angular head. "From the early days she was always screaming: 'Guy, what're you doing so long in bed?' No matter where I was whatever I happened to be doing or thinking, I was doing it too long for her. In the old days, and believe me, Daniel, I was a normal kid and I'm not ashamed, when I'd get a new copy of the *Police Gazette* and get into bed for a long, drawn-out, relaxed read, she'd be hollering something at me. I could spend hours looking at the pictures of girls and when she'd barge into my room, what could I do but say that I was reading about the new evidence that they had about Hitler night-clubbing in Argentina and dancing *frailachs* in Buenos Aires while Jews the world over suffered and that my mission in life was to get there and find him and bring him to justice. I spent my adolescence with my peter locked in the center fold of that magazine an inch or two from Hitler's nose as he was galloping through the pampas to his vacation place. My Wilbur's still got scars from where the center fold's staples stabbed it. All the time my mother is yelling at the top of her lungs: 'Study, Guy, or you'll wind up a nothing.'

"When *Night and Day* took over from the *Gazette,* I had a love affair with Eve Meyer, the woman with the world's most perfect tits. Issue after issue, I suffered with her, sweating it out until inch by inch we got into basic tit. I almost had a heart attack—I did develop a six-month murmur—when I actually saw her nipple. The size of an English Rose under my magnifying glass. I think I must have dropped five hundred loads on Eve which was no easy matter when I heard my mother screeching: '*Bulvan, fercocked paskudnyak,* you'll *gay in drerd* if you don't know Civics.' "

Indicating a longish parcel of cheekbone, meticulously barber-shaved and a sideburn carrying the lingering suggestion of Alberto VO⁵, Guy as though entreating imposed an examination on Daniel.

"See, my skin's clear. In those days I was a mass of pimples . . . my eye muscle every minute gave a twitch like I was a lunatic. Still shrieking at me, my mother took me to Dr. Greenspan, the neighborhood sadist who was supposed to be a skin specialist. He put these dark goggles on my eyes with an elastic string that cut into the back of my head and spent fifteen minutes a week burning my pimples off with an X-ray machine while I cried from agony and my mother yelled from the waiting room to lay still."

"You thrive on noise," Daniel said.

"The sad tales of Guy Rabinowitz," he said with clucking tongue. "For my wife I need sounds of explosions. I got this old Hi-Fidelity record which when they first came out with Hi Fi, they used to peddle for a buck. It's got Niagara Falls, a dam bursting, an atomic bomb going off, so that's why it's important, understand, that I sus out a true-blue screamer."

Sidling over to Pam, now spent, his lavender shirt, with the Swank cuff links, darkly stained under the armpits, Guy nodded reluctantly, ready to proceed, in spite of the fact that Pam had not cut a demo so that he could determine if she was chart material or not. Giving Daniel an iron-clad birthday handshake and an affectionate back tap, he said:

"Sorry I lost my temper before, but this is a natural preserve, and Irv had no business sending that yo-yo up here." He goosed Pamela. "I'm taking a chance on love."

"Guts, Guy," Daniel replied.

Taking in a big pot on which he had called both high and low, Christopher got up to give Daniel his money back but intimated a certain ambivalence.

"I'm thirty ahead. Your twenny brought me luck. I could give it back now, but if it's okay with you, I'd like to hold onto it till I bust these bullshitters out."

"Hang onto it," Daniel said, walking toward Kit's office, a table-seat combination that housed the telephone and her orange-jacketed looseleaf binder to which she was applying fresh reinforcements. Head cocked to one side, she covered the mouthpiece.

"It's Pauline, doll. She's stuck at La Guardia because the cabs are packing groups in before they'll move into the city."

"Tell her to wave a fin at a cop and hustle her ass in," Daniel said turning his watch in Kit's face, revealing three thirty. "I'll reimburse her."

After repeating Daniel's instructions to Pauline, Kit apologized.

"Sorry to hang you up, but what can I do? I can't count on anybody." Tilting an ear to the bedroom in mystification, Kit said, "What's that noise?"

"Guy," Daniel explained, "is getting his rocks off."

"Why does it always have to be in stereo?"

In attempting to elude the complications of swinging a chick, the romance of steak dinners, weaving in and out of discotheques, glad-handing headwaiters for a numero uno table, he had strayed into another form of iron-clad predicament—the total unreliability of Kit's soggy cheese puffs.

"Don't excuse me for saying this, Kit," he said sharply and with ill-concealed exacerbation, "but you're turning unreliable."

"Me!" Her Joan of Arc protest. She looked over at the poker table for a helping hand, a rebuttal. When none was forthcoming, and, on the contrary, Tony Palazallo's added confirmation:

"You could say that again, Daniel. I been waitin' three hours for my special, too . . ." Kit's face—usually masked in indifference, her standard reaction to complaints—turned a chalky white. It appeared that the insurrection was gaining advocates.

"I control transportation and traffic? Have a heart, Daniel."

"Mine's not flying in," The Pal said angrily. "I been at this location since one thirty!"

"Kit, what's happenin'?" Leo demanded. "You got a call out for Tony or what?"

"Someone's coming over from Max's on the West Side. Everything is my fault that you guys have weirdo tastes?"

"You still screwing pigs, Tony?" Daniel asked.

"Only my wife. And she don't really count. She's too damn pretty."

The Pal, a small burly man with a pasta gut, carried with him the bouquet of clams oreganato, a scowling beefy face with a blue-black shadow and the strangest obsessional appetites of all of Kit's clients. As a consequence, he was the most difficult and finicky. Some manic process of reversal had tuned him to a band wave, so special, so beyond the ken of imagination, that he was an object of astounding interest to Daniel.

Before Kit began catering to him, he used to hang around mission houses, women's correctional institutions, in order to pick up the most slatternly drunk of all. Just as a man fusses over a woman's demeanor, her figure, to insure that she is the closest blend of his ideal characteristics, so The Pal inverted these principles of selection.

The dirtier, the grimier, the girl was, so Palazallo's excitement was heightened. Louse-infested scrubbers, girls lassoed out of rivers after failing suicide were his special province. The increase of narcotics addiction among women fell as manna from heaven for his exemplary ($- \times - = +$) algebra. The more beat, straggly-haired, track-marked a girl was, the more pronounced her state of dereliction, verging on the subhuman, the more he was prepared to cough up.

He was, Daniel thought, the sexual geek incarnate, closer than any man he'd met to the total and pristine animal state. Thriving on coprological delusion, he existed in the ambivalent forms of family man and alter-ego wolfman, operating a book for years in the silk stocking district of New York, residing over the bridge in Fort Lee as a concerned paterfamilias. Daniel marveled at the balancing act that frenetic split demanded. For The Pal, Kit literally had to dig deep.

Checking out his attitudes regarding necrophilia one day, Daniel, utterly enthralled, asked point-blank: "Ever screw a dead woman, Tony?"

A Garcia y Vega cigar was the natural furniture of his mouth, and he teased it from side to side like a thermometer which had been forgotten. When the cigar was absent, The Pal banged Planters nuts into his face from a closed fist.

"No, but like everybody else, I've thought a lot about it," came the harmless reply.

Exquisitely couched in a bayou of depravity of which he was not aware, he seemed to Daniel an incorruptible specimen of savagery in a world of straphanging, compromising conformists. Kit had promised him a real beast for the afternoon, and he looked contemptuously at the attractive partners she had organized for the daily festivities.

The Pal had been absent, oh, perhaps four-five months when a virulent outbreak of the mysterious N.S.U. had been traced to him. Like foot-and-mouth disease in Aberdeen, Kit's flock of regulars had been threatened with decimation. To prove that it was not him, he had sprung several of the main hunting party (Reno, Christopher, and Guy) to a group treatment by Dr. L. L. Lefkowitz, the East Coast's Mr. Skin, an eminent syphilologist, whom The Pal kept on a retainer.

"All they got is herpes simplex," The Pal pronounced, a version of subclap and a second cousin to shingles which the adept Lefkowitz claimed was still incurable and treated like diaper rash with Lassar's paste and a 2% solution of gentian violet, resulting in the unholy trio for a month, flashing purple shafts upon which a design of suppurating dingleberry muffins had begun to harden. They were instructed by Kit to employ gossamer Trojans, which she had purchased on their behalf.

Oddly enough The Pal remained immune to both plague and disease, having worked up some extraordinary defense to communicable viruses and bacteria which defied all extant medical theory.

In an aside, Christopher informed Daniel, upon the completion of the examination: "Them bugs is ascared shit of The Pal," which Daniel took to be gospel.

This everyday aspect of behavior was, Daniel realized, the very core, gristle and sinewy grit of human life. They disgusted most people, but somehow not him. He was firmly convinced that knowledge and truth ennobled and that he was a better man for having learned the revelations of sewers.

Under a meringue of black curls and deeply tanned from some Caribbean winter wonderland, Herself, the mythical Pauline Bianco, emerged from Kit's darkened corridor like a Pacific sunrise. She wore a pastel mink coat, high beige suede boots, and her face had the lustrous candescence of intelligence applied to experience.

"When I was leaving the plane, the steward asked me the usual nitwit question about enjoying my flight and I said: 'Baby, if an airline could ever fuck itself, I hope yours is the first one to try.' Leo, shove the Ammies in the Frigidaire."

Daniel gave Kit a slow nod. No question about it, she was worth waiting for. He found something admirable in the pouting, arrogant truculence of Pauline, who did not even bother to size up the goods in the other room, heading straight for Daniel.

"I hope you're worth the trouble," she said to him, offering him a snort of coke, which she unfurled from a dainty Irish linen handkerchief.

Her drink was a quasi-dry blend of Christian Brothers California champagne, and Kit had laid in an ample supply. For once, Daniel saw her really activated, hustling out the long-stemmed tulips, like a topless pro slinging booze on commission. But moving. Leo also got off his can, emptied ashtrays, gave the bar a wipe-down, scooped up the two decks of Tally Ho, shoved them into a sideboard drawer.

"Smell of green in the air," said Daniel. He nicked glasses with Pauline. "The question is: are *you* worth the trouble?"

"You'll find out soon enough."

"Ass on the table," he said with a smile, coming to life, balls swelling from a home-brewed injection of testosterone.

"Pauline, baby, I missed you," said Kit. "Need you like a pint of blood."

"It's a one-day favor. I'm cutting out to Jamaica mañana."

"Kit turned her out," Leo advised Daniel, steering his three-inch-high platformed shoes to the rail, his shell gray pinky sapphire wrapped around a glass.

"What did I know? A seventeen-year-old piss-pot," Pauline replied in a friendly needle.

Arm draped over Pauline's chocolate brown couture creation, Kit bubbled proudly. Could have been Press Maravich with Pete after the Pistol signed that dotted line. Happiness.

"Like the mink," Leo said, massaging the soft hairs on his cheek. "Come from a heist or just boosted?" he asked academically, as though the skins' derivation were of paramount importance.

"Laid on me by a union meatball. I forgot to ask where it came from. Wanted to leave his old lady and marry me. Fifty if he was a day, counting weekends and union meetings. Kids, the whole scene. What's the matter with these tools? Spunk in their brains. Man, I am a business girl and that is my element," she informed Daniel to forestall a similar offer, in case he had one in mind and was, well . . . mulling it over. "Dollars in my kick for doing something I'd do for nothing strike you as a bender?"

"I think you're on a winner's diet," said Leo.

"Know thyself." She burped up some champagne, held up her glass to check the bubble distribution. "Warmish."

"Ice-bucket it, Leo," Kit said, for at this hour Leo took over the barman's duties. Spring and fine weather he spent as a "Yours is the model house in the area" siding closer for an Allentown outfit that printed contracts with disappearing ink.

An incredible piece of merchandise, Daniel thought, joining numbers in his head as though for a kids' coloring book until the composition was complete. A body reader without peer, he decided she was worth being late for, hanging up Casa Brasil, where he was expected for dinner, and suffering a lockout by the lady who ran the place and came on in Brazilian when she didn't want to get the message.

"Better, Leo," Pauline said approving the rechilling.

"You've got to give me a break and stay till the weekend."

"Sorry. N. O. I'm here for Daniel B. and possibly a short time with Rich Larry. I'm through knocking my brains out for forty-cent Wilburs, Kit. And that's final."

Kit came out in a mini heat-nerve rash. Money discussions were always conducted in private for a special, during which her wheedling, conniving appraisal of how much the traffic would bear could be chewed, cudded, rechewed, so that an outrageous *prix fixé* would be agreed. The hot-pants guy would be pacing outside, banging back doubles to slow down the progress of the explosive come.

Cuties who might be laying out a hundred dollars often cut first to the bathroom for a rapid starch removal. They'd walk out, with an ear-to-ear smile, lobs still granite hard but jismless for at least three-quarters of an hour. The two-finger nurse-administered karate dick-chop was just so much bullshit, unless you had a clamp holding your guts together, and the nurse was one of those big hairy jobs who meant business and was shoveling down your dinner with the other hand. Daniel had pulled that number in the early days, been caught, eventually utterly humiliated by the girl and forced to admit that he'd done a little limbering up by himself as an appetizer. No kidding a chick who tossed a hundred lays a week. Once the girl had the meat in her hand she knew exactly when, what, how, to expect the firepower. Which . . . is precisely why she was being paid in the first place.

"We've got to talk this over, Pauline. I've made a half a dozen bookings for you."

"Isn't it great to be in demand?" Pauline told Daniel, rolling her brown eyes to the ceiling. "A thrill a minute."

Shapely hands with clearly defined moons lit by neutral polish. The eyelashes were riveting and fanlike, boldly black and slick. If they were phonies they were the best he'd ever clocked and markedly different from the butterfly wings Sonya glued on.

"What's so important about Jamaica that it can't wait?"

Pauline opened her handbag and fished out of the mirror

sheath half of a thousand-dollar bill, passed it around for a courtesy inspection.

"I want to marry it, if it's okay with you," she said, tugging it away from Leo, who also seemed to be considering nuptials.

She had thick, black, luxuriant hair which was waist length. Daniel liked the way she toyed with the ends then tossed it back when it blocked her vision. She had a violent, irrepressible nature which aroused him.

"Don't ever change, Pauline," he said.

"Me, never . . . unless . . ."

"Unless what?"

"I meet somebody tougher and he kicks my ass in. Not physically, you understand. But like, there's always a sharpshooter someplace."

"It goes both ways," Daniel said, beginning to enjoy himself, loving to match wits with a new face.

"You get hooked on somebody. The world might think the cat's A-1 dirt and like what do you see in him. Mr. Nobody. But he's got your number. You can't fight the chemistry, right?" She tugged down the wide leather belt of the dress which had started to creep up the rungs of her ribs. "I'm an aware chick."

"You were from the word go," Kit said of her subject as though confirming a biographical fact for a meeting of scholars. "I knew you'd go places and wouldn't wind up deadassed in a joint with your eyeballs locked into the TV screen."

"Growth," said Pauline. "That's my song. Leo, pop a cork unless"—she fixed her eyes on Daniel, gave him a pert smile, indicating wholesome even teeth that had a natural Macleans message—"Daniel's got to catch a train. If you want to go now, I'm ready."

"I caught the train," he said extending his glass.

By five, they were still yakking when The Pal suddenly came to life. Madame Gruesome had arrived. About five-eleven, weighing eighty-three pounds to give her the benefit of the doubt, hairdo by a family of foul-tempered ravens, possibly consumptive to judge by the racking cough, and blacker than a goat's turd. Lovelight gleamed in The Pal's eyes.

"Two, Tony, is free."

Pulling Daniel away from his company for a moment, Tony treated him to some genuinely affectionate, avuncular advice.

"A word in your ear, Daniel." He wagged his head critically at Pauline. "I jus' don' know how you could make it with her. Man, she turns my stomach."

"A little compassion, Pal. To each his own. Not every guy's man enough to chew a spade's box to shreds."

The Pal, he heard, thrashed them into julienne strips.

"You don't know what you're missing," he said, gingerly high-stepping to his loved one and taking her hand like a swain.

"What was that that walked in?" Pauline asked Kit.

"Garbage. I've got a collector that pays a C for the privilege."

5

A little unnerved by the "Beat the Clock" obstacles strewn in his path by Pauline's tardiness—and he wasn't in the mood to start shooting ping-pong balls through a hoop to see if he could collect a discontinued Philco TV—Daniel sat on a nubbly toilet seat covering which featured a portrait of a Scotty or a Yorkie, or some midget dog that had hooker appeal. Apropos of dogs, Pauline's chartreuse poodle had been checked at the La Guardia pound and while paring her arms with globules of sparkling Sea Jade bubbles, she expressed serious concern about the fate of her *bel ami.*

"Do you think they'll walk Brandy like they promised?"

Of dogs, cats, household pets, pests, the speech advancement of the parakeet, he did not want to know. Dog kissers, in any event, made him simply nauseous.

"If he shits on someone's two-suiter they can't ask him to clean it up. So if they took him in the first place, they probably have a hangar or something so that he can crap his head off."

"I can't imagine him lifting his leg against a Jumbo, can you?"

She had complained of being hot, sweaty, shagged, and the rest, and insisted on a bath, so he wasn't going to fight with her. Invited him to keep her company while the purification was taking place. He caught a shave with Leo's new treble-headed

Norelco, although he avoided electric razors like the plague, since they broke him out at the borderline of neck and beard.

"Boot it home," Leo had said with strange excitement when Daniel followed Pauline inside as though cheering him on to complete a Daily Double with a big price. "It's an absolutely sensational piece," he added ruefully. Groomed as Kit's lapdog, he was forbidden, under threat of going out and getting a job, to touch the candy.

"Brandy's my one human contact and a kind of loyalty is like there with us," Pauline continued.

"Mind if we change the subject. Your dog's bowel movements sort of turns me off," he said rubbing his skin. The fucking razor *had* irritated his face.

The er . . . equipment, was in a word—OUTSTANDING. A bra inspector from way back, he ran a check on the manufacturer's claim, cordoned the label on his index finger. LOU: made in France; 95. The conversion table on the back stated: Europe: 85B; U.S.A.: 38C. Numbers!

"Ever get the silicone job?" he asked her as she swaddled one of them under her chin.

"Nature, Daniel. And if she couldn't do it, I'm not crazy enough to buy cancer."

"My wife, if she married her pair, could get into one side of your bra and still have elbow room."

"Are you some comparative statistics freak?"

"Recall a guy called Irv Spigleman who you put out of commission for a while?"

"Name me no names. What did he look like?"

On the neck-brace part of the description she replied: "Contact! The guy with the phony whiplash. I remember him clearly."

"You gave him a little trouble. That's his story."

"Hmmmmmmmmm. As I recall, he wasted about twenty minutes"—she tossed out a leg to depart and he toweled her glistening, jeweled back—"trying to wring dick compliments out of me. Did I like the size? How did he compare? True-blue goon feelers"—she lifted her hair and he dried the back of her neck—"of a kind that I thought I'd never hear again after I gave up schoolyard feel-ups. A peter-meter freak if I ever met one."

"That's Irv. Did he offer to sell you stock?"

"A bell has been rung," she said, lacing the inside of her thighs

with some Estée Lauder talc from a makeup kit which contained
—at least it so appeared to his astonished eyes—about two thousand pots, jars, vials, containers, tubes, pencils, crayons, felt-
tipped Pentels, lipsticks, Chap Sticks, minute easels, brushes,
eyelid and finger cutlery; creams, a spectrum of bases, shadows,
tonics, oils, cleansers, skin milks, cocoa butter, Mary Quant
Jeepers Peepers, special eye cream, moisturizers, Bleachine
cream, blackhead cleansing grains, orange skin food and orange
sticks, eye repair masks, shampoo from the four corners of the
world; and a Ronson Rio R1 4 dual voltage hair drier with two-
and three-pronged plugs. Not to mention scents.

"Were you in on a hijacking or what?"

"Believe it or not, I'm traveling light." She slapped her belly.
"This is the machinery and it has to be oiled or it starts to rust,
you understand." Her skin looked absolutely laminated. She
wrapped a towel around her extended fingers, plunked powder
on it, barber-fashion, and patted the arrival lounge.

Calling The Fly back to the forefront of her head: "I gave it
to him but good. Half hour of constant heave-ho and, man, I
thought he'd explode, that yo-yo. I'm pleading with him to fill
me for his own good because over the horizon is one of the most
agonizing cases of blue balls I've ever read. He was like strangling
himself. He finally uncorked, then spent more time writhing on
the ground than he did in me. His balls must of been the size of
a cantaloupe. My fault?"

"Big eyes," Daniel suggested. "I come up here—I at least don't
want to make a career of it—drop my pants, release the poisons,
and go on with my life."

"Let's have a little wash, shall we? You this time."

He straddled the sink, the honored member limp until she
seized it. A class filly. Breeding, not like the usual guff who tried
for a semijack-off, justifying the treatment in the interests of Kit's
principles of de rigueur hygiene.

"When you go to the john," he said, as her fingers and wash-
cloth took the wang on a soapy carousel ride, "you lift it up,
slap it into the palm of your hand and see yourself as you actually
are. It's a man's autobiography."

"Never thought of it like that. Makes sense." She unfurled the
skin, rolled it down to check for bumps, lumps, sores, gently pres-
sured the head to test for discharge, the yellow peril. "Kit was the

first one who showed me how to roll back a dick. Man, I was so green I thought, well, all I've got to do is give it a rinse and away we go. Which is more than I was doing previously." She dried him tenderly, returned his property. "Okay, Daniel, follow the leader."

Greeted by fresh maize sheets, it was obvious to him that Kit really put herself out for him. Probably collecting only a 25 per-cent split from Pauline rather than the usual 50 percent, which was what she nailed the house authors. Two pillows each side sloped like a Cape Cod roof. Inviting. Still, any way he cut it, the angle of elevation equaled the angle of ultimate depression. Basic human trig. He'd start, as so often before, as the protagonist of the drama, and wind up with a bit part, barely remembering the lines.

Another . . . magic . . . box, one of a set of soft hide twins. Chinese box affair, this one. On the top shelf of the case he dis-covered Pauline's variety of religious experience. A copy of the *I Ching*.

"What's this?"

"I had a flirtation with Scientology and an affair with The Process, but I lost my heart to Linda Goodman and the *I Ching*."

Perhaps the retailing of sex always imposed such helter-skelter quibbles with destiny, he thought.

Pessarily speaking, she had nothing on show. When quizzed, she explained that years before while the U.S. Government was trying to show basic friendliness to India and had offered them freebie rings, they needed to test the damned things, and called upon public-spirited volunteers to advise and consent on the device.

She had been tested, and now years later, some Institute of World Snatch Study in D.C. funded by an international front of the Department of Commerce checked her out biannually or whenever she wrote complaining of pain and required a smear. Imagine, taking an interest in the Kiss of Death's vitals. Govern-ment doctors rushing wildly about to check for parabola forma-tions on their twat graphs.

Made him feel better now that he would be fortifying himself with U.S. Govt. Inspected:

PRIME . . .

The mirror, one of those antique gold jobs, braided with plywood open-mouthed cherubs shooting arrows from quivers that kept dropping off and which Kit kept right on gluing back on again—almost a contest to see who would tire first—had been tilted for full auto-projection. He made a slight adjustment to the rear-view mirror, hanging over the headboard, so that if he got into the position of tailgating himself in an upside-down crazy lurch, he wouldn't lose himself.

Another shelf containing her amber, aquamarine, and zircon collection, Pauline had settled on top of the dresser. Standing over the display case, she crooked her finger.

"What's all this?" he asked.

"Tools. Have you got a favorite?"

Never before had he seen such a collection. Worthy of a museum. Dildoes in red, white, and black, and in different sizes, what was more. Vibros with an assortment of heads attached to a black velveteen shelf and held under small elastic straps so they wouldn't move, like a mechanic's garage box with different drill and screwdriver heads. A . . . batter-rrrrr-y recharger. Miniaturized Nip product which she said came:

"From Hong Kong. You can get anything there." He lifted something with a long salmon-colored hospital tube, attached to a rubber ball which looked like it was stolen from a blood pressure gauge. "Easy with that . . . it's given me trouble before. Temperamental, kind of."

He put it down gently.

"I don't mean to be inquisitive, Pauline, but how . . . what is its primary use?" he asked, so slow to undress that he must have been holding a shirt button for five minutes.

"When you're into international things like I am . . . and you cater to all tastes, you've got to be equipped." She screwed it into a small valve attached to the underside of the red dildoe balls which were ridged and all in all a fine repro of someone with a ten-inch red dummy. Could it have been sculpted from life? Racially, what kind of guy owned such a peter? "See how it works?"

"Frankly, you've lost me . . . mechanically inclined I'm not."

"I boil up some cream, or milk, funnel it in here"—she held up a plastic funnel, baby's bottle type—"and when the party's ready to come, I squeeze the ball and searing hot spunk fires out of the top."

"A simulation. But . . ." he pondered. "If I'm not mistaken, you'd be the guy."

"So? You've never heard of chicks who like chicks? I've also got a few latent, maybe not so latent, homosexuals on my books and much as they'd like to, they've never cut it with another guy. The gutless wonders of the world, because I don't see anything wrong with two guys making it. What's abnormal about that? What is abnormal is going to a shrink and having him scoop things out of your head that rightfully belong there. Making you crazy with tranquilizers, so that you're in a trance and liking other guys is supposed to go away like a bad dream. Or this other thing I heard about awhile ago where they show a guy a movie of two men making it, looking thrilled because why shouldn't they if that's their scene, and the poor John who's watching this gets electric wires strapped to his balls and they negative him when he's tuning into what he'd like to be doing. So who's sick? The guy watching the film? The parents who are footing the shrink bill? Or the doctor who turns the switch to jazz the John's balls with electric current? My opinion is that the doctor ought to be put away, he's the frear-zeeking menace who gets *his* rocks off making someone who's perfectly normal suffer!"

He took a deep breath. Approved of what she said. On the lower level of the case which was platformed as though a prop developed by Q to assist James Bond in a jam, he saw an assortment of—

SCUMBAGS . . .

Nothing under the sun like them. Maybe thirty or forty different models, he thought. Demon faces with pointy beards, small rubber spikes, one he flicked with his finger did a somersault, movable parts, ratchet wheels, tubes, tubularities, nodulized, dredging gear, oil rigging if you wanted to jam the weasel into a bottle of 3 in 1 oil to see if there was any left, a small rubber-shoveled one for an archaeological dig . . . undoubtedly; a minuscule Zulu spear if caveman was your bag, spikes, pikes, picks, double and treble-pronged for . . . tuning (what else?); thorns, piercers, stabbers . . . All for Daniel!

He was becoming delirious. Pinched his own cheeks in the mirror. A living witness of a God-given *mitzvah*. He removed his trousers, got the seams straight, opened the top drawer of the dresser an inch and slipped the bottoms in and closed the drawer on them. Hanging straight. Shirt on the chair, tie over it. He had the sensation that he was walking in a slow-motion farming film about to seed . . . himself.

A knock on the door. He didn't hear it.

"Daniel, maybe you better see who it is. Won't be for me."

"Yeah, who is it?"

"Gary," came the reply. "It's important!"

What could possibly be more important than his present occupation? Opening the door a wink.

"Gary, for disturbing me at this moment you should get lock-jaw."

"Sorry, but a call came through from Zurich. The bank guy said that an Internal Revenue creep offered him fifty thou for info on your account."

"Well, call back and offer seventy-five thou, so we'll see who the fuck is bluffing who."

"It's also getting late, Daniel."

He slammed the door, returned to Pauline with a serene Taoist smile, praying for noninterference with the course of natural events.

"Where do we go from here?" he asked, giving a languid stretch.

"How about me warming up a little?"

A hand reached into the magic chest, scooped out the red tool. She held up the tray of marionette condoms, inviting him to pick his favorite. Not simple. Befuddlement in fact. A dynamic conflict between one attached to three turning ratchet wheels and a Satan with fingernail-long rubber spikes for a beard. He decided to leave personalities out of this, and went for the wheels. She removed a fresh one from the inventory drawer, dressed the dildoe with it—a costume change—and smiling from ear to ear, slowly, tortuously began the descent. He couldn't believe his eyes, for in seconds it had all but disappeared. Then . . . a heave, like a *gevalt*. Never, but never, and casting his mind back over his life, had he . . . twatwise, and short of a Bob Cousy feint on a basketball court, seen such a move.

"That's warming up? Easy, it's precious, Pauline."

He hunkered a breast in his mouth, part of one . . . just up to the midfield stripe. Any more and he'd choke on her. Her fingers glided-glided over the windjammer and she said, or at least he thought she said:

"Uummmmmmmmmmmm. Uummmmmmmm. That's a fucking cock."

He was in danger of swallowing his own epiglottis.

"How can you be sure?"

"With a curtain rod like that, you would've fired off flares when I showed you my gear . . ."

"Ah-hah, so there was a certain psychological approach to all of these implements?"

"You read me."

"Maybe I better not talk to you while you're . . . you're loosening up. You seem to have stopped."

Wham! Removing a piece of frayed Dental Floss from the tobacco crumbs of his jacket change pocket, he set the white dildoe on the bedside table under Kit's Merrie Cavalier lamp for a fast circumference estimate. Round about four and a half inches. Now if he could just remember the goddam pi equation, he'd have a fair idea of what kind of progress he could expect when it was his turn to come to bat in the servolab.

"So this is what galvanized rubber is all about," he said, seizing her wrist, forcing her to desist.

"I was almost there, again," she said.

He looked apologetic without meaning to, no intention whatever of pleading for boons.

"I don't want to throw you—"

"You won't," she replied. "Something bothering you?"

"Just . . . to put it as delicately as I can. Do we stick to Family Dinner B, or can I get a little à la carte with you?"

"Name it."

He carried over the tool kit. Eyes proctoring various devices. She seemed temporarily at rest, but there was still no sign of the red humdinger. The balls had also mysteriously disappeared. A little worrying when he came to consider that it might be his lot to share her, play second fiddle as it were. *Buckas*, or, claiming *ackies* with the evanescent, bachelor stilt—not a bargain he was prepared to strike. She moved a few inches and he saw that she had been sitting on it. He was relieved to discover that he was not a victim of black magic . . . The Process. A "garoooooop" accompanied the ejection of the spurious ding-dong . . . Exposure. The coated condom window-dressing it shone slick with the secret recipe of her bouillabaisse.

"I've come to the conclusion," he stated, "that I'd like to get a little more contemporary. Sort of trace the history of electricity with you." He placed the vibro in her hand, taking from her at the same moment Big Red. Done with the dispatch of: "Here's Colonel Abel for Gary Powers," another triumph smoothly engineered by the masterful Gehlen Bureau.

What a noise it made—"Wha-wha-whaaaaaaaaaaa"—like one of those industrial floor polishers. Turning, twisting, rotating. This was becoming nicely narcissistic. He stood back to monitor the exercise in the rear-view mirror while she selected a head and put Chief Red Dog back into stock, firmed him into his Frankenstein's clamp.

"This really turns you on . . ." she said, readjusting a pair of pillows under the shapely *toochis*, so that she appeared front and center in the dual mirror setup. It was like two TV sets, one recording live action, the other instant replay. Only thing missing was Howie, Dandy, and Giff, analyzing the action for the fans out there.

"I'll let you know when to stop," he said, crossing his legs and sitting meditatively at the side of the bed to avoid obscuring his vision and somewhat out of range in case she decided to polish him off with a sneaky swallow.

"I can work on you at the same time," she volunteered.

Through the door, Gary's voice boomed the latest on Daniel's financial situation.

"If you can hear me . . . I beat the manager down to sixty-five g's, and he's going to report the Revenue guy to the prosecutor who got Edith Irving's scalp . . ."

"Gary, no more reports. Please, I beg you."

He patted Pauline's flat waistline, tanned the color of Lüscher brown. Obvious that she baked herself without benefit of bikini , . . sort of the sun and me and all that vitamin D. Nothing did he have to spell out for her. She commenced firing immediately, working the gyrating Apollo head into orbit until it too disappeared from view into the Sea of Tranquillity. Serious problem tracking the goddam thing. She said:

"Oh, shit," when the thing had gone from "whaaaaaaaa," to "w-u-u-zzz," fizzing out.

"What do we do now? Abort the mission?"

"I must've forgotten to recharge it . . ."

"Ahaha."

6

Daniel watched her with middle-class fascination, he who could not change a plug, feared fuse boxes—one of the jobs he assigned to Sonya in the early days of their marriage, for the world was not going to fold up if there was one ex-stewardess more or less; no TV funeral for that *schtumie*. For sure. But for the elected, chosen member . . . ? Kept away from the backs of TV sets. The linearity lost its mind, let it. Six feet seemed a safe distance from bathroom shaving plugs. Radios in the toilet, never. In his teens he once heard of a girl who got electrocuted that way on a Saturday morning because she didn't want to miss a word of Martin Block's "Hit Parade." A hot car radiator cap, his hand had never touched. The oil stick might blow up in his face if he went near. Even flashlights made him nervous; the backs of transistors with their miniaturized circuits brought him out in a cold sweat; never in contact with a phono needle which could make an unnoticed insidious puncture mark and before he'd know it, a case of unarrestable tetanus, freezing his jaws. From hot water systems, central heating pipes, he ran for his life. What, was it impossible that they could burst, scald him so that even with the skin grafts, he'd have a hard time recognizing himself? With light switches and the automatic changer on the phono, he was a big shot, fearless, even though in cold weather the carpeting sent electrical shivers through the funny bone and he'd wince, screw up his face agonizingly. Thus, for the repair job of her twat chopper, he was not offering assistance. Stayed out of range as she attached two wires, a red and black, live and not so live.

"Positive and negative," she explained.

"Very interesting." He held a coverlet up to his chest, affecting chills. Object: insulation in case of fire. If he saw a spark, dead certainty that the tool would shrink into obscurity like a turtle under pressure. Just another memory.

"How long does this usually take?" he asked.

"Just until this needle on the gauge moves past two amps. You'll hear a buzz."

"A buzz, like crackling?" wondering where to retreat.

If only he hadn't made the suggestion of the machine aid, stuck with true and tried pre-Industrial Revolution home industry. Hand Power, but unfortunately he'd behaved like one of those tourists on a package holiday who steps off the plane and in three minutes flat expects to see all the sights and points of interest that the travel agent conned him about.

During the mission, Pauline had given him a skimpy but chronological rundown on her past performances, which acted as a buffer, distracted him from the gnawing fear of being I.R.A. exploded any second, all of this interspersed with a wide range of précis'd info from *Popular Mechanics*.

Arcane . . . Pauline . . . facts. A quarteroon P.R., her mother's mother, in short, her *Bubba*, had left the land of sun-dappled climate and Mafiosa gambling pits to settle on U.S. soil some time back. Marveled at Pauline's pronunciation of the place Puerto Rico; the *ue* came out as authentic "where," conveying the definition: rich port, having little to do with his recollection of the island.

Miss Pauline Bianco gave him a thumbs-up sign.

Recharged.

All systems go.

Dare he beg her pardon, explain that he was ready to tour the precinct, and had been victimized by the technological revolution? Too late. She resumed her frenzied drilling, as if pavements, sidewalks, depended on her. He assumed that she was used to noise—no bucolic wisteria whisperings in the breeze, or cicadas clucking for this one. Like a dentist whipping through cavities with his Siemens Special water gun, the whole exercise was second nature. Conversation she gave, and conversation she expected in return. Gewgaws spun, rattled, a proper assortment of Jujubes danced through his head. Would music, WNEW, interfere with this *tumuler*, break the concentration?

He learned, via the department of incidental intelligence, that she was a child prodigy, began her craft at twelve—went through the complete medieval training program apprentice, journeyman, craftsman—in Harlem schoolyards.

Reassuring.

"You started at the bottom," he said over the din. Not quite a holler, but decibels higher than usual for intimate encounters not involving Sonya.

"At a buck a shot," she replied. "The boys used to be finishing their punchball, and no kidding everybody was in Tap City. Just enough change for a Pepsi or a Coke. Then they'd all wait in line for their deposits back." Thirst taking precedence over orgasm among these spicurians. "Chip in . . . and then when they got to a buck, everyone would gather in a circle and play 'one potato, two potato, three potato, you.' Whoever got two fists behind his back first . . . got it from me."

"Another success story in the face of incredible odds," he noted. She had a faster growth record than I.B.M. Multiracial, mixed media setup undoubtedly, but still he made further inquiries. "Any Jewish kids in your area?"

"No, they were miles away. West End Avenue or C.P.W. I didn't know that they circumcised dummies till I was at least eighteen."

Out of the window, two thousand years of *moile* tradition, the world's finest surgeons, prophets without honor among the Puerto Rican spore culture.

One undeniable, irrefutable fact as clinical as a chest X-ray: her health. What, with low, high, cholesterol diets, macrobiotic madness, weight watchers, organic food faddists who broke out in psoriasis, *fressers* of nut cutlet specials, the yogurt crazies, volunteers for the latest hormone trip, water, nonwater advocates, all of them could learn a lesson from this spunk swallower. A spot-free complexion—the face was like velvet—not a crooked tooth, not a single sag-bag under the luminously clear eyes. In spite of the dimensions of the breasts, no snapped cords forced a retreat to the belly. No shards of glotty fat bounced on the backs of the *pulkas*, not the merest suggestion of incipient steatopygia could be detected by Daniel's penetrating examination.

"Do you work out—exercise—much?"

"You've got to be kidding."

"Then how do you account for . . . your condition?"

He grasped her hand, the one feeding the vibro. Didn't want her to wear it out.

"Few things. Like I don't worry. Besides, I've got no sexual frustrations."

"Even I could tell that."

"I love what I'm doing. The action and the bread . . ."

"Key to life," he agreed. "You must do pretty well financially."

"I've been banking a thousand a week for almost four years. Which I keep in Mexico because of the big interest they pay. And I've got a couple of boutiques in hotels there."

"And it's all beautifully tax-free."

"Tax? Who's that?"

"You don't feel under any special obligation to Uncle Sam and his mechanics who do the annual ring review?"

He was beginning to feel like a guest in his own home and decided it was invitation-to-a-beheading time.

"You've been pretty good to yourself. I hope I can count on similar fair treatment."

"How good depends entirely on you. You've got the cannon."

She stopped the vibro, a sound reminiscent of a plane's engine reverse on landing, and he thought he detected a certain forward-backward unwilling recalcitrance characteristic of machinery with a lot of go. She placed it on top of her case, filched out a jumbo-sized Lavoris bottle and drifted off to the bathroom. Listened to thirty seconds of well-coordinated gargling, and in a spirit of mischievousness wondered how she'd react if he hid the vibro. The condom headdress had frayed. An open and shut case of friction fatigue.

In his nostrils the spicy, cinnamony, cheeky fragrance of Lavoris. A toe-to-head worker, she commenced with a series of shank kisses, filling her mouth with little bits of ankle meat. Not his style.

"Pauline, could we sort of get down to hostilities. Like right away?"

"You're calling the shots."

He received customized, individual attention, falling, reeling, with that heady sense of confidence when the big Cancer Man at Sloan-Kettering does the biopsy. Something definitely Chinese mandarin in her style. Each ball caught tongue slaps, loosening him up. Not painful either. A rhythmic ping-pong style. This magician he didn't have to instruct to get the hair out of the way. A powerful clasp held the pony tail in traction. One item in the repertoire he was not crazy about. She stared at him, un-blinkingly. Big saucer eyes from that angle.

"Pauline, what's with the looks?"

"Turns me on . . . your reaction."

"Maybe it's a mistake to say this—heaven knows I've been plenty wrong before—but if you could concentrate a little less on my reaction and more on the experience itself . . ."

Should have kept the big mouth shut. A muted "uh-oh" escaped from his lips. On the receiving end of an internal examination, the penetration of which made him jerk as though from a dreaded electric shock. She seemed to be visiting with all of his distant relatives, a look in on the alimentary canal, a wave to the liver. An anal treasure hunt so special, so different, so . . . vascular . . . Obviously he'd wasted himself on Sonya and Norma.

He gave her the hi-low, palm slicing the air, poker call, when out of mammalian urgency, she came up for air. An answer to the tacit question, of course: half-French, half-fuck. Rather than go all one way on a first encounter, he decided to strike a generalized posture, pile the plate, then select the favorite. Entirely reasonable, they both agreed. Favoring a body bisection stance rather than the up-and-down on the knee seesaw, she swiveled across him in one of those ice-skater roundhouses; one of the marvels of balance, when the girl swirls an inch from the ground and never touches it. Seizing the trencherman's cane, he made an earnest inquiry:

"Well, what do you think?"

"Oh, another candidate for dick compliments . . ."

A mind reader. Actually, he did want to ascertain how he compared: size, coloring, a general purpose statement on the condition.

"A nice, healthy portion, isn't it?"

"Daniel, I'm not picking out skins for a coat. What does it matter?" Pausing. "But I suppose it does. Everybody asks . . . Bigger than average," she concluded.

He shrank back. Offended. Not the best? The biggest? Tapping concealed infantile hangups. By way of apology, she provided him with the standard dick projection scale which was based on the antiquated—but still accurate—sock measurement test.

Fists. Closed. Climbed up the peter-meter.

"Three fists," she claimed, giving him the benefit of a ring finger; an unrounded statistic might make him cry. She knew all about these Jewish guys: when they weren't counting their millions *aloud,* so that only ninety-two thousand people could hear them, they were worried about Wilbur shrinkage. "You satisfied now?"

Naturally he was. Like being able to rap a Spalding two sewers in punchball. Not many walking around who could.

"You don't have to be so curt about it."

"Look, we both know that size has nothing to do with skill."

"A fact . . . but still . . ."

Getting down to it, her head in a slow-motion pavane began consuming him by degrees, all the way down to the stump. Tongue flailing, chasing itself, disengaged. No words to this song.

"I don't want skimpy service. You don't have to worry about me popping off and then bitching that you cut corners."

"Just say when."

"I don't want to live by the clock. So just assume that you're trying to get back from New Jersey via the Lincoln Tunnel and that there's a lot of traffic piled up. The time it would take to wheel into the city under those conditions is the time you should take."

Ululations . . . pullulations, jaws tensed, she actually re-created the time conditions he'd insisted upon. More, she was going like the roads were icy and caution had to be observed. Her mouth sucked in as though doing an imitation of a fish. A little rotation thrown in for good measure. She actually managed to create a halo around it. On maybe the seventy-fifth lap, she eased up on the acceleration. Doing a circuit analysis, checked the gauges, and determining that a pit-stop was unnecessary. The utter, unbelievable orality of it.

At about quarter to seven, he was showing signs of wear and tear, thought he heard heavy breathing outside the door. Gary? Technical faults were showing up left, right, and center. Slow . . . . leak. Frantic flag waving from the pit. The technician diagnosed the trouble instantly, preventing a devastating, horrific, blowout. Spla——tt——er.

"You're pretty close," she said.

"Can't last forever."

Slow lift-off, while she sympathetically encouraged him to cool down, recover his balance, so they could get down to some serious work. For two hundred dollars a shot, he received coaching, the management's kid gloves for the bonus baby. The head pulsated uncontrollably, like an idiot, then flaked out on the top part of his thigh.

"You could have had it . . . and I wouldn't have kicked," he said.

"You wanted half and half and that's what you're going to get."

"You know something, Pauline. I really like you."

A half-time smoke of a bomber joint and he was back, cheering himself, as apprehensive as a diehard fan grown restive shoveling Stevens hot dogs in his face, and swallowing piss-warm beer. The cry for action was not vocal. He jolted into the air like an altar candle. Aflame. The second half called for a change of positions . . . the north goal, right into the face of the prevailing wind.

No holdup at this toll gate. He dropped right into the slot while she checked ceiling slopes, went round and round the garden like a teddy bear, and he detected that the box had a series of unmistakable calibrations. Wall-to-wall carpeting. Then . . .

Something went radically wrong. He slipped out.

"Galoooooooomp."

Rejected like a stranger's organ when the transplant tests had decreed otherwise.

"This has seen a little traffic. I don't want to say anything," he continued, moving on his side, "but I'm like on the Major Deegan. This isn't just room, it's lanes."

"I didn't fix the position. You did. You see, pleasing another human being means doing exactly their thing, so since you didn't ask what would be best—"

"—Technical data," he interjected.

"Sort of. I didn't want to tell you your position would be a waste of time."

"Such consideration . . ."

"If you let me get on top of you, I'll show you what I mean."

He stretched out like a corpse.

"Don't spare the razzle-dazzle."

She engineered her feet behind his ear lobes, extended her hands behind her, palms downward, spanning the foot of the bed, and reinstated him. Temperature: Equatorial. The ass balanced in a death-defying gravity stunt. Pirouetting him in slow whirls, he discovered that she was taking him through gear changes. First . . . second . . . third . . . OVERDRIVE. Fully synchromesh. No double-declutching in this model. Like being in a convertible, and speeding hell for leather through unbelievable curves, then up to mountains, down to the valleys. She had a muscle that caught, trapped, squeezed him, in some sort of blitz defense. Wherever he moved, he was getting double coverage. The coup de grâce was a final wrench, like being caught in a flexed Steve Reeves bicep.

No hero . . . Daniel.

Exploded. Not to be another patient for The Fly's sock. He registered shock waves. With an incredible move, another spirited illustration of her legerdemain, a dusty-pink washcloth appeared out of thin air which with that instinctive reflex action marking greatness—Brooks Robinson going into the hole—she reached the nook. Not a single spunk pearl fell. Marveled at her, truly. Pauline hopped to the bathroom, leaving him for dead. After this, he expected to cough blood . . . what else? He had to jack his neck up on an elbow for a view of his front end. His dick looked like it had gone through a blender . . . emulsified.

Loved it . . . the actuality . . . the el supremo quiddity of it. Where hadn't that box been? Slobbered over by *schwartzers*, ripped apart by the neighborhood reamos who stood on Amsterdam Ave. with satin fuchsia neon LORD jackets conducting the music of their lives from behind a toothpick. Experience, she invented the word.

Semi-semi dressed, she reappeared wearing a pair of panties and the bra slung over her shoulder. He made an involuntary shrink away from her when she came near him, fearing that she planned to continue the vendetta.

"Well . . . ?" she inquired after her patient, "how do you feel? Christ, I'm still dripping. I caught an oyster."

He peeled off two crisp magic C notes from a three-inch high roll, and a fifty.

She looked at the money like a dopey kid his first two-wheeler, and he sussed out that cash was her trip. If bills could be fondled, that's what she was doing.

"Kit told me that you drop green like an angel and you've helped her out in the past."

"Oh, that . . . ?" An old loan when she'd had a pair of back-to-back busts a few years ago. "I remember. I arranged a Ford Foundation grant so that she could continue her studies."

Corralling her breasts into the LOU bra—committee work—she still waited for critical commentary and her eyes worked over him with that expectancy of "it's your turn to say something."

"The extra fifty is a tip. It was worth it," bringing a . . . blush to her face. "Still I can't figure out how someone gives you half of a thousand-dollar-bill on the come."

"I'm into an entirely different scene"—she zipped one and a half feet of boot zipper—"it's real constructive . . . involves counseling. Coming back to the city was a favor to Kit. She told me that you'd been asking about me for a long time." She sponged him bone dry, then picked up a vicious-looking instrument which turned out to be a talc schpritzer. Any hot oil around and he'd be ready for breading.

"Counseling what?"

Like summer camps? And taking on the whole camp on a retainer basis?

"Marriage, Daniel."

He winged into his trousers, dressed in a minute, and she gathered together her equipment. Tying his knot, he detected the telltale ruckled V on his forehead, indicating puzzlement.

"Marriage counseling? Are you putting me on?"

"No, seriously. I like go way for the weekend with a married couple. Let's say they're still like youthful forties, attractive, good clothes, but those home fires need like a piece of flint. They still dig each other and no way want to split. But ten days in the sun, swimming, swatting tennis balls together . . . gets a little boring. Mrs. Wife is raring to go in the sack after three days. Her skin is starting to tan. She does a lot of body investigating in the full-length mirror. Nothing wrong with her! He looks great. So what's stopping them from really starting a four-alarm? Each other," she said as though it were the most obvious fact in the world. "If she gets lucky, she might catch a single in a week because he's on this uninteresting timetable like dog walking, vacation or not. So I get recommended . . ."

Both fully dressed, sitting on easy chairs, smoking cigarettes, looking directly at each other. Only thing missing were the radio mikes and Susskind's list of questions.

"You go away with them . . ."

"A friend of a friend, or whoever, suggests that they contact me. We like interview each other over drinks and dinner. Nobody comes on. Then if the vibes are good we make arrangements and shoot off to wherever they want to."

"What's the wife got to say about all this?" he said leaning forward, getting hooked.

"I don't create jealousies, I dissolve them. No favorites."

"A kind of merry trio?"

"I usually start with Mrs. Wife . . ."

"Why the wife first?"

"She's the bomb and she's got to be defused. A real friendliness gets going. I'm not looking to steal her old man and I don't want to make a leather jacket out of her, you understand. I make like nice to her. We get out front and they've got something different on their vacation. We're like family and friends after a day or two."

"Wouldn't surprise me . . ."

"But the joint thing like Kit's setup I'm totally out of. I don't mind the fucking . . . it's the sitting around. Eyeballing. Listening to stories of other business girls. Zonks me into like stuporization. So . . . I wind up dropping leapers, downers, snorting coke, smoking grass all day long just to get into my own head because the company turns me off. . . . Listen, Daniel, much as I'd like to go on talking to you, I've got an appointment."

"Any of the locals I might know?"

"No, it's not business now. I've got to hit my dentist for a gum recession treatment."

He stooped, picked up her cases like a rushing bellhop.

"What happens afterward?"

"I have to check with Kit to see if Rich Larry is going to show. Then probably I'll wind up with Kit and Leo somewhere . . ." She shook his hand. "You handle yourself real well."

Traffic conditions were reaching Labor Day intensity in the living room at this hour. A battery of men—strange faces—were hiding behind newspapers, closeted under room screens. Waiting. Kit bustling, weaving back and forth like an out-on-his-feet headwaiter, called names from a list she compiled on shirt cardboard. Leo, and Christopher, were wheeling drinks around. A great believer in atmosphere, Kit was very generous with liquor. But after six, nobody was allowed to smoke grass in the public rooms. She didn't want any new face—friend of a friend—freaking out on two belts of a joint, and losing his train ticket back to his playing fields. She wasn't running some lost and found department. Kept a train schedule by the telephone for such emergencies, so that those in the waiting room with their fat knockwurst printed ties, cool tinted shades, breaths frenched with Binaca Frosty Mint atomizers, and Bonwit's roué gear could plan ahead and not make a home of her dwellings.

Leo dropped off three drinks to a group of embarrassed hiders, then cornered him.

"Listen, Daniel, Kit and me feel so cruddy about this being your birthday and all and doing nothing about it—and by the way, Gary went back to the office and he says to meet him at dinner. But getting back to how we feel . . . please do us a favor and meet up later, so we can at least have a drink. After twelve we'll be at Sally's."

"I'll try . . ."

Kit stopped calling numbers for a minute and kissed him. Everyone would have to sit tight before "Bingo" was announced.

"Sally's, Daniel. Please. We'll have a few laughs, I promise," she reiterated.

He'd been there before once with them. A fruit and nut establishment, like a free zone with its own laws; grass was openly smoked, pills and H exchanged hands; every known variety of sexual free-for-all could be bartered for; the back room was a plush shooting gallery for those well fixed financially. Sally kept out the riffraff by making it "members only" and charging a ten-dollar cover for each guest.

"I'll see," he said.

"Do I have to ask you how you made out with Pauline?"

"I think I'm breaking out . . . finally."

"Not to do anything crazy again?"

"Could be. I've got just what I needed . . . a new woman in my life."

Kit helped him on with his coat as the commuter group stared at him. How did he rate such service? A few of the men were inspecting the available girls, and Daniel paused to watch them. He himself experienced a trembling discontinuity of thought. He visualized the slack-mouthed girls as babies: adored, powdered, mollycoddled, little Miss Sunshines, lighting up the empty galaxies of their parents' lives.

Who would have thought that they . . . ? How could he make plans for his daughters when they'd choose for themselves? His daughters . . . Dear God.

At last, Daniel felt a cozy sense of well-being. He was going out to dinner with his two grownup girls, and he had reached a decision.

"You know, Kit, I do know what I want."

iv

EATING OUT

When I am grown to man's estate
I shall be very proud and great,
And tell the other girls and boys
Not to meddle with my toys.

—STEVENSON

1

The night had turned raw-black, and the diseased body of the city, with its frightened streets from which all signs of human traffic had disappeared, swallowed Daniel. He walked quickly and nervously toward the safety of his car. Remembering moments from its glorious past, and the new reality of night in Manhattan, the city now seemed to him mourner, pallbearer and victim of a violent death.

The doorman outside the Carriage Top, still slapping his gloved hands together and groaning under his breath, leaned against the iron post of the canopy with a special air of bereftness. There was a casualty in Daniel's life, and he listened to a garbled report of destruction while examining his car.

"I was up on Second tryin' to get a cab when I hear gunfire. Three or four of them bastards was scoring junk when the cops closed in on 'em."

On the passenger door of his car a series of random dents, slush marks, and dirt maculations, highlighted by a legible scrawl which illustrated the most recent art form swaddled in the city. A graffiti poet had scratched with a nail or skeleton key:

FUCK YO

Having omitted the *u*, the author had scored the door like

pork skin. Daniel winced at the sight of it. A symbol had no defense but itself.

"Young Lords or them Warlocks, who knows. But when I try to get back to the entrance the cops stop me. Mr. Barnet, what could I do with them bullets flyin'? Tell me, please. . . ?"

He handed Daniel back the five-dollar tip he'd been given earlier, but Daniel said: "Keep it. Shit, I've never seen such a mess."

"You got yourself a car like that, you don't go near the lots 'cause they bang hell out of it. So you trust it to me and I look after it. This fucking city . . ."

Daniel started the engine, let it idle and lit a joint to make the damage disappear. After a few moments, he flicked the roach out of the window and went into his evening stock of leapers. Tranquilizers during the day and speed in the evening. He swallowed a Desoxyn and entered the paradisal state of UP, then shot through red lights with Diana Ross on tape melodiously informing him—"Ain't no mountain high . . ."

Possibly. He got properly hung up pulling into a spot down the street from Casa Brasil. Images of Rubens' *Three Graces* which had been the adolescent high point of his interest in art, via the *Universal Encyclopedia*, shimmered in an oscillating daisy chain of mental transparencies. A new holy sexual synthesis of which he was the master.

He walked past the restaurant, saw by a clock at the Seaman's Bank that he was late. Inclined to wander and stare into darkened shop windows, he shivered uncontrollably. The chill factor went right through his bones, restraining oblivion, but allowing him to forget the car.

The snapping voices of the culturally attuned, advertising that specious fact in stereo, and the lights in the restaurant dazed him. Smiling at strangers, he observed women shrink from him and whisper to their men, for in civilized places like New York, the purposeless grin was a dangerous sign.

"Where have you been?" Gary said, standing lookout at the foot of the stairs.

"At Kit's."

"All this time? You better wipe the smile off your face because I told them you were involved in an important meeting."

"Where was I?"

"Wall Street." He eyeballed Daniel. "You blasted off, I see."

"Anybody wounded yet?"

"A miracle has taken place and I don't know how you've pulled it off, but like everyone's behaving and laughing."

Since his morning departure, Sonya had obviously spent six hours at the hairdresser. Result: a curled silver-haired skull which reminded him of the back of an old TV set before transistors. Wires . . . exposed. A red satin blouse with puffed-out sleeves billowing on her wrists, a skin vest of python or something that had once crawled, over a midi American Indian embroidered hide skirt. Calf-high snake boots supported it.

Sonya wished him happy birthday; Marlene reminded a God above that He should bestow everlasting life on Daniel; and Norma, in a siren lime green satin dress exposing her silk-soft laminated cleavage upon which no obtrusive bauble might conceal her natural splendors, said:

"Happy Valentine's Day, Daniel." He had cheek-hopped to her and in the folds of her dress she secretly squeezed his pinky. "At long last we're out *in* public . . . with Sonya and Max."

"How'd the meet go?" Max asked. "Daniel is so mysterious at the office that the people who work there are the last to find out what he's done."

Norma had bought him a navy blue suit, and after a strategic weight loss, he was now an actuary's dream of fifty-year-old health.

"Fine, Max, just fine."

Creeping up with the stealth of a linebacker sniffing out a quarterback's telltale audible, Sonya was upon him.

"We've been waiting an hour for you."

"Tied up," he said with a twinkle, and the absence of remorse her presence inspired.

She observed in her tricksy-tricksy voice, modulated so that only the person just beside him might catch it, an apparent carryover from her stewardess career: "Looks like somebody got his rocks off." She pressed her purple-black lips close to his mouth, and Norma self-consciously averted her eyes. "You've got Lavoris on your breath, and somebody's Jolie Madame on your cheek . . . We wear Calèche, don't we, Norma?"

"I do," she snapped, ever-easy to reveal distress.

"Sonya, I don't know if I should answer you or just whack you across the mouth."

"You don't usually get violent when you're high. As a rule, you roll over on your side and snore."

"Now come on, kids," Marlene found herself mediator, "we're birthdaying and we want to have a few laughs." She gave Daniel a wheedling smile, pressed his hand affectionately, "Call a cease-fire, just for tonight."

Sonya turned her back on him, eyes becoming suddenly animated as a man peered at her. Her lips puckered and she tossed her head back provocatively and large triangle earrings jangled from her lobes. She usually resorted to these tactics—throwing herself about—to attract attention. A constant source of embarrassment to Daniel. In public he frequently pretended she was attached to another man.

He realized that she was also high and found himself oddly perturbed by this discovery. He'd never known her to smoke.

"With all your connections and all . . . why do we have to stand here like slobs?" Sonya asked. "I don't even like the food. It's pretending to be chinks."

Max leaned across Norma to get Daniel's attention. Even at play, Max recorded a universe in jeopardy.

"Your friend Spigleman came up to the office and saw Don," Max said. "Claimed you gave the okay. He's peddling what Don knows are stolen bearer bonds. He oughta lose our address."

"You are not still getting yourself involved with that crook, Daniel, are you?" Sonya demanded.

The questions bombarding him seemed to belong to another time, another place, filling him with confusion. Norma's eyes were on him, registering disapproval.

"I never gave him the least encouragement. Saw him by accident at lunch."

"I just wondered, Daniel. 'Cause a deal with Spigleman could set off a four-alarm . . ."

He signaled Gary to draw Max off his neck, and Norma closed into the space by his side. She had her pert nose close to his ear.

"What did Sonya mean about the perfume?"

"I know what goes on in that mind?"

"Well, Daniel, whatever you've got on isn't just innocent after-shave, is it?"

"Norma, don't start trouble."

"I thought that was my job," Sonya interrupted. "What I can't understand, never will"—she shook her head as though to unclog a water-filled ear—"is how a nice woman like you ever got involved with Daniel."

Stepping right into the eye of the throbbing, swirling vortex, Gary, with a faint frozen smile on his face, advised the trio of lovers of a pertinent, lugubrious fact.

"They've got our table ready."

Behind him, Marlene's hand slashed the smoke out of the air.

"I think I hear rumbling stomachs. I don't know about you all," she stammered, then halted as electric carpet-shocks crackled. The faces of the group zeroing in on their long-postponed rendezvous indicated that the safety of the table was just one more perilous step toward the unknown.

2

Never one to confuse the gallant gesture with his own comfort and self-interest, Daniel attached himself to the seat at the table with a view of the human traffic. Norma was to his left, and Sonya had a direct view of the wall and mementos of Brasilia. To his right, Marlene provided sotto voce instructions on how Gary ought to behave:

"Now don't you be a big shot and start grabbing the check. Understand? We've gone for plenty on the present . . . and Gary, they want to argue, let them. You keep out."

Visibly shrinking before his eyes, Gary just nodded, a proponent of the yes-yes-yes-yes theory of managing his brittle domestic empire with the hawk-jawed Marlene. She had made dissatisfaction a way of life, and blaming people for anything that went wrong had become second nature to her. To break up the bird symmetry of her face, she had stenciled several beauty marks on her chalky skin. As champagne was poured, Daniel watched out of the drugged glaze that had settled over his eyes, places being changed next to him. Having forced Marlene to shift to her seat, Sonya was now within clawing distance of Daniel. She leaned across Gary and, in a voice, revealing the absence of harps, said clearly:

"I am the boss's wife and no waiters are going to hit the back of my chair."

In a sense, Daniel agreed with the detestable ethics of her case, forcing the weak to give ground, but the execution and the manner had become habitually cruel. He could now see how deeply he had implanted his own unkindness on her. An unhappy revelation: she had cultivated his own lack of grace. It had been possibly a year since they had had dinner out together with friends, and the change in Sonya seemed to reflect the lack of people. A new enraged surliness informed Sonya's easy manners.

Norma twittered soothing love concoctions under her breath, wetting his ear in the process. Romantico and a bit inane, she was starting to annoy him. Norma's featuring her breasts as blatantly as the Jackson Five did their moppet prodigy, belonged to a time he had outgrown. A great believer in affectionate foreplay, she had never smoked grass with him or engaged in a speedy bang. Norma always needed coaxing and conversation and glasses of chilled wine and closed with a medley of her whimpering hits. He'd been listening to the same recording for years. By comparison with Pauline, his two women had been plucked from another age.

Max was deep in conversation with the waiter about the origins of Brazilian cuisine and the correct pronunciation of Fei Joada, while Gary, who had brought the champagne, was feeling bottles and wiping his hands on the corner of the tablecloth tucked underneath for the benefit of such patrons.

Children of earlier and less sophisticated climates, and with the service more hypothetical than observed, an unveiling of presents took precedence over ordering. His people were in the habit of thrusting large boxes at him in crowded public places which led directly to commentaries about wrapping paper.

He unveiled a gleaming black crocodile attaché case, compliments of Gary and Marlene. His initials in lower-case gold letters were below the handle.

"Baby skins," Marlene advised him. "Know what's so thrilling about giving you a present like this," she added with a damp eye, "is it cost seven hundred and fifty dollars and we can afford it—"

"Thanks to you—" Gary interposed.

Marlene's eyebrow lines were raised by remote control.

"—Gary, *I* was speaking. . . . And we didn't look for a wholesale break on it either."

"It's pretty," Sonya said, "but Daniel never carries an attaché case."

"I will carry this one, proudly," he said leaning over to kiss Marlene and Gary.

"Perfect you're not, Daniel," Marlene continued, moved by her own eloquence, "but a lot of people would go to hell for you."

"I'll buy the tickets," Sonya said with a wicked giggle.

"Doll, what's steaming you up? If you missed your monthly, don't blame me," Daniel said in a gay offhand way which was intended to disarm Sonya and reassure Norma.

"We've come a long way from Babylon and lousy plumbing, haven't we, Sonya?" Marlene said, about to begin counting blessings.

"Daniel has not moved an inch from the moment we met."

"I don't agree," Max advised her. "He was quite a handful at Princeton, but he could sure move business."

"Personally, I mean," Sonya added like a witness thought to be mad but in reality sane, if only the corroborating evidence would appear.

"I think he's a much better person," Max insisted. "In business, he's got real imagination and a certain craziness that rubs off on the people he deals with."

"Like hiring you to work for him?" Sonya asked, doing her irritating wide-eyed number which never failed to enrage Daniel.

Somewhat abashed, Max sipped his champagne, winked innocently at Norma and avoided Sonya.

"I mean, Max, honestly wasn't it incredible and weren't you surprised—when Daniel asked you to join him?"

"Max is the best office man in this city," Gary said.

"Well, I never heard Daniel speak of Max without praying for his death, and it has always struck me as beyond belief that he'd get you to work for him."

Although a history of modern cosmetics had found temporary lodgings on Norma's face, she managed to flare, redden, and erupt through her Touch & Glow.

"Is there any reason why you have to insult my husband?" Norma asked. Her left eye twitched, and Daniel recognized the possibilities: either nerves, or heading for climax uno.

"Since when is the truth insulting?"

"When it comes from your mouth," Daniel said, hoping to avoid messy public surgery on the mother of his daughters.

He wished that she would leave and return to whatever was her life. Hardly the moment to announce that their days together were indeed numbered, for it would drop him irretrievably on Norma's lap, and all he required from her was visiting privileges. Sonya hedged her bet and offered Norma a dose of champagne.

"Sonya, let's forget we're out celebrating my birthday," he said lifting her wrist and toying with the idea of severing it so that he might recover the emerald bracelet on it; a purchase which *crenked* him like a spasm of angina. "Let's give you a minute of our undivided attention, so you can tell us what's disturbing the mind."

She gave the impression of cranking up a barrel organ, the eyes submerged under lacquer-slick lash extensions darted from face to face in search of an Axis partner. Gary developed his itchy nose wrinkle when it became evident that she had elected him to retail her grievances.

"I will bet that all the gals feel like me." Sonya paused for support, but no one hurried to her side. "I am wearing an Yves Saint Laurent blouse which costs ninety dollars. A skirt of hide, price four hundred and fifty dollars. The snakeskin vest another hundred and fifty dollars. Boots, a hundred and fifty dollars, not to mention my jewelry, new hairdo, my 'draky' mink coat upstairs. All in all"—she reckoned on her fingers—"maybe fifteen thousand dollars' worth of attire. And do you think this man would have the decency to tell me I looked nice?"

"You wear my wealth so elegantly, Sonya, that compliments die like roses on my lips. Actually, you dressed a whole lot better when you had your airline uniform on . . . because to you price has now become everything. Taste does not know from expenditure." He halted, smiled affectionately at her, and took up her fingers. "One other thing: when you're on the prowl for a new husband, and you can get him to spend sixty-five hundred—and that's wholesale, Marlene—on a mink coat for you, you've got a moral obligation when showing contempt for it to pronounce *drekhy* correct."

Ever resilient, here she was smiling through the beastliness of another day that had seen Bud Van Allen developing supernatural immunity to her charms. He had casually wheedled her for money, and they had had a virulent argument. Then she'd cruised without luck for an instant companion.

"We fight like hell, but I do love him," she announced, leaning over and startling Daniel with a noisy kiss.

He did not recoil, which surprised him, discovering a certain piquancy being out with this lunatic whom he'd left to toss herself off the previous night and too many others to recount. He scrutinized the index and middle fingers, both beringed, and the chunky thumb which recently had joined in the action, and was used as a sometime spring to hold the index before it flicked out powerfully against the mossy cave. He had been attending this elective course for years, and until this moment the frequency of the activity had never seemed excessive or extraordinary. Similar to having a close relationship with a chronic nail-biter. After a time one simply did not notice it.

BUT . . .

Some little lift-off accomplished earlier by Pauline attuned him to

SONYA.

Almost against his will, he encountered, to his amazement, growing secretly as though a bulb in a darkened closet, the emergence of something hard pressing against the zipper of his trousers.

Sonya had given him an erection. A fine distinction that he drew between hard-on and erection. A new girl instantly inspired the former, a wife plugs for an erection. Ignoring the seafood cocktail, he instituted a search for the last known date of a true, unaccidental matrimonial *rite de passage*. Ticked off the months, working backward.

February, January, December = 0

That closed out the winter. A change of year too!

November, October, September.

The fall season, also *fartik*.

A fuzzy recollection in July. Both of them drinking gin and tonics after they ran out of Tom Collins mix and attempting to fathom the mysterious skills of croquet which he had set up on the lawn. Dead drunk, the two had jumped bare-ass into the pool. And then . . .

Marlene interrupted his trend of thought by calling his attention to the high incidence of mercury in the seafood he began to toy with.

In the orangerie, his eyrie, Sonya had been egged on to perform the impossible dream. An ice-cube French treatment. She'd almost choked, a cube had lodged in her windpipe. While she gagged he shoved it in to cut his losses. One of his sub-four-minute miles with the Missus.

Thus, around the time Cancer was making way for Leo, he and Sonya had consummated their last fling.

Observed her savoring the black bean soup. Fact was, some men might find her attractive with her whirligig haywire permanent. Kind of weird, this extravagant fricassee of clothes, jewelry, makeup, youthful face—a fine snub nose she had inherited from pioneer stock—lips almost black in this lighting. Definitely something different. Through the alchemy of neglect, a reedy figure in animal skins, Sonya had been transformed into a STRANGE PIECE . . . or had he in some fearful Pal-like reversion developed sinister urges for a pig? When she stared open-mouthed at him over the soup, the perpetrator and the recipient of the restaurant thigh feel-up regarded each other with downright shock. Once over her surprise, Sonya went back to her food, and Daniel thought he detected an odd constraint. She had not objected to his stroking her, but he got the impression that it had no effect on her, and the habitual touchings of men was a hangover from the indifference she'd developed as a stewardess when dirty paws had been the daily currency of her job.

Attached to him as scientifically in place as the wires of a

Keeler Polygraph, Norma registered that irresistible manic heat
fueled by jealousy. Another amazing revelation twisting genie-
like through the speed haze: Sonya definitely looked younger
than Norma. A teen queen matched up against a fortress of a
woman.

Her marriage to Max had aged Norma prematurely, or was
she simply one of those girls who have that postpubescent flourish
which is annulled when thirty wags its wicked finger? No question but that Norma was as preposterously handsome as a Mer-
cedes. Built for comfort, reliable, and uncompromisingly dull. A
clotheshorse who displayed herself brilliantly and pined for romantic lays. But after the coach-work had been admired, what
more was there to say?

How would she react to one of his matinees at Kit's? He'd
thought of broaching the subject during his swinging-couple
period—just as a gag—to see how she would react. Ultimately he
decided that she would never sacrifice her career as an emotional
blackmailer purely for the sake of pleasure. Norma, with her
magnetically sad eyes, had, he knew for certain, no entertainment value.

On the other hand, his inadvertent rub of Sonya excited him.
Rumblings from the ashes of a dead volcano. It was turning him
on in a peculiarly insistent way which defied explanation, spinning him on a revolving wheel. The very absence of contact had
regenerated desire, but there were differences which might be
worth exploring. She was beginning ever so slightly to shift her
leg away from him and he leaned over to whisper to her.

"You holding out on me?"

"I thought it was the other way around," she said without
enthusiasm.

"I've got a big investment in you . . . years of my life."

"About the only thing I'm sure of with you is that you like to
fight . . . for everything. All the rest is one long pure mystery
which I will never get to the bottom of."

The Rubins ceased their attack on the razor-thin slices of pork
which along with ten other national Brazilian delicacies had
been laid out on the table, leaving Max an open field.

"Can this be possible?" Marlene asked Gary who stopped
chewing to hear better. "Daniel and Sonya talking to each other,
like civilized?"

Norma selected dignity on her emotional chart, feigned not to notice Daniel's mischief. There was safety in writing him off as a professionally naughty boy and arguments as to his true feelings were suspended or shelved. One day though, he suspected, she'd lie in wait for him, and when he was unprepared, she'd try to ram it up his ass. He assumed her recurring fantasy was an end in itself.

The clatter of plates, knives, and forks presided over by Max's explorations and forays into foreign territory shielded Norma's bleat.

"I don't know what you're doing. But I don't like it one bit."

"You insisted on coming," he explained, "and you can't expect Sonya to welcome you with open arms."

"I can expect you not to make passes at your wife."

"Norma, relax, I was just kidding."

Marlene veering ever so slightly had fallen in love. Her new attachment was Dom Pérignon at twenty-five dollars a bottle. She had on special occasions tested New York and California varieties, at fashionable bar mitzvahs and continentally inspired weddings. But for her, French culture was emphatically exotic.

"I love this as my beverage," she informed her husband. "Get some more from that waiter."

"At last Marlene is into the better things," Daniel said innocently, failing to observe signs of impending drunkenness.

The suburban housewife sloshing champagne on an empty stomach was a homemade short-fused bomb when separated from her kitchen and standard meat loaf.

"Daniel, you haven't touched your food," Norma said.

The speed had made him forget and certainly aborted his appetite.

"Norma, I think I'll call you Momsey," said Sonya.

He picked at beans, pork, medallions of beef in a thick syrupy gravy, Brazilian peasant fare which cost half a lay with Pauline.

"Sonya, leave off Norma, will you, please?" Max asked quietly. He was the first to finish and was ungluing his undershorts from his seat.

"Gee, Max, I didn't mean anything," Sonya said. "It's just that everybody watches Daniel so closely and worries about his welfare that I feel out of it at times. You know, what's left for Sonya?"

"Empties," Marlene chortled.

"Ah, Marlene, a fellow sufferer. How about you, Norma?" Sonya's eyes had a fine malice. "Some things we gals have to stick together on."

"This is not a ladylike discussion," Max said, pressing forth his skills as arbitrator of social discourse.

"How come you haven't opened up our present?" Norma asked.

It was a solid-gold key ring with his initials on the back of a four-leaf clover. He kissed Norma in that stiff, standoffish manner which ancient intimacies impose on indiscreet men and which attempts to camouflage a history of carelessness. He shook Max's hand over pork ends.

"Gary, champagne!" Marlene commanded in the voice she used on unlistening children.

"Just relax," he said. "I think you've had enough."

"Never once have I had *enough*," she snapped, catching Sonya's eye, "of anything . . ."

Actually, the subject of who was getting what from whom had more than academic interest for Daniel. What exactly did the women do to relieve, arrest, the resident sexual doldrums which crept over their lives once frisky exploratory passion had ceased to be? Well, obviously the men searched for fresh blood, testing candidates for a night or a month. Oddly enough, he'd never thought about *them*. He knew perfectly well that Gary—in all the years they'd been friends—had never been on a retreat or a pussy fast. The electrifying crackle of her voice, wedded to an intolerable noisiness, suggested that Marlene had a prima facie case of *frustration*. His own doll unquestionably had other interests: rather touching in fact that she who had apparently been beyond education was now taking courses in . . . ? Well, she was searching for knowledge.

And Norma? The owner of an elderly collection of love themes from great Hollywood epics, featuring such heartrending unforgettables as *Duel in the Sun*; early Beatles; Dionne Warwick and the Bacharach syndrome of tearsiness—what of Norma when he wasn't stalling her, double-talking her out of the sack, plying her with Sonnerman's Delphic wisdom?

Max, come to think of it, was not a bad-looking man. Having surmounted his bachelor grossness and a certain intemperateness when free food and drink was in the offing, he was now in the full healthy flower of maturity. He couldn't exactly ignore those resilient pillions next to him in bed. Norma was not the most modest of women. He could hardly imagine her undressing in darkened rooms or locked cupboards, while Max staggered through the precinct wearing double-knit pajamas and a blindfold.

Occasionallllllllllly . . . something. Sinatra must have torched through their mini Fisher bedroom speakers. With a glass of chilled wine at her elbow, resting on a coaster, to be sure, Moonlight in Glen Head, L.I., although not precisely the Arabian Nights, would have served admirably as a suburban lab for Kama Sutra investigations.

It seemed clear to him that the miraculous accident of Benji, giving him legitimate "Uncle-Daddy" status in the boy's life, had also attached him to a listing ship.

Across the table something unmusical had forced Gary into a slouching position. Marlene had been denied . . . what? A public ass-whipping was in session, and Daniel was tempted to lean across and rap her teeth in.

". . . As I was saying, Sonya. Five minutes of intimate contact on a seasonally adjusted basis grates my nerves. . . . All I ever hear is Daniel this, Daniel that. Daniel needs me."

Max lowered his eyes, deciding that a systematic rape of both his and Norma's strawberry tart would be more intriguing than entering into the conversation. He gave Norma one of those knowing husband-to-wife warnings to keep out of it.

"How do I figure in all this?" Daniel asked.

"You don't," Gary replied. "Marlene just can't be taken out in public."

"That is the way Daniel talks to Sonya. You, mister"—she menaced him with two wagging fingers—"don't open a mouth to me or I'll wipe the floor with you."

"Every inch a lady," Daniel said. "You married one of nature's defenseless flowers."

"Gary is not going to California for two weeks without me. Understand, Daniel?"

"We're opening a new territory there?" Max inquired.

"I've got a few people for Gary to see," Daniel said.

"Gary's been opening entirely too many new territories this year," Marlene protested, sloshing more champagne, then glaring at Daniel. The cool purity of her hatred had the perfection of jade. Daniel reached out to fondle it.

"Marlene, for a long time I watched and listened and I'm really curious about one thing. . . . When you're eating Gary's balls, do you use a spoon or just the side of your fork?"

"Gary may be your friend . . . your *employee* . . . and Sonya your custom-made punching bag, but I, my dear, won't take any shit from you for a second. Now do we understand each other?"

Sonya did not look up from her plate. She would be satisfied with just a commentary. No visuals needed.

"By the way, what balls?" Marlene asked, insinuating that from her point of view the remark was abstract. "When he gets back from the office, there's nothing . . . but nothing left. Except a guy with graying hair, a very noticeable stomach sag, because no matter how good your condition is, if you spend your afternoons, every one of them, drinking booze, it has to show somewhere. I play hostess to a man coming out of the throes of his hangover. He enjoys my cooking, falls asleep at eight thirty and has a hand for one purpose . . . signing checks."

"Marlene," Max began, turning choleric. "I don't like that talk in fronta my wife."

Sonya gripped Max's hand and petted him, smiled angelically. "I am so glad that there is a real man here."

Next to Daniel, Norma was already shoving little handkerchief corners in her eyes.

"This is upsetting me, Daniel," Norma said, shrinking back.

He knew from his habitual encounters that she had not become one of the nation's finest criers without practice. Usually she irritated her eyes, forcing them to tear. From there it was one easy step to hysteria.

"When Gary leaves the office, I'm not responsible for him," Daniel said, narrowly gazing at him sitting stricken between them. A hostage bound and gagged.

"But maybe by following your example day in day out, exhaustion overtakes him the moment he puts his key in the front door."

"Much as it would flatter me to take full credit," Daniel said in a reassuring manner, "I'm not responsible for the fucking you're getting, Mrs. Rubin."

"Let's can this shit already," Gary cheeped through.

"Is that what they do?" Sonya inquired in her dozy choir-girl voice. "Fool around? Ye gads, Marlene, you mean to sit right there and tell me that my Daniel is not the loyal, faithful, truthful, respectable father of my two daughters?"

"Why can't Max go to California?" Marlene asked.

"Because you are not running my business. And if I send Gary that's my decision."

"Maybe Norma *wants* Max to go," Sonya suggested, still holding Max's hand. "With Max away, it would give you a little freedom. I mean, I am so happy at times to see the back of Daniel . . ."

Norma's lips moved in full synchromesh preparing for an aural blubber before the flood gates opened.

"Take me away from all this," she crooned to Daniel.

"Daniel is ruining our marriage, Gary. Can't you see he's a bad influence?"

"Marlene, you're drunk. If you weren't I'd tell you to fuck off."

"She is behaving very sober as far as I can see," Sonya corrected Gary. "Fact is," she continued sublimely relaxed, "that I am proud of Marlene for standing up to Daniel. I had her down as the ass-kisser of all time."

"Well, Sonya, you're goddam wrong. It has crossed my mind over the years"—she glared at Norma—"to have certain lady-to-lady discussions about unnamed but not entirely unknown parties."

"He was right about you," Gary said with resignation. "I never should have married a loudmouth like you who was gathering dust . . ."

"*He?* By he you surely don't mean that *nothing* across the table who suddenly became *important* when he fell by accident into the insurance business. He could not be the man who drives an inconspicuous white Rolls Royce in case anybody wondered if *he* had *money?*"

"I think you ought to thank God that Gary does give you five minutes of his time every month, Marle."

"Don't you call me Marle."

"One thing I never knew about you, Gary, even when we were kids, was how strong your stomach really was."

"Does not matter," Sonya mused aloud, "how much pussy these boys get every day. It is still impossible for them to have a pleasant dinner with their wives. Excepting Mr. Hoffman."

"Puss—?" Norma began, faltered, frowned, dabbed.

"Boys and girls," said Max, "what the hell are you all fighting about? You understand, Norma?"

Flashing through Daniel's mind as he flipped out his fresh hundred-dollar bills was that isle of tranquillity: Pauline Bianco. For a man she had all of the advantages of ownership and none of the headaches. She would become obsolete, not him. Yes, Pauline was just what he needed—a leasing agreement.

3

The plan, such as it was, called for an appearance at Raffles. Through the kind offices of Adele Weintraub, Daniel signed in as the luggage king. They received his usual table off the coast of Reykjavik, somewhere beyond the ten-mile limit.

But . . .

The group had kissed, forgiven, embraced, each vowing eternal friendship. Norma, however, remained aloof, nurturing reproofs, and clinging to her unforgivable coyness. She and Max had wandered to the dance floor.

Marlene had left her belligerence at dinner and she recommended a group Barnet-Rubin-Hoffman-Slotnick-Ackerman plot at Mount David cemetery, so that even underground she would have opportunities for coffee klatches and gossip. Whoever survived would insure that the headstones were polished and that colorful stones would be regularly supplied to make a good impression on the pilgrims with cameras who might venture out.

To make matters even more delightful and to relieve the gloom occasioned by the damage-inspection of the Rolls, Marlene and Sonya agreed to make a serious attempt to get high with the boys, so that idiotic solo gigglings and manic cravings for food might be shared family-style.

Apparently Marlene of them all was the most distressed by the damage to the car.

"It's a desecration. No matter what I said before. I am now talking from my heart."

"Don't you think I'd like to see you and Gary driving around in one?" he replied.

"Yours . . . damaged, what would it run?"

"Well, they hold their values. For you, Marlene, give or take a buck, thirty-five grand."

"I don't believe it." Over the thunderous music she reckoned aloud. "What with the insurance, and that must be a fortune—about gas I'm not even going to ask—you can't be just like wealthy, you've got to have *money*."

Sonya dropped her head on Gary's shoulder. He still revealed the wounds of dinner and was wandering through his failure period. Marlene gently prodded him.

"Come alive, sweetheart. . . . Gary, I have forgiven you, now dance with me, and pretend you're opening a new territory."

He allowed himself to be pulled up from the table, leaving Sonya and Daniel peering red-eyed through the gloaming of navy blue smoke and million-dollar lighting. Daniel had never seen Sonya zonked.

"I didn't even realize you could inhale."

"There are quite a few things you don't know about me."

"Really? You mean there are mysteries . . . still to discover?" he asked as they abandoned the table for T. Rex.

"I would like another one of those cigs to smoke."

"You can do that in the open in some places. But here I'm not even a member and being asked to leave would distress me. So, doll, let's see what I was missing."

Another surprise. Sonya could dance. Weaving and gyrating the lithe body, she seemed almost double-jointed, leaving most of the women on the floor for dead.

"Hey, you don't look at your feet anymore," he said, but she was not listening. Eyes closed, fingers snapping, she whipped herself into a happy frenzy. Across from him through a forest of bald heads shuffling the green in their pockets with youthful companions—could they all be the roommates of daughters?—Norma wiggled her belly in ever-diminishing circles and Max rolled his head. She struck him as a belly dancer from some third-rate stable of Turkish entertainers. He gave himself to the dance and reflections of Pauline. Next time a weekend in the sun. Sweeping aside such plans, he found himself tum-to-tum with Norma, while Max with stuttering feet attempted to keep up with Sonya.

"She thinks she's Tina Turner," Norma said critically.

"She ain't bad," Daniel observed factually. "I don't think I've been dancing with that woman since Don's kid got bar-mitzvahed . . . like two years ago?"

"I've had to wait longer."

"What about New Year's Eve? Anyway, you're one of nature's great waiters, Norma."

"I don't think you're being one bit funny. To put it mildly, Daniel, I'm fed up to death with you."

"Ah, come on, don't be so intense. What do you want me to do? You pushed the dinner and I couldn't have handled things any differently."

"Do you love me?" she asked in a little-girl voice which did not quite fit with the ski-tracked breast fighting for release. She'd do fine for a Bunny Mother.

"Of course I do. Even though you're putting on a little winter coat."

As usual he'd offended her. She moved with the unwieldy gratuitous hand motion that characterize women on one of those starvation dance diets. With Max, what else? Opting for security with Max, Norma had been trundled into middle age, and he sadly reflected that he was to blame. Out of the wonderland of their affair, a child had emerged, but he was being raised in the Hoffman tradition, and Daniel would never know how it felt to have a son as his pal. Only at such moments did Daniel experience the pain of his predicament. But it was no longer the soft malleable wound of the past, rather the stony gristle of a calcium deposit at the elbow.

"I think we've reached that point of no return, Daniel," she observed severely.

"Oh, airline lingo and you're not even a former stewardess."

"Cut it out. Either we straighten ourselves out tonight or . . ."

"Or what?"

They moved off the dance floor to the bar and Daniel ordered two Armagnacs and popped another pill. Norma put her hand in his jacket pocket and fished out the bottle.

"Beautiful combination," she noted. She shrugged her shoulders and looked at him fidgeting. "I guess we spend so little time together that I don't know what you do."

"You really care? Or is it just easier to spin the whole thing out?"

"You know damn well that I love you. I mean, Daniel, honestly, do you ever wonder about Max and me?"

"You make adjustments very easily, Norma."

"Well, what do I do at four thirty in the morning if he wakes up and reaches over? Call the police?"

"Let's go back to the table."

"You don't want to hear, do you? I'm tired of being used. I'm not a convenience or a receptacle or a lost and found department. I've wasted my youth on you and all I have to show for it is one illegitimate son, a lifetime of waiting by telephones and the infrequent screw when you can spare the time. And that's all."

He had always possessed a wealth of compassion for himself and once again the career professionally-injured party sprang to his own defense.

"Why now? Just this minute?" he said.

"Maybe it's the weather, or Benji, or Max nagging me to get the hell out of New York and move to a warm climate. He's got enough money and he can read an insurance table and he isn't going to last forever and he doesn't like bussing or putting alarms in the house or feeling faint if the phone rings six times and he expects me to be in. So he keeps talking about wanting to pack up and get out. . . . I've waited long enough for you, and there's been too much left unsaid between us . . . because it suited you."

She disengaged herself from him and as he was about to follow, Marlene took his arm and led him back. Women from his past and present hemmed him in, making demands and registering protests. It seemed to him only at Kit's could he find a sanctuary.

"You really upset me before. Imagine saying I cut Gary's balls off. Daniel, we're supposed to be friends."

"I told a lie?"

"In a way you did. I couldn't cut off what never was. Can you imagine my frustration for just one second . . . ?"

"I'll try," he replied, inspecting the bar for strays who might at least provide a place, other than Marlene's face, for him to rest his eyes.

"You are Gary's oldest and closest friend." He nodded. "I live with him and through all the ups and downs, I believe I got to know every side better than any person on the face of the earth . . ."

"Agreed," he said, overwhelmed by the tedium of a housewife's confessional.

"But *you* know him better than I do. That's what's killing me. You were his friend before we met, you're still his friend. You know the truth, Daniel, and I live on a diet of illusions, self-inflicted guilt—that maybe it's my fault we're not so terrific anymore. I blame him, he blames me. Would you tell me what Gary is really like?"

Draining the last of his Armagnac, Daniel recognized the familiar danger flares of Marlene's inquisition. Gaining his second wind and fully alert, he guardedly replied:

"How can I? Marlene, only *you* could rate his performance."

"You're suggesting that it's pretty good."

"I'm suggesting nothing. You're the wife, he's the husband."

"But would it be asking too much to give me an indication of what he was like before we met?"

She paused for breath and he hoped she would not regain it. These women were coming at him in waves, as unremitting as the tides.

"Gary is the only man I've ever been to bed with . . . and I've never been sure if I'm with Muhammad Ali or a dive artist."

Max and Norma were beginning to snuggle close to each other on the dance floor, and out of his weariness a diamondlike form of indestructible anger took hold of him.

"Don't ask me all these silly trick questions. Gary never discusses your personal life."

"You discuss yours with him?"

"Never," he said with finality. Denial—constant, meretricious, inviolate—was his creed.

"You ever thought what . . . I would be like in the hay?"

"Seriously?" Her open face hedged him in. "I'm married to two women as it is."

"Am I asking you to leave Sonya and Norma for me? No. I just asked has it crossed your mind . . . us."

"In a perverse kind of way, yes, I guess over the years I have wondered."

"Why? So you could say that you laid your best friend's wife? Now come on, let's have the truth about my Gary. Which pig is he keeping?"

Dumped her at the bar. At the table an assortment of empty liqueur glasses explained the passionate conversation of Gary and Mrs. Barnet. Intruding on them? He stopped short, a little too short, for Marlene stepped on the back of his shoe.

"Gary . . . order me another drink. For the first time in ages I am really getting charged up. Another thing, I think I like marijuana. I would like to *do* it again . . . but running to the car in this cold weather, then back here . . ."

"How have you stayed married to Marlene?" Daniel inquired.

"The same way you and Sonya stick together. With a little glue, a piece of string, and a skate key," Gary replied.

"I am feeling just wonderful," said Marlene. "What would really make me very happy is the truth. Golden, shining, the sunlight, the health, the perfection, of the TRUTH."

"I've heard of a place," Daniel noted, "where you can sit around, smoke grass, put headphones on and do exactly what you feel like."

"It's getting late," said Gary.

"Are you about to chicken out?" Marlene thundered at him.

"I'm frightened of you? You're kidding, Marle. I give you your own way because it just doesn't matter to me," he explained.

"Sounds to me like we are all prepared to put our little asses on the table and yours truly is not the teeniest bit afraid," Sonya piped in.

"That also goes for Max and me. If we're not intruding on you, Daniel," Norma said, hovering above him.

"Where now?" Max asked, checking out his chronometer and yawning.

"Downtown," said Daniel. "You can have a late morning for once."

"Why is the truth always downtown?" Marlene inquired.

The men waited while the girls prepared themselves for the occasion with fresh coats of lipstick.

4

At the long, scuffed bar in Sally's three bartenders dealt drinks with the speed of faro dealers. Before Daniel had an opportunity to duck he was hemmed in by The Pal and John Reno, locked in a camaraderie of shot glasses and cigarettes smoked to the length of roaches. Sitting in her cozy corner with Leo, Kit, only marginally drunker than she'd been that afternoon, was gaily singing to herself and a bottle of Jack Daniel's.

"How far is this going to go?" said Gary.

"No whispering, you two, or the whole point of this exercise is defeated," Sonya yelled ahead as they attempted to lose her in the crowd and warn the team that they had brought amateurs with them.

Marlene had burst forth as a diehard recruit, holding her breath, choking, gasping, blowing out her cheeks, constantly demanding of Gary and Daniel the answer to:

"Am I high yet? I can't stop talking . . . but a conversationalist I have always been."

"If you were quiet," Gary suggested, "I'd give you a verification." His nervousness angered him. "Why don't you just wander around and discover . . ."

"I don't see what's worrying you," Daniel replied before entering the charmed circle. "What's at stake, except your wife? If you live another forty years, can't you visualize yourself without Marlene?"

"I'm just not sure. But I don't want anything to come out that could be embarrassing."

"To who? You or Marlene?"

Gary always shrank from combat, ducked confrontations whenever he could, for uncertain fears conquered and governed his character, and there were moments when Daniel despised him.

The opportunity to resolve the two strands of his daily life waited patiently, just a few feet ahead or light-years away. The opportunity was tailor-made for self-revelation. In showing the women the duality, a resolution of some kind might be the next step to a just exchange: the lie for the truth. In a sense the precarious balance of every married man was at stake and in spite of unforeseeable consequences the crucial element of danger attracted Daniel. Here in the flesh was the factual summary and record of his life with Sonya, he reflected, and she deserved a chance to see where she had driven him.

"The worst that can happen is that Marlene will forgive you. She can't be jealous of you laying hookers."

"We're talking about *your* idea of my wife, and what she is. Two different people."

"Well, leave if you think it's going to be too rough. If Marlene can't look at the facts, you're going to spend the rest of your life kissing her ass. Come on, Gary, grow up."

"I think Sonya's got herself picked up . . . by two chicks."

"She'll find me when she wants to."

Norma watched Daniel through an assortment of mixed nuts while Max found himself conjoined to a group of male hustlers who looked at him and wondered exactly what kind of time he was on the prowl for. Daniel crooked his finger at Norma and she edged uncertainly toward him, guarding her purse.

"What is this place?" she asked with a shudder, gripping his wrist.

Under the Old Spice, the smell of grilled meat leaped from Reno's hair.

"That Daniel, he don't never fuckin' stop. Orways got himself fresh talent," Reno said.

The Pal did an instant body-reading of Norma and informed Reno of his verdict: "No drums, no trumpets."

"I'm seeing you, Daniel, seeing you, you know."

"It's about time."

Turning to his friends at the bar, Daniel felt himself drifting to a state of lucid consciousness. The Pal elbowed some customers away to make room for him.

"This is Norma," he said to the group. "She isn't our idea

of talent, she's the nice respectable wife of my office manager."

"Yours here too?" The Pal asked.

"Who are you?" Norma asked.

"Who am I?" asked the Pal. "My name's Anthony John Palazallo. And I'm a friend of Daniel's. His asshole buddy."

She shrank back, greedily gulping a brandy that Daniel had shoved in her hand.

"Why? Why?" she muttered.

"You guys are nuts," said Reno, who had overheard, "bringing your wives here. I'm shocked . . ."

"Which one's yours, Daniel?" asked The Pal.

"The blonde down the end."

The two men leaned forward, craning their heads over the bartender on their mission to view Mrs. Barnet. The lighting, smoke haze, and constant regrouping of people provided them with only a glimpse.

"Yours isn't bad, Gary," said Reno. "Reminds me of my number two. . . . Still got a soft spot for her."

Leo left his place at Kit's side and wormed into the pack. He carried out an eagle-sharp inspection on Norma, a housewife buying by weight.

"Where'd you get the retread from?" he asked. "I think Kit can use them knockers. California Charlie ring again lookin' for the outsize department. Where you working, honey, 'cos if you want a bookin' we might wing you in latter part of the week."

"I am Daniel's mistress," she said with pomp and an air of profound disbelief that these were his friends.

"What, for the hour?" Leo said with a nasty chortle as his eyes darted over her legs and ankles.

"Daniel wears 'em out real fast. Kit's best 'scream uncle' when the master gets going," The Pal said reeling drunkenly.

Leo snapped his fingers at Kit. Business? An audition. She shifted her stool from the caddy corner closer to the boys.

"Daniel and Gary brought their wives and this is—what?—like Norma. Claims she's straight."

"Daniel, when are you going to get normal again and stop putting us on?" Kit said with a flighty chuckle that stopped abruptly in a head-on collision with the twisted disclosure of pain imprisoning Norma. "For real? For real, Daniel?"

"I'm not his wife. He just cheats with me . . . and on me."

Norma regrouped her forces and pushed to the center, for once the focal point in Daniel's life, and determined not to back down.

Kit climbed off her stool and touched Norma's shoulder.

"You're not a business girl," she said in a clear sober voice.

"Norma is a part-time woman and a full-time conscience," Daniel said, beginning to wobble again. "Norma, you're not crying!"

"You and Gary are out of your heads," Kit said angrily, like a teacher reviling malicious boys. "Well, me, I don't know either one of you."

"It's Daniel's fault!" Gary explained, terror-stricken.

Gary hesitated, rocked back and forth on the balls of his feet. Still time to leave. Disengage himself from Daniel for good. The awful powers of male friendship connived against him, impaling him on the safe fence he had dangled his legs from since he'd been a boy. He had permitted Daniel to tear a way through the jungle so that he might walk fearlessly. And now, in the easy, thoughtless fashion of a man *only* along for the ride, he knew that Daniel would be placing him in jeopardy. Marlene staggered toward him.

"Gary, I need some air. . . . I thought this was a club. It's just another bar with lousy lighting. . . ."

He took her by the arm, nodding farewells, and creepily whispered: "You got away lucky at dinner . . . but this is a bad mistake."

"Well, Daniel," Kit said in a tone of resignation, "one of you isn't an asshole."

"Kit, what's wrong with you?" Leo demanded.

"Listen, piss-pot, I've been hustling in this business for ten years, and I'm not going to go through any shit with wives. You think I want to fall again? And what do you think is going to happen if I get princesses from Long Island steamed up at me? You guys want to play games with your old ladies, then do it without me. I'm splitting. Get the tab, Leo. Christ almighty, Daniel. I know you've got trouble with your head now that you've got more money than you know what to do with, but baby, you're looking down a gruesome street if you don't cut out right now."

"You've got no business talking to clients like that," Leo said aggressively. He grabbed her face in the palm of his small hand. "I'll slap your teeth down your throat, you fucking cunt."

Calmed her down. The stern whip hand of the little jockey. The wild menace in his eyes terrified her, and she loved it, crumbled, the human glue of the booze spattering.

"Leo, we'll wind up blowing the whole business," she pleaded.

"One more word and I'll kick your ass in. Here and now! Daniel's done us favors. You got a pretty short memory, you lowlife bimbo."

"I haven't forgotten a thing and I can see what's coming. . . ."

Daniel placed an affectionate friendly arm around Kit, but she flung his hand off.

"What can happen?" Daniel asked calmly.

"Anything. I've come a long way since I was dealing Spigleman blow jobs and I don't want to go that route again. Taking a rap as a business girl is nothing, but getting hit for keeping a joint again . . ." she shuddered. "They'll bury me this time."

"Whatever you want, Daniel," Leo said.

For once Norma just listened, and Daniel was overwhelmed by a curious mixture of elation and respect. No romantic illusions remained to entrap them. At the far end of the bar, Sonya was surrounded by a butch group plying her with drinks while Max, lighthearted and laughing raucously, prodded her on.

"Know what's effed Kit? Rich Larry didn't show and she was stuck two hundred for Pauline. Because when we got a call out, it's our responsibility to see that she gets paid and not the client," Leo explained. "And Kit's spent the whole evening trying to con Reno and Pal into cutting the expense if they'll shell out the bread."

Daniel fed two hundred-dollar bills into Kit's hand.

"You're now off the hook and in profit," he said.

"See," Leo shouted at her, "you piece of garbage, what it means to have a gentleman for a friend." He wrenched the bills away from Kit and dug his long nails into her wrist and when at last she nodded her head in defeat he let her go.

"Where's Pauline?" Daniel asked.

"In the club," Leo said. "Should I tell her you paid for the privilege . . . again?"

"When I'm ready. Make it up with Kit. She's crying."

"I would . . . but maybe you didn't know . . . her scene is abuse . . . and punishment."

Kit a woman? Daniel had admired her cool disdain, her organizational abilities and unflappable manner since she had set up in business. It gave him the geeks to see her sit back in the corner shuddering. Something inviolate had been struck down in the temple, and a five-foot-one-inch former jockey with large yellow teeth and hair slicked down with some gooey wave set which on windy days blew off his head in a thick clustered hank, each night took charge of her. The little baby-size-five boot which the maid Ethel dusted weekly and polished monthly was driven right into Kit's ass.

She, *her, Kit,* just another woman, who put in fourteen-hour stretches, chased, grifted the lost, meek deranged victims of marriage and lovelessness, so that Leo could piss the hard-earned dollar away on limp ponies, based on info that scored once every ten times. A broke, deadbeat jockey who cringed before Daniel and whined for the loan of a few thou so that the bookies he owed would not push his face in, tear him limb from limb.

"Daniel's made a lifetime study of punishment," Norma said. "He just opens a woman like one of his new territories then rips her belly open."

Leo looked at her as though she were insane.

"Somethin' wrong with that, sister? You seem to be thrivin' on the treatment. My ole lady sops up abuse, eats it the way some chicks swallow cock."

Norma pushed forward like a lioness about to attack.

"Are you the butcher where Daniel shops?"

"I'm the man that knows the value of women. I clean 'em from under my fingernails every mornin'. They ain't shittin' on my head."

Savage and wild-eyed, Leo leaned behind the bar and yanked a bottle of Jack Daniel's off the shelf and slid it along to Kit, who sat in woebegotten shades of gray-white, unable even to turn the screw cap, a service which Leo performed stylishly and with a flourish.

"See, Leo knows what the lady needs. Well, honey, that settles the problem of Pauline. I'll let her know upstairs."

Before Daniel's eyes, Norma was slowly but systematically

beginning to fall apart, but still striving, imploring herself to remain intact. She began, for no apparent reason, to roll her head from side to side.

"Who is Pauline?"

"One of my valentines."

"I love this man," Leo said hugging Daniel. He turned on The Pal and Reno. "They been hangin' around all night waitin' for Pauline to reduce the price. What have you cunt-eaters got to say for yourselves now?" he needled.

"If you were a foot shorter I'd be able to piss on your head without moving my ass off the stool," said The Pal.

"You couldn't fight like a gentleman, you guinea shitbox," he said, jumping like an animated dummy and weaving, setting his minuscule fists in motion. "I'd shoot right in that belly—bam goes the ravioli in your gut—splat-splat, the orange goo disintegrates and I'm standing over you kicking your head in. Yeow, man, I love you guys."

Norma leaned her head on Daniel's shoulder, weary and battered.

"I guess somebody's prepared to go to hell for you."

"I loaned him a few thousand last year when he was in trouble."

"And that was enough?" she asked quietly.

He placed an arm around her.

"For some people, favors like that change their lives. Office manager I once worked for took a personal pride—no matter what I did—in carving me up for years and I was so shit scared of him and being thrown out that I kept my balls in the desk drawer. But did I repay that favor? Sure, I just hired him and pay him three times more than he's worth, so that a lady I love and our small son can have the best things in life."

"Do you hate us? You see, Daniel, I'm trying—trying so hard to understand."

"What is there to understand? The only way to deal with extortion is bribery, the only thing worth paying a price for is freedom. Kit, I'm going upstairs, so if two people come looking, make sure they find me."

As always, Norma followed meekly behind.

They passed into a small darkened anteway lit by a single green-painted bulb which threw off a sallow sickly light. At the counter stood Sally, a man of indeterminate age and sex. Daniel had seen him in both a tuxedo and an evening gown. For ten dollars a head he provided a set of headphones and the liberty of a cork-walled room which was chopped up into alcoves with tables set back in black gloom. Cushions and headrests and innumerable outlets for the headphones were the amenities of each section of the room; and on the four walls, lights mixing with pornographic films flashed subliminally, so that Norma found herself alone for the moment as she turned her head full circle to watch what was going on.

"You shock me. Paying this money just to watch dirty movies," she said. She stopped and gasped at a live display in one of the rookeries.

Through the murk, he detected, sitting in a corner, a familiar figure and a lingering perfume scent tickling his nose.

"I heard you picked up on me. What do you want to do?" Pauline inquired. She opened her small daintily embroidered handkerchief and offered him a snort, and when he seemed to hesitate said: "Don't get so worried, Daniel B., it's just a little coke."

"Why is Leo so pissed off?"

"His junk connection stiffed him, and he's on a search-and-destroy mission."

He turned to look for Norma, but in the permanent night-world of upstairs at Sally's she was invisible.

"I brought my girlfriend . . . and my wife, along for the ride."

"Well, that's the outfield and the pitcher," she said hinting at unexplored possibilities . . . infinity.

He found himself growing puzzled and uncertain of his motives, as he lifted off with a snort, finding a new level, but hunting for a "safe house," and respite from an unmanageable predicament. And yet, he sat riveted next to Pauline. Touching her hand, he thought he'd finally found a woman he would not abandon.

"Sooooo, Daniel? Are you scared? See, me, when I get paid I've got this middle-class bug about . . . delivering. You've gone for four-fifty today and I feel under an obligation. Kit and Leo covered the short, but with your green in my hand, well, it's like unfair . . . ."

"My wife . . . ?"

"Or your girlfriend?"

"How do I decide?"

Pauline took a long snort, then sipped her Fresca, the perfect engagement of no-cal pleasure. She had found the answer to mystery.

"Depends on who can cut it without getting panicky."

"Maybe that's what I want to find out. You know day in day out for years I've been covering the same fucking territory without either of them. What would it be like?"

"I'll be cool. If when you're ready to go, you change your mind, I'll still owe you. You can collect whenever . . . all right? I just felt that you're one good guy and I don't want you to ever think like I hustled you . . . or Kit did for me. Check it out and don't look so worried, I glue marriages back together, I don't bust them. They won't be jealous, you understand. Nobody ever is . . ."

The sinuous shape moved off into the blackness, leaving him in his permanent state—alone. As he was about to slip on the phones, he heard the fearful eerie whine of a woman. Could not place or identify it. A woman in pain, or coming? Both sounded the same to him. No more tidy compartments for him, he thought, unlike the two Germanys, he would become one with himself. Unity. But before that quite took place . . .

Norma's shrieks overpowered the room. People partially dressed poked out their heads like mice. A stomping of feet, a nerve-rending whine from the amplifier, dropped works, half-smoked joints were flung down.

Kit pulled Daniel off his cushion, and in the center of the room dim images of hair, breasts, and genitals belonging to no one had found a home, and splayed across Norma's face. She had lurched into the line of the film projector.

Green-yellow ick-drik-ich shot uncontrollably out of Norma's mouth. It seemed as though old diseases had been remaindered in her gut, and suddenly spewed forth. A multicolored explosion. Bits of half-chewed undigested tomato in a slush slime of internal gravy splattered over her stockings.

"Oh, Max, help me, please."

Daniel stopped short, for the wrong man had been called to the aid of his country. Norma sat down on the floor and looked up at him.

"Oh, Christ. You . . . filth," she groaned feebly at him, before she was seized with another bout of retching. Scalloped bits of meat and sour booze, and something at the back of her throat she fought to expel, forced her to surge forward and press her palms on the butt-laden floor. A wheezed hacking-rack of a cough with no phlegm shook her body.

"Uch, that Leo pimp was injecting himself and he tried to touch me . . ."

Out of the festering swamp, a clean-cut American beauty walked as though gliding over the Nile.

"Norma has always had a weak stomach and a loud mouth," his doll, primping at her hair, advised him like a weather recording.

No wide-eyed cornball hick, the former Sonya Anderson, National Southern's own professional housekeeper, just a mean grim chick. Daniel was almost proud of her. She'd been forged out of steel. He lifted Norma off the floor, but she disengaged herself.

"You're the saddest man I ever met," she said.

"No! He is not . . . not yet. Daniel, would you like to see your guests home?"

"Where's Max?" he asked.

"I'll show you."

At the side entrance, lying in the alleyway with the wreckage of uncollected garbage hanging like colloid suspensions from the rims, Max sat with a gash over his eye. Alarmed prowling cats and rats drifted past his feet. The cold had become tactile and putrid smells hung frozenly embalmed in the windless cul-de-sac.

He rose to his feet, still apologetic: "Them girls took me here to show me *what* they do."

"You okay, Max?" Daniel asked.

"Well, I got robbed. I guess I was a schmuck to go outside. Where's my Norma?" he asked after his crown jewels.

"She had too many drinkies," her hostess said.

Feeling obviously better without dinner and Dom, Norma reached Max. She held her mink coat away from her dress. It was said that vomit infected both cars and fur.

Sally fended for a cab. Did not want any trouble, and Daniel laid fifty on the driver, gave the address and forcibly had to close the door, for Max was busy thanking him for dinner and apologizing yet again for having abused his hospitality.

"I'll be in sharp, though . . ."

As the cab pulled away to a globe-circle of Glen Head, a coatless Daniel breathed in the fresh purity of clean February air.

"Sonya, you amaze me. But it's three thirty and if you want to quit , , ,"

"Your party, Daniel. I'd like to see more freaks."

"We've got each other."

They walked to the front, sheltering under the ragged canopy that had gone through a dozen aborted names before emerging as Sally's.

At the curb, his ass propped under a massive orange foam-rubber cushion, Leo pressed down the electric window of the Eldorado.

"How's that party, Daniel?" he shouted as Kit and Pauline huddled, freezing, before sprinting to the car.

Sonya extended her hand, shook with Leo over the wheel, Kit and Pauline.

"I'm Daniel's wife, Sonya." She stabbed an accusing finger into the soft territory of Daniel's stomach. "Why am I the last person to meet Daniel's friends?"

"Ask Daniel that," said Kit, attempting to shut the window, but fearful of catching Sonya's fingers.

"Where are you going?"

Pauline leaned across Kit from the middle of the front seat.

"Join us if you like."

"Leo!" Kit barked.

The window closed. Sonya and Daniel stood shivering and stared at their damaged Rolls.

"Don't you want to show me what you do . . . and where you go . . . when you are not with either of us?"

"Either who?" he said, jamming the key in the door.

"Me or Norma."

5

Kit seemed uneasy back at the apartment. Her horoscope, and the *I Ching*, prophesied events which would have serious repercussions. With a faltering tongue, slurring and slipping,

forgetting which point she intended to make, she failed to com-
municate to Daniel the vision of destruction clouding her red-
rimmed blood-flecked eyes. Leo's hands were all over her,
pinching her flesh, his teeth digging into the soft, flaccid skin
of her neck until she screamed with pain. Sonya wandered from
room to room, in the manner of a prospective buyer.

"Wallllll, one thing we have at home that you have here," she
said, setting down her highball glass on the table in front of the
sofa. "Contour sheets . . ."

"My wife is so observant and practical-minded," Daniel said.
"She used to make a bed like a champ, but sometimes she's for-
getful about unimportant personal things."

"Could it be that I am not too anxious to encourage you?"
she said with a sly grin. "Now if I knew where you had been,
I might be more obliging."

"You're blowing my mind, Sonya," said Pauline. She ran her
fingers on Daniel's stubbly chin. "You got yourself a real sharpshooter and you never knew."

"He is so naive as to be untrue," Sonya said.

"I'm naive?" Daniel croaked. His throat was raw from all the
rough dirty twig-filled grass that he'd smoked, for Leo was too
beat to bother cleaning it. "When you don't get what you're
after at home, you find it elsewhere. Paying for it makes it painless."

"That is where you are wrong. Involvement is what makes it
exciting. But the type of man you are, you might just as well
be boring it into the ass of a sheep."

Prancing about gaily, and not the least bit winded, Sonya reminded him of a new bride about to take possession of her future
home. That she could outsmart or outthink him still seemed as
remote a possibility as parallel lines converging.

But he began to notice something . . . well, a little odd about
her. A quivering outline that harkened back to his early Miami
encounter with her. Sonya had been a cinch *lay*.

In exploring the sexual wilderness of their life together, he
was confronted by simple biological logic. She had to be getting
it somewhere. On the other hand, who but Daniel Paul Barnet
existed for her?

Who could his doll pull? A single man would run for his life,
and nobody was going to destroy a home for her. The U.S.A. was

waiting for Sonya to return to a legal state of singleness? No, he'd never lose Sonya unless he decided to push it.

Kit had taken the precaution of telling him not to blow the TOP SECRET aspects of her apartment.

"She might turn vicious," he was admonished.

"You don't know her. Not a mean bone in the body."

But he did wonder how she'd respond to the truth about Kit's. Probably giggle madly. In the area of human feeling, Sonya had a permanent vacancy disguised by an excess of nervous energy. While everyone flaked out, the worse for wear, she darted like a curious lizard through the bedrooms.

"You're making me nervous," he complained. "It's enough already with the walking. I'll take you home."

"Why don't we stay here? Kit's got plenty of bedrooms."

A hint of ambiguity. Could it be that soiled, semen-stained sheets, the stacks of dirty towels and washcloths littering all of the bathrooms had given Sonya the idea that she might be in some type of boardinghouse or pension?

"You're always welcome to stay," said Leo. "It's awful late to cut that long drive."

"I don't mind," Sonya replied. "And Daniel is beat, isn't he?"

Danger appealed to his instincts. Under the same roof were the elements of all of his fantasies and he suspected the resolution of his difficulties. The shadowy walls, the rooms now empty containers, the sleepy people, the mauled bar with its gimp wooden temporary leg which Leo had been promising to fix for years, all suggested that the history of Daniel's life had somehow been detained each day he spent there. In a sense Kit's stopped time, confined him to eternal youth and represented some schoolyard for male adults, and as the girls came and went so did the seasons of sports. Along with the absence of time was the stillborn twin of guilt which had never roused its sleeping head to haunt or accuse him. Without guilt, there were no memories, only sensations . . . fragments of himself, totaling nothing on the divine balance sheet.

Sonya followed him into Bedroom Three. She was beginning to weaken, sat down on the highbacked chair, the springs of which had been so heavily damaged by the mass of human traffic that the coils inside as though inhabited by metal parasites tore, whirled, and squirmed inside each other. He had sat on the chair hundreds of times when concluding a half-and-half treatment. The girl down on her knees blowing him to kingdom come, while he himself the recipient of the labors thought of something else.

She, Sonya, was obviously of two minds: to yank off the boots and flake out on the bed with him, or to put on her coat and doze off on the drive home.

"Daniel, what is this place?" she asked as he slumped down on the bed, resting his back on the headboard.

"You don't know . . . ?"

"I want you to tell me."

"Guess," he said abruptly.

"I've never been in a whorehouse before, but I'm pretty sure that is what goes on up here."

"Keep joining those numbered dots. . . ."

"Kit and that little man run it . . ."

"It's like you've had a brain transplant."

"How often do the two of you—you and Gary—come here?"

"That depends entirely on you. . . . I'm only speaking for myself."

"I see," she said pulling off a boot. "I guess I've known for some time," she added without surprise or emotion. "How long have you been . . . ?"

"Years . . ."

"And Gary of course plays follow the leader. At his age it is pretty sad."

"And at my age?"

"Well, we have been sharing a failure since we met."

She got up and brushed her hair, dabbed some perfume behind her ears, then went to the window to look out and saw only an opaque smeared pane.

"There is a rotten odor in here. But I don't expect you would notice," she said without sarcasm.

"The poisons of the body."

"I am surprised at you. I thought, if he is going to a place it will be elegant and have a certain class that Daniel thinks he wants because he doesn't have any himself. My dear man, this is a slaughterhouse."

"All I care about is convenience. I don't want romance, and sad songs don't make my eyes cloud with tears."

"I don't suppose that anything affects you any longer. But you

do have attachments. Norma's been pretty constant," she said.
"Did you know about her?"

"Gads, for ages. Don't understand what you found so fantastic
about screwing that tub. Ahhhh, the convenience. When you
were at Princeton. That's why you hired Max. I figured it out
then, real quick."

She tugged off her other boot and massaged the squashed toes,
ran her fingers through her hair and the set of her mouth disturbed him, for it reflected the deepest form of irony. Sonya
was actually gay.

"All this time, my man has been drinking coffee out of a
machine."

"You can claim all the credit for that."

"Bull-sheeeet. You have never given me a chance. You care
about just coming. Not about what happens to me."

A reference to his sometime forced entry of her without due
preparation irritated him. She did not understand that this
method gave him heroic stature, had developed into an act of
burglary—the raging, anarchic vandalism of a Hell's Angel—for
he who, like most men, would never have the opportunity or
inclination to heave through a locked door.

"I still do not understand why you want to spoil everything
between us."

"Like what? What is there between us that hasn't been
smashed?"

"Well, there is the fact of our hatred which has withstood all
sorts of tests and there is that emotion in our sex. My reluctance
to fuck you which turns you on, and makes you a crazy man."

"I touch you and you jump away."

"I have been giving you exactly what you want from me. If I
did not reject you, we would have split up ages ago. I mean to
say your comings and goings have been so out in the open that it
is no longer gossip. Most people assume we have agreed to go
our separate ways. Which is fine."

Felt a grudging respect for her which defied reason.

"You were never hurt?" he asked, beginning to get the cold
tired uneasy sweats.

"I have a long history of hurts . . . way before I met you, I
had been humiliated so often when I was a kid, and then later
on, that you did not matter one bit to me."

"Why do you think I brought you up here?" he demanded.

"To see how far you could go with me, and to humiliate me."

"How far can I go?"

"Well, Daniel, arm yourself . . . with spurs."

She was beyond pain with him, and all of the others. Sonya had entered a dimension where devils abounded and cruelty was King. She stripped down to her panties and bra, then flung across the chair the familiar pantyhose.

"Oh, I love it," Daniel said. "Boy, you should have told me you had it in you."

Always she could hit the nerve end as though she had practiced acupuncture for the Chairman. Never failed to incense him. The blood rushed frantically to his head spurring him to action.

"Should I whip that piece of tail in here?"

"I am in your hands, Daniel. I am not afraid."

"You implying I am?"

"Show me."

His hands trembled and he stood irresolutely in the doorway. Confused by the exchange of roles. Leading her, he discovered he was being led. There was a sly mocking expression on her mouth, the bottom lip pushing and overwhelming the top, engulfing it.

"You're sure about this? Because Pauline is very mechanically inclined."

"Isn't everybody nowadays?"

"I wouldn't want you to panic."

"I have been flying on one engine for so long that it does not frighten me at all."

"One other thing, Sonya, if this upsets you and tomorrow it just might, if you start hollering lawyer, I promise to bury you alive."

"What in the name of heaven would I want to get a lawyer for?"

He stumbled from one room to the next, where the threesome were tuned to the insomnia chiller on Channel Nine. Leo got up from the sofa to make room for him, while Kit's eyeballs remained glued to the screen. In between viewing, Pauline pampered her toenails with an orange stick, thwacking cuticles.

"Made up your mind yet?" she asked. "Because like seven thirty tomorrow morning I'm winging it to Jamaica."

"Daniel, if you want some friendly advice, I think you're making a big boo-boo," said Kit as a commercial offering blacks a piece of the action bombarded the sleeping airwaves. "You set it up with Pauline for a sun and fun fling, it's one thing. But here and now could be bad news."

"Why don't you keep your nose out of other people's business," Leo said truculently. "Maybe this is what Daniel wants here and now. Could be he needs it."

Pauline popped a pair of spansule leapers, swallowing them noisily, then plopped barefoot on the floor. She opened the hall closet, where Kit and Leo apparently had stored every bit of forgotten clothing they'd been landed with.

Pauline brought out her sample case.

"I still don't think it's right," Kit said.

"Close the yap before I kick it in," Leo snarled at her. "Daniel is practically supporting this place and *you* don't tell him a fuckin' thing. . . ." He handed Daniel a couple of joints. "Your Missus is an improvement over that big momma. Go to it, Daniel, and give 'em hell. I wish to God my hangup was as simple as yours. You don't know what it's like to match wits with three thousand horses six days a week. Man, that's a big habit. If only I could get myself so loaded on grass or lose myself with a piece of ass, my life'ud be one long beautiful symphony."

Sonya had not moved from the chair. Staring into space, she appeared not to notice the entrance of Daniel and Pauline. He had a profound sense of disbelief when the two women were together. Face to face. Sonya's presence and restraint shook him. All of them interlocked in some recurring nightmare, the meaning of which he could not penetrate immediately. A low ululant sound wailed in the still room and he wondered whether it came from the women or himself. Under the window, he realized that the troubling noise was the hissing clang emitted by the central heating. Like a spectator at a sporting event waiting for the commencement of the game, he sat on the edge of the dresser watching the two women size each other up. His heart palpitated irresponsibly.

The veteran of many such scenes announced that she would use the bathroom first.

"She is fantastic," Sonya said admiringly. "No nerves, no feelings, just nothing. How did she ever get to this stage?"

"It doesn't matter," Pauline shouted over the running water.

"It's like a chink dinner six months ago. If you remember any-thing about it, then you had a heartburn and lose the address."

"Like you and me?" Sonya said, strutting like a peacock and smiling at herself in the mirror.

"I remember everything. That's the trouble."

"Were you ever really in love with me?"

"At that point only, my memory fails. . . . Why, is it important?"

"Not especially. I just wondered, that's all."

"Look, there's nothing wrong with trying this, is there?" he asked, hoping for a reaction.

She refused to reassure him, pet the head of her small boy. Hummed to herself.

"I did start off—you and me—with romantic intentions," he admitted with a sad chill. "But you killed them right off. Getting pregnant before I knew what hit me."

"And I wanted a baby? Daniel, my dear man, you were a crooked bum working for Spigleman . . . until I forced you to get a steady job."

"Yeah, I'm eternally grateful for all the years I bled slowly to death at Princeton."

"But dammit, look what it got you!"

"It fucking well was not worth it. And if not for the children, I would have dumped you ages ago. You're just not my type, doll, and that's the truth. We should have called it a day. . . ."

"Norma was stopping you," she protested. "Not me!"

"Yeah, sure," he said skeptically. "You're ready to walk out on thousand-dollar wardrobes, mink coats, and a house that set me back four hundred big ones. That's why you swallowed all the abuse and pretended not to notice the truth."

"Which is?"

"That I've been cheating on you from the word go. But with a meal ticket like you've got, you're not moving an inch. Isn't that what you told Norma as 'one cunt to another'?"

"You're not going to make me cry."

"That's a hopeless enterprise and it always was. To cry, you'd have to care, and you don't."

"Not two shits, mister. You never knew how to treat people except when you got yourself a team of deadbeats, with Gary as chief. He hates you too."

"That's a fucking lie, Sonya, and you know it. Listen, I sussed you out pretty quick. An anti-Semitic piece of garbage is what you are. It's an impossible job getting you to assimilate into the human race. In all the years we've been together, have I ever met a personal friend of yours who wasn't some shithead like Bunny from the glorious flying days? You were a transient bang, only I married you."

"You know why I'm going through with this with you?"

"Not a single idea comes to mind. Why?"

"Contempt for you."

Pauline stood silently outside the bathroom, waiting for hostilities to cease.

"I don't play favorites, kids. Now who's going to be first for a wash?"

Sonya stood up, kicked her snake boots angrily out of her path and confronted Pauline. Eyed her suspiciously. Next to Sonya, Pauline looked plump and beckoning with soft friendly curves in contrast to his angular bony doll. Dark against light hair struck him as an imposing contrast. Pauline, he noticed, backed off.

"I've never made this kind of scene with my husband," Sonya said. "Or a professional . . ."

"Well, if you'll just relax and let me—"

"—I am not a dike and I have no intention of going down on you," she interjected. "What you do . . . is your business."

"Sonya," Daniel said angrily, "if you want to cut out, I won't stop you. Pauline and I can resume where we left off this afternoon."

And yet, he knew he did not want her to leave. The display of spirit, and the do's and don'ts she insisted on, gave a semblance of order to a situation threatening to get out of hand. But what made his glands and gut churn was the ambiguous intimation that Sonya had not entered into such an arrangement with *him*. Had she before meeting him? With a dozen girls sharing men, cans of beans, clothing, charge cards, bills, rent, perhaps they had from time to time shared other intimacies. The possibility until that moment never occurred to him. His judgment began slowly to crumble, giving birth to doubts.

Sharing . . . there had never been an attempt by either of them. Both resided firmly in their private worlds. No emotional space-walk had ever united them. No common cause, save their daughters, had enabled them to reconcile their differences. Out of his self-loathing and grotesque confusion about himself as a man grew the ultimate agony, the suggestion of which blinded and tortured him. Perhaps . . . she had fooled him, living a very, very private life from which he had been excluded.

"Could you tell," he whispered to Pauline, "if she's been through this before?"

"Probably. One thing for sure," Pauline said, "she isn't scared. Even you can see that."

Even he? So obvious that she'd experienced . . . what? Troilism? Sonya and another woman with a single man, Or Sonya and two—? Slowly he felt himself losing his grasp. He kneaded his hands, then rubbed them over his face. Paced the room like a lunatic incarcerated in his own vision of hell.

She came out.

Naked.

No swells or baubles of fat danced on the trim shape. The long legs with narrow thighs, the glazed expression—she might have been reading a newspaper—the serene casualness of her movements without the hint of embarrassment, astounded him. With a leer she said: "Now, Daniel, don't disappoint us." She extended her right arm in invitation to the bathroom. "Are all the married men you deal with bum lays or just my Daniel?"

"I'll be right back, so don't go away."

"They're giants," said Pauline smiling. "Never screwed one who wasn't King Kong. You're a very attractive woman," she said as though admiring a piece of furniture. "Your kind of figure is a blessing. It doesn't age. You don't have big tits to worry about. No stretch marks. You'll look like this when you're sixty. Me, though, if I go off my high-protein diet for a day, I'm in trouble. I pick it up in the breasts which I need like another hole . . ."

He examined his face in the splotchy mirror. Under the blue-black beard, his face had a yellow unhealthy pallor and his red eyes were haunted. He had succeeded in shocking himself, finally.

"Daniel does not feel so wonderful. His gal said adios."

"*Shut up,*" he shouted from the bathroom.

"You getting nervous, Daniel? We are waiting patiently."

The voice of doom, digging at his manhood, cutting through his other life, had at last found him out.

The women stood huffing, puffing, and chattering before the mirror. The conversation took on its usual elevation as Sonya held the floor. The low incidence of airline fatalities when statistically compared to other modes of transportation. Dismissing Pauline's—the scared flier's—fears. On and on she chattered about the martial discipline of pilots and their fitness, the skills of all connected with airlines.

Somehow he managed by a supreme effort of will to take charge.

"Show her your collection, Pauline."

Sonya curiously craned the neck over as Pauline revealed the multinutrients of her trade.

"Christ, Daniel, do you need all these . . . these weapons, just to get laid?"

The women resumed their gossip and subtly boasted about where they had traveled, as if the geography of the Caribbean Islands would relieve the blight of being stripped for action at four thirty in the morning in a bleak sleazy apartment in Manhattan. The three of them might have taken a rain check on pleasure.

"It's always been a question of orgasm. Mine . . ." Sonya confessed.

"Like how?"

"He's never been able to get me there. He has always quit on me at the crucial moment. How do you explain that to Daniel?"

"I could show him," Pauline said as though conducting a tutorial among scholars.

"It's a little too late. I do not care about what he does or who with. Have I lost something valuable? What is there to be jealous of?"

The statement pierced him like a nail. He had organized his own crucifixion. Sackcloth and ashes for breakfast. Oh, for the soft, yielding touch of Norma and the confirmation of his godlike stature. . . . But he had been playing games with himself for so long that he had reduced his view of what really was going on in the mind and body of the woman he had legally married.

"Well, you're in a pretty fair financial shape from the looks of things," Pauline said with that unrestrained admiration which makes a virtue of an accident.

"And that is about all. He is a producer and I whipped his ass real good so that he wouldn't find out he was a complete failure."

"As long as nobody shits on your head," Pauline sagaciously averred.

"But what does it matter? *This* . . . is shitting on my head."

Sonya examined the contents of the magic case and became enthusiastic about the assortment of dildoes.

"I've seen these advertised in *Different*."

"Half the time you send your money to them and they rob you. Me, I shop cash and carry."

"Who do you use them for?"

"Girls and . . . boys. It's a steamup. For myself too. Here, I'll show you."

"What is *Different*?" Daniel asked.

"My dear man, a whole new thing is going on outside of Kit's parlor. Just open those eyes."

Pauline reclined on the bed, spread her legs, and slipped in a huge black Afro tool. She was correct. It stimulated him, the now silent spectator.

"Gads, it is so far inside. Doesn't it hurt?"

"No. Do I look like somebody who'd hurt herself? This is painless pleasure. Captain of your own ship, you understand . . . It's a freakout. I mean with or without a guy, in fifteen minutes, you're absolutely wasted."

He felt helpless and retreated to the bathroom as the two conspirators forged their loyalties without him. Intimidated by the sisterhood of women whose relationship no man could breach. It seemed to him characteristic of his status with Sonya: at his own orgy, she left him out. But for the best reason in the world, Daniel was compelled to withdraw. He had gone soft. . . .

The girls might have been having a picnic on the grass, as they innocently and affectionately explored each other. Only his Sonya could rob perversion of its sanctity. Reduce it to an absurdity. She rolled one of Pauline's plummy breasts around in her mouth, as though tasting a new cheese dip just on the market.

His equipment failed to react and of all the betrayals that had haunted him or ever would, this was certainly the cruelest, the most invidious. When he heard his name called, he played deaf, turned the water on full blast.

Would he require shots, or a shrink, or both, to elevate his firepower and capability? The animal shrank away from him, refused to obey, hid covertly in fleshy folds of glut. His mental condition would pay an exorbitant price for this act of disobedience. Would physical exhaustion excuse him? Had the high intake of alcohol, speed, hash, damaged his system? His strenuous exertions of the afternoon?

Or had Kit's over the years, and the constant, apathetic, to no purpose firing of spunk, at last taken its remorseless toll on him?

None of these defenses satisfied him so—

He *blamed* it on Sonya. Reassured himself. And . . . delighted in the renewal of glandular performance in his Wilbur. It just jutted out as though waking from deep dreams and stretching. Fully pulsating and quivering maniacally he courageously presented himself to the ladies. Thanking God, his lucky stars, and the talismanic baby mezzuzah around his neck for rescuing him from this brush with death.

He was now ready to fuck.

"I wondered where you went to," Sonya said, relaxing her grasp on Pauline. "I guess I forgot for the moment how abnormally clean this man gets himself before he can cut it. Daniel's balls must be the best powdered pair in the East."

"Watch an artist at work, doll," he said, indicating Pauline, who began to consume him slowly, metrically, by centimeter, until she had reached the stump of what in an arboreal mood, he considered his *redwood*.

"He hasn't even got a big tool," Sonya carped.

"Sonya, if you don't want to play with yourself, or us, then cop out now. And for your information, Miss Bianco, who is an expert on these matters, gave me a Triple A credit rating in the department you're now criticizing."

"Bullshit."

He eased Pauline's jaw off him and demanded corroboration.

"I never said you were gigantic."

"You didn't?"

"No, you're not some kind of freak. I thought we went through the compliment bit this afternoon," she said petulantly.

"This is a new day, and you will remember that I didn't have my Missus along."

"I don't care what she says," said Sonya. "She is being paid to provide a service. You, Daniel, have a short, snub-nosed Jewish dick, and if any lady tells you different, you are being conned." She lifted one of Pauline's mighty giant dildoes. "This is the size some men carry."

"They can't be American," he protested. "From Arabia or Equatorial Africa I don't know. But where I come from, seven inches is no sin."

Pauline resumed him, refusing to take sides and also with her free hands began to conciliate Sonya, who sat cross-legged on the bed, a vision of true Socratic skepticism, demanding concrete proof of his claim.

"She's miles ahead of you as far as I am concerned," Sonya advised him, commenting on Pauline's handling of the viola. "She made me come without even trying."

"You kept it to yourself pretty well," he replied. "I didn't hear any groans of ecstasy."

"That's only for a major orgasm. And it's got to be with something a little bigger than a .22 pistol."

"Your tongue should fall out for that lie. If there's a God you believe in, He should strike you dumb for this libel. Never made you come. You haven't got the intelligence to know when you've had an orgasm, you dummy."

"Can we cut this crap for a minute. I'm losing my concentration," Pauline warned them. She straightened up for a moment, checked out her tits for wrinkles because of the awkward position Daniel and Sonya had engineered. "Look, I have a suggestion. I can work on you both at the same time. If Daniel gets on his knees behind your head I can French him and work a dildoe into you. What do you say?"

"As long as Daniel doesn't come near me," Sonya replied.

"Who wants to? For years now I've avoided your cunt like it had rabies, so you've now got the *chutzpah* to make demands that I leave you alone!"

Pauline strapped the tool around her waist, adjusted it to the proper level for Sonya, then placed one of her friendly personality condoms—a centaur with a spear—on the Monster, lubricated Sonya with a few flicks of her pinky finger and set about her various tasks of mercy.

"I just beg you both to do me one favor when I'm working. Don't ask me questions, please. . . ."

"Did you hear that, doll? Keep the face shut."

"I'll think about that."

Sonya began, as he knew, to sulk, wanted to be wooed back into the fold.

"Come on, Sonya," Pauline said, "this can be a trip."

"No it can't," he said forcefully. "Not until she takes the chewing gum out of her mouth and stops with those fucking cracking noises."

"He's got a point," Pauline advised her in an affable coach-player huddle.

"Now you know why men leave home."

"All right. But it is for Pauline and not you," she said placing the spent piece of Juicy Fruit in the ashtray on a lit cigarette naturally so that now the sickly sweet smell of burning gum permeated the room.

He left the bed with the ashtray and dumped the contents down the toilet bowl, flushed it, and returned to operational headquarters with a fresh plan for the campaign.

"Can we all work together and stop chewing gum, kill all cigarettes, and refrain from speaking. If you both agree, so will I."

"Agreed," said Pauline.

"Seconded, you bastard."

"I choose to ignore that curse." He raised his hand. "When my hand falls, silence."

Dropped his hand, maneuvered back into the crouch that Pauline requested and waited for the professional to call the pitch. Silently of course, like a big-league baseball catcher.

It appeared to be going well for about three minutes, but then nature played a dirty trick on him once again. His foot fell asleep and a treacherous drowning cramp flowered through his calf. He pulled out of Pauline quietly, not so she'd notice, and started to hop, then walk, around the room.

"Daniel," Sonya crooned. "Could you stop that? It is distracting me from my goal."

All smiles and with her back arched, Sonya's legs flailed the air, the toes interlocking and forming a scissors over Pauline's head. The sight of a professional probing deeper into his slap-happy bungler gave his wife the status of a stranger, for he had never—as a detached observer—caught her in this position. She was demanding more: Depth Charges.

"Get away from there," Pauline called over her shoulder. He had meddled with various objets d'art in the instrument case. "If you want something, just ask," she chided him.

"I warned you, that man is impossible," Sonya said wiggling a hip and lifting her shoulder off the sack as though to avoid a pin.

He had selected the . . . the . . . well it resembled a spare intestine. He squeezed the salmon-colored rubber ball knob and heard a slow-register "whooooosh."

"It had an airlock," he explained. "She fills this up—"

"—Put it down, dammit," Pauline shouted, her hair disar-ranged in a glorious fluster.

"Don't stop," Sonya said.

"I've got to readjust the strap, it's slipping down my waist."

"Look what you've made her do now. I was almost there, you sonovabitch."

"Shut up, you weren't even close. I told you you couldn't tell." He presented the coils to Sonya, dangled them like a fear-less handler of dangerous snakes. "This is a Spunker for your information. Pauline doesn't leave the house without it. Custom-made with her two little hands after years of extensive research."

"A what?"

"She fills it up with hot fluid and attaches it to this torpedo, then screws the two together. Whenever she squeezes the ball you've got hot running jism from the reservoir. I'd like her to use it."

"Why, did you lose it already?" Sonya asked.

"No, but since you've got serious complaints about the way I handle myself. I thought the two of you could function with-out me. And I haven't lost anything, I just had a cramp in my leg, and that's not a crime. She had me bent like a pretzel."

Pauline's eyes roved from one to the other. With a damp wash-cloth she patted the sweat beads on her forehead.

"What is it with you? I thought we were doing fine."

"He has always been all talk."

"Hate, Pauline, is too private and expensive an emotion to share with a stranger. Now fill it up."

"With what?"

"I don't know. Hot water," Daniel said.

"I couldn't. It would hurt her, you understand. You don't want to burn her insides? No, never with water."

"Then you tell me. You're supposed to be the expert."

"Well, what's wrong with what we're doing? We had some very good sounds going for us."

"Are you trying to tell me in a nice way that you're quitting? And after that long spiel this afternoon about depravity and strange tastes? Like all chicks, you're basically full of shit. The mouth goes, the stories unfold, but in a crunch you pass the buck."

Paid for her docility and the employment of her body, Pauline was in danger of having her first client beef in years.

"Milk," she said. "You ought to really be asking yourself if this marriage is worth saving."

"Only as an example to others," he replied, slipping on his trousers. "A warning, like those billboards with mangled bodies after car wrecks: 'This could be you.' "

"Go get the milk, Daniel. I will not chicken out."

"Don't you think I know that about you? Don't you think I've been wondering since I met you how many guys . . . when, where, who, how? I don't believe you've missed a trick. Anybody, but anybody, can put you away . . ."

"And have," Sonya replied fiercely.

"I'll be back."

Kit's head had fallen on her chest and her legs were bunched up under her. She snored violently as though the sound would purge her gut of alcohol saturation. Neutralize the acid. Leo sat on the bar stool, with the *News* and *Times* spread out at the sports section. He crunched a Lifesaver on his back teeth and ground it when he saw Daniel prowling around the kitchen.

"If you're looking for ice, there's some on the bar," he said.

"Have you got any milk?"

"Should be," Leo said without looking up from the papers.

Daniel stepped over mounds of towels stacked by the washing machine in the kitchen. The multicolored refuse of the day's sexual carnage.

"There's no milk."

"Have a Coke instead. Pauline treating you kids okay?" he inquired without interest.

"Leo, I've got to have some milk now!"

"Now? Hey, Daniel, I don't do the shopping here." He thought for a moment, studied the intent, tight expression on Daniel's face. "I'll try Pedro. He's on the door." Left his seat and pressed the buzzer half a dozen times without making contact. "He should be there unless he stepped out . . ."

"*Hola,*" came the tinny voice.

"Daniel, how's your Spanish?"

"Doesn't exist."

"*Hola, Pedro . . .*" Leo turned to him. "Maybe I should go down to ask him."

In his blue-striped junior-sized pajamas the shrunken little man seemed to him to have been the victim of a hacksaw.

"I don't want to put you out . . ."

"I'll wake Kit."

He shook Kit's chin, then tapped her cheek with the palm of his hand like a kid testing Mommy's reflexes. She stirred fitfully, rolled her eyes open, then closed them.

"What's wrong . . . ?"

"Daniel needs milk. It looks like he's got an ulcer attack."

"Milk . . . ?"

"Pedro's on the house phone. Ask him to bring up some."

Daniel watched as Leo, in a moment of tenderness, assisted Kit to her feet. She leaned on his shoulder and stumbled to the paint-peeled finger-marked house phone.

"*Pedro. Por favor. Tiene leche?*" Through half-closed eyes and supporting herself on the wall, she indicated that the answer was *no.*

"Can he get some?" Daniel asked.

"He's not supposed to leave the door," Leo informed him. Underneath the scowl, he was a frightened city-dweller.

"For five dollars, he'll shift his ass," Daniel said. "It's important."

"*Emergencia, Pedro. Una propina de cinco dólares.* He's going," Kit said at last, then peered through the shutters of her purple-veined lids. "You're still here, Daniel? How come?"

"My wife hasn't had enough."

"Oh, wow . . . I'm so sleepy . . . See you tomorrow. You coming to bed?"

"Yere, honey, in a minute."

Daniel stood by the window and watched the handyman dash to where a green all-night deli arrow blinked on and off in the black pall of the early morning.

"You want a little Alka-Seltzer?" Leo asked.

He did not hear, but stared attentively at the street below. The shape of a man emerged from the shop carrying a bag. Except for a lineup of lit cabs parked at the curb, there was no traffic on the street. Daniel sat on the arm of the sofa, dangled his legs. The spasmodic jerks of exhausted muscles roused him when his head drooped. The doorbell rang, and Daniel reached in his pocket for five dollars and offered it to Leo.

"*Gracias, Pedro,*" he said, returning with a brown paper bag and handing it to Daniel. "Well, my friend, I hope this makes you feel better. I'm closing down, so if you want to stay over . . ."

"Good night, Leo."

Daniel opened the noisy rough brown bag and saw a fat midgie can of Carnation Milk, lost in the bottom. He removed it, held it up to the light. He egged himself off the seat and returned to the kitchen, found a beer opener and made two holes in the can, poured it into a saucepan and listened to the tinkle of an even flow of milk. When the can was empty he tossed it onto the already full bag of garbage from which coffee grounds like an army of germs had started to ooze. He turned on the gas and watched small bubbles buzzing in the pan.

Thumping bare feet came from behind him, and he sprang suddenly out of his stupor. Pauline and Sonya, in league against him, both naked.

"It's not going to work," Pauline said. "Nothing even I can do about a dry well."

The milk surged and erupted over the top of the pan onto the grimy range. Bleary and exhausted, like a fluted warbler he

migrated back, returned to Sonya's ravaged quail breast for comfort. He wrapped his arms around the stringbean body and
rocked.

6

Daniel's afternoon at Kit's had overrun, and instead of a parking
ticket he had a paralytically stiff neck and a dormant recollection of a tingling Lavoris kiss from Pauline doing her bye-bye
number and a looped voice informing him to "keep in touch."
Imagining that Sonya had been transformed into a sixtyish black
lady seemed perfectly consonant with his mental condition.

It was 10 A.M., and rain or shine Ethel vacuumed, stuffed the
mouth of the Bendix washer-drier with the moldy sheets and
towels of the previous day's casualties. A new dawn roared into
being at Kit's.

"Who you . . . ?" Ethel asked calmly when Daniel dragged
himself into the kitchen and leaned on the refrigerator for
support.

"It's okay, Ethel," Leo called out. He was sitting at the poker
table in the alcove, straightening money. "Lay in some coffee,
Daniel, grab yourself a shower, and you'll feel better."

"What happened?" he asked.

"You took the count, and Pedro got Sonya a cab home."

"How was she?"

"Quite a customer you got yourself there." The phone rang.
"That's The Pal with the morning line."

Ethel handed Daniel a cup of coffee, but he waved it away,
and lurched into the bathroom.

After a shower and a shave with Noxzema, he felt his circulation had improved and the neck-ache had been lulled into a
nag. The occasional involuntary muscle twitches around his
mouth and arms would disappear after a night's sleep.

Ethel had given his suit a press and his shoes a shine. Leo fed
him a double Alka-Seltzer, and three belches later with his
stomach tuned to UHF, he took his leave.

"Listen, Daniel, check with Kit later. There's a major piece of couze due in from Buffalo this afternoon. And I'd never forgive myself if you missed this vintage."

As he stepped into the even texture of one of those resplendent crisp pollutionless New York mornings that stifle all complaints with the fiery candescence of midwinter sunshine, the city almost seemed to be gloating in its revival.

Wearing a smeared loop of chicken-shit parking tickets, which Chris would quash, his car had miraculously withstood the threat of being towed away. He avoided the eyesore of the passenger door and the first order of business in the crowded office with priests sitting on the assembly line and in various stages of insurance documentation was to Jeanette.

"Get Zage Rolls Royce and tell them that my car was scratched up. I'll bring it in tomorrow and I want another Rolls to use while they're repairing mine."

"You're in a charming mood," she said peevishly.

"I'm hung over, that's all. See if you can find some V-8 juice for me somewhere."

"Are you taking calls?" she asked slipping on her glasses to read off the list to him.

"Get Sonya for me."

"What about Norma?"

"Norma is over."

"Oh . . . well, you couldn't have really talked to her because Max is home. He said he wouldn't be in today."

"I'm not surprised. For my part he can stay out forever."

He flung his jacket on the sofa and fended through the pile of yesterday's messages, then buzzed through to Don Ackerman.

In a moment Don presented himself as fresh and cared for as an oven-ready bird.

"How was your evening?"

"A disaster."

"I don't wonder," he said hiking up his trousers and crossing his legs. "You take too many chances."

"Maybe in my personal life I do, Don. But not here. I was told that Spigleman came up here with stolen bonds."

"That's true."

"You're not encouraging him, I hope, for your sake."

"All I said was that I'd see him and raise the matter with you. He's got a package and it's his opinion that we can move in three million dollars' worth of Triple A's without anyone knowing. It would cost us a million and a half—that's how far he'll discount them."

"Don, at times I think you're fucking insane."

"Since when are we getting so fussy?"

"Since now."

"Okay, Daniel, anything you say."

"I don't want Spigleman in here ever. We're not running some shit-ass boiler room."

Through the flack of the shouting, Jeanette appeared, carrying the elixir he had ordered.

"Drink this and maybe you'll feel better," she said.

He gulped down the V-8 and hiccuped violently. Don took the opportunity to slip out. All the men in the office had come to fear this side of Daniel, for through the cloudy unpredictability of his character, there were never any quibbles or backbiting regarding the astuteness of his business judgment. Slotnick even suggested that Daniel's jungle talents were fed by the scandalously unwholesome aspects of his personal situation.

"Sonya isn't home, and Gary won't be in today either," Jeanette announced. "Thank God your birthday comes only once a year—you've put half the office out of commission."

"They say where she went?" he asked softly, his body groaning unheard ultrasonic pitches.

"No. Is that all? Daniel, I realize you're hung over, but what are you so angry about?"

Himself, he thought, picking up the *Wall Street Journal* and staring through the maze of prices and sales, then crumpling up the paper and flinging it on the floor, too fatigued to begin designing his prelunch glider. He dozed on the sofa, one of those dreamless overpowering voids in which the flesh quits on man. When he awoke, it had just touched noon and he decided to gather his slender resources, do a spot check on the new luminary coming in from Buffalo, then cut his losses and head home for a sauna and a sleep.

Daniel had never been at Kit's at this hour, and was surprised to find the place jammed. For her early-bird special, Kit had Danish and coffee on the bar, laid in by her caterer. Reno presided over nubs of wearied cold cuts that he'd lifted off the fat tray at Deli City along with rolls which had the chilblained cheeks of rough handling from coarse industrial bags. Daniel located a small Hoomintash stashed in the corner and wondered how it had found its way into Kit's. Reno laid some coffee on Daniel, and after tasting it, Daniel was tempted to cut his slipper collection into small pieces.

"So, John, what happened to your partner at the frank counter?"

"Dint show up, that cocksucker. Know what they done to me . . . switched me to dairy. I ain't a dairy man. Know what it's like to deal tomato herring and mash that shit on a whole-wheat toast and seaboard it for a spick? So I quit."

"I can imagine," Daniel said wearily.

"That turd's got industrial dyes in it. I change two aprons . . . I look like a mass murderer after an hour. You stay away from that stuff, you hear."

"What's with this crowd?"

The early-bird special, a form of sexual American Plan at $22.50, included snacks and coffee for the lunch-at-twelve-back-at-one office weasels. In charge of the wholesale trade was Carmelita, yesterday's siren. She wheeled in and out muttering, "*Al punto,*" as she turned out a Jayhawk every five minutes so that he could attempt a Marty Liquori mile back to his office.

Men brushed by him into Bedroom Two and Daniel heard noisy cheering. The place did not seem the same to him and he realized that the afternoon regular big spenders were actually few, and that Kit had to rely on volume to help with her nut.

"Between twelve and two Kit deals out live action and movies. We got two doses of rough trade doin' a special-material number. Spades," Reno said contentiously. "This type group digs drumsticks for lunch," he explained.

Kit staggered in, pulled an eyelid up forcibly, and asked:

"Where is Leo?"

"Out for change," Reno informed her.

"Shit"—she had her usual complaint—"my head is splitting. Somebody bullshot me before I leap out of this freaking window."

She stopped her peregrinations, and the rims of her eyes like flesh wounds were Murined into focus.

"Daniel? Little early for you."

"Leo talked me into Miss Buffalo."

Chris lumbered in from Bedroom Two where he performed his guard-dog duties.

"Hey, Daniel. You left your case. It's in the closet. There's something else—shit, I lost it, but it'll come to me."

He brought over the Gucci attaché case and Daniel found it unmarked. He opened it and smiled grimly at the gold four-leaf-clover key ring. In the corridor, two dark, naked, dripping wet torsos, slapping ass, marched into the bathroom for purification rites.

"They smell like C.N., Kit," Chris complained. "I think we oughta 'liminate them animals and stick with movies."

Daniel had intruded at Kit's . . . a . . . board of directors meeting was taking place in front of a client and Kit silenced Chris with a slashing brush of her hand, recognizing the incompatibility of bargain basement value in the presence of the caviar trade.

Reno mixed a pair of bullshots and handed them to Kit and Daniel, while Chris, somewhat abashed, returned to the bedroom, but not before she pulled him up short.

"Run a flick and turn these yo-yo's out. I'm hitting the showers."

"Keet," shouted Carmelita. "*Quién es la próxima?* I waitink."

"You caught us a little behind schedule," Reno said, failing to disguise the mistress's discomfort.

The drink settled Daniel's stomach, inspired him with a food appetite. He sat down quietly and took inventory of his bleak stocks. It would not be the same again with Sonya, and he was tempted to call Sonnerman to reinstate her irrevocably in his will. He blacked out their evening. No question but that he had let it get out of hand, and he was left with a problem now that would require more than a fur coat fence-mend.

Reconstruction . . . or . . .

The roiling voices of office Charlies intruded on his thoughts. It was movie time at Kit's, and a divergence of opinion by seasoned veterans of the hard circuit did little to mellow the air or relieve throbbing temples.

"This is a whorehouse, so keep your voices down," Chris ordered.

Daniel handed Reno his glass for a refill and attempted to

settle the issue of Sonya. Obviously a vacation in the sun. With
Pauline or without her? Should he be alone with Sonya?

A key in the lock turned and that nutty flavor of bonhomie
engulfed him with Leo followed by The Pal and Guy. The club
was back in session.

"Aha, I should have known that the maître would beat me,"
Guy said. "You're waiting for the soprano from La Scala Buffalo,
I presume."

"The same," said Daniel, livening up.

"Hey, Daniel, how are you?" The Pal inquired. "With you
guys in a sec. I got to check the spread." He picked up the phone
and began to dial, but went gooey-eyed at the two black girls
passing through on their way back to the street.

"Hey, Leo, long-stemmed roses. Why didn't you tell me . . . ?"

Kit reappeared wearing a thick terrycloth robe and a towel
around her prewig scrag. She blinked herself into existence and
fresh still-undefined scents tickled Daniel's nose and embellished
her person.

"Afternoon, gentlemen. Another day dawns."

Reno handed her a bullshot.

"They're gettin' earlier and earlier. But it keeps 'em off the
streets," Leo said, getting back into the shrimp perspective that
Daniel liked so well.

Kit's, Daniel knew, was

HOME

Rubbing the thick sagging bags under his eyes, Chris emerged
chuckling to himself, and slapping at the hanging fatty tissue
wielded around his ribs.

"I don't give a crap what nobody says. You can't beat them
amateurs. Man, we got a movie, lit by the prince of darkness
and featurin' spares like you never seen."

"Keet . . . *espero*," Carmelita in mid-Listerine gargle whined.

"Them amateurs, man, we got one chick givin' the other a
French lesson. Keep your Paulines excetera. Gimme them amateurs anytime."

"You're terrific for business," Leo barked.

"We'll hand him our Ad account and get him to write copy
for us, Leo," Kit said, pointing Chris in the direction of Bedroom Two. "It's twelve fifty and those Johns have to punch in,
so clear them out."

"This is different," said Chris. "Daniel sent up the film."

"Oooooooooh a première," said Guy, wiping the lint off his glasses. "Am I dressed for such an occasion?"

Hearing his name in this strange context, Daniel, never one for practical jokes unless he was pulling them, bolted up.

"What kind of shit is this, Chris?"

"I swear to God." He gathered little-used brain paths into some form of orderly distress. "Daniel, that's what I was tryin' to recall."

"Yere, like you did for the Knapp Commission," Reno said.

Daniel recognized the navy blue letter paper and the white typewriter ribbon. A color combination favored by the former Sonya Anderson.

FOR YOUR VIEWING PLEASURE
WITH COMPLIMENTS
DANIEL BARNETT

"It's Sonya," Daniel said. "No question of that. She's misspelled our name."

He let the others peel out of the room while he stared at the note. His mood turned mildly apprehensive. He picked up his attaché case rather than trust the motley group of interlopers on the early-bird. Laughter and chattering and rousing guttural cheers.

"From the museum of primitive arts," Guy shouted. "A poker player Chris may not be, but a *mavin* of blue for sure . . ."

Apart from his gang, there were half a dozen new faces in the mini-cinema Bedroom Two had been converted into. So much of this tired refuse around that he barely looked at the rumpled sheet improvised as a screen. Wrinkled faces and unironed limbs and squashed toes wriggled in a weird St. Vitus dance.

"Look at that belly," shouted The Pal. "Man, there is a history of Baskin-Robbins. Every flavor . . . that pig *spazzino'd*."

Daniel saw a leech of long blond hair and a wiry goy, abashed and irritated, shielding his face from the glare of the lights.

"Hey, somebody get that tub to move her hair."

Almost by magic, the woman lifted her platinum fall and Daniel thought he recognized a face from some hamper of soiled memories.

"Christ, I know her," he shouted. "Bunny—"

He did not complete the identification, for a shining, glazed hand, oily slick, shoved the fat face off the man.

"Hercules I am not," Guy called out, "but this peter belongs to a pygmy."

On the screen the hand stretched, wearing a crescent-shaped cocktail pinky ring, adorned with knubby chips, which Daniel clearly remembered purchasing. One of his undeniable victories over city sales tax: a phony Nassau County address. A blond wig ensconced in an Alice band appeared. Knew it intimately: he'd given it numerous lifts boxed in clear plastic.

"SONYA!"

and . . . her crew of naked merrymakers, experimenting, frolicking, and making an awful mess of perversity.

"Linda Lovelace she will not replace in my heart," Guy said.

"Sheeeeeet," Leo shouted. "Ain't . . . THAT?"

Kit stuck her face in.

"Turn off this noise. My head is fuckin' . . . Oh, wow, DANIEL."

The Pal viciously grabbed Daniel's arms and flushed his eyes closed with a breath of fiery garlic.

"I tole you guys this was great," Chris bleated in the confusion.

"Daniel, with the wildest piece of gash in the city, you been comin' here?" The Pal asked with exasperation. "My wife I never seen naked 'cos she's got these hangups . . ."

Daniel stood up, knocked the projector off the plastic kitchen table, stooped and ripped the film out of the gates. He picked up the reel of film, and his attaché case, and walked slowly down the corridor.

"I tell you people, no wives here," Kit shouted.

In the living room, Daniel was stopped and his hand seized and shaken by a man wearing a chartreuse cashmere turtleneck sweater, white flannel trousers, rings, amulets—and could it be Miss Dior?

"Daniel Barnet, *this* is C. Bernard Waterman. I was up the office yesterday, but you were still here. This man, Bernard, should be an example for you. *He* always has his nose stuck in a pussy. Bernard is taking my suggestion and is going to try again."

Opened the door and left, carrying his case in one hand and his film in the other. He sat in his car slumped over the wheel, clinging to the evidence of the photo-finish in the Barnet Stakes, a claiming race toward let's-pretend land.

In search of a priest, Daniel naturally turned to his lawyer.

Whenever possible, Sonnerman avoided litigation. He settled, or else. If a client wanted to sue, fight forever in the courts, he invariably used two words to express his policy:

"Go elsewhere . . ."

Thus, an innocent accused of murder, or statutory rape in some unenlightened state—no matter what the personal relationship—had to swallow this dictum.

"For murder: Bailey or Foreman. For personal liability: Melvin Belli. A political favor: Paul Weiss, Rifkind is still the best. Divorce and famous names: Greg Bautzer. You want to raise money on a derelict building, screw your tenants with a Dracula lease, or take a company public: ME. On my staff I have Keats, Shelley and Byron. My province is romance."

Daniel slammed past Sonnerman's secretary and into his office. Sonnerman stood up and waved him to the sofa.

"I assumed you'd come to see me," he said eerily. "We've got ourselves a very serious problem." A painful sigh. "The Treasury lawyers have decided to rip your whole tax avoidance structure to shreds."

Daniel brandished the film in Sonnerman's face.

"I've got all the evidence I need right here to finish Sonya, I've been married to—"

Sonnerman slipped a piece of dried fig into his mouth, and Daniel realized that he was not paying attention.

"Daniel, I'm going to be very rude to you. When are you going to stop this shit about your domestic life? Nobody is really interested whether you divorce Sonya or not . . . You must've had some celebration. Why don't you go home and sleep it off to prepare yourself for the big crunch."

He lifted up a yellow legal pad, scattering through sheets of scribbled notes, then plopped on the arm of the sofa.

"The money from the Cayman Islands goes to Zurich into a numbered account . . . the bank using its name buys stock for you and other foreign currency when . . . we do a little gambling. No tax is paid. Well, Internal Revenue people were at the bank and I've got some kind of garbled version of a bribe offer. Apparently the story *they* have is not the least bit ambiguous." Sonnerman shook his head sadly.

"Sonya . . ."

"Listen, Daniel, Sonya's *not* important. She doesn't exist. We're playing around with numbers. You offer to bribe a man, so does Uncle Sam and he's got more money. You might offer a hundred thousand dollars, the Internal Revenue will take say twenty-five percent off the top in cash. You got four million dollars, they'll drop a million into a manager's hand, and grab the other three and then bury you . . ."

Daniel had stopped listening. He picked himself off the sofa and passed, silently and calmly, out of Sonnerman's office, thoroughly composed, at last finding a clear straight line out of the dilemma of his personal life.

It had begun to snow, and the morning sun was just another memory. Sharks' teeth of blinding white flakes accompanied by the termagant howl of the wind made the drive on the expressway a precarious venture. Several times, Daniel was tempted to pull off the road and wait for visibility to improve, but the dauntless traveler sped on, trusting to the broad smile of fate. He had not survived the ordeal of Kit's merely to die a statistic . . . on a highway without tolls.

The route to Glen Head was so familiar that he virtually coasted on automatic pilot until he reached Norma's home. His good, patient, loving woman had been badly treated and had earned the necessary straight and honorable path he'd sidestepped through the years.

Norma's car was in the driveway and Daniel breathed in the rich, crisp air and rang the doorbell. Max stood wearing a powder blue robe, maroon bedroom slippers, and the lime pallor of a man whose stomach had triumphed over his character. Daniel was silently ushered into a small—by his Roman standards—living room, rather chintzy, damask, brocade, rather Norma.

"You missed her."

"Her car's outside."

"I took her in mine with Benji," Max said. He was sipping tea with lemon from a glass. "She left for Florida . . . early, Daniel."

There seemed a terrible stillness about Max. Not angry or indeed cowed by Daniel's unexpected visit. Max at home.

"You're not surprised to see me, are you?"

"No, not really. I was not going to come to you to discuss personal matters. And offices and bars were not right either. So welcome to my home. I got an Alka-Seltzer if you can use one."

Daniel accompanied him to the *Good Housekeeping* kitchen where copper frying pans were mounted on the wall, and a new-rage butcher's block stood next to the Westinghouse Giant refrigerator. Max dropped two of the fizzlers in a glass of water, then offered Daniel a chaser.

"How long is Norma going to be gone?"

"Oh, that's hard to say. It takes time when you're house hunting, and we still got to unload this one. When she's found somethin', I'll hop down and give the okay."

"So you've decided to resign?"

"Belch it up and you'll clear your stomach," Max advised. "No, no resignation. Me?"

Out of the kitchen window, Daniel saw a sliding board, a plastic pool with an ice glaze, and neat, carefully tended geometric frozen flower beds which in a way had the effect of organizing the snow into molds.

"Well, I'll retire you then."

Max plopped another tea bag into his glass and filled it with boiling water.

"You know, Daniel, I wish I understood you." He leaned on the sink and smiled at a frying pan. "All this balls about passion and romance that you fed Norma with . . . Her and me . . . we're friends. She don't want no part of you. You spin her out for a reason . . . ? Well, she told me the truth. Everything. Benji . . . I was her friend. Norma'd never leave me because she's afraid of uncertainty."

"Which is why she married you in the first place."

"That ain't a bad reason."

"Well, maybe it's good that you know, so we can clear everything up finally."

"It's done," Max said.

"You'll give Norma a divorce!"

"Whaaaaaaaat? What're you readin', the comics? I'm retirin' on double pay and you'll give me a contract to that effect."

"Max, don't be an asshole."

"If I was you, I'd get some legal advice on the matter. I hand over to the government all the green sheets I Xeroxed, plus all I know about the deals you done. They grant me immunity and you ain't a pretty sight when they haul your ass into a federal court."

Daniel was so utterly startled by the suggestion that he began to laugh, weep, uncontrollably.

"You'd never, Max."

"Maybe, if revenge was my story, I might. But I want to live real well and you'll make it possible. Sooner or later you had to fall down"—he looked to the ceiling—"so's I could piss on your face. See, I worry about me. I do what's good for me. Me is what counts."

Max knew the secret more deeply than anyone.

He left the kitchen, and Daniel waited a moment, looking out at the garden, then felt a biting draft enter from the open front door.

"You're terminated, Daniel. I'll be in touch. You'll get a letter with the terms of my contract and I suggest you sign real prompt. Don't trust the mail, have it delivered."

"Fuck you, Max. I'll give you anything your little heart desires. It'll be a pleasure getting you and Mrs. Hoffman out of my life."

On Max's face, Daniel saw neither pleasure nor anger, just an image of
reality.

Daniel skirted his own house for the better part of an hour, sensing the wonders he had been privileged to view. He held his own life in the palm of his hand. That exquisite knowledge, the revelation of mystery was interrupted by a more mundane detail. He pulled the car on a cockeyed grass shoulder. A sin of undefined magnitude sealed his afternoon, and he began walking. He'd run out of gas.

The event did not go unnoticed. Honking the horn and dressed as an Indian maiden with plaited hair, Weintraub was upon him.

"Hey, you're home early," she said, shoving her head out of the window. "Pass any good-looking, strong, snow clearers? I'm out doing a little headhunting. You busy? I'm a real live Indian." She slapped at her mouth with the palm of her hand. "Wooooo-Woooooo."

Stepping carefully on his sleek, iced, driveway, he knew that all danger had passed. His house was alight and he fidgeted in his pocket for the keys.

Sonya opened the door. Bright, smiling, relaxed, and with a welcome glow illuminating her ash-gray eyes.

"Hel-lo, doll . . ." he heard his voice, as though from some distant land, hang still in the frozen air.

"Hi, Daniel. Fish cakes and spaghetti for dinner . . . or would you rather eat out?"

This is for Lori Latham,
whose unselfish contributions
made a rough crossing
an occasion for rejoicing.